For Steven, my imagination buddy for life.
For my family, who didn't think me too insane.
For my friends, who were just as crazy.
And for that starry void in our heads that we call wonder.

Copyright © 2018 by I. A. Ashcroft.
ISBN-13: 978-1-944674-03-8
ISBN-10: 1-944674-03-9

Printed in the United States of America.
Editing by L. McCaslin.
Visit I. A. Ashcroft on the web at ia-ashcroft.com.

Eclipse of the Sun

Book Two of Inoki's Game

I. A. Ashcroft

THE STORY SO FAR
New York City, 2147

Since the nuclear bombings 125 years ago, the place where the U.S. once stood is a harsh land. Some modern cities remain, protected from radiation in the wind and water by Barriers—but survival is more tenuous than anyone would like to admit.

In this world, an orphan lives: Jackson Dovetail. Amnesiac, adopted, he grew up suffering nightmares and bursts of uncontrolled shadow magic. Desperate, he throws himself into managing his family's delivery business after the Mage Order cast him aside. But his prophetic dreams never cease. In them, long-extinct ravens fly, and a starry-eyed man calls him "Chosen". He worries his sanity is slipping.

Financial desperation forces him to accept a smuggling deal with Agent Jaden Walker of the international Coalition government. And in their cargo, he finds Dr. Anna Matthews, a woman who died over a century past.

Before the Bombings, Anna was a scientist at a nuclear analysis site. She gave her life warning the world of a terrorist attack, one related to the apocalypse to follow. Breathing her last, she closed her eyes… and when she opened them again, Jackson was looking down at her.

She now brims with magic of her own: radiation and healing light.

Fate has connected them in ways they cannot understand.

Of course, the Coalition has long tried to examine and exploit the magical. This was the fate of Jackson's childhood friend Tony—a boy with wild, dangerous powers, groomed to slaughter the government's enemies. The Coalition seizes Anna too.

Fortunately, Agent Walker, consumed with guilt, arranges for Anna's jailbreak. Jackson offers his aid, hiding her, getting dragged into her whirlwind. The government chases after. The Mage Order and their devious Archmage joins the pursuit too, their eyes on Anna, their wrath on those who help her.

And in a display befitting only a master showman, Jackson's boyhood ally Tony returns. His breathtaking magic and cracked rage throw all plans into chaos. Driven mad by former Coalition masters, he frothed with violent prophesies and curious hungers, ruling over a deadly underground arena. Though friend to neither government nor Archmage, his help was deadly. As his price, convinced only life and death struggle would awaken Jackson's potential, he pitted his friend against the fearsome Tiger, a gladiator of peerless skill. And Anna… she was next.

Jackson prepared to die, knowing the Tiger from his dreams, seeing so many before him crushed and broken.

Captive, anguished with her memories, Anna too almost despaired.

But she was always a survivor, and she held rare resourcefulness and courage. Seizing control of her new abilities, Anna broke her chains and lead a pursuit after Jackson, convinced she had to save the only friend she had left.

In the end, they earned their escapes, their path fraught with blood. Tony is dead. So is the Tiger. Anna and Jackson are finally free.

But the Coalition and Mage Order still lurk, searching.

Jackson's advisor Frank sends them now into the no-man's-land beyond the Barrier, where uncontaminated resources are scarce, and raiders terrorize the unfortunate. They've been promised protection by a group of bandits who owe Anna a debt—she saved one of their own from Tony's death matches.

However, will these thieves honor their word? Anna's fallen into a deep sleep, overspending her healing powers in a bid to save Jackson's life. Recovering, he too worries for the future. His magic comes easier. But the ravens follow. The visions beckon.

Only time will tell if these two will learn what they are meant for.

But out in these wild lands, monsters dwell among men, and nothing is as it seems.

PROLOGUE
A Wolf at the Door

"Blood and vengeance," the stranger whispered.

Baldur turned to face the man. His arthritis groaned. *Who…?*

His stomach dropped. He had no memory of coming out here. It was deep in the night, and yet, he was in the middle of the fields.

This stranger frightened him—he'd appeared from thin air. Bones were woven into his midnight-dark braids. His fingers were long and thin, nails sharpened to points. And his *eyes…* they could freeze a soul. They… they…

Baldur wheezed, dizzy. Every time he tried to meet that gaze, his heart would almost burst.

A ferocious, shaggy hound prowled at the stranger's side. Its stare was wide and golden, its teeth long and stained. Some half-remembered fairytale from Baldur's youth whispered one word: *wolf.*

A shaking started in his knees, one that betrayed the old warrior he thought he once was.

Casually, the stranger withdrew a gore-spattered bone from a sack at his side, proffering it to the hound with a sly smile. The beast perked. With a lightning-quick crunch, the bone was shattered in its jaws.

"Blood," the man whispered again. "Vengeance."

The wolf stepped forward, slavering, a furious hunger in its snarl.

Baldur woke trembling.

His wife made a sleepy noise. She pulled him close. In her hands, strong, safe, he tried to forget.

When dawn approached, Echo rolled from his side and stretched her arms to the sky. She was the first to bound out of their furs, her only clothes a bright smile. Baldur, in comparison, stumbled out exhausted. The aches swelled his joints where the frost had bitten him long and hard as an orphaned boy. His left forearm throbbed down to the bone. It took him a moment to remember that the limb was still missing, as it had been for forty years.

"Come on, lazy," Echo teased. Her laughing brown eyes lit the room even through the last shreds of night.

Baldur's heart eased, and so did his pain.

The village was already waiting for the pair outside. They were indeed a sight: he, the muscled old warrior with but one true arm, and she, a small, willowy woman, black hair swaying in the breeze. Yet, she was the one that made crowds stand aside. As they passed, the people tapped their throats in respectful greeting. Baldur smiled, even though the salute wasn't for him. Echo had donned her helm, the skull of a deer, and in doing so, she'd become something more than his beloved wife, something more than a mother or sister or friend.

She strode to the east, confidant, powerful, to where the heads of the sunflowers pointed. The villagers' eyes turned with her, watching the antlers on her brow, ready for her guidance.

Baldur held the story of this crown close to his heart. All here did.

Echo's forebears had come here from far to the south. There lay a great city under a protective barrier, a place where Baldur was told he'd been born: New York. A sanctuary. A paradise. But long ago, when the bombs had fallen, food ran scarce. Disease ran rampant. The land beyond New York's little Barrier turned to poison.

The citizens decided some of their own needed to be sacrificed for the good of all.

These offerings to the land were the prisoners, the poorest, and the sick. They cleansed the soil even as it killed them. They planted the seeds of the future they were never expected to see.

They looked to the stars, dreaming.

They were people of many backgrounds and tongues. They had nothing in common but the knowledge that they were meant to die.

Still, dreaming of tomorrow anyway... doesn't that transcend language?

The story often changed regarding the how, but the enslaved escaped their keepers. With them went satchels of seeds, hopes for the future. With them went the dreams of living and dying on their own terms in this strange, frightening new world. With them went their songs.

They walked for many days. Food ran out. Some got sicker. Some starved.

But hope came for them again.

A young buck, innocent, bred true, bounded through their camp. Its presence told them of safety nearby, of untainted food and water. One deer led the tired refugees to safety. Now, over a century later, crude homes dotted this little valley, sheltered from the radioactive particles on the wind. After so many years, the soil was purified, the crops many.

Hidden in this shattered land that was once a vast nation, these people had grown themselves a pocket of peace.

And Baldur took deep pride in it all. He may have been born a New York citizen, but that was a lifetime ago. These were his people now, and his wife's crown made his heart sing.

Echo arrived at the fore. She spread her arms as if embracing the sky. And then, the sun began to rise, spilling its warmth and life, her antlers holding it aloft. From her lips sprang the beginning refrain. It was a work song once sung in New York's fields over a century back. All of the farmers and warriors in the village knew it still.

It was not long before they all joined in, one grand chorus.

The final planting of the season was here, and they would greet it with a smile.

Baldur beamed up at his wife, his queen. This was not the future his Coalition parents envisioned for him. He was sure they'd meant him to be a trader, just as they were. It was the very reason why they'd left New York to found a settlement.

He knew they would have loved Echo regardless.

And he knew they would have loved their grandson, too. His boy Tiger was a man grown now, tattooed and strong with an unbending back, someone who would one day wear the helm in his mother's place. He was a fighter, that much was certain. And though his son was quiet, Baldur saw wisdom in his eyes. Already, most of the village had taken to calling him Father, the honorific of leaders.

My fierce, brave boy, Baldur breathed in his mind, pride swelling in his heart.

The future was in good hands.

Even if it felt like something was amiss right now.

The old warrior rubbed the hard metal of his arm prosthesis. The phantom sensations remained. In spite of the peace of the dawn song, everything in the air itched, like it had in his dreams—like a storm was coming.

Maybe he was just getting old. Most out here didn't live longer than fifty, and, well… he'd made his peace. His life had been a good one.

But his stomach wouldn't stop flipping. After the work of the day was done, he embraced his wife like a life raft.

And in his dreams, again he was in the fields.

"Blood and vengeance," the dark stranger whispered. The wolf snarled and paced. This time, Baldur dared to meet the man's eyes. They were black pits, liquid void. In their depths, fury burned.

He shot awake, sweating and shaking.

"Can't sleep again, love?" Echo mumbled.

"Yes…" Baldur shook his head, trying to clear it. "I'm fine. Go back to sleep. Dawn will be here soon."

She smiled and curled the furs tighter. Baldur padded out of the house, full of aching age and exhaustion.

The summer was upon them. The crops were going to be bountiful, all the hopes of the year fulfilled. But the atmosphere's electric charge rattled his teeth. His phantom limb groaned. Even the watchdogs were growling and pacing, drooling, hackles raised.

Yes. A storm was on the way.

When the dawn ceremony came, no sun came with it. Clouds thick and black crowded the sky. The breeze turned to a gale. Cold, acidic rain began to spatter. And then came the thunder, the lightning. Back inside the farmers ran. Stopgap shelters went up over the fields.

Baldur watched the storm from his home, miserable. His wife wrapped a blanket around his shoulders and whistled as she prepared tea.

"This could seriously damage the harvest," he whispered. "If the rain is too far from the west, the radiation…"

"It'll be fine," Echo laughed. "This isn't our first storm. You worry too much."

The wind howled on. Trees splintered, branches falling with mighty cracks. The deafening thunder roiled for hours.

It ended long after any good work could have been done, and the only thing left was to repair the damage. Some crops that had been flourishing were snapped and battered. Much had to be collected straight away before it was lost entirely.

As they worked in the damp chill, a great, booming shout came over the valley. "I found something!" Baldur jerked his attention away from laying fresh thatch on his roof.

It was his boy's one-day second-in-command: Shark. This man was a mountain who had taken to filing his teeth in the way of the raiders beyond the valley, his smile fierce as his fists. He was practically a favorite nephew to the family, a canny and curious creature, mind like a steel trap when it came to learning the layout of the wilds. It was for good reason that he was the head of the scouts and patrols.

But in all of Shark's findings beyond their borders, he'd never run towards Baldur's home with such fire in his legs. "Mother Echo! You must come!" His gaze was surprised and wondering. Baldur found he did not like the look.

The problem in question was in the middle of the tomato patch. It was metal and shined, lumpy and misshapen, as big as a man's head.

"What is it?" Echo whispered. She kneeled, scooping it up, turning it in her hands.

Snapped propellers hung limply from its side. They broke off and fell to the earth.

And a tiny red light flickered at its front. An eye.

A memory slammed into the old warrior: his first mother's call to come inside... buzzing red lights in the night...!

Baldur smacked the device from Echo's hands. As it fell, the camera eye lolled around the crops, seeing too much, sending too much! With a fierce battle-shout, he slammed his foot down, crushing it. He stomped and kicked, grief for his parents coming in wave after wave, fury and fear rolling after. Shark backed away.

"What's gotten into you?" Echo demanded. Hurt and confusion burned in her stare.

"Coalition," he panted. "Coalition drone. The wind must have blown it off-course."

This widened their eyes. A dark silence took root.

That night, Baldur dreamed of standing in a field again, but not that of his village. It was the field of his boyhood settlement. His father and mother were talking to a man in Coalition black and gray.

"Come on, it's just a bit of land," the visitor said. His words were full of oil and false cheer. "Let us buy it legally so we can mine. You *are* citizens. We'll give you a fair price."

His mother was white-knuckling her cane. "Baldur," she whispered. Her face was angry and sad. "Go and play, okay? We're having an adult talk."

Baldur turned and obeyed. But as he left, he heard his father's words, the ones that would doom them all.

"I don't care what's here that you want. It's taken us years to build this place. This is our home. We can't leave. *We won't.*"

Baldur began to shake. He looked up to the sky.

Up there, there was a swarm of buzzing, as if someone had rattled a beehive.

There were so many little red lights.

Walking by his side again, there was a stranger and a wolf. The bones in the man's hair rattled in the droning wind.

"Blood," the man said. "Vengeance." Baldur saw now that the stranger was smiling, his teeth as sharp as his beast's. "Will you run forever, little coward? For you could be so much more."

Baldur woke.

Doom came only days later.

He'd known in his heart that it would.

The sun was at its highest when Shark burst through the valley, screaming war. His scouts were not by his side. His right arm was shining red from a bullet wound. Echo rose like the proud queen she was, the tide of battle standing with her. Farm tools became staffs and swords. Old guns came off the walls.

Whining rose in Baldur's ears. Buzzing.

The drones dove out of the blue sky with no warning, nearly twenty of them: a robotic hive. They hovered for a long, lifeless minute.

Waiting. Watching. Recording.

Shark picked up a rock in his good arm and flung it. One toppled to its death.

A loudspeaker screeched, relayed from the airborne eyes, sending people covering their ears.

"BANDIT AND RAIDER SCUM," the loudspeaker accused. "SURRENDER. YOU WILL BE TAKEN INTO CUSTODY PEACEFULLY. YOU ARE ON COALITION LAND. SURRENDER."

Echo barked a laugh of disbelief. "*Your* land?" she challenged. "*Bandits?*"

"Echo!" Baldur grabbed her elbow, pulling her close, a tear sliding down his nose. "We don't have a choice. You know this is what happened to—"

"They would come here too then, and take what we made?" Her teeth bared. "They would call *us* thieves after what *their* people did?"

"Love, we need to run."

"No!" She wrenched her arm away. In her eyes shone a thousand arguments.

"If we don't run," Baldur gasped, "They'll kill us. We can go through the cave by the brook. They likely don't know the tunnel is there. It is better to run than to be *exterminated!*"

She stared.

And he knew his pleas wouldn't reach her, because she wasn't just his wife, wasn't just a mother and sister and friend to her people.

She wore the skull of their guardian savior, and she was something more.

"My great-grandparents would have died before they became slaves to the city again," she hissed. "Take the children. Take those too old to fight. Go through the tunnel and wait for me."

Baldur bowed his head in defeat.

"My love?" She cupped his face, smoothing back his hair. Her hands were so soft, so cool. "Of all of us, you know the world outside. Help the others. Love them as you do me. And know: I will come back to you one way or another."

Then she was gone, gun at her side, feet swift.

Baldur reached out for her far too late.

If you love her, he reminded himself. *You must do what she's asked.*

He did. It was the hardest burden he'd ever borne, gathering up those who could not fight, hiding with his tail between his legs. But he did it.

The minutes crawled as he huddled in the secret tunnel with fifty others—injured and sick, old and young. The sounds of shouting began far away. Guns fired their furious reports.

Shark was standing in a corner clutching his wounded arm. He looked enraged that he wasn't by Tiger's side, that he dared to be injured, that he couldn't avenge his scouts and friends. And just as Baldur decided to speak to Shark, to give him some encouragement... their world fell silent.

Fifty heads raised, clinging to hope, as their people always would.

The thunder of feet began to resound through the cave. "Hide," Baldur hissed, but there was nowhere to go.

It wasn't Coalition. It was a band of those who had been fighting, perhaps fifty.

When they'd gone, there'd been nearly a hundred. Patiently, Baldur scanned the tunnel beyond, waiting for more.

Waiting.

Then, there was one, last straggler.

His son Tiger.

For a moment, Baldur smiled.

But in Tiger's arms was the skull of a deer.

That day, an old warrior's soul dropped into nothingness, leaving just an empty shell behind.

The fighter group was injured and silent, eyes wide, the sinking sensation of loss rolling before them. They were bleeding, frantic.

Shark stepped forward to meet Tiger, his gaze hard. "I know a way out," the sharp-toothed man said. "I know a path through the wilds."

Tiger nodded.

That was it, all that could be said. There was nothing to do but walk.

Baldur did not let himself look back. No one dared speak: an entire village, quiet as the grave.

And when night came, hours later, Baldur was not the only one to fall.

It was his son who came to him as he gasped and choked on his own air. Tiger kneeled. They trembled together with grief and longing, sorrow and rage. In Tiger's arms, there was clutched the weight of leadership, the symbol of their unity. "Father..."

Looking into the nothing-eyes of the skull and then to those of his son... Baldur could see no difference.

"She told me to give it to you."

The old warrior blinked, not understanding.

"You came from the place beyond Sunrise. You know this land. Mother said you would know what we must do. And I'm... *I'm not ready.* I couldn't even... couldn't..."

There was a bullet hole in the helm, just above the eyes. A long crack stretched in its wake. In a faraway place, Baldur saw the blood, saw the single, long, dark hair between its teeth.

"Father..." Tiger's hands shook as he held out his burden. He was a proud man, a strong man.

He was a boy too, a boy with a mother slain.

Like me.

Not knowing what else to do, Baldur took up the skull, cradled it close with his false arm, and with his real one, he pulled his son into an embrace. Together, they wept.

That night, their rations tasted like ash. They shivered into their furs. These stars, these trees—they were hostile, foreign.

Under them, there were only fitful dreams.

And there, the dark stranger waited. "Blood and vengeance," he promised, holding out his hand.

CHAPTER ONE
The Book of Stories

Two months later

Jackson shivered in the lonely wasteland night. He had the ominous feeling he was never going to see home again.

"Two weeks, kid. That's all." His dearest advisor Frank was nodding at him in that gruff, get-on-with-it kind of way. Jackson grimaced. A lot could happen in two weeks. But Frank seemed to hear his words unsaid. "With the credits I've promised this lot, they won't dare hurt a hair on your head. Hell, they would take bullets for you."

"…How many credits again?"

A sandpaper chuckle answered. "Trust me, I've made bargains like this before. It'll be just like camping until things blow over back home. The big guy claims they haven't seen a fight out here for a long while. So you're gonna be fine—and people like this, they know how to protect what's valuable to 'em." He gave Jackson's shoulder a pat with a thick hand that carried the scent of gunpowder and cigars. The other hand passed over a small satchel. "Everything ya need."

Accepting the bag, Jackson kept silent about his bone-deep unease. Belaboring the point would get him nowhere, and he was exhausted enough. He'd just finished fighting men who could snap him in half with their fists or their minds. He'd nearly bled to death twice *today*. What he really wanted at the end of it all was just to have a drink and sleep until next week. He'd love to share that drink with Frank here, the only sort of family he had left, or Anna, the woman who'd saved him, who was now stuck out here with him too.

But New York was miles behind them. The Barrier was a blue, gemlike dream on the horizon.

They were fugitives.

Frank's dark eyes flashed goodbye, because gods knew, he'd never say it. And that was that. The van fired up and peeled away.

The vulnerability of the open sky and the ruined city pressed down on Jackson's heart.

"We'll be okay." Anna came up behind him with a smile bright and dreamy in the moonlight. Her blond hair cast a tangled halo around her head.

How had that grown back so fast? Probably part of her healing magic. Maybe her optimism was too. Jackson knew that for everything he'd been through, she'd been through worse—fighting and running and grieving all she'd known. She'd *never* had a home to go back to in New York. Not in this time, and not in her own over a century ago.

But her hand was warm and reassuring in his, and that, at least, was something he understood. He squeezed it, unused to the companionship but liking it nonetheless.

Thick, dark clouds were beginning to creep across the stars.

There was no time to feel sorry for himself anymore. Anna had fallen in and out of consciousness during much of the drive to the far outskirts of this raider camp—and they needed to walk the rest of the way. Their patron had insisted that if they'd approached while in a vehicle, they might have gotten shot at.

What a lovely welcome.

And that was when Anna's hand went slack again.

"Hey…!" Jackson barely caught her. Her skull sagged only an inch from the concrete. Her eyes rolled back in her head as she shivered violently.

"Woah, what's wrong?" Their mountainous guide moved on surprisingly nimble feet. This giant—Shark, the raider had said his name was—flashed his filed teeth, kneeling, reaching out. Jackson mistrustfully moved his body to block him. Raiders were slavers, by and large. Everyone knew it. Everyone read the Coalition reports.

How good was this one's word, even if he owed them a debt?

Something simmered in those dark, wild eyes. "Easy." The thick, unfamiliar accent almost made Jackson bare his teeth. "I help. I promise. I won't hurt her."

There was the buzz of magic, the cool, soft shadows of the night on Jackson's skin. Could he fight if he needed to? Like he had against that nightmare gladiator in New York's underground, the Tiger?

Yes.

Okay.

Slowly, he eased back.

Shark kneeled closer, brow furrowing under the red tattoo ink that covered his face. A thick finger extended, pressing itself gently to Anna's forehead. It was the movements of an elephant handling an egg. A low hiss escaped his lips. Jackson knew what he meant. Anna's hands were afire too, like tiny furnaces.

"She is sick?" Shark muttered.

"No. Not sick." Jackson winced as a foreign pull trembled in his chest. A strange connection or thread or *something* had sprung up inside him since Anna had knitted his ruined lungs and made him whole. It wrenched in near-agony now, a sickening vertigo.

He could feel her waning consciousness. It was like they were both falling.

"She saved my life," he whispered. "And… and she hasn't been able to stay awake, and…"

Shark's frown grew. "We need to get her back to camp. Now. The rain is coming."

"Do you have a doctor?" The question was a weak one. What could a doctor do for her? He was certain there was something wrong in her *magic.*

Shark's shoulders seemed to shrug *maybe.* It didn't instill confidence. Jackson slung his satchel over his shoulder anyway and lifted Anna as best he could, easing her onto his back, supporting her legs around his waist with his arms. Her grasp hung loose around his neck. Her eyes fluttered, and she leaned into him, making it easier than it might have been otherwise. She wasn't fully present, but it seemed she could hang on.

"Are you sure you don't want me to…?" Shark offered his thickly corded, tattooed muscles.

Jackson barely felt her weight at all. Perhaps it was because he still had her healing magic running in his veins. Perhaps it was because he was terrified.

Either way, he shook his head no.

"Then move fast." The big man launched into a half-sprint. Jackson could only follow.

Anna would grow much heavier, but they didn't stop, not even when the predicted rain began to splatter. Shark let out curses in his native tongue. The cold wet exploded on their skin, alien and frightening. This was the first time Jackson had ever felt *rain*—the Barrier always absorbed it before it could reach him. The city's water was pumped into the dome and purified. Now it soaked into his hair, matting it to his head, mixing with his sweat and making him shiver. He desperately wanted to wipe it away.

But on they ran.

Anna's hair was soft and damp on his neck. Her fragile breathing kissed his cheek. "Where…?" she mumbled.

"It's okay. I've got you," Jackson panted.

It was not okay. The rain was beginning to itch. It began to *sting.*

His skin was burning.

"Shark!" Jackson cried out in alarm. He shook his head, desperate to keep the water out of his eyes.

"Don't stop!" Shark was rubbing his flesh. Angry welts were erupting down his tattooed biceps. "Almost there!"

A horrific crack of thunder punched Jackson in the ribs, vibrating his teeth. Lightning scorched the sky. They ran until they both were gasping, until Jackson's entire body screamed. Derelict buildings and ruined lots passed them, barren of life.

Suddenly, a reedy tattooed man sprung out of *nowhere.* Jackson was knocked off his feet. The butt of a rifle cracked into his side. Anna went tumbling with a weak cry. "No…!"

Jackson's attacker peered down, training a gun barrel as if about to take a head shot. A gruff, questioning noise came from behind a knotty beard, something that sounded like, *"Ayeh?"*

And Shark *howled.* He was screeching in his pidgin tongue, waving his giant arms.

Nine others suddenly appeared on the abandoned block, angry specters springing from hiding. They were armed and baring teeth. Jackson moved in front of Anna again, drenched in the shadows and the lashing wind and the storm, and wondered if he was quicker than their trigger fingers, quicker than their fury and greed towards two Coalition refugees.

But the next words to drop out of his assailant's lips were only, "Shark?"

The mountain made an agile salute with four fingers to his throat, chattering something. A gap-toothed smile answered him. The gun almost wavered a little.

What a lovely welcome, Jackson thought again.

The rest was a rush, getting herded, getting a slick cloak draped over screaming skin. It was barely enough to cover him and Anna both. There was running, and there was more yelling, and the world was thunder and chaos and Anna's weight pinioned on his back.

He was tugged into one of the ruined buildings, shouted at in a language he couldn't comprehend. The smell of mildew and decay swallowed him whole.

This might have been an apartment block once, but it was now a century past maintenance. The air was stagnant. Raw baseboards squealed underfoot. Somewhere, the hiss of water was leaking through the roof.

Another crack of thunder vibrated the walls. One could hope that this storm wasn't what finally collapsed this wreck, but it didn't look like hope counted for much out here.

It burns...

Jackson felt a whine building in his throat. He wanted to scratch off his skin—throw it away, grow something new, something that couldn't feel like this...!

A woman stepped before him holding a candle. For a moment, he forgot his pain, entranced with this singular light in the darkness. A bit of cloth was tied over the holder's right eye, her skin leathery and severe from sun. Her clothes were thin and ripped. "Shark says your friend is sick. I can help her."

"Doctor?" The one word was all Jackson could manage. His legs and back and brain were shrieking.

She nodded. "Maya." Her hand directed him to follow her into a nearby apartment. A man with a rifle hovered nearby, peering suspiciously.

Jackson kept his head down, and no one started a fight.

There was another woman in this room, small, standing by a lumpy hunk of mattress. Her back was bowed with age and care. When she spoke, it was to one-eyed Maya, and it was in a new language, tonal and ringing. "We need to lay her down," Maya said, "And we need to get both of your clothes off. You weren't out in this rain long, but it *will* get bad if you don't clean up and get dry."

Jackson obeyed without question. Gently, he eased Anna to the mattress. A handful of thick woolen blankets were hoarded in the corner, stained, smelly, but they sang to him, as did a pile of canteens resting by their side. He turned that way as the women worked at Anna's clothes, sending self-conscious prickles up his spine.

His shirt came off first, a button-up from his favorite tailor—once white, now soaked through with water and blood. He hadn't really let himself think about how horrific his injuries had been. But… there was a *lot* of blood.

A little dizzy, he ran a hand over his tender, wailing chest, pausing at the ragged scar where the Tiger's spear had run him through.

He still couldn't think about it. Not now.

Jackson grabbed a canteen and started dumping fresh, clean water over his scalp and skin, then started to scrub. The blanket got him dry, but couldn't stop his faint whimper. His entire body was red and tight like a blister.

But slowly, the worst of the sensations faded into a sore numbness. Jackson threw a second blanket around his shoulders, letting it drape down to his knees. With that tiniest bit of privacy, he removed the rest of his clothes, kicking them into the corner, drying himself all the way. The bag he threw into the nearby bathroom, deciding to worry about it later.

Now he was a shivering, aching vulnerability in the dark.

But he could think.

He hooked another blanket under his free hand and walked backwards, passing it to the mattress. The doctor took it, and he heard skin getting wiped down, the two women chattering. He didn't like their low voices, their concerned hush.

He especially didn't like it when the elderly lady shrieked. He spun. The woman was just standing there, gaping, pointing.

Anna, mostly wrapped up in blanket, was *glowing*.

"Oh," was all Jackson could say, addled. "She does that."

There was a ticking, a whining. His eyes fluttered to a nearby table. On it rested an old Geiger counter.

"It's not harmful levels of radiation, in the short-term," he added lamely.

The old woman fled the room, muttering, eyes wide with fright. Maya stared at him, then back to Anna. There appeared to be a lot of words working in her throat, and it looked like she was having quite an ordeal putting them together. Finally, what fell out was a businesslike, "I've cleaned her up. The swelling from the rain will go down soon. By morning, it will be fine."

"That's... good. What about...?"

"The glowing?" There was an edge of hysteria in the question.

"No, no, don't worry about that, it's fine."

"The *radioactivity*, then?" The edge winced louder.

"That... will also go away."

"The Warlord is going to know about *all* of this." She gathered up a small bag in the corner, something that clinked with medicine and tools.

"Wait. Don't go." Jackson moved in front of her, clutching his blanket tighter, not sure he wanted someone named *the Warlord* to be informed of either of them. "...Please. I know it's a lot. Maybe I can explain it later. Just... she needs..."

"She needs what? We don't have any medicine, not even for ourselves. And... and I don't know what's *wrong* with her. There's nothing I can do."

"Is she dying?" Guilt reached icy fingers into Jackson's heart and squeezed.

The doctor closed her eye. "Her pulse is *very* weak. Her temperature... it keeps going far too high, then *much* too low... If she was anyone else, I wouldn't like her odds making it through the night, never mind all *this*…!"

There was the odd sense of floating, of unreality under Jackson's feet.

A note of sympathy flashed across the woman's face. She bit her lip. "I'm sorry. She might make it… if she's strong. But… just… if you care about her, then stay with her. Other people need me. Keep her warm, or cool if the fever goes up. Give her water if she needs it. Other than that…"

There was a helpless shrug.

"Oh," was all Jackson managed, hollow and broken.

The doctor fled. The door opened and shut with a weary creak and slam.

The connection to Anna in his chest trembled, pulling him closer. It urged him to tug the blanket higher over her now-naked shoulders, to try and ease her shaking. Her forehead glimmered with sweat.

He brushed the hair from her eyes, her skin still hot under his fingers. "This is all my fault. I'm so sorry."

Her eyelids fluttered. A reply floated from her lips. "Sing…ing."

"What? Anna?" His heart pounded as he leaned in.

"She's singing again." She said this like it was the most obvious thing in the world. Her eyes rolled back, and she was still.

"Anna?"

The rise and fall of her chest was so slight, he had to put a hand to it to make sure it was real.

"*No.* Not now. Not after everything. Okay?" His voice started to shake.

This wasn't just about someone who fate had thrown in his path anymore. Yes, she'd been like him, lost and with powers she couldn't control. Yes, she'd needed his help, but… now…

Now she knew his secrets, and she didn't even care. She called herself his friend. She'd put so much on the line to keep him safe, was hopeful, positive, and strong, even when she had no right to be. She was a smile in the darkness, a promise they might make it.

And she left this raw heat in his chest… this ache of familiarity, a quiet insistence that there was more to her that he needed to understand.

He couldn't *lose* that now. Couldn't lose *her*. He was starting to realize that the thought of being alone again in this world filled him with a slow, agonizing dread.

Jackson slumped against the wall by her side. A breeze whistled through the room, chilling his agitated feet. He tried pulling them under the blanket, but it was just too short.

"You're going to make it Anna," he whispered. "There so much for you to live for and see. It's just two weeks with us here. Just two. And then Frank is going to get us. He'll have cleaned up the company. We'll find a place that the Mage Order doesn't know about."

He checked again to make sure she was still breathing. She was.

"We'll get you a new identity. Some work. I'll find a way to get the Coalition off my back. You'll find a home. More friends. You probably don't have any problems making friends. You'll be happy."

He knew he was rambling. It all sounded weak, even in his own ears, promises he couldn't keep. Who were these promises for, anyway? He didn't really know what she wanted.

The minutes passed with the bitter smell of the room and Anna's soft sighs. The rain echoed, hard, endless clattering on the roof.

It was then a voice that wasn't his own sliced the air: a man's. *"Helpless."*

"What?" Jackson rose. "Who's there?"

There was another voice, a woman, as close as if she'd whispered in his ear too. *"Hopeless."*

Jackson jumped, then squared his shoulders. He stalked from one end of the room to the other, peering in the bathroom, into the barren kitchenette.

No one was there.

"Hello?"

"Weak. Another Chosen to be sacrificed." The new, gravelly baritone turned the sweat on his neck to a chill. He stiffened, feeling the shadows gather under his hand, preparing himself to lash out. The rain hissed against the window, lightning sending stars into his eyes.

"Too weak. He'll never win."

"The Last."

"Too late. Too old."

"But does he hear?"

"Does he finally hear?"

And Jackson realized: the voices weren't from anyone nearby. There was nowhere to hide.

They were in his head.

Not now. Not now.

Back thudding against the wall, Jackson rubbed his straining eyes. The poisoned tea the Mage Order had been feeding him was gone forever. Whatever it suppressed, he was going to get it all back: his magic. His visions. His terror.

This could have been what happened to Tony. Perhaps the voices had come first, before he started "seeing secrets" and getting murderous nervous tics.

The whispering was getting louder.

"Does he hear? DOES HE HEAR?"

Jackson pulled at his hair, slapping at his ears, trying to jar some part of himself into stopping the hallucination. *It's just in my head. Not now. Anna needs me.* He slumped into a cross-legged stance on the floor.

Something crashed against the window. Jackson leapt up. Lightning tore open the world.

A dark shape perched on the sill: a raven. It stretched its vast wings against the gloom of the true night's sky. The glass thudded as it beat the window frame, over and over.

Shaking, Jackson stepped forward. He could scream at the creature, that which had followed him all his life. He could ignore it.

"To hell with all of you," he said instead.

He undid the latch, shoving the window open. The rain battered his skin, angry, stinging. The gale howled, blowing his hair back, thunder pounding.

The raven gave a long croak in greeting.

"Well, then," Jackson told it, spreading an arm outside of his blanket in challenge. "Come on in. Why don't we talk? Eh?"

He'd expected the bird to flee, as it always did. But it ducked its head low and squeezed through. With a long *quooork*, it shook its feathers free of the wet and fluttered past. Jackson edged from where its talons clicked the floor, shutting the window with a creaky slam.

The storm fell muted. The whispers still marched up and down his skin. "Okay. W-what now?"

The raven, an oil sheen against the darkness, lifted its beak from where it was smoothing its primaries. It cocked its head. *"Rawwwk."*

"That's v-very helpful," Jackson snapped. "Thanks."

"Awwwk."

Jackson quieted. If he was losing his mind, it wouldn't help if everyone here knew it. Yet, that was the thing, wasn't it? He wasn't sure if he was crazy. After all, even if Tony had been very, *very* broken, he'd seen the ravens too. "Why am I hearing voices?" Jackson muttered, kneeling down into a perch to match the bird's. "Why are you always there? *Why?*"

The creature stared up at him, beady eyes reflecting the light from Anna's skin. It opened its beak.

Jackson snorted. *Why do I expect you to answer?*

"Seeeeecrets."

The word was a harsh, inhuman thing. Jackson scrabbled away, wide-eyed.

"Seeecrets!" The raven hopped past him in a waddle-flutter, stopping just around the other side of the mattress. It rapped its beak on the ground once, twice, *thrice.* Its obsidian eyes sparkled with challenge.

Jackson, shaking, followed. The whispers were swirling around his ears, so close, repeating in an endless refrain.

"*Too weak.*"

"*Too late.*"

"*Does he finally hear?*"

The ghosts in his ears suddenly spoke as one. "*JACKSON.*"

Then silence. Nothing. Only his breathing remained, shallow and scared.

"*Awwwk,*" the raven said.

Where it had knocked... the floor sounded hollow.

Something's there.

An intense urge seized Jackson's hands, lighting up his spine. For just a second, he knew he glimpsed something important, a crack in the veil of mysteries, mysticism, and visions.

A secret!

What if it meant no more fear? An answer! Hope!

What if it meant he could do something to help his only friend?

That was all he needed. He tore at the floor, cutting his fingers prying, working the rotted wood. Splinters dug into his fingertips.

Destiny, Jack, a voice in his head muttered: Tony's voice. *Gotta get your destiny!*

The fevered mood wrapped around him tighter. The board popped free. Jackson stared down into the black hole it left behind.

"*Rawk!*" the raven cheered.

Reaching inside, Jackson was like a man possessed, unable to see, expecting a rat to bite him. The shadows in the hole felt as if they were bending *around* his fingers, thick and soupy.

His grasp met something. It wasn't a rat. It was rectangular, hard, and smooth. Sucking in a breath, Jackson pulled it loose. The sides of the boards scraped his knuckles raw. "Gah!"

There it was. He sat back, taking in the mystery object.

An old book.

The black, leathery cover was scuffed and dinted, uneven and blotchy. Jackson squinted, seeing no words on the front, only ragged leather stitching and waxy, yellow pages. Good gods, was that *vellum?* Whatever it was, it should have been in a museum, not buried under some hovel.

There was a paper slip sticking out of the pages, but it was no antique. It was folded neatly in half, one edge exposing the outstretched wings of a dove.

This book, miles from home in a derelict building, had his adopted father's stationary tucked inside.

What the hell...?

With quavering hands, Jackson took the paper's edge, sliding it out, taking in the familiar whorls and loops.

Dad...

He read the impossible page, the paper alight under Anna's glow.

My dear son,

Please, before doing anything else, understand this: you have been my greatest pride.

His throat tightened, and for a moment, Jackson had to look away. All these years had passed, and this particular hole in his life had never stopped hurting. It was then he realized the raven had vanished. His mouth dried. His hands shook harder.

The bird's barely real anyway. Why should it have stayed?

Trying not to examine this thought too deeply, he kept reading.

When this book appeared on my shelf, it was the week I brought you home, and... well, you owned nothing, so I thought it couldn't have been yours. I thought maybe Catherine bought it before she died. Pre-Bombings books—that's a love you share with her, you know. But this specimen was all blank. So, I brought it to my office, wanting to take a closer look.

It disappeared. I thought it was stolen. But when I looked at our shelf again at home... there it was. Twice, this happened. Uneasy, I threw it away. It returned. I was afraid; I didn't understand why this was happening. I tried to burn it, bury it, tear it apart.

It always came back.

In the end, I went to Huxley. I heard from my own father the sort of bizarre work he did during one of the coups. Occult—well, you know.

Jackson's lip curled.

Son, the look on his face when he opened these pages... he was scared. He said it wasn't haunting me—it was following <u>you</u>. Waiting for you to notice it. He said it was a curse, a trap. He said there are those that hate people born like you, and that the less I knew, the better.

He swore he would help you as best he could. And I just don't know what else to try.

Yes, Huxley had helped, alright. Conniving bastard almost killed him.

We may never know who put this burden on your shoulders. But, reading this book, Huxley claims, would be your death.

We couldn't destroy it, no matter what we did. I'm so sorry. We could only hide it nearby.

So now you know why it's under the floorboards in your room. I prayed you'd never find it, though if you're reading this... well. I never was a good servant of God. I suppose He chose not to answer my pleas.

But Jackson, until the day I die, I will protect you, and I know Huxley's people will protect and guide you after that. I <u>know</u> you are a curious one. But leave the book. Spit in the face of curses. Live your life instead, and become the incredible man I know you will become.

Love always,

Dad

Jackson rocked back on his heels, sitting heavy. His core shuddered, and he gathered the blanket close, trying to think.

Spit in the face of curses? That really was something Dad would say—and it was great advice. This book was clearly magical, if it had followed him from under the floor back home, all the way to under the floor out here.

But words from a dream man also came to him. *The book of stories. Secrets kept from you. Secrets that are rightfully yours.*

Tony's final prophecy rang in his mind too: *"He's waiting for you. In the walls. Under the floorboards. He's listening."*

Jackson re-folded the letter and set it down.

The ravens wanted me to find this. Maybe I was finally ready to find it, without the Order's poison slowly killing me.

The magic was pacing his mind, calling to him. It was a steady hum in the room, a pulse. He couldn't just un-remember something like this and stuff it back where it came from. After all, Huxley was a *liar.* His father couldn't have known the old man's advice came with dark ulterior motives.

In the here and now, Anna was still breathing, and that might not last long. Could finally finding this help…?

Jackson placed a ginger touch on the cover. An electric shock coursed up the tough leather, connecting into the hum in his mind. Warmth! The buzzing swelled and harmonized, singing down his spine. Jolted, Jackson tore his hand back. The sensation faded.

He breathed in wonder. This time, the magic didn't turn his stomach. This time… it felt *right.* It felt like the connection with Anna when she'd healed him under the fading sky, as if he was bonding soul to soul with another. It was pure. It was as if everything was as it should be.

This is my book. The thought settled into his body, into his clenching hands. *It's mine.*

It was in his grip before he could think better of it. He was breathing in the scent of musty pages and antiquity, hugging it to his chest. His body tingled pleasantly.

Live your life and become the incredible man I know you will become.

The cover fell open almost of its own accord, and the whispering swelled, a thousand voices giddy and warm in greeting. They rang in a chorus, then peeled away one by one. Finally, only one singer remained, a familiar baritone leading them all: the rich, laughing voice of the starry-eyed man of Jackson's dreams. His words became clear as day.

"Welcome, Chosen! Welcome, at last!"

Then the room faded, and Jackson realized there was nothing around him anymore, only him and this book, him and this divine song.

No ceiling.

No walls.

No *floor.*

His heart twisted. His stomach flipped with the weight of gravity. Jackson let out a startled scream.

And then he fell, deep into the darkness that had swallowed him.

CHAPTER TWO
Sunrise

Anna slumbered, dead to the world. Her fevered heat was a tight fog, casting her mind inwards.

Anna dreamed.

She walked the wasteland as she'd seen it only hours before, an echo of a song she didn't know in her ears. There was no Jackson here this time, reassuring her, getting her through. No guide.

No moon, either—the sky was endless and black.

Why weren't there any stars?

Under her skin, her internal light sputtered and faded. She'd leaned on her strange powers too much, desperately pouring almost all of herself into saving Jackson's life.

She didn't regret that. After all, he'd pulled her out of a prison, becoming a backbone of friendship, safety, and kindness in a world she no longer knew.

But... what would happen if her light went out entirely?

What would she do, alone and blind in the dark?

What else might be out here with her?

Her teeth chattered, insides quivering with cold and fear. At the nape of her neck, her skin prickled, her stomach dropping as if something was watching her. But when she tried to peer into the night, she could find nothing.

Why did Jackson and Shark leave me…?

Her steps found their way through the mournful emptiness of homes, parks, and lives that used-to-be. It was all dirt and rotted building frames now, abandoned when her world died in hellfire and poisoned air.

Her cheeks were wet. Startled, she wiped the tears away. Crying wouldn't help.

But her lonely heart ached like it had been bared and ripped open. The crying was going to happen whether she wanted it or not. The wind made strange noises as it scraped through this dead place: old ghosts moaning. Anna wrapped her arms tighter around herself, trying not to let her mind drown in the empty sorrow of this wasteland, this echo of the home she'd lost forever. Her inner light quavered like a dying coal.

Suddenly, there was scrabbling to her left. She whipped her head to see.

In the blackness of the night, she thought she saw a form shifting through the rubble. She blinked and rubbed her eyes, wanting to be sure.

Two pale orbs flickered, reflecting her glow. Then they were gone.

A fear-soaked memory came: mutant dogs in the subway tunnels, pale, slavering, tumor-riddled beasts. Anna's hands sunk into her pockets, but she had nothing—no weapons, no hope of defending herself. Her breath came in frightened pants.

The wind changed direction with a *skreee, skreeeeee* noise, like it was laughing at her. It froze the sweat trickling down her neck.

Another pair of pale orbs blinked down the road. She spun.

Another pair flickered to her right.

How many of these things…? She couldn't tell. But in some deep, instinctive place, she knew they were hunting her. Primordial dread leached into her bones. She couldn't run forward, back, or to the side. Beasts prowled in every direction. She saw now the shifting shadows of bodies, drawing in a tightening circle, a noose.

A hiss came from behind her, a warm breath on her chilled skin. *"Dr. Anna Matthews."*

She spun with a shriek, throwing her hands up, shielding herself.

Just at arm's length, there stood a man. He was well-muscled, pale-skinned, and blue-eyed, hair shorn in a military buzz cut. His boyish face was that of a stranger. But his gaze, it was hollow and old, eyes of a man that had seen too much, *caused* too much. His combat fatigues were blotted with blood, dark and drying. She knew then in an instant who this man was, even though she'd never directly looked on his face.

His pistol was in his hands by his side. That gun was the last thing she'd seen before he'd murdered her: the dark barrel of cold steel. The name on his uniform was obscured with blood.

"You," she breathed. "You're *dead.*" He had to be dead. *Everyone* was dead.

"Yes." He smiled. "And you're *supposed* to be." The pistol raised, came level with her face. "So how are you still breathing? What gives you the right?"

Time slowed as she stared down that barrel once more. The animals in the dark were tightening their ring. She'd be dead before they even reached her.

Run? He would have shot her before she'd gone a few feet. *Not again. Oh God, not again.* Hot tears leaked from the corners of her eyes. "Please," she whispered. "Please, no."

"Why are you breathing?" her murderer hissed. Blood began to seep through his teeth, running down his chin. It flew out in his spittle. "It's... not... your... right!" Smoking bullet holes began to shred open his shirt, the ones Anna guessed eventually ended his killing spree. He stood as if nothing about this fazed him.

Dread wrenched her words. "Stay away from me...! You...! You're dead! You, you can't hurt me!"

The specter blinked. The smile twisted wider. His eyes began to melt from his head. The whites ran down his cheeks in a curdled stream. Anna felt bile rise in her throat, a horrified scream building. "We burned. Everyone burned." In his eye sockets now rested dark pools, endless, infinite, fury burning within. "Everyone but you. But you should have burned with us. Died in our blood and vengeance! *What gives you the right not to burn?*"

"*Get away from me!*" She screamed, staring into those hateful pits. Her hands rose to protect herself. "*Get away!*"

Flames roared up before her, the light searing her sight. The fire tore the shadows back. Her murderer screamed. The blaze caught the edge of his gore-spattered uniform, and he flailed, the fire raging across his body as if he was made of tinder.

Then he simply dissolved, smoke in the ether.

Anna collapsed, panting by the fire. Silence. *He's gone.* A sob shook out of her throat.

For once, Anna let her questioning mind live without the answers she couldn't give it. She didn't even care that these sudden flames were burning merrily on the mud, needing no fuel at all. Their warmth hugged around her. The light told her one primal truth: *I'm safe. He's gone.* And so were the wild animals in the darkness, scattered by the flaring bright.

So too did the crushing sorrow flee from her heart, just a little.

She curled her knees up to her chin, inching as close to the guardian flames as she could without singing her hair. Smoke and ash stung her nose. *What was that thing?*

There Anna sat, wringing her hands, aching and queasy. When she realized she had no answers, she tried to plan. Where was she going to go now? How long would this fire last? She'd been a Girl Scout for six months, but unfortunately, she'd learned nothing of navigating the wilderness. She'd only gone on one camping trip, during which she just missed her mom for three days.

Memories bubbled to the surface of that time, when she'd been sashed with green by another fire, learning songs that helped keep the homesickness at bay. That was when the world had been whole.

She breathed in the heat. It was soothing. So long as she looked into this fire and not behind her, her good memories didn't seem so far away.

Then, something new caught her eye.

There were two more tiny moons bobbing in the light at the fire's perimeter.

The hairs on Anna's neck rose. *Are those animals back?* She looked for a stone to throw.

Something was strange about these eyes, though; they didn't weave low to the ground. Despite their reflective quality, they were at the height of a human, a person walking towards her.

"Stay back," she whispered. The sound didn't even carry over the fire's crackling. "Stay back!" she said again, standing, trying to make herself bigger. *No more ghosts. No more crazy monsters!*

The eyes stopped and stared.

"Anna?"

The tenor of the man's voice floating to her was… familiar. She clenched her fists, swallowing hard. "Who are you? Don't come any closer!"

"Anna? It's, it's *me!* It's Jackson!"

Anna gasped. Now the eyes were bobbing closer, and as he came into the light, she saw it really *was* him, lean and disheveled as usual. His relieved smile beamed at her under a shock of tousled black hair. Relief almost cracked her heart in two.

But he was wearing… a dirty blanket. He might have *only* been wearing a blanket. His bare feet were filthy and looked to be bleeding. In one arm, he was cradling what looked like a book.

"Jackson!" She didn't even know what else to say. His appearance was bizarre, but so was everything else she'd seen in the last twenty minutes. "Why are you…?" He shook his head in a helpless way. "Where have you been? Where are we?"

"I don't know." He crept closer to her, squeezing the blanket tighter. Anna realized he was shaking. "Are you alright?"

"No," she said. "Come here. It's really cold."

"Y-yeah," he agreed. He sat, and she settled next to him, looking at his pale shins and bare feet. His toes curled in the fire's heat, as if he was working feeling back into them. "C-couldn't have fallen into a bad hallucination while dressed, could I?"

She snorted, leaning into his side, sharing her warmth. "Hallucination, huh? Is that what we're doing?" This hypothesis both frightened and reassured her.

"Yes," he said, nodding solemnly.

"I wish it would stop." She couldn't stop her voice from hitching.

"Me too." There was a cool, tentative brush on her hand, and she realized it was his fingers, poking out from under the blanket, trembling. She took them and squeezed, relieved. He licked his lips, chapped, cracked. "I'm not totally certain you're real," he said. "But I'm worried about you."

Anna drew back. "Real? Why would I… I *am* real." It was the only thing she was sure of. But suddenly, she wasn't so sure about *him*. "You're the one that almost bled to death. You're the one wandering around the wastelands with just a blanket and a book! Why?" She didn't even know if they *made* books anymore, not with those crappy datapads everyone seemed to have.

Jackson swallowed. Anna peered at the pages by his side, left open. They shimmered strangely, as if ink was spilling over them in pools and whorls, dancing mirages. A sharp pain lanced her eyes. She winced.

Not wanting to think about it, about anything else so unnatural, she turned back to his face, flushing with embarrassed heat. "Seriously, where are your clothes?"

He laughed. But, something about it made it seem like it wasn't because things were funny.

And before he could say more, the distinctive noise of a clap rang through the air: slow, lazy applause.

Anna jerked her head away from her friend. Just across the fire, though no one had been there before, a person sat cross-legged on the dirt. He was, Anna thought, far too well-dressed for this dusty, dead place, tailored up in a business suit and shined, black shoes. If he hadn't made a sound to announce himself, her eyes might have passed over him many times before realizing he was there. Everything about him seemed to bleed into the night beyond the fire. His hair, his clothes, his skin, his... his eyes. They were void-like orbs, like the ones that had been lodged in the head of the bleeding specter of the soldier. She shuddered, afraid. And yet, in these eyes, there was something beyond just the shadow. There were... lights? Tiny, cheerful lights?

She drew in a surprised breath, unable to understand what she was seeing. Looking in those eyes made her thoughts ooze to a contented crawl.

"I told you I'd see you again, Jackson," the man spoke.

"What? Who are you?" Anna said. She shifted her stare to his hands. His thin fingers were drumming together in a musical pattern.

Jackson had gone very still beside her. "You," he whispered.

Anna heard the smile in the stranger's reply. "I was waiting here for you. I was beginning to think you'd never come." His fingers stopped thrumming, instead forming a steeple. This, he pointed to Anna's nose. "*You*, however. You are not supposed to be here tonight. How is it you touch this place? I did not invite you. And you've been drawing the wrong kind of attention, that is *certain*."

Anna's vision blurred and stung. A lonely ache sprung up in her chest. The man's question was an echo of the words the specter had spoken. *Not supposed... to be here.* Her fists clenched. *Not supposed to be alive.* She swallowed. "I don't know why I'm here, but you can deal with it."

There was a long silence. Then, the stranger began to quiver, vibrant giggles filling the air. There were dark things in that laughter, dark secrets. As if forced by the sound, she looked up. His pearly smile seemed to float in the shadows, his starry eyes hypnotic. "Ah. I see. You burned your fires too low, so now you walk the veil. And your power... you wound it up with his...?" He pointed at Jackson and sniggered. "Did you at least buy him dinner first?"

"What are you saying...?" Jackson growled.

"Do you know this... this..." Anna's lips kept trying to form the word *man*, and wouldn't. *This can't be real. None of this can be real.* This being, this *creature's* presence, that mocking, piercing lilt in his voice... it was the final straw for her suspicions.

I'm dreaming!

The realization hit her as if she was dunked in ice.

"Silly woman. Off you go," the being said with a laugh. "It is not your time. And this is not your path. *She* is here for you, to guide you home, not ready to let you go, it seems." He made a shooing motion. "Though I... am intrigued."

Anna turned to Jackson, feeling something tugging at her core, something intangible and powerful. She was suddenly drifting, not away from the fire, but *into* it. And, something about this, wrapped in the ineffable logic of dreams, felt right. The flames licked around her, and yet they didn't hurt. There was something beautiful in the crackling, a note she hadn't heard before—music.

A song.

Wait. Jackson! I can't leave him here alone in the dark with these monsters! She turned from the voice in the fire.

"Anna...!" Jackson shouted, surprised, reaching for her hand again as she fell away. He passed through her grip, like she was becoming vapor. Warmth infused her bones, all the way to her center. "Wait! Where are you—!"

She awoke to the morning sun splitting the room through a window draped in broken blinds. Groggy, she lifted her head. There was a song she didn't know in her ears, but it was beautiful, even though she couldn't place it as it faded.

Her skin was glowing, filling her with warmth. Shocked, she willed it to dim, and it did.

She was breathing hard, like she'd been running or fighting. Great. Another nightmare. An awful one this time, something that was making her stomach quiver. But now that she was awake, she was just left with a sense of alarm and puffs of a fading dream. Stars. Darkness. Blood.

A... a fire?

Wasn't there a fire?

Her head was searing open from the inside, some horror in the back of her mind. Her legs and torso burned, hard, fiery spots... the places where bullets had once taken her.

Don't think about it. She'd never put much stock in dreams, so she tended to forget them on waking. Anything that made her feel like this, well, she didn't mind letting it go.

So she breathed in and out, looking up at the ceiling. It was pockmarked and foreign, all rippling stains and crumbling holes. *Where am I?* She didn't know this place. She didn't even have the memory of climbing into bed.

Sitting upright almost made her throw up. She swayed, dizzy, and forced herself to stand. Her ankles felt, at first, like they'd break. She stayed up. They didn't. Somewhere, there was a steady dripping of water, the echoes long and piercing.

Anna swayed. Around her was a red, scratchy blanket—had someone taken her clothes? Embarrassed heat began to swell across her face. But the chill of the baseboards made her concerned with socks most of all. She let her eyes pass over tattered curtains and mangled flower-print wallpaper. The floor groaned in an alarming way as she began to walk. A hundred unkind years had passed through this place, just as they'd missed her entirely.

She kind of remembered her wasteland journey now... the acrid tang still hanging in the air must have been from the rain.

Her world suddenly tilted a few degrees.

She threw a hand out, catching the doorknob, bracing herself. Her vision swam. *Easy. Take it easy.* What had she done to make herself so sick? She went to one knee, unsteady... and there before her was a minor miracle. Her socks. They were lying out as if they'd been put there to dry. Grateful, she regained her footing and tugged them on. The rest of her clothes were nearby too, and she wrapped herself up in them like they were the finest discovery in the world.

Then, she saw another bundled blanket curled up in a corner on the floor. *Jackson?* One of his bare feet stuck out from underneath, though the rest of his body was tightly bound up in a ball. Something made her heart beat faster, a sense of déjà vu. He was shaking in the morning air. *Did he sleep here on the hard ground all night?* Guilty, she lifted the blanket from her now-dressed shoulders, unfurling it and draping it over him and his exposed toes. His shaking quieted.

She settled by his side, tired, confused. For a moment, despite her anxiety, there was a little warm tug in her chest, in the spot that had tethered Jackson to her during the healing. Sitting with him here, it felt familiar and good. It felt safe.

She was struck then by the desire to squeeze his hand or put her arm around him. But an apprehensiveness of uncertain boundaries made her stop.

There was something else sticking out of the corner of Jackson's blankets though, something he was cradling near his chest. An edge of... old leather? *Is that a book?*

Something dropped in the pit of her stomach, a powerful memory. The dream she'd dismissed flickered in the back of her mind. Overpowered by sudden curiosity, she lifted the edge of the blanket to see the book better.

And with a crash, the bedroom door swung open, hitting the wall.

She jerked her hands back, bringing them up in defense. There, towering above her, stood a mountain of a man, a hulking muscled figure of tattoos and very, very sharp teeth. He gripped an automatic rifle in one hand. His gun swung wildly.

"YOU LIVE!" Shark cackled. "Good! GOOD! Because it is time for *WAR!*"

CHAPTER THREE
Outcasts

Jackson sat alone in the wasteland dark. The man with stars in his eyes was bearing him down.

"Anna!" he called out. The fire flickered pleasantly, as if it hadn't just swallowed his friend whole.

"Just you and me," the being across the flames chirped. "It's about time."

The fabric of Jackson's anger was fraying, the threads about to snap. His head pounded. He'd fallen in this beast-ridden hellhole clutching nothing but a book and a too-thin blanket. He'd looked around in wonder and fear into the whipping wind. And the voice in his head had echoed, *Welcome Chosen, welcome to the Shadow!*

There'd been baying in the dark, the calling of hunters.

He'd run.

And when his breath was about to give out, as the panting and snarling of the monsters drew close, he'd seen a miracle. He'd seen light. And he'd torn for it. The fire had kept the beasts away. Why Anna had been there waiting for him, he didn't know. Maybe it was because it was her he'd been searching for.

Now she was gone. Again. There was only this laughing creature who'd tormented him with mysteries for long enough.

"What the hell is going on?" Jackson spat. He drew up the book, shaking it. "What is this thing? Who *are* you?" His final question made his stomach broil. "What did you do with her?"

The man frowned. "We don't have time to discuss irrelevant matters."

"Irrelevant? *No*—I don't feel they are."

"We don't have time to discuss your feelings either."

Jackson rose, knowing he wasn't the least bit imposing, clutching his blanket to his body like an uncooperative toga. "I opened that book so I could help her! Where is she?"

The darkness around the man seemed to shimmer in waves. He was only sitting, and yet, he towered. "Help her? Is *that* why you finally started listening?" He giggled. "I granted you the gift to see in the dark… but you don't look very far, do you? What are *you* supposed to do for her? And that tone! Did you know that once, your people *begged* for my favor?" Jackson shivered. His breath began to puff in icy bursts. "Did you know that once, they sacrificed? That once, they remembered that I could simply pluck them from the tapestry of the universe's story, cast them in the void, as if they never were?"

A sick wave of vertigo billowed forth from those cosmic eyes.

Then the being chittered, jiggling his knees with laughter. He was so overcome that after a few moments, he wiped away a tear. "So serious. Look, she didn't need you. Another has her. Lucky, yes? A dangerous place she ventured, her light near spent. So, so close to just…" He made a slippery gesture with his hands, puffing air like he was blowing a tiny life into nothing. The motion punched Jackson in his solar plexus. "She will handle herself. It is wiser for you to focus on your own problems. The wolves circle closer, Jackson." His eyes took on a hard glint. "*Ever closer.*"

There was a brief shine of a beast's eyes far off in the dark. The creatures out there weren't leaving. Jackson tensed into a tight coil.

"But, you've found the book!" the man continued, speaking

quickly, ignoring the night prowlers. "So the first part of your life, all you were—it is over. It does not matter. For you are now my Chosen."

Wait. What? Something about this statement made Jackson clench his fists. He spoke in a hush this time, even though his teeth were on edge. "You've never even told me who you are! Stop making me fight you for answers!"

"Fight? I've been quite clear if you're clever." The being licked his lips thoughtfully. "My name, if it's really that important... well... I have been known by so *many*." He cast a hand at the dark sky. "The Dreamwalker. The Great Storyteller. The Star-Stringer. I am he who pulled your people to greatness a very, very long time ago, and he who would do it again. You've heard another of my true names, have you not?"

Jackson ground his jaw, his bones aching in recognition. "Tony said *Inoki*. I haven't been able to get it out of my head. That was you, wasn't it? He saw visions of you. Of the ravens."

"Very good!" The man began a slow, steady applause once more. "Tony *always* remembered. Yes. Such a good boy. Slowly helping you put together the pieces of your destiny." The humor in his voice faded. "Very slowly."

The chill in the air kept creeping in, no matter how tightly Jackson pulled the blanket. *Such a good boy.* A strange definition of those words.

Then cocking his head, Inoki stood.

And the absent moon suddenly rose with him in the empty sky. Jackson's jaw dropped.

The moon was a shining halo over those midnight braids, and the being strode closer, a careful, purposeful walk. The moon moved *with* him, as if it were a crown.

A god! Jackson's bones suddenly told him, shivering, aching, recoiling in fright. *He IS a god!*

"Yes," Inoki whispered, lips parting in a pearly smile. "You finally start to understand."

Jackson didn't *want* to understand this. He didn't want this creature near him, suddenly a small speck of life before a towering mountain—and Inoki wasn't just the moon, not just the man, but the darkness that surrounded it all, the air here, the earth, and the shadows in between, it was all... all him...!

Even as his brain screamed to run, the sheer vastness of what this creature was froze him in place.

Inoki kept walking, aura moving with him, stifling the air, suffocating. Jackson couldn't breathe. The weight of presence was about to crush this fire circle and everything in it.

But it didn't.

The god simply kneeled, outstretching one finger, tapping the book at Jackson's side. The roiling wave of power broke. It was possible to breathe once more.

The tome made a shocking thrum of what could only be described as *delight*.

"My gift to that which is mine." The god's soft whisper came. "Your answers. It will tell you the stories. It will prepare you. Teach you. Guide you. Because your purpose..." A damp sadness glittered across his starred eyes. "Is to survive. One day, it will be to tell a new story of this world that is not so very tragic. It will be to turn the tide in this game."

"...Game?" Jackson managed.

"For now, your purpose is only this: *live*. My opponent... he would have your cities choke on war and poison and terror. He would destroy all you hold dear. He is the Fear in the Dark, and he walks the Shadow as surely as I, whispering into ears, plying minds. He has manipulated you. He has tried to kill you. Just as he has killed so *many* before. Hundreds of years... slaughter, terror, famine, bombings, nothing but blood spilled, over and over and *over*."

Jackson's jaw worked as he reeled. "I... I am a businessman, and I am a *smuggler*, and... and I am a lot of things, but... I'm not... I mean, what do you expect me to—"

"What you *were* does not matter. I have said this. Only what you *are*. I want you, little one, to learn what it means to be a hero. Good versus evil, yes? That is simple. Think of it that way, if you struggle so. You will evade death, fight the bad, save the day, and you will try to... er..." The being waved a hand on his wrist as if trying to fill in blanks. "Get the girl or something? That is an exciting goal, right?" The gleaming teeth flashed.

The sluggish cold in Jackson's blood slowed his mind. But he bristled. A hero? In his experience, nothing was simple, and good and evil were never so *plain*.

"You should learn quickly." Inoki's smile widened in a peculiar, fraught way. His form began to waver, as if he were not entirely there. Darkness bled through his body. Jackson, still clutching the thrumming, warming book, reached out in surprise.

His touch went through the god's body as well, just as it had Anna.

"A new war is coming," Inoki whispered. The wind blew harder. The fire shuddered and swayed, flickering.

"What do you mean? There has to be more you can—"

But when Inoki's lips moved for the last time, they said only one word: "WAR."

A crowing bellow tore through Jackson's mind, a resounding echo. "It is time for *WAR!*"

He launched up, out of the vision, out of the darkness, rocketing into the morning. He was on his feet, adrenaline firing and singing in his ears, and there was a gods-damned raider in his face, brandishing an automatic rifle. Jackson let out a holler, and part of him was in that place called the Shadow still. It reached out, into the crevices of the room where the sun hadn't touched. It clutched at the darkness there, and the shadows began to bend and waver, ready to become impossibly solid in his defense.

"Hey! Hey, it's okay!" There was a hesitant touch on his bared forearm. He whipped his head around to see Anna, awake and well.

The raider was laughing harder now, swinging the gun away from them, slinging it up onto his back. *He's not shooting us. He's… he's… what the hells is going on?* "Anna? Where…?" Jackson closed his eyes and shook his head, feeling a sickening sway of vertigo. Reluctantly, he let the shadows go, heart thundering, breath quick.

The raider kept laughing, the merriment starting to squeeze out tears in the corners of his eyes. Jackson recognized his ugly face now, that wild, throat-tearing grin: Shark. "Sorry I interrupt! It's time to go. Get clothes! Go, go! You don't make the Warlord wait!" Shark waved a meaty hand over his broad shoulders and stomped back out, clearly expecting that they would follow.

Jackson breathed, trying to get his heart to slow. *What? Is this real?* He had no idea if he had a proper hold on his mind anymore. *Clothes…?*

It was then he realized his blanket had sagged when he'd bolted to his feet, and he was now standing there, mostly naked, important bits only *barely* concealed. A stiff breeze would change that.

"OH." Jackson darted his hands down and wrangled the blanket close, mortified. He hazarded a glance at Anna. She had turned away, hands wringing, her face a brilliant red. "Uhhhh," she said.

Jackson's words failed him. Regardless, he scrabbled for a sentence, trying to string together… anything… a distraction! "You're… you're looking… okay?"

"Um. Thanks!" She was still not quite looking at him.

"I mean, that is, you were really sick. And now you look better."

She nodded frantically. "Mmm-hmm! Feeling better."

"Really glad you're okay!"

"Mmm-hmm!"

"Good!"

"Yep!"

He began to back away, hoping to salvage some aspect of this morning. "Going to… going to find my clothes. Probably dried out by now."

"Okay!"

He turned, walked with intense purpose into the bathroom, closed the door, and escaped.

Good job, he told himself, sarcastic even in the comfort of his head.

But she was okay. She was safe, made it through the night. There was a mess of heat in his chest now, his heartbeat tripping over itself.

She's okay.

Thank the gods.

...I'm an idiot.

The mud and howls and cold, it all still was right at the edge of his nerves. His brain was still struggling with what he'd seen, or what he'd *thought* he'd seen... or...

Of course, he'd let all of it get to him and came swinging out of that nightmare vision, letting his ass give her a good hello.

Get dressed. Clothes will help.

Wait. His uniform was stained through with blood and forgotten outside the door.

Jackson braced himself, realizing he needed to leave the bathroom to get it... but then, something on the back of the toilet caught his eye. A pile of brown cloth. Concerned, Jackson hooked the fabric with a suspicious grip, unfurling it. It was a pair of pants made of mismatched brown hide, hand-stitched. Under it was a yellowed and handspun cotton shirt. *Raider gear.* The garments were a little torn, but one might imagine that they were almost his size. Someone had painted a black insignia over the heart; it appeared to be some beast's antler. A deer's? He'd seen them in books.

Jackson felt his mood sinking even more, his lip curling. These sorts of things... he could be mistaken for one of *them*. A scavenger who made their living harassing and stealing with no regard for life or property.

But there was nothing else.

A sudden pang of alarm coursed through his veins. He dove for his bag that he'd thrown in here last night.

It was undisturbed.

He breathed a sigh of relief. Inside, untouched, was a full cache of Quarantine, the radiation resistance drug. He'd be due for his dose tonight. *One shot a day, keep the poison away.* Such medicine was gold in this place—and beneath it was a small stash of ration bars. If the raiders found any of this...

Jackson smiled. Nestled next to the food was something that made him glad Frank was his contingency planner: a long-range emergency communicator. There was no screen, no datalink access, no bells or whistles. It was no more than a heavy-duty walkie-talkie, really. Yet out here, it meant he wasn't cut off from home. Not entirely.

Not alone. Thank you, Frank.

Jackson bit his lip and reluctantly pulled his new clothes on. The pants were too loose, as most pants were for him until they'd been tailored, but a knotted rope at the bottom of the pile let him pin them up. The shirt sagged on his frame. He felt as if he was wearing a costume.

Luckily his old shoes and socks had been laid out neatly on the tub's edge. Those at least were his size, and though they were dirty, they'd been spared the worst of his injuries.

Braced, he swung open the bathroom door. Waiting there were two wide blue eyes.

Anna was again wearing the old courier uniform Frank had given her. In her arms was something that made his heart skip: a ratty old book, covered in dark leather. Tucked inside was his father's stationary. "Hey..." she mumbled. "You had this. It looks old... I don't know if you want to leave it behind..." She proffered it up. Wordlessly, he accepted it, a lump in his throat.

This was a real thing, right out of his god-laced hallucinations and into his hands.

"Thank you," he whispered. Uncertain, he darted a hand behind the door and picked up his satchel. Now, it would also hold this book. He wasn't sure if his whispers and visions would come back with touching it for too long. Right now, he didn't want to experiment.

The unfortunate thing was that he barely knew how to handle Anna either. "Sorry, about… earlier. My clothes were soaked through… the rain… which was why I…"

Her cheeks tinged brighter pink, but she nodded. "Ha, it's okay. We're even now I guess." Jackson raised his eyebrows. He remembered how they'd met: she'd been naked in a box under the bare sky. "You know," Anna muttered, "I keep wondering… if the Coalition was the one to find me outside New York, why couldn't they have given *me* a blanket or something? At least you had that."

Jackson snorted, heat creeping up his neck. Thankfully, she was smiling, even if it was awkward. His heart beat a little harder.

"Well," he said past the lump in his throat. "Coalition's a lot of assholes. But I guess we should see what the crazy raider wants."

"I hope," Anna said, her voice fragile, "That 'war' is a figure of speech out here. Guns are… I mean… I can't handle more of them right now. I can't."

Jackson nodded. The shots in the dark from the subway tunnels… he saw her remember too, saw the fearful whites of her eyes exposed. "Two weeks. That's all." He hoped she found his words reassuring. She nodded and began to pad away, eyes downturned, hands wringing. He quietly followed after. Should he reach out, squeeze her shoulder? Would touching her like that be unwelcome…?

It was then that the book satchel warmed unnaturally into his ribs.

It *pulsed.*

It felt… *pleased.*

Jackson stumbled to a stop. His thoughts blanked.

Even though he'd always had nightmares, everything always felt more together, more real, come morning. Dreams didn't leak over to the dawn. He could always have a nice cup of tea to banish them entirely.

That security was leaving forever.

What you were does not matter. Only what you are.

"You coming?" Anna turned to look over her shoulder.

Jackson's heart hammered, uncertain, afraid. Suddenly, he was unsure if he was ready to face anything at all now. "Yeah," he said, putting up his smoothest mask. "Just… almost tripped on these pants they gave me. A bit… overlong."

"Oh, okay." She shrugged and turned away, looking lost in her head.

Sweat beaded on his neck. She'd accepted his lie. But guilt crept through the cracks. It wasn't long ago that he hurt her by hiding his magic, letting her think she was alone because he assumed she was too overwhelmed to handle his secrets.

Of course, now they were about to tromp outside into a raider camp, and this seemed a *terrible* time to discuss crumbling reality, ancient religion, and magical books.

Alright. He was just putting off the conversation. He would try to tell her, he promised himself. He would.

Inside, he remembered the questions Tony had posed him in that dark hole under the city. *You want your destiny? You want to know what the man by the fire wants?*

He'd said *yes*. Now it looked like Inoki was endeavoring to give him exactly what he'd asked.

What are you? he thought to the ancient tome, as if it could answer. *What am I going to do?*

There was no reply of course, and there was no time to pry. As he and Anna walked out the crooked apartment door, two guards peeled away from their posts and fell beside them. They were armed with automatic rifles, likely stolen. The first was brutish and tall, hair in a ponytail, eyes little black beads. He could have been Shark's brother. The other… *huh.* An odd detail Jackson hadn't expected sprung forth. Raiders were often slavers, treating women and children like resources to be exploited. Yet here, the second guard paced to his right, looking well-versed with *her* weapon. Her scarred, taut frame moved with the ease of being used to combat. A tumorous and scabbed bulb bulged on her chin.

These two were silent, but their tight flank ensured he and Anna were not diverting down any path except what they wanted. It was clear they had done this before.

A clear sky and a beaming sun now cast over broken streets and pools of rainwater. The smell of the storm was in the air. Jackson saw no fences, no working cars, and no tents or banners—he wondered if he and Anna had been placed at the camp's furthest reaches. Crumbled buildings stretched down the city block to both the left and right.

Small groups of two or three bandits in tattered, homespun cloth skittered down the road, most heading in one direction, the direction he and Anna were being herded. They were all adults, an almost even mix of men and women, inked and battle-marked. Some led dogs. The canines' ears were cropped and alert, their bodies pulled inexorably along by their sniffing noses. Their hackles were fluffed in anticipation. *True breeds... not mutants.*

There was one boy, about thirteen, kneeled in a dirt patch where the concrete had rotted away long ago. His torso and feet were naked. A tattoo of a snake curled on his young back. He was digging with his hands. Little mounds of upturned earth were all around him. *What is he...?*

A furious yelping and barking tore Jackson's attention away, and he dismissed the boy. A lone duck erupted out of a water-strewn alley, taking flight. The dogs across the way leapt and pranced, straining at their collars, but their owners held fast, shouting sharp reprimands in a foreign tongue. Jackson rubbed his arms, nervous, glad they were on the other side of the street. His childhood memories kept him wary of dogs.

These people... they were guards, warriors, and attack beasts all.

No slaves. Whatever was going on, they were expecting a fight, men and women both. Coalition reports were very clear on dominant raider culture near New York. If things were bad enough that women were allowed to have arms and be on the front lines… perhaps this band's numbers were low. Perhaps they were desperate.

Or perhaps the Coalition reports were inaccurate. In which case, he was even more adrift.

"Haven't seen a fight in a good long time," Shark had told Frank. Liars.

He stared closer, trying to learn, not caring if they stared back. Some did. There was no enthusiasm like what Shark had. Their looks were resigned, distrustful, and haggard. Their dogs' ribs were clearly visible under their fur.

This isn't good.

After getting led down several side streets, their destination became clear. A crowd was gathering around a raised stone platform. The statue it held had long since toppled and been dragged away, cracks and scrapes in the concrete marking its passing. A blackened plaque remained, unreadable.

In the statue's place was a man towering above them all. His palms were raised to the sky, the corded muscles in his tanned arms bulging as if he were holding up the weight of every last bandit gaping up at him. This, no doubt, was the *Warlord*. On his long, wild dark hair rested a savage crown: the sun-bleached skull of a buck, antlers cresting around the sun. This man's burning eyes peered out from under those sockets as if the beast had been reanimated by dark magic.

His voice was rolling in the strange pidgin tongue the raiders here favored, gripping, sonorous words. A few of the crowd were even humming in song. But then, those fiery eyes locked onto Jackson, and the world fell silent.

The man made a lithe leap off of the stage. His people parted like they were making way for a storm. Striding forward, his bare feet glided over the dust and weeds as if he was part of the earth itself, a spirit made manifest. He was massive—even without the crown, he would have towered a foot over Jackson's head, even more over Anna's.

He stopped just an arm's length away, raising his hands. One of them was hacked clean away at the elbow, a brutal prosthesis of rusting metal and twine in its place. Jackson's eyes fixed to the center of the skull crown, to an ugly hole where a bullet had clearly shattered.

It seemed as if this brutalized giant was here to pass judgment on them both.

The crowd was a hundred quiet, wary, hungry eyes. One word, and Jackson sensed they would not hesitate to tear him and Anna apart.

Then, the Warlord simply nodded, dipping his head in a respectful bow. Jackson blinked. Anna seemed taken aback, but she smiled, bowing her head back, mimicking. The crowd began to mutter, as if unsure.

With a snap of the Warlord's good fingers, a tattooed man jogged up, handing his leader a bowl. From there drifted the familiar smell of roasted mealworms and cracked wheat. Jackson's mouth watered, remembering the globs of the stuff he'd subsisted on in the orphanage, and craved it for the first time since those years. He'd barely eaten in almost two days as his body flushed out poison and hardship. It was so simple, the poor man's sustenance, but *any* food right now…

The chieftain handed the bowl to Anna, both his natural and synthetic palms up, a symbolic weight in his eyes. *Sharing food. A friendship gesture.* Jackson's shoulders creaked in relief. Perhaps Frank had been right. Maybe these people really did offer shelter for credits.

Anna looked hesitant, but took the bowl. She looked over at Jackson. "Do I eat it?" she whispered.

The Warlord chortled. A bead charm, tied to the antlers, rattled. "Yes, Anna of the city. Enjoy breakfast with us. You have my protection."

Jackson wondered, prickling, that the Warlord's deep, rich voice held clean and standard English, no accent, no bends. *Who is this guy?*

Anna took in the aroma of the nutty ground mealworms—she

hadn't eaten for a long time, either. "Thank you!" She beamed and immediately began upending the bowl into her mouth. "I have no idea what this is, but it's good. Way better than Coalition porridge." There were nods in the crowd now, murmurs of approval. Jackson breathed a little easier.

The Warlord's stance shifted. The skull turned Jackson's way.

Jackson bowed his head in respect, hoping he had read body language correctly. He willed his mask to stay calm and summoned his most pleasant business smile, as if it was a lovely day in this gods-forsaken ghost land, and he was very happy to meet this barbarian king.

"You," the Warlord spoke, his eyes boring down. His voice was harsh now, dragged through wind and rain. "You slew the one we call the *Tiger.*"

Jackson's mind darted. Shark had seemed to take the fight as an honorable thing, even going so far as to congratulate him. So, he stood taller, tried to make it seem as if he was proud. "Yes. I… mostly. Yes."

The Warlord held up a silencing hand. His mouth tugged down into a grim line.

His judgment passed.

"So it is you, man of the city. *You* killed my son."

CHAPTER FOUR
Treaties

Anna choked. The hot cereal went down the wrong pipe.

The crowd was muttering again, some in rage, some in disbelief. There were snippets of English mixed with the unidentifiable language of Shark's people.

"*He* killed Father Tiger?"

"That's *impossible*."

"Coalition *filth!*"

"Death's too good for—"

Jackson was freezing, his words failing.

The Warlord's stone-hewn frame was *shaking*.

She thought of the empty, dead eyes of the fallen gladiator in the arena. She thought of Shark closing them respectfully, of the fierce, powerful fury that had once been in that form.

So she clutched the bowl of gruel to her chest and edged between the chieftain and his target, looking up into that piercing stare ringed with dark paint. His psuedo-hand of heavy steel and twine was raised as if it was about to crush a skull. Even though she knew how strong she was now, her voice shook. "We can explain. It's not his fault."

"I have heard the story from my faithful Shark," the man replied, voice taut, not even looking at her, staring over her head to Jackson beyond. His voice cracked with barely-contained grief. "It's why I haven't killed you where you stand. So speak, Coalition citizen. She who helped my people—*she* can stay. But tell me why I shouldn't snap your neck! Why I shouldn't *spit* on your credits!"

There was a familiar mountain standing off to the side, though next to the Warlord, he seemed small. Shark. His face was drawn, looking wan now even through all of the bright red tattoo ink. He was gripping his hands together, pale-knuckled. Anna had never dreamed of seeing that expression on him. The crowd was leering closer. There were at least a hundred of them, clenching fists, grumbling throats.

"Tell me of my son and his death," the Warlord repeated.

Anna heard Jackson shuffle. His stance deflated. "Sir. I'm sorry. I'm... so sorry." He cleared his throat. "We didn't want to fight, you must believe that, and he died very..." There was an audible swallow. "...Honorably."

Anna knew this was a lie; nothing about the forced death match was honorable. But she felt Jackson's hand on her shoulder. She let him step in front of her so he and the Warlord stood face to face, though she didn't like it, her body stiff, her heart pounding and insistent that it was wiser for her to be his shield, not the other way around.

"He and I met in an arena," Jackson continued. "Where prisoners were being forced to kill each other. There was a madman running it..." He trailed off, and Anna shuddered, thinking of a velvety sharp voice, of a man that squeezed her heart with his mind until it almost burst.

"The red demon under New York," the Warlord growled.

Jackson paused. The crowd murmured, notes of morbid curiosity drifting to Anna's ears. "You all knew of him," she whispered.

The antler crown bowed. "Yes. I saw him."

"You *saw* him." Jackson drew breath sharply. "Then you know that neither your son or me could have done anything except what he asked."

"Yes," the Warlord hissed. "If things happened *as you say*. The demon, we found him wandering from your city, raving, asking if we'd heard singing, if we'd seen the *sky* open. The Coalition soon followed. But he killed them all… and when he was done, he came for us."

Anna's brain whirled, trying to put the tale together as Jackson tensed even more. She'd been found north of New York too, she knew. She'd been surrounded by dead Coalition.

"He took my son," the Warlord continued. "He said it was destiny. And when we tried to stop him…"

The crowd shuddered. Anna sensed a creeping dread there. It leached into her heart, reminded her of a cracked smile, blood, fear, and uncertainty. "Is that how you came to New York, Shark?" she said.

"Tiger was my friend," the mountain whispered. "I came to find him. But the red demon… he knew everything we were going to do before we did it. We had no chance. I never even saw Tiger again." He leveled his thick finger at Jackson. "Not until I saw him fight you. Not until the Coalition came and shot him dead."

"The man in red, he wasn't a demon," Jackson continued uneasily. The Warlord narrowed his vengeful eyes. "Not always. The Coalition warped him, twisted him into their killing machine. When he escaped, he just started bringing death on his own terms, his mind gone." His voice was quiet. "I'm sorry again for your son. But there was nothing any of us could do. And honestly? Tiger killed all of his opponents, and he would have killed me too if he'd been given any more time. He was stronger than any man I've ever seen." He started to rustle in his clothes, taking off his shirt. "He wielded a spear, and he gave me this."

The scar. It was blotched and red, right in the center, where he'd been pinned through like a butterfly under glass. In Anna's memory, a crowd was roaring with approval. His chest, when she'd healed him, had been so cold under her hands, so close to lifelessness. She hugged herself.

"You lived through that." The Warlord raised a hand, tracing the scar in the air, not touching.

"Only thanks to Anna."

Anna closed her eyes, trying not to let them sting. *Chin up. Everyone's looking at you.*

She heard a rustling again, and wearily looked. Jackson was putting the shirt back on. "I don't think I really won. It was good enough for Tony... the red demon. But it was the Coalition that ended the match, that killed him."

The Warlord's fiery stare dimmed. "Coalition." His last question was a solemn, quiet whisper, just a hint of unsteadiness marking it. "More than you know. And Tiger's captor?"

"He's dead," Jackson said, tone flat. "Him, I did kill."

The Warlord was silent. He inhaled, exhaled, a long, dry *whoosh*. The world was quiet, the crowd around them murmuring, on edge. "My son traveled with me, believing in my path. He thought I would lead us well. He thought I would be the one to find what we seek. And... he died because I brought us here. Because of the road I laid out. Because the Coalition, even when we flee them, continue to take everything."

The air was tight in Anna's lungs.

"But if you speak the truth, as Shark says... you killed who took him for sport. You killed who made us unable to leave this place, for it would have been abandoning Tiger. You killed a Coalition monster. And this is why Shark came with joy. Because Tiger is free... because we are free again too."

He held out a hand. The helper by his side looked unsure, but passed over a second bowl of gruel.

"And you bring us, I admit, an opportunity my people need. So speak your name, man of the city, slayer of demons, for I... I allow you here." His voice cracked. "I will *not* forgive. But I allow." He held up the offering as if it was far heavier and difficult to grasp than it was. "Will you eat with us today, aid us? Will you honor my son and all those we lost?"

Jackson slowly accepted the gift, looking just as stiff and uneasy as the giver. "My name is Jackson... thank you. I will."

The Warlord dipped his head again, brought both of his palms together in a sort of salute, but Anna saw the conflict in his face, the sorrow and anger. His teeth were baring as he turned away. "Jackson and Anna are under our protection now. Treat them fairly. They will work. And Shark will speak for all they do."

The crowd rumbled. They seemed deeply unsettled. But Anna saw the more important thing: the rage had gone inward. Now they just seemed tired. So tired.

The Warlord turned and paced back to his stage. His good hand was flexing like he desperately wanted to destroy something with it now that Jackson's neck was no longer within reach.

Jackson himself was gulping down the gruel, eyes wary and alert. None of this seemed lost on him, but like her, he looked hungry. Anna offered him a weak smile of relief and resumed eating.

"We have things to talk about later," he muttered cautiously to her between bites. "Alone."

"Yeah."

"That aside, I never thought I could miss mealworms this much."

Anna snorted, her chewing coming to a cold stop. "Wha…?" Her eyes focused on her bowl. There were toasty, crispy bits in there, unidentifiable. Her stomach flipped.

And with a mental shrug, she kept eating. Hunger won.

The Warlord was raising his hand in the air now, commanding the group's attention. "Today," he announced, seeming to continue his speech in full English, perhaps for the newcomers' benefit. "You heard the alarm raised. It is as I said would happen. A caravan approaches." The crowd mumbled in assent. Anna wondered what it was they seemed to agree so sternly about. "This is our last fight here. A test! Make it matter. There will be no more dead on this day. Now go. Walk the earth, through light and rain."

An answering call sounded from the assembled, a beautiful, song-like strain Anna couldn't interpret. They began to disperse, shouting in foreign tongues with purpose, fists to the sky.

"Blood… and vengeance!" the Warlord bellowed above it all.

She did not like the sound of this.

What's this about? What's going on? Readjusting their rifles on their backs, the group was splitting off into buildings, some quickly monkeying up rusty fire escapes, positioning themselves on rooftops. Before long, only her, Jackson, the Warlord, and Shark remained, the last of which was starting to chow down on what was left in the gruel pot. Everyone else was hiding. Watching. She could feel the weight of their eyes.

It seemed a plan long ago discussed was being put into motion.

"What's going on, uh, sir?" she said, though the urgency in the air pressed her voice into a thin whisper.

Their leader made a grave nod. "As Shark spoke to you: *war.* As we've been locked in for months. I foresaw a caravan coming from the southwest. It was said there would not be many, but that they are well-armed, their vehicles armored, and they could tear through the center of this camp like knives through soft necks if they wished."

Jackson made a querulous noise in the back of his throat. "Foresaw?"

The Warlord gave him a hard look and continued, not answering the question. "It is a test, for our courage and resolve. Tiger's loss made us weak. Made us stop. And we must prove we are worthy to continue before we can move on." His voice caught again. "We must prove we will honor his sacrifice."

Anna blinked, processing.

"Wait," Jackson muttered. "The camp is moving?"

Again, the chieftain did not answer, his head turning instead to the horizon. The wind whispered hollow, man-made noises in the empty wastes. Tires. Shouting.

"What do you want Jackson and I do?" Anna asked.

"Defend yourselves. Or, stay silent. Whichever is best. I won't throw you under their cars. But these are not safe lands. Survival is your own responsibility."

With that, the Warlord flagged his prosthetic hand to the southerly end of the street, towards the alcove of what might have once been the entrance to more apartments and shops. Shark followed the silent directions, beginning to head that way, and the Warlord himself was not far behind. Not knowing where else to go, Anna scurried after, Jackson in her wake.

It was strange, she thought. Once everyone was hidden, it was as if no one had touched this road for a century. If this entire band vanished from the earth, it would be as if they were never here at all.

No one would know where she lived or died.

Like heck was she going to let that happen.

From behind cover, it wasn't long until rumbling tires grew louder in the dead air. A slow minute passed. The first of the intruders to show themselves was a ten-wheeler, cracked black solar panels glittering on the roof, though a puff of gas exhaust also rose from behind it. It seemed an ancient thing, rust eating the body through. A dented and warped sheet of metal was welded to the grill, clearly a primitive ramming contraption. On this, a wild insignia of a laughing fox was painted bright.

Whispers murmured between the Warlord, Shark, and a few of the others: uneasy noises.

"Foxhole," Jackson hissed beside her. "Of all the bands we could run into..."

By this ten-wheeler's side, two smaller semis and three vans kept pace. Metal protections were haphazardly welded on their forms too. The only things that tied them together were the cackling fox splattered on their doors and the thickly muscled men at the wheels.

Anna had seen enough movies to know that the holes in the vans were, in fact, from bullets. She wondered if this caravan would charge through and wreak havoc as the Warlord suggested.

But then, they slowed. They stopped.

The driver's door on the ten-wheeler opened and slammed shut, a red-bearded man in hides and cloth hopping down and adjusting his wide-brimmed hat in the sun. The other vehicles eked out a defensive cluster around him. He cupped his hands around his mouth and bellowed. "Halloooooo?"

Several of his people got out and flanked him, guns by their sides… but they weren't actively aiming. All things speaking, they seemed wary, but casual.

"Perhaps traders after all?" Shark muttered.

Jackson just glared at the caravan. He didn't seem convinced.

"We will find out," the Warlord growled. "I want thirty of us with me out there. Such is the size of most traveling bands; they will think we are mostly present. Maya, you tell everyone else to stay ready, *out of sight*." A nearby woman with one eye made an acknowledging grunt and scampered further into the dark building.

"Halloooo?" the red-bearded man called again. "I know you're out there! No harm here. Just a merchant!" He beamed at no one. "Looking to make friends."

The Warlord uncoiled and strode from the shadows like a wraith. His people and their dogs rose and walked with him.

Anna found herself drifting with them, wanting knowledge, but hands pressed her back, behind cover—or, rather, they pressed *Jackson* back, and he grabbed her hand, preventing her from going. She grimaced. Right. He was worth credits to them. And… well, maybe her curiosity would get her in trouble if she listened to it. It often did.

So she simply peeked around a doorframe's edge, straining her ears as the group left to meet the visitors.

The trader was giving them all an arched-eyebrow stare. His tanned face remained full and smiling. His clothes were a little uneven, clearly handspun, but the vibrant patterns and clean wear spoke of someone who could enjoy new things. The force of this well-fed, grinning presence seemed to fall like a brick on the silent, grim, and hungry faces before him.

"Hallo," he chirped, waving two fingers. Thankfully, his voice carried well. "Aye, well met, well met."

"Indeed," the Warlord boomed. It seemed they were both happy to broadcast their conversation. Anna decided that was likely for the benefit of their backups, as if to say that any trouble the other started would immediately see a response. But of the two, it was the Warlord that truly loomed, towering over the newcomer with his crown, his people bunching behind him. His eyes burned in their dark-painted hollows. "You're from Foxhole?"

"Aye, what gave it away?" The trader let out a wild guffaw, pointing at his truck's grill and the insignia there. Anna felt Jackson tense again. "That voice ya have there... sound like a *citizen*, ya do. But I was told that folk bearing the *antler* had, for summin' or other, left their lands up north. 'Sunrise', you call that stretch? So which'er you? Citizen far from home? Or antler-folk?"

"Antler," the Warlord said brusquely, crossing his arms. "I was born a citizen. Another life. We've been avoiding your claims on purpose. Does Foxhole have concerns about our presence?"

"*Concerns* 'bout *presence?*" Chuckles rippled out of the man's throat in jagged bursts. "Aye yeah, city really did stamp ya. But if ya say so... no, no, you're too tiny a lot to make *concerns*. But Foxhole's *curious*, ya 'stand? I hear ya got a real nice setup going on up north, with real land, happy people. Hell, I've heard some of us tried to rob ya once or twice. Why'd you come south to this rot? Nothin' to grow out here, is there?"

Anna didn't think it possible, but the Warlord's back jerked and sent him another inch higher. His words were seething electric current. "Our land, our claims... well, you can try to rob the Coalition—the land's new masters—if you want. It would end as well for you as it did for us."

The man sucked in a furious hiss between his yellow teeth. He made a skin-crawling *hork* and spat on the earth, face contorting up in rage. "Bastards!" He looked like he was about to slap the Warlord's shoulder in sympathy. His hand fell short, though, as if he thought better of it. "I heard they were on the march. Foxhole's been worried they might get bold and try to strike us from two fronts if they get comfy. How many did ya kill for their trouble? I hope it was a *lot*."

A growl came low in the chieftain's throat, a sorrowful groan beneath it. "Not as many as we needed to."

"My friends…" The sympathetic rage turned to a speculative stare. "I understand. How many of you make it out?"

"Enough."

"Aye." Shark sauntered up by his leader's side, clearly intent on intimidation through his existence. He bared his filed teeth. "And we were not *all* good at farming. Some of us were the reason no one like you took Sunrise for a hundred years, eh?"

The red-bearded man acknowledged Shark's combative stance with two raised and open palms, as if to prove he was reaching for no weapon. "You a big boy, ain't ya? But we have no fight now. Though this close to the city, you can bet the Coalition might tangle a patrol or two in your business. Ya might try a bit further back, along the coast, right?"

The Warlord scratched his chin with his thumb, as if perplexed. "So you're not here with demands? You're not here to make war?"

"Naw. I'm fine with ya. Antler folk are known for bein' friendly, even out here! Just keepin' to themselves and growin' food. Who wouldn't want neighbors like ya?" The smile was back. "Foxhole proper might come later, asking to make partnerships. I think we'll cozy to each other right fine. Ya know, since we're so close, the Coalition might not shoot ya up every time they get bored."

Anna sensed a deeper truth in those twanging words. "Jackson," she whispered, tugging on his sleeve. He leaned in. "He makes it sound like they'll have to pay for protection."

"Yes," Jackson said, hunching close to her ear, breath a warm puff.

"Foxhole's a brutal lot. They wouldn't let anyone be out here unless it was useful to them somehow. But… I've never heard of Sunrise. Or Antler-folk."

The trader was rolling on. "O' course, I bet ya could benefit from tradin' with a friendly face right now. Why wait for the big boys to come visit, Clan Father? I've been out makin' runs, and got a full goods train."

There was an uneasy ripple in the crowd. The chieftain's words were tight. "You do me honor with the title, but I'm no Clan Father. Our last Clan Mother… she's gone now. I am only the Warlord."

Anna squinted. Jackson answered her with a confused shrug.

"Ey… *Warlord*, ya say?" There was an awkward disbelief underlying the question. "I, uh, I confess, haven't heard of ya Antlers keeping a *Warlord*. I mean, yer the types what would even take in washed-out citizens… and maybe an old Foxhole raider-boy or two, eh?" He winked at Shark. Though Anna thought it impossible, Shark somehow squared his shoulders larger, a displeased scowl his only reply. "I don't know your face, but ya got the look. Reminds me a bit of someone I used to know that tried visiting your Sunrise once…"

The Warlord simply placed a hand on Shark's back, his sharp-toothed second almost *vibrating*. "Enough. You say you want to trade?"

"Aye!" The merchant latched onto the question with open arms. "I think we'll be fast friends!" He clanged the truck grill with a steel-toed boot, and the others in the vehicles responded as if it was a signal. Four men in similar clothes hopped out carrying boxes. "Just a sample, of course," the trader winked, grinning. "But see if you like it, yeah?"

Anna squinted. She couldn't get a good look, but the crates seemed to be filled with everything from electronic scrap to little vials. There were cracked datapads, dimly lit orbs, and yellow-stamped kits that seemed to bear both the Coalition seal and a medical cross.

One of the crates being toted around had a stamp of a dove printed on the side, a logo she knew. Wincing, she looked over to Jackson. His fists were curled, his face turning red. "You see that too, huh?" she whispered.

"What I'm hoping is that my driver for that crate made it back home," he hissed.

"Got more than what's in a box," the red-bearded man added, drumming his hands on his stomach. "Mickey, get 'em." A beady-eyed, weaselly man scurried to the back of his eight-wheeler. "You people, you look like you could use a few hands to help out around here while you get settled."

The assistant opened the door and tugged a line, shouting. A bare foot came into view, uncertain, dirty, shaking, sinking Anna's heart in her chest. A body followed the foot. Then another. And another. Three people marched off, their heads bowed, their necks, wrists, and feet tied, all shuffling forward at the man's insistent yanks.

The first naked, filthy toes in line belonged to a boy, barely a teenager, red hair matted, eyes hollow. "This one," the red-bearded man said, "He's very responsive. Got him from an old friend who owed me, ha! Just needs a few directions, and he'll go. Small thing, but works hard, and *very* quiet." The second prisoner was a tanned and muscled man, his hands calloused, his stare never swaying from his feet. "This one's kitted out as a fighter," the trader introduced. "Ya know, he'll keep away those damned sick packdogs around here, or lift the heavy things that need liftin'."

Anna almost cried out as her eyes alighted on the final member of the lineup.

Of the three, this woman looked out defiantly at the horde, teeth bared. Her dark hair was drawn up with a leather strip, clothes only just showing their wear. But her look of fiery defiance was what Anna recognized.

It just... it can't be...?

The name tumbled from her lips, marring the silence.

"Nyx?"

CHAPTER FIVE
Raid

Jackson heard a startled, pained whisper from Anna, and he whipped his head to the side, seeing her eyes squint in confusion. Something in his connection to her began to throb in turmoil.

This is the first time she's seeing slaves, he realized. It was for him, too, but he'd heard reports. He'd been bracing himself for it since he first stepped foot into this discarded strip of city. From the way Anna was covering her mouth, wide-eyed, it was breaking her heart.

His chest tightened in sympathy and worry. If she spoke up, tried to do anything, this delicate and strange bit of diplomacy from these well-armed Foxhole traders was going to go bad quickly.

Of course, if no one said anything at all, he could barely fathom the hell these chained souls would go through.

"This one," the trader sneered, tilting up the bound woman's chin, "Is fresh caught."

Her eyes glittered in fury. "Just you wait, asshole," she sneered.

The trader chuckled, though he pulled his hand away. "Got her runnin' up the backpaths, probably a fugitive from the dome, ya stand? And ya know how it is. Needs to be learned a bit. But she's lovely, ain't she?" He shrugged noncommittally, wiping the humidity from his tanned brow. "Now, any of these three, I'd get top dollar for at Foxhole, but I'm makin' slower time than I like, so I could cut ya a good price, a very good…"

Jackson sensed his speech was rehearsed, the measures being tread a thousandth time.

The mood of the Warlord's people had shifted ever so slightly as the shackled merchandise had entered the negotiation space. Where once there was wariness, there were now white-knuckled grips on guns, muscles flexing, tendons popping out against skin.

But the trader was only staring at the Warlord, that immovable, stoic creature at the fore. His lackeys at least clearly saw the tension rising against them, and their eyes were growing wider, nostrils flaring as they shifted their rifles in their hands pointedly.

Move an inch, their glares said, *and we'll destroy you.*

"…How did she even *get* here?" Anna muttered. "Jackson, what are we going to do?"

"Do?" The nervous thrumming in his chest was getting faster as Anna clenched and unclenched her fists. "I don't know if there's anything we *can* do." He began to back up, slowly. "I actually think we should get further back. This is a powder keg."

"…Of course," the lead trader was continuing, "If ya wanted some of the medicine, and maybe a radio, a combo deal, is what I'm sayin', I could cut down the price a little more, and—"

The Warlord's words were quiet, but sliced through the red-bearded man's amble like a knife through butter. "Sunrise. We're from Sunrise, our town, our home that was stolen. You know that's where we're from, but you offer us this anyway."

Time to go, Jackson's well-crafted business senses screamed. He tugged at Anna's wrist.

She dug her heels in. "I can't—"

The trader tapered his words down, peering back at the dark-rimmed stare under the skull. His lips made a confused pucker.

"Do you know our history?"

"Uhhh… no, can't say I do, heh. Ya'll are so secretive up there. No one even right knows where ya sleep."

The Warlord leaned down until the tip of his crown's nose rested on the trader's forehead. The trader's eyes seemed like those of an entranced mouse before a snake. "New York lives because my people's elders were chosen to die. They were slaves that escaped and found a place of their own. And we will never keep others in chains. No matter your wealth, Foxholer."

Jackson swallowed a dry lump, startled, confused by the words, by statements he'd never heard in the histories. The trader backed up, looking spooked, barely audible. "Aye, well, if'n ya don't want slaves, that's not my business." He laughed, a brittle, thin sound, and waved at the man with the leash. The man shrugged and started tugging his stock away once more.

It could end like this: an awkward bit of failed diplomacy, a mutual nonviolent parting.

But Jackson spied an odd bit of motion. The Warlord's hand had fallen behind his back. It was making strange signs. Signals.

Oh no.

"Wait," Anna whispered.

Jackson saw her move and reached out to grab her hand again, but she'd already lunged forward and slipped from his open fingers. His stomach plummeted.

She made it all the way to the fore when the Warlord's massive hand caught her shoulder. "Be at ease," Jackson barely heard him growl.

The Foxhole team's arms were growing stiff around their rifles, like they itched to stretch their fingers the last two inches to the triggers. If Anna hadn't been so slight a woman, he was certain they would have fired already.

The defiant slave woman was stopping the march back to the truck, her jaw dropping under that dark, greasy hair.

Wait.

Her face... was that *recognition?*

Jackson felt again the strange tilt of fate under his feet.

The trader nervously shrugged and continued to the Warlord, "My friend, if you don't want these goods, I still have medicine and other things. And I'm *very* sorry if I caused offense to your soft and kind Antler hearts."

Jackson's heart pattered as Anna stood on her toes, saying something to the Warlord like it was the most urgent secret she'd ever borne.

The man leading the slaves yanked his line tight, hard, the boy up front making a *horrible* choking noise that made Jackson's teeth hurt, and even the staring woman was stumbling away again—

The Warlord made a long, slow blink, and held Anna's shoulder tighter. Jackson couldn't hear a word, but... he just *knew*, from that look. He was making a deal. And if he'd judged anything about this situation, it was that the Warlord would want extra protection and increased access to Anna's powers to benefit his tribe.

Anna was already nodding.

"I want your *word*," the man said. That much was audible.

In that second, Jackson knew *exactly* what Anna would do. She was kind and she had powers other people didn't. She was still reeling at this world he knew to be so much harsher than her own. But above all... he knew that despite his pretty promises to her in her sleep, she had nothing she was living for, nothing that would make her cautious.

"Wait—" he began.

Her blue eyes were glittering, the gold in her hair catching the sunlight. "I promise. I'll do everything I can to protect you for the next two weeks. Anything."

Jackson stopped, stomach growing cold. Nearby, Shark was grinning, shaking his head, as if he thought her very brave.

And the Warlord was turning to the trader. He made one final signal behind his back. "Very well. We will take your slaves after all.

For I see now that this is our test."

"What, ya change your mind?" The red-bearded man laughed. "Maybe you're not all as soft as I heard, eh? Strange man, ya are, but I ain't gonna argue. Well, then, let's talk price—"

"We will pay with blood," the Warlord growled. "And vengeance."

He sliced two fingers in the air.

Every last gun his clan carried was raised, through windows flanking them, from rooftops high.

A hundred guns fired as one.

<hr>

Anna shrieked and dropped to her knees. The world exploded. Her ears ruptured.

There was a memory locking her mind: a soldier with a gun, thundering, life-ending shots.

Her better instinct told her to get behind cover, but a tidal wave of panic mowed her down, her lungs strangling, joints freezing.

The lead trader was blasted back into his truck's grill.

The world roared.

She shook and choked on her own air. Shark leapt over her head, a bounding, sharp-toothed, smiling mountain, bloodlust alight in his eyes. She'd seen it before when he'd jumped into a crowd intent on the kill, and now was no different. The Warlord simply stepped over her as well, shielding himself behind the trader's truck next to the man's dead body. He took up a rifle a woman passed him, his dark-ringed eyes dead as he pulled the trigger over and over.

Anna finally got ahold of her legs and tried to crawl away, to at least not have a panic attack out in the hail of bullets for god's sake…!

Arms were around her: a flash of dark hair and brown eyes. Jackson had her, the both of them backpedaling behind cover as she remembered how to breathe in the thunder and madness and death.

"Stay down, it's okay, stay back here…!" he was shouting, and she could understand, but the sound of his voice was thick, murky, and so far away.

There were so many parallel, ferocious thoughts in her head that she could barely process.

Run run hide not again PLEASE NO STOP—

Get up! Get up and help Nyx! Don't be worthless, don't you even freeze, not like this—

What if someone dies because of me…?

NO! DO SOMETHING!

Tears were streaming down her face, but she stood in spite of it, and her inner light was *burning*.

Suddenly, there was a man at her left with a gun and a virulently red headband over vengeful blue eyes. He'd rolled under the truck and sprung up, breaking her and Jackson's cover, and his gun was leveling at the Warlord's back, and—

She swung, not even thinking anymore, the uneven shouting in her head blurring together into a panicked slurry. Her open hand slapped the attacker's gun, of all things—she wasn't even sure if she'd been consciously aiming at it. But with the power in her arm, the shot went wide. A bullet ricocheted off the truck instead of the chieftain's head.

Jackson let out a startled yelp. She remembered he was at her right, that he'd never really left.

And he, clearly just as panicked as she was, managed to do something just as brave and stupid. He slammed his lean body into the raider's in a shoulder tackle as the man turned his gun on her. Even though Jackson clearly didn't have the superior weight to throw in this fight, his long arm hooked around that thick neck in a sort of stranglehold. The man, red-faced, surprised, tripped and slammed head-first into the truck.

The slaver bared his teeth and rammed an elbow backwards into Jackson's ribs. The hold broke. Jackson's face crumpled with a pained hiss. The raider found his feet and brought around the gun again, this time aiming for his attacker's knees.

Anna yelled and dove for the rifle. With strength that still surprised her, she grabbed and yanked the barrel, sending the gun firing wide a second time. The metal turned lightning hot under her hand. But the pain lasted for just a second. Her scorched skin was already healing over.

Jackson's hands flexed with sure grace, his eyes alight. The shadow under the truck made a strange wobble. It pooled under their attacker's feet, whipping him backwards. The raider's head hit the asphalt with a crack. Anna, nerves shot, stomped on the man's wrist. He let go of the gun with a pained shout, struggling.

Suddenly there was a one-eyed woman with graying hair and an old shotgun, stepping forward from the Warlord's ranks: the one he'd called Maya. Her mouth was a tight line. Her coming heralded an ear-shattering *BOOM.*

The raider stopped struggling.

"Good work," Maya's mouth moved, though Anna couldn't really hear. She refused to look down. Red was in her peripheral vision. Bile was in her throat.

Jackson's hand closed around hers and it was the one thing that made her not throw up. For just a second, all the conflicting, panic-soaked chaos in her head went quiet.

"Come on," he mouthed. It was like a line in her chest pulled her along with him, made her feet unfreeze.

He ran, and she followed.

The shattering reports of firearms exploded behind them. Jackson dragged himself and Anna back into the cover of the nearest building, pushing through a window frame that had long been broken. He sent a mannequin flying that had been modeling an ancient bleached sundress, sassy hands on plastic hips. Together, he and Anna ducked behind a brick wall.

Anna was hyperventilating. He was dizzy, and realized he was hyperventilating too. But his blood was hot and bracing—he could hardly believe he'd fought like he had with a gun in his face, and they'd *won*, and he really was Chosen by a god! His magic was coming easier, more powerful, and… and together, they…!

"We have to help her," Anna said.

"What?" He was certain he was misunderstanding, his ears ringing from the gunfire.

"The chained woman!" She grabbed his shoulders, fear in her eyes, catching her breath. "I know her! She broke me out of the Coalition facility! We have to get her out of there!"

Suddenly, everything that just transpired fell into place. "Okay. Okay, we can go through here and cut back around." He gestured to the ruins of the store, to a window on the far end. Every cautious nerve in his body screamed not to do it, but he was starting to wonder if anything was impossible anymore. Besides, Anna wasn't going alone.

The gunfire was slowing.

"*What the hell?!*" someone screamed.

A burst of heat and light billowed through the air through the broken window. A chorus of screams rose, and he peeked around the corner, just in time to see both sides of the conflict fleeing.

The ten-wheeler had burst into flames.

The slave woman with dark hair was screaming, and for a moment, he thought she was on fire, too.

She kind of was.

But those were not screams of pain.

"*Come and get it!*" she roared, hurling a ball of flames at the man who had been leading her by the leash, her shackles burning orangey-red around her wrists.

"She's a mage?!" Jackson hissed.

"Um." Anna was peeking too. "Yep. She does that thing."

Well. Okay, he thought. "I think she's taking care of herself just fine."

The woman called Nyx looked like she was taking no prisoners. The shackles tying her to the other slaves melted clean through. The rest of her fellow captives were fleeing for shelter, back into what looked like the truck they'd been taken from. One of the Foxholers saw this, started yelling—he made to run for the cab, perhaps wanting to get his stock the hell out of this war zone. Nyx saw this and sent another fire blast hurtling, blowing him off his feet. "Don't even think about it!" she screamed, full of triumph.

The Foxholers were falling back to their other vans, though.

First priority is to save their inventory, Jackson knew. *Businessmen. Of course.* "They're going to try to flee," he breathed.

"Oh—!" Anna pointed.

Another driver was barreling to the slave truck again. Nyx flung a blast his way, but he was having none of it, grabbing and lifting an old garbage can lid like a shield. It deflected the hit. Hair smoking, he dove into the cab, and Nyx squared her stance, letting out a furious, cheated roar.

"She can't hit him in the truck!" Anna said. "She could set it on fire like the other one, and…"

"…Hurt the people in the back." Jackson stood. He sensed Anna straining next to him, shaking, like she wanted desperately to move, to help.

"What do we do?"

The man in the slave truck slammed the gas, wheels squealing. It was slow as hell to get going, but if it got up to speed, it was going to be unstoppable. Already, it revved right for the line of the Warlord's people in the road. They scattered. The caravan started to follow in its wake.

They were coming this way.

A split second later, and there Anna went, tearing across the earth, hair beaming in the sunlight, bounding like some warrior woman of old. Jackson's heart leapt in his throat.

Two things occurred to him:

First, this was a very stupid thing to do, and of course Anna was going to do it, because it was brave, selfless, and so, so reckless. What did she have to lose? How many could she save?

Second, he was in awe, perhaps falling a little in love, and his feet were already following.

⁂

Anna had no real conscious moment when she made the decision to play chicken with an accelerating, armored, eight-wheeled freighter. In fact, she was shaking and about to throw up.

But, despite it all, she was certain she could do something. Her subconscious was whirling with on-the-fly calculations.

The vehicle was still gaining speed, straining with what looked like its odd hybrid solar/gas engine. She skidded to a stop in front of it, blocking its path.

The driver looked as if he had no qualms about running her down.

On instinct, she leapt. Part of her remembered how it felt in New York to dive into danger, to save people from getting mowed down, of when she'd *flown*, no logic to it, physics not her master.

She didn't fly now, but it was more of a jump than any normal human had any right to make.

"Oooof!" The landing knocked out her wind as she smashed onto the sun-baked hood. Her whole body went numb. Power and anger revved through the engine, and she faintly heard the driver screaming at her from his seat. She yelled right back, though it was more terror and pain than war cry. The truck lurched, swerving, trying to throw her. Anna did the only thing she could. She scrabbled for purchase and dug her fingers into the hood's seam.

"Annaaaa!" Someone yelled. The truck blew by a mess of dark hair. Good God, Jackson had followed.

He shouldn't have done that, she thought. It was crazy and stupid. *This whole thing is crazy and stupid! What am I doing?!*

But the driver was reaching for his rifle now in the other seat. Anna almost froze, realizing she hadn't considered that.

And something else was happening, too. For a moment, the driver flinched, then swung his fists, eyes wide. It was as if he was fighting something invisible. The truck swayed, unsteady.

A shadow knocked the gun just out of his reach.

Thank you, Anna wished to her friend, and resumed focusing on trying not to pee herself.

She'd once seen a few mechanics on the Nevada test site working on a freighter, a giant monster of wheels and cargo. She remembered how the engine access swung up at the base of the windshield. She just didn't know how to trigger it. So she gripped the metal body as hard as she could, yanking, straining.

Her shoulders popped. Her back screamed.

The driver made another grab for the rifle.

She let out one last shriek and pulled as hard as she could, focusing only on the unnatural strength now hers, on the fists that could shatter reinforced glass. Fire flowed in her veins.

The latch screeched and broke. The hood sprung open, and she lost her grip, getting flung, hitting and rolling the asphalt hard enough to punch out her wind again, sending a lancing shock through her body. The caravan roared past, missing her by inches.

But now, the driver couldn't see at all, the raised hood in the way. He finally slammed into the line of derelict cars by the roadside. Furious metallic screaming echoed along the street as the paint on the truck was sideswiped into oblivion.

The truck swerved one last time, smashing and squealing, out of control, tires lifting on one side. It somehow stayed up, but in a haze of burning rubber, it skidded to a stop, torqued, blocking the road.

The brakes of its followers screeched. The caravan ground to a halt.

None of the slaves were going to be taken now she knew, none of them to be sold at some market somewhere.

The Warlord's people descended on the stalled merchants in a hail of gunfire. She couldn't see the last of the slaver men, couldn't see the blood.

She shut her eyes, heaving.

It hurt to breath. It felt like she'd sprained every muscle in her arms and back. Her head whirled in a seasick stew.

They need you. Someone needs to heal the wounded.

One more time, Anna fought herself up.

It was done.

Jackson looked on in disbelief as the firing stopped, as black smoke and flames boiled around the abandoned ten-wheeler, as eerie silence followed in the wake of the last execution just up the road.

And a cheer sprung up amongst the Warlord's people. It was overpowering, gasping, like they'd all battled their way up for air from under the ocean.

Anna stumbled to his side. She looked sick and shaking and determined all at once. She was covered in dust and bruises, but her blue eyes were shining with inner conviction.

Beautiful.

What on earth had happened to that terrified woman he'd rescued from the wastes just weeks ago?

Her bruises were turning purple, then yellow, then fading to nothing, her scrapes closing in the sunlight. She turned to him then, eyes moist, a small smile of relief blooming.

Jackson realized he was staring like an idiot. Something deep in his chest was chiming again in familiarity, asking him to pay attention, and he couldn't shake it.

Her smile winced a little, hair falling in her eyes. In that moment, the fierce warrior that had just run into the fray slipped under the surface again, an awkward, lost woman he knew better resuming her place. Suddenly, her arms wrapped around him in a hug, her chin embracing his shoulder. "We're okay," she said. "You *are* okay, right? No life-threatening wounds I gotta do another light show on?"

"I'm fine." He chuckled, meaning it. He was uncertain of his hands though, realizing she smelled like earth and sweat and flowers. It made his head hazy. "I'm fine."

Eventually, he remembered that people who hugged others often expected the gesture returned.

But she was already nodding and pulling away, seeming to put herself back together.

"Glow-witch!" a deep voice called to their left.

Anna flinched again. "Shark… you can call me Anna, you know…"

"Wow!" Shark enveloped each of their shoulders in his huge hands, looking as if he intended to wrestle them both. "Amazing! Great fight! You both… ha! Oh, I am glad I got you both from that city, eh?"

Jackson found he didn't have the strength to lie about this being a good fight; his head was whirling and nauseous.

"Does anyone need my help?" Anna whispered.

"Yeah," the mountain rumbled. "The once-slaves. Chains broken!" He threw back his head and crowed, a strange, animalistic call, and immediately a few of the raiders well enough to respond cheered back in kind. "Aye yeah!" he added, pumping his fists.

"What about…?" Anna pointed. For the first time, Jackson noticed a terrible gash had shredded itself along Shark's right bicep, blood trickling down. The hand that had clapped his shoulder had left a red stain behind.

"Bullet!" Shark shrugged. "Just scraped. Is fine! Go help people that need it."

Anna turned and jogged off towards the cargo rig, and Jackson found his feet moving to once again follow her.

The Warlord was standing at the back of the slave truck, thrusting the cargo doors up. Another by his side held thick bolt cutters. The rest of his people were gathered there too, a smiling, dirty, bleeding welcome committee for those they had saved.

He said this was a test.

For a moment, reality seemed to blur just a little. Jackson shook his head, a fog descending.

Suddenly, atop that slave truck, three ravens were perched. Beady black eyes turned towards Jackson, burrowing down into his soul's depths. Beaks opened, greeting him softly.

Jackson stared, staying quiet.

He thought of the raven that appeared on his father's desk the very last time they'd talked: an omen of death to come.

A cluster of new people were emptying from the truck, some staggering through rope shackles, some dirtied and beaten. There were perhaps fifteen in total, many sporting a crude metallic collar, marker of their status. None of them had tattoos like the tribe that freed them, so they were perhaps citizens, maybe settlement-born. All, however, had eyes wide with fear. Perhaps it was because they were falling from one set of owners and into the hands of another: constant pawns.

"Come here," the Warlord said, voice even and calm. "Line up."

They did as they were told. Their stares were clouded, all averted to the ground, clear in their lack of challenge.

Bolt cutters rose up to the first in line, a man who squeezed his eyes shut as if he was expecting to take a hit. Instead, the Warlord's helper took the tool and wrenched and squealed against his collar, until, with a startling snap, it broke.

"You are free," the Warlord said simply. "You may stay with us for food and shelter for a time."

The stares of the slaves were no longer at their bruised and filthy feet. They were alert, shocked, wary.

The freed man's mouth hung open, collar still dangling broken on his neck.

The Warlord made one more step. Up came the bolt cutters. A woman flinched. Her collar fell.

"You are free," the king decreed. "You may stay with us for food and shelter for a time. We are not the monsters the Coalition tells you we are."

And he stepped one further down. Now the slaves were staring at each other, aghast, silent, sparks of something new flashing in their eyes.

One woman didn't need the bolt cutters though: the woman Anna called Nyx. Her chains were already gone, melted to slag. But there'd been a price to pay for that: angry, bleeding, painful looking burns around her neck and wrists. Patches of her hair and eyebrows looked to have been singed away.

She stood silently off to the side, all present eying her with no small wariness.

Except Anna. She was brimming with surprise and delight.

"Nyx!" she cried.

"Gods," the woman replied, voice raspy with smoke. "I am one lucky bitch."

Anna practically flew to her, wrapping her up in a tight hug. "You're okay! I can't believe you're safe! I can't believe you're *here!*" For her part, Nyx smiled as she leaned into Anna's shoulder. Her grasp was shaking, and her eyes closed, looking as if they were overwhelmed with emotion.

"Hey girl. Good to see you again. Good to see you made it."

Jackson crept closer, curious.

Nyx opened weary eyes, looked up at Jackson, then blinked. "You… I know you, don't I?" she said.

"Oh!" Anna said. "This is Jackson! He took me in after you got me out of that Coalition facility. We've been traveling together ever since…

and saving each other's butts." She smiled, her spirits clearly recovering. Jackson felt a small bit of warmth in his chest and nodded, offering this friend of Anna's a smile.

"No way," Nyx said. "Jackson Dovetail. My gods." Slowly, she stepped forward and reached, cupping his face between her palms. Her skin was strangely soft and cool. "You've grown up so much."

Looking in those dark eyes, Jackson suddenly knew her face, knew this voice—the black hair, the gentle touch. He'd felt it before. He'd been just a boy when she'd come to the orphanage after Tony's bloody outburst of magic, standing alongside Agent Walker. She'd cupped his face then, too.

She'd erased his memories.

Jackson stepped back. "I'll thank you not to mess with my head again."

Nyx recoiled, dropping her hands.

His friend grimaced. "Jackson, what are you...?"

The woman's expression was turning even more exhausted. She shook her head. "No... no, it's okay. We know each other. I'm sorry. I didn't know you'd remembered. I probably seem like... like a horrible person for altering your mind like that."

"No," Jackson said, voice soft. "It was a lot for a boy to live with. You wanted to spare me the nightmares. It's... okay. But don't do it again. Seriously. Don't." He glanced over at Anna's questioning stare. "Right now... I'm just glad you and all the other prisoners are alright. But what's a mage doing out here?"

"It's a long story." Nyx didn't say more.

Anna gave them both an awkward look, but slowly, it faded. She took Nyx by the elbow and began to guide her off, probably to get her medical attention. Jackson noted that of the group, aside from burns, Nyx was in the best condition. Her skin didn't hang loose from deprivation. Her eyes weren't so hollow. She was dirtied up, but she hadn't been in this for long, perhaps only days. His mind filled in some blanks that Anna had begun to explain: no doubt she was one of the unnamed people Agent Walker had wanted to stay behind for.

Had *Walker* let her loose out in the wastes, hoping for the best, only for her to get captured?

What *luck*, then, that she'd found her way to them.

Jackson frowned, wanting an explanation, feeling all the paranoia Frank had ever imbued in his head. Some unseen hand was at play here. As he'd learned the hard way back in Tony's metro tunnels, nothing in his life was simple coincidence. Nothing.

It was all destiny.

CHAPTER SIX
Good Neighbors

Nyx limped and winced along, and Anna helped. They were ushered into a jury-rigged medical area, one that wasn't inside the sheltered, damp, and stinking ruins. Instead, this place was under the sky, a stained stretch of canvas its cover. Maya the one-eyed huffed and paced and prodded, patching, cleaning up injuries, and snipping out orders in foreign tongues.

Anna's stomach turned, head getting dizzy again. It was chaos. At least two dozen men and women had collected here. A few lay near-unmoving, red stains streaking their bodies. One man wept, biting down on a chunk of tree branch as a helper dug into his bicep with a pointed bit of metal. Blood streamed. Finally, a bullet squelched free in the medic's grasp. The man gave a muffled scream.

This happened because I asked them to do this, she knew. Slaver deaths, she found, she could move past. But the cost…

The one-eyed doctor whirled on her, as if noticing her for the first time in the rush. "You!" she snapped in English. Quick as a hornet, the woman snatched up a Geiger counter from a nearby spread of tools. She pressed the cool device directly to Anna's chest like one might a knife, glaring in challenge.

The counter hummed, but it didn't click.

Anna stared. *They know.*

Only then did the doctor ask, "Why are you here?"

"My friend is…" Anna gestured to Nyx's burns.

The doctor stared, dispassionate. "Go to the end. Sit. And if this starts clicking…" She shoved the Geiger counter in Anna's hands. "Then leave. Run, *whatever* you are. Before you hurt anyone." With that, she spun to face her next patient, a man who looked as if he'd gotten his chest slashed open. She appeared to be reaching for thread and a needle.

Subdued, queasy, Anna skittered to the far reaches of the sick and injured. Nyx hobbled at a brisk pace. Together, they more or less collapsed at the back of the queue.

"So, ah, we might be a while," Nyx laughed. It seemed a miracle that she might think anything was funny. Pained sweat clung to her forehead. The sensitive, scorched nerves at her wrists were probably screaming. All the same, she just shook her head. "I'm not as bad off as some of these guys, at least."

Anna slouched. She had a hard time looking at this kind of blood and pain, regardless of whether or not she'd seen so much of it lately.

In fact, a rebellious notion was whispering in her ear, and it was getting stronger.

You asked for this. It's your fault. But you can help fix it. You can help make it right.

She knew there were limits to her abilities. Saving Jackson's life had almost stretched her to a breaking point. The state afterwards… it was like slipping in and out of a coma. She couldn't shake the feeling that she could have severely hurt herself—she didn't feel entirely recovered *now*. Adrenaline was a great drug, but…

…But could she let it matter if she could do something about all this, even something small? "Can I see your wrists?"

Nyx blinked. Gingerly, she held out her hands. They trembled a little.

Anna pocketed the Geiger counter, then softly, softly, let her fingers rest on the scabbing and wet flesh. Nyx cringed at the touch. "Don't move," Anna whispered.

And she reached inside.

The healing light was there, a swirling ball at her core, a puff of warmth, happiness, and knowing. It tingled through her fingertips.

The other woman gasped. "Wait, that's not...?"

Slowly, the burns congealed and softened. Pink, tight, fresh skin grew in their place.

Anna opened her eyes. "I think," she whispered, "I'm starting to get the hang of this. Your ankles?"

Gaping, Nyx just nodded.

"What the hell are you doing?!" the furious, one-eyed doctor was storming across the concrete. Her hands were still bloody, bandages in her grip. She snarled at the light under Anna's skin.

And she watched Nyx's leg burns fade, the skin blooming.

"What... what are you doing?" she asked again, softer this time, with awe.

Anna stood. Her soles were cold and numb, but she felt in control, useful, and right. Her friend was rubbing the new skin, grinning. "Woah."

"I want to help," Anna whispered. This was the truest statement she'd ever said.

The doctor narrowed her eye at the Geiger counter. It was silent. She bowed her head in resolution. There was a cold practicality in that measured stare. "Aye. Alright. Come on. Follow me."

Anna waved to Nyx, getting a happy *see you later* in the answering smile. And she turned, ready to do her duty.

The line of patients was long, but it was about to get much shorter. Anna kept her eyes on her hands and inward to her heart. After a while, even the blood stopped being so nauseating. The doctor would point, rap out her judgments, and Anna would gingerly touch, feel out the matter with her new senses, and observe how cold and numb the fixes left her. And then she'd nod, ready for more.

The doctor did not point her at every problem—just matters not threatening to kill. There was healthy suspicion and skepticism in that intelligent eye, and Anna didn't question it. She was being evaluated, like every other medical tool.

"My name," the doctor told her after the hours passed. "Is Maya. You, city-woman, are Anna, yes?"

"…I'm not really from that city, if it helps you feel better." Anna sighed, rubbing her wrists, trying to get feeling back in them.

"It does." The woman hazarded a tiny crack in her severity: a brief, toothy smile. She paused to grab a canteen, rinsing the blood from her hands with a thorough, methodical air. "You are slowing."

"This… takes a lot out of me."

"Then sit. Breathe the good air, not like in those ruins. You have done, very, very good for us."

"But—"

"Sit."

Anna did. The doctor passed the canteen, and Anna washed away every patch of red, every shred of guilt she'd felt walking under this canvas. There were still patients, but so few now. Some of the previous ones were even showing off their new scars, pointing at her from a distance, smiling widely.

There was a cluster of former slaves further away. They watched the proceedings with wary, glittering eyes.

"Do you think there's anything I can do for them?" Anna asked.

Maya shook her head. "No. They need something more than a few cuts fixed, yeah?"

Regardless, Anna offered them a hesitant grin and gave a tiny wave. They ducked their heads down, but for just a second… one returned the smile. "I can't imagine what they've been through."

"I can. Maybe I will tell them our story—of our great-grandparents who were like them, and how they escaped, how they found happiness. Maybe I will give them hope. That will help better than anything else, though it takes a lot of doses."

Anna suddenly realized Maya was in fact a very good doctor. "So your people used to be slaves too?"

"Aye yeah. For the city."

Stomach growing cold, Anna set down the canteen.

"After the world-fire." Maya shrugged. "Long time ago. But not long enough. Someone had to fix the poison land, make good food, help them spread their Barrier wider, eh? Someone had to die to save them all. Most of us did. Some of us did not. Some of us got our own happy ending, right?"

Anna just stared. She put her face in her hands.

That after everything, *everything*, an advanced and progressive city would still turn to slavery when their backs were against the wall...?

"You know," Maya chuckled. "My great-grandma, she used to say there was a reason we escaped. That there was a woman in the tent next to hers that could do..." She clicked her tongue, like she was trying to settle on a word. "The things people can't usually do. Like you, but not. She used her ways to distract the guards and set us free. I didn't believe my mother, telling her grandma's stories. But now..."

A strange, rhythmic tapping started to drift on the breeze, accompanying the setting sun.

"Ah," Maya nodded. "The celebration."

"...Celebration? Of what?" It couldn't be all this blood, all this pain.

"We passed our test. So now, we are free to move again. And before we do, we must honor those who live. Those who died. There are many of both." Maya gave an assured nod, squaring her feet. "Our road is long. Hope is always needed to walk it. So go on. You've done much. I have the rest."

"Are you sure...?"

"Aye. Follow them. It's not far. You'll see." Most of those gathered nearby were starting to stomp their feet, to chuckle, to holler. They were moving as one to the west as the sky began to grow dusky and deep.

Anna rose, feeling adrift, sad… but better, like she'd made a difference. "Thanks—good luck. And let me know if you need anything else!"

Maya winked her one eye—or maybe it was just a blink. It was hard to tell. "Thank you. You know… I would like it if you stayed with us to the end, Healer Anna. Regardless of the…" She waved awkwardly at the Geiger counter in her helper's pocket. "…just, keep that. But you could be needed here."

That simple offer was just the medicine Anna needed. Her heart swelled. With a lightness in her step, she began to follow the path of the setting sun and the drums.

⁕ ⁕

Jackson tread carefully through the camp's center. Along the way, he collected a number of stares. He was getting used to it.

He'd been asked to help pick the trucks clean for supplies. Or, rather, Shark had scooped him away to do it, and that was that—he wasn't going to argue with either a smile or a grip that strong. Besides, he sensed the best way to get along was to be helpful. It wouldn't take much for this crowd to turn on him again.

Out of one cargo bay came guns—Jackson's breath nearly stopped to see the racks all the way down the hold and back. The unloaders hooted and clapped each other's shoulders.

For raiders, he supposed, this was a very good reward. He tried not to think about how Foxhole was managing to obtain such fine, new inventory.

Beyond that, however, the dead trader's goods were mostly junk. For people beyond the city, it was probably *useful* garbage, but still. Old clothes, ropes, and rusted tools were their lot. None of the datapads worked. What Jackson wouldn't have *given* for an unregistered datapad right then. An internet connection, however unlikely, would have been a fine way to pass two weeks.

Dissatisfied, Jackson bit his lip in the now-empty cargo bay, looking about.

"Hey, come on," Shark called, the last of the boxes in his grip.

"Hold on." Jackson kneeled, feeling at the floor seams, pressing, searching. There had to be something—

And as he was about to call it a day, his fingers caught a section with just a *little* too much give. Grinning, he shifted his weight, clicking the panel down, releasing the springs.

"What the…?" Shark gaped as the lid to the smuggler's cache came free.

"Always hide the good stuff," Jackson said, pleased with himself. He counted two dozen sealed bottles of brown, bubbly alcohol, and one packet of crumbling, purple-brown mushrooms. He let out a low whistle. New Age Nightcap. There was a least ten-thousand credits worth here.

Shark lifted a bottle of the home-brewed ale, a reverent gleam in his eye. Jackson sensed that maybe tonight, people might think a little better of him when they lifted their glasses.

They brought back what little medicine and food there was alongside this cache, and were greeted with a chorus of cheer. Jackson's spirits lifted on that upswell too. A few people even smiled at him.

Blessed are those who bring beer.

When they were done offloading, Shark took Jackson by the shoulder, a celebratory bottle in his hand. He pointed merrily to the horizon—and he announced his new friend needed a tour of their home.

Ambling, they came to a tiny park, green weeds and ivy overtaking the rusted fixtures of yesteryear. "Aye, it is not fancy, but it is good." Shark spread one hulking arm wide. "This is where we gather for food, morning and night."

Where he gestured, a large group was springing up, chattering and socializing, comparing injuries from the battle. Already some of the hurt warriors, now bandaged and tended, were drifting back from the doctors. A cookfire was at the center of the commotion. Someone was passing out gruel bowls.

In Jackson's memory, a looming chieftain handed him food in a grudging peace offering.

To be honest, Jackson still wondered that he'd been allowed to live. *I helped kill his son.*

What twisted ways fate wove. And a web was indeed here... a *tapestry*, as Inoki put it. Everything was connected.

It began with a mage man, one with a rune-carved beard and ice-eyes who tried to murder him as a child. But Tony stopped that man. And that was when this Nyx woman had met him for the first time, Agent Walker by her side, to collect Tony, to take him to that Coalition program for children with magic. Project Esper, hadn't they called it? She erased Jackson's memories. This was the first thread in the tapestry.

When he found his way to the Order, the rune-bearded mage had been there again, though Jackson couldn't have known. And he was denied training, slowly poisoned, his abilities crushed until they meant nothing. That was thread number two.

Then Tony, broken, eventually escaped Coalition custody. He'd been unleashing his shattered mind and fury on raiders and criminals— enemies Project Esper brainwashed him to hunt. The Order mages eventually found him. One of them had been down in those tunnels, a healer, claiming they'd figured out a way to manipulate him into disposing of their problems. Thread number three.

She'd also said Tony had utterly lost what was left of his sanity after going for a wander in the wastes, where he'd found Anna and a mess of Coalition agents. On that same day, apparently, he'd come back with his newest gladiator: the Tiger. All of the ravens' whispers in

Tony's head, they'd pushed him this way and that along fate's design, and he just followed it, thinking some puzzle called *destiny* would eventually fall into place.

Maybe Tony was right, because it was a very small world in which Jackson would end up not a day later alongside that dead gladiator's father: a man who mentioned *foreseeing* things, who spoke of tests, who didn't like answering questions.

A bowl was suddenly forced into Jackson's hand, breaking his thoughts.

"Eat!" Shark crowed. "Just staring off into nothing! No good of it."

Hungry, he complied. Frankly, his head hurt, and he had no more data left to sift through—there was only a cold emptiness in his stomach, the notion that he needed to hunt down more information. But he had nowhere to begin.

Hmm, his brain noted, feeling out the chunks and textures with his tongue. *Rat bits in this batch.*

It had been a very long time since he'd been forced to have rat, and it wasn't as bad as he remembered. He hardly expected four-star cuisine out here, so he ate, and he hoped that at the very least it had been properly decontaminated. "Thanks," he belatedly added to Shark, feeling his belly grow full for the first time in a long time. It was strange; though this raider was loud and brash, he seemed… well, alright.

The big man clapped him hard on the back, almost sending him spitting. "Of course! Ol' Shark got you, eh? Anyone that runs at those trucks like that? Who finds us beer? Of course he gets to eat."

A short distance beyond the cookfire, another flame sprung up. There, a man and woman were filtering water through a tight cloth of some sort, adding it to a cauldron and bringing it to boil. Around them were piles of canteens. These all bore clear Coalition brands. The man had a handful of iodine tablets at the ready too, probably for further decontamination work.

All their wool blankets were red, all their bowls a uniform

stamped tin. At some point, these people had to have brought down a government supply truck to get this inventory.

Very ballsy. Very desperate.

"That is where you get your daily water," Shark continued, gesturing to the cauldron. "They give you your canteen. Give it back before sleep, yeah? They fill it again for morning."

Jackson licked his lips, realizing they were cracking. "I don't suppose I can get one now."

"Ah yeah. Right. They won't give you one until tomorrow. Here. Have mine."

It was somewhat startling, having the container generously pressed in his hands. Jackson wasn't quite sure what to say. "Are you sure?"

"Don't want you falling over, eh? Shark has beer! He is fine." As if to demonstrate, the man took a swig from his bottle and worked his biceps, making his tattoos dance.

It was difficult to argue with a flexing mountain speaking in the third person, so Jackson drank from the canteen happily. He'd never had rations beyond the filtrated reserves of New York, and this was new. The tang of lukewarm iodine burst on his tongue, bitter and nose-wrinkling.

There was no point in questioning if the water was really safe; they were trying their best with what they had. His Quarantine would just need to work overtime if it wasn't. He'd no doubt get a full checkup once he got back to the city anyway—and a full detox.

"So I ask *you* questions now?" Shark settled on a rock as they finished their gruel. He leaned in eagerly as Jackson took a seat.

"Okay?"

"Where is your... ah..." The man made a gesture as if to indicate everything about Jackson's entire body.

"My what?"

"Your..." Shark's face screwed up. He covered his mouth, making a wheezing noise.

"I'm not sure I understand."

The man continued to make the odd sound, his eyes shining with mirth. Then, the dam sprung forth, bursting guffaws, uproarious and consuming. "You're naked! Hahaha! Like baby! *Where are your paintings?*"

Like everything he seemed to do, it drew the attention of anyone within twenty feet. Jackson shrunk in on himself.

"Naked like baby!" Shark crowed again.

Even a child stopped running by to stare.

"I, uh…" Jackson swallowed. "You mean…?" He reached out gingerly and tapped the big man's arm. There lay a coiled image of a dragon overlying a thick scar.

"Yeah!" Shark's head bobbed in a furious nod.

"Tattoos. Right. Well." Jackson chose his words with care. "In the city… ink like that's not considered good. People think it's…" Really, the simple fact was that tattoos made a person look like a criminal, a *bandit*, and who would do legal business with someone like that? Maybe he'd get one if he wanted to wear his illegitimate dealings on his sleeve, but… why?

Fortunately, Shark seemed content to accept that it was just a city thing. "Pffft, whole dome, running around like little babies!" He giggled, wiggling his fingers like he was conjuring the image before him. "Don't worry. We fix that for you."

"Wait, what do you—"

"My friend, she is very good with painting. She will give you the good rites, I am sure."

"*Well.* Um." Jackson finished his gruel, trying to smile. "We don't need to rush into the *rites* and all. I mean, seeing as I'm not even staying for long—"

Shark waved a hand. "No no, can be very quick, I bet even tonight! A warrior with no painting… that's silly!" He turned his head on his thick neck. "HEY! NAKAMA!"

Jackson spied a gangly, tattoo-laden woman at the far end of the gathering, directly at the end of Shark's line of sight. She looked like she hadn't heard. Shark inhaled for what looked like a repeat bellow.

Oh no, no thank you, no needles, no surprise friendship tattoos. "Actually," Jackson tapped the hulking shoulder. His companion's chest deflated with a confused burst. "If you don't mind… I'd actually like to learn more about your people and your leader."

Such an innocent and eager smile spread on that face. Thank the gods, the distraction took root. "Like what?"

"Well… the Warlord seemed to say you've all been on the move. He said we'd be moving again soon. I… I have to say, I'm a little concerned about that."

"OH!" Shark grinned wider. "Yes, we've been searching. End to a path—the Warlord guides us. He is wise to this country! But we can't stay in one place long, this close to the city. Surprised everyone was still here when we got back."

Jackson blinked. "You mean no one might have been here at all when that storm hit?"

"Would have been fine. They would have left a message. We'd go after them. That's all."

With Anna on my back? Jackson couldn't help but wonder.

Shark continued, "He stayed so long because of Tiger." The smile disappeared. A darker look took hold. "Family makes us not wise."

Jackson licked his lips. "Oh?"

Shark shifted. "Hope. Hope lies, makes people dumb. But now he knows there is none. Our soon-Father's gone. My friend." Bowing his head, the mountain sighed. "Gone. All gone." He trembled. "But not your fault. Do not let anyone say it's your fault. You didn't choose to fight, but still gave Tiger the death he wanted—fighting with all his might against the city. And you did it honest. Most of them don't."

Jackson shifted, casting his gaze around for any who might be listening. It was hard to tell. He let the silence stretch out of respect.

A single tear wound down the red tattoo ink coating Shark's face, losing itself in his stubble.

"Shark?"

"Yeah?"

"What does he mean by foreseeing things? Your Warlord. He said he saw that the caravan would come. That it was a test."

Shark frowned. There was almost an air of embarrassment there. "…Nothing. He, just, he knows the land and the people very well, that's all."

Jackson's eyes narrowed. He knew lies, knew them through countless negotiations and posturing and ulterior motives.

Shark was not a good liar.

But faintly, on the breeze, the sound of drums began to pulse.

Fierce lights dawned in Shark's stare. "Ah. There! Soon time to honor the ghosts."

Flustered, unsatisfied with his answers, Jackson swallowed. "Ghosts?"

"Aye yeah. You too have many ghosts, right? Something about how you look… I bet you do." The man rose. He clapped his hands and hooted. Several others responded with their own applause and happy cries, especially as he lifted his bottle high. "And this? Best way to tell the dead, they do not need to stay. Best way to tell them that we miss them, but we're going to keep living! We see them one day soon, but not until we're done!"

"Shark! Shark! Shark!" A group nearby rose and began chanting.

"Ha!" The mountain spread his arms wide. "Yeah, Shark is back!" The chanting turned to cheers. Despite Jackson's grim mood, the joy was infectious. "Back from the dead! And I love all of you! And Tiger did too! So we honor him!"

Many voices rose, agreeing in a score of tongues. The gathered started to finish their food, to scatter.

Jackson started standing too—it just seemed like the right thing to do. He slung the canteen over one shoulder and his bag over the other. "A celebration?" In spite of everything, perhaps that would be nice. He felt about ready to crack in half from always looking over his shoulder and puzzling out the motives of gods.

"Music! Planting! Dancing!" Shark gave his back another mighty clap, making him stumble. "*Drinking!* We freed slaves today, killed bad people. Tiger would have loved it."

At the dead man's name, the persistent tension between Jackson's shoulder blades turned into a dull ache. "Really?"

"Yeah, just wait. Many fires will light up tonight." Shark prodded his chest with one finger. "Maybe you dance with Anna, eh? Or maybe I do!"

Jackson straightened his back. "I... well."

"Shark sees you looking."

"No!"

"Aye yeah, sure. I have your back if you have mine, but I dance with the pretty glowing lady if you do not!" Another booming laugh ricocheted from his chest, filling the clearing with its cheer.

Grimacing, Jackson felt a self-conscious twist in his stomach.

Had Anna noticed his gaze lingering for maybe a second too long? *Gods, I hope not.*

The truth was, even if he was drawn to her, it wasn't like out here there would be opportunity to...

Well, it wasn't as if she'd dance with him anyway, right?

In lieu of engaging with the teasing, he only sighed and rifled through his bag. At least Tony's goons had made sure he kept his toothpaste and toothbrush—hospitable of them. There was really only so far he could salvage himself right now, but he dipped his brush in the canteen, pasted it down, and began to scrub away at his mouth.

"You... you foam." Shark sounded unnerved.

Jackson spat. He was somewhat startled that his new raider friend had never caught wind of basic dental technology, given that he appeared to have at least most of the pointed teeth in his head. "It's to clean your mouth. Look, if I'm going to dance, I'm not going to stink."

Shark began to giggle again, slapping his belly. "That's what chewsticks are for, you naked babies."

Surprised, Jackson revised his own assumptions, feeling an odd sense of kinship to that. *Chewsticks.* The orphanage had preferred them, as broke as they were, though this toothbrush substitute was said to be a bit uncivilized after he'd been properly homed. He washed away the toothpaste with another chug from the canteen, careful to ration out what little remained. "Maybe I'll start using those again out here."

This earned him a smile of approval. "Yeah! You do not need to defend the city or their ways. I think maybe, after all they did to you…" Shark shrugged. "I do not think you are really going to go back, you know?"

Jackson's wind deflated like he'd been punched in the chest. He stared. "I…" *Of course,* his mind whispered. *Of course I'm going back. Home and the company and my life… it's all waiting for me.*

But the ominous feeling in his heart pulsed louder.

A soft horn billowed through the neighborhood. Shark hooted again happily, as if he had no idea how badly he'd rattled his guest. "That's the call," he said, tugging his companion on. "The war is taking a break for now. Come on. Is time to live."

CHAPTER SEVEN
Dance

At the end of the crowds was a bright red stretch of canvas, a simple shelter. Underneath this flashy cloth, the growing twilight at his back, was the Warlord.

As the sun set, it looked as if it was simply coming to rest between his antlers.

He was looking at all gathered like they were his children. Though his face was severe, when they filed up, opening their hands, they smiled. One by one, they pressed their foreheads to the skull's nose. There was an exchange. Their leader's huge hands grasped theirs together, one leathery and one metallic, gripping as if he was bestowing upon them the secrets of the universe.

When they left that place, their steps were alive.

"Uh, hi again," Anna said, one of the last to mosey forward, awkward, unsure what all of this meant.

This close, she could see the deep lines in the Warlord's face, the gray melting across his hair. Not knowing what else to do, she imitated what she'd seen, cupping her hands together in supplication. Wordlessly, he reached into a nearby pack, scooped, and let his huge grasp give way over hers, a torrent of sunflower seeds showering into her palms.

"These are for good luck," he whispered. "So our successes live on."

She smiled back, not understanding. "I know this is going to sound dumb, but what do I do with them?"

This earned her a bark of laughter, like she'd asked how one walked or breathed. For just a tiny moment, his dark eyes glimmered with joy. "You plant them," he said, voice hushed and low, as if he spoke of the sacred. "Go, see the fields. Honor the life still here—because life grows from death, as it always has been, as it always *will* be. Life from my wife. Life from my son. That is what me and my people were chosen to do. You will see."

Anna nodded, confused, and turned on her heel, deciding she didn't want to hold up those behind her.

Twilight was still falling, the ruins casting long, dark shadows. People scurried about coaxing up campfires, one every hundred yards or so. And there on the corner, staring at his cupped hands in a baffled way, was Jackson. She trotted to his side, nudging him gently with an elbow. "Hey! Were you waiting for me?"

He nodded. "Do you know why we're being given these things?" His hands were full of seeds as well. "Shark got them for me—he said I might want to give the Warlord some space, but then he kind of just…" He rotated one of his shoulders like it ached. "…Slugged me in the arm, smiled in an *extremely* disconcerting way, and took off."

Anna laughed, shaking her head. "I think he likes you."

"Uh. Hm."

"I'm told we plant them."

"This is a *strange* raider ritual." He chuckled. "Better, I guess, than heads on stakes or drinking the blood of your enemies."

Making a face, Anna looked again to her palms. Sunflowers indeed seemed a gentle gesture. It reassured her down to her soul. *Life grows from death. Like me.*

It was then she noticed. "Hey, one of mine's already sprouted!" She smiled at this tiniest hint of tendril snaking its way to life, the healthy new green of a flower being born. An excited niggle began in her chest.

"C'mon, let's do this!"

Jackson looked over at her hands and scanned the movements of the crowd. Slowly, he turned with a silent *I might have found the way* in his body. His feet followed a few other people with cupped hands and smiling faces. She trailed after.

Together, they came upon a series of empty lots. Coiled, rusted chain link and old bricks were lumped to one side, cleared away. People were talking and laughing while hunched over patches of earth. Little upturned mounds of dirt were everywhere, even where chunks of asphalt and concrete had been cracked or destroyed, exposing the soil beneath. *The fields. Got it!*

She nudged Jackson again, spying a spot that so far seemed untouched. Most of the Warlord's people looked to be finishing, many returning to the fires throughout the camp, wiping earth from their fingers. The drums were growing louder, and singing had started too. A few of them were dancing, a gyrating, stomping flurry. Some were quickly gesturing with their hands, like they were telling stories. *Honor the living.*

As she settled down against a dusty, weedy patch, she felt a little bit of her tension seep away. This was a moment of peace, of life.

Enjoy it while it lasts.

Mimicking other planters, she pawed aside a tiny bit of earth, carefully placing the sprout. Jackson was watching, kneeling beside her, not yet digging. "This reminds me of a lot of things," she said, wanting to fill the quiet between them. "Back in Las Vegas... Mom... she's... I mean, she *was*... great." Despite her mood, using the past tense ached all the way to her bones. She soldiered on. "You would have loved her. *Everyone* loved her. She looked a lot like me, until Frank told me to hack all my hair off." Jackson nodded. "Blue eyes like mine too. And she loved to garden, spent all her time in the dirt planting orchids. Wild ones: black and orange and purple! I first got into science testing the pH levels in our soil." There was a catch in her voice. "Did experiments… with ladybugs. Um. Yeah."

She sniffled, covering the sprout with dirt so it only peeked through. It was so fragile, wasn't it? Would it survive?

"That's a good memory," Jackson whispered. He set his own seed pile down, and with an uncertain touch, he started to shift aside a little soil near his knees. "She sounds important to you."

"…Yeah." A surge of guilt welled up in Anna's chest, knife-edged with raw sorrow. She hadn't given her mother a proper visit for two years before this all had happened. She'd stayed away from home after graduating college. How must it have felt? Had her mother thought her only child didn't care anymore? What had she done when she heard her daughter was dead?

Anna's chest shuddered. She was about to break when Jackson's hand touched hers, a soft comfort—a distraction.

"I didn't have a mother I knew," Jackson said, though it wasn't said with any sadness. "I did have my adopted father. How about you? Any father?"

Anna bit her lip. "Yeah." He'd been the reason she'd stayed away from home. She started burrowing a tiny hole for the next seed.

"What was he like?"

"Dad was… Dad." Her throat felt thick. Here was something she hadn't wanted to examine either, not yet.

Jackson raised an eyebrow. "I… see?"

She snorted. "No, I mean… I don't like talking about him much. He's… he just…" She paused her planting, coming to the sudden realization that she hadn't cried once for her dead father. Hadn't even thought of him at all.

I'm a horrible person.

"Are you okay?" Jackson was actually burying his seeds faster than she was. Some of his holes, she suspected, were too deep. "We can talk about something else if you—"

"I'm okay," she mumbled. "Well… I don't know. I guess I'm not.

I just, I don't know if I'm sad or not that he's gone—! I mean, I'm supposed to be sad, what kind of monster wouldn't be *sad* that their own dad is…!" Her voice cracked, and she dropped a couple of her seeds, her hands shaking. Jackson's face grew alarmed. His grasp settled on her shoulder, and somehow, as she searched his eyes, she found her breath again. "It's just, he made me so *angry*. We didn't get along. He hated what I did. Said it wasn't my place. I mean, science. He was really *traditional* sometimes. Fundamentalist. You know?"

"A fundamentalist what?"

Jackson's blank reaction made Anna reel. It stopped her spiral in its tracks. "Religion's still a thing, right?"

"Oh! Yes. Why?"

His disconnect pulled her in a welcome way from the ghosts of her family. She veered from the roiling ball of emotions that had yet to be dealt with, finding comforting explanations to give. "A couple of Christians have really specific ideas about women's roles in the world. You know. Stay at home. Cook. Whatever. Make the babies. Raise the babies."

Jackson squinted. "Huh."

Anna couldn't stop a burst of laughter tearing out of her throat. *Oh. Oh my God. The world ends, but it took all of the fundamentalists with it?* "You have no idea what I'm talking about."

"There was a Christian group funding my orphanage, but I never heard of that nonsense."

"Maybe," she said dryly, "The bad ones went up with the Rapture like they always said they would."

He snickered and she leaned against him, glad he was there while her hands furrowed new holes in the dirt, glad she wasn't facing her memories alone. "I might not be a reliable source," he said. "I was never a churchgoer of any stripe. But… Anna." He sighed. "I'm so sorry about your family. I know this is hard. I… when I realized my father was gone…" He swallowed and said nothing more, but he didn't have to.

Her eyes passed over the wasted, dissolving buildings of another era. She didn't know what to say. Home, she knew, was going to haunt her for a long time.

Home.

Hadn't Walker said Las Vegas had a Barrier? Was it possible that her friends, her family, had been some of the lucky ones to make it inside? "Jackson," she finally managed. "Do you think it would be possible to go to Vegas someday? Catch a plane?" Of course there'd be no one she knew there anymore, couldn't be, but… if she could see the city she'd left behind, maybe, somehow, that would make it better. Maybe she'd find something, anything, that would help her wrestle with her grieving.

"Plane? I don't know." He ran a touch over his jaw, the dirt black under his fingernails. It was getting stubbly, and this seemed to make him frown. "They don't just let anyone fly from dome to dome. You need special approval for it." She sagged a little, but the arm around her shoulder squeezed tighter, a half-hug. She was already snug against his side, and this made the center of her chest light up with warmth. "I might be able to arrange something. There's some cargo vessels in my fleet."

That was all Anna needed. *Home.* There had to be something left of it all: something familiar, something to cling to. She smiled up at him. "Thank you. That means *a lot* to me."

"Mind you, it might be an uncomfortable trip. Under the radar, in with the cargo."

"So," she said, eyebrow raised in a teasing way, "You're going to smuggle me."

He smiled. "It's what I do."

"You're not even going to hide that."

"You're smart. I know you've figured it out. I mean, I keep Frank around, right?"

She laughed. The work started going easily now as they talked.

"But I promise," he added, "That I don't ship anything bad. Not *bad* bad."

"It's okay. I'm not judging you at all. Honestly, I'm really glad I met you."

He straightened, looking pleased. "Oh?"

"Yeah. I mean, where would I be right now if I hadn't?"

Jackson smiled. They fell into a thoughtful silence for a long, companionable stretch. Then, he whispered, "Do you trust them?"

Startled, she blinked. "Who? The Warlord and Shark and all of them?"

"Yeah… I don't know if I like this talk of foreseeing things. Of tests and *vengeance* and moving camp."

Anna bit her lip. "Is there anything we can do about it? Other than help where we can? I mean, we don't really have anywhere else to go. And, well, vengeance against slavers probably isn't the worst thing they could be doing—at least they're not robbing Dovetail trucks, right?"

He was quiet in the face of that.

She didn't know if she should say that she'd been invited to stay. She didn't even know what to think about it. It was so good to be needed, to make a difference.

"If things go bad, we'll figure it out," she decided, not knowing what else to do.

"Yeah." He looked like he had reservations to that, but she couldn't imagine it being any other way. Things were a lot dicier between him and the Warlord, after all. It was doubtful he'd be extended an invitation, no matter how friendly Shark was.

Besides, he really did have a life to return to.

Most of her seeds were buried. Jackson was working with only one hand, keeping an arm around her, but she found it comforting, so she started burying his seeds too to save him trouble. Perhaps even two days ago, this closeness would have been alien to her, far too much, but now… it put her at ease.

She realized that when the choice came, she didn't really want to go separate ways.

And as the last of the young plants went into the ground, a thought dawned on her, surveying the hundreds of little mounds as the diggers joined the fires. The music was swelling louder. "Oh my God!" she said. "I just figured it out."

"Hmm?"

"*Sunflowers*. Oh my God." It was brilliant.

"…What about them…?"

She pulled away and stood, looking out over the streets, every patch of dirt planted. "They're *purifiers*, Jackson. Sunflowers can be used for cleanup of contaminated areas!" He rose with her, expression not quite understanding. "Look, some plants suck up heavy metals from the groundwater and earth, especially the sorts of particles that are radioactive, right? Sunflowers are amazing at it. There were some experiments… you can get a place de-contaminated within a few years. You can plant again, and the food grown will have less of a chance of being harmful." She rubbed the grit between her fingers, brushing it away. "They really *are* farmers!"

He seemed incredulous. "You're sure?"

"Look at this place. They're planting in every patch of dirt… why else would they?"

He brushed his hands free of soil, eyes guarded. "I've been thinking. A lot. My only real interaction with the people beyond the Barriers has been to deliver to official settlements and to beat back the hoards of thieves and killers and slavers that try to intercept us. It's clear these people, they're no strangers to violence, but… I don't know. They *are* different from Foxhole. That much is obvious."

Anna nodded. The drumming was insistent now, upbeat, the people around the fires cheering and chanting. One of the former slaves, the big man put on display as a 'fighter', was edging closer to the crowd. A red ring still imprinted the flesh around his neck. His face was gaunt… but he looked like he was finding his place too, his first night of freedom in who knew how long. "We did something good today," she breathed. "I know it. We helped make some things alright. And maybe… maybe I'm going to be alright too." Despite her exhaustion, the music was starting to get under her skin, make her awake and glad to be so. "So. You want to leave all the thinking about the future for the morning? I think we should join the party."

Jackson regarded her, his eyes reflecting strangely in the growing shadows. For a moment, she was struck with an inexplicable sense of déjà vu. It was like his look was something she'd seen in a dream. "Alright," he conceded, holding out a dusty hand, a tentative question. "Well, in that case… maybe you might honor me with a dance?"

The unexpected offer made her blink and stiffen.

The drums said, *this could be fun.*

Her historic lack of coordination argued, *no no no, it won't be.*

She fidgeted, anxious, trying to laugh it off. "I don't really know how."

The crooked grin she was starting to know him for started to dawn, just a little. "It's alright if you don't want to… but, anyone can dance. It's easy. I could teach you. Maybe it'll help get your mind off things." Again his fingers waggled, beckoning.

She swallowed. "Um." There was an uneasy, but not unpleasant, tingle in her solar plexus. *After everything,* the feeling said to her, *this is what you're scared of? If you can learn nuclear physics or beat up a supervillain, you can learn to dance.* She steeled herself, taking his warm, outstretched fingers. "Okay."

Jackson's pleased, mischievous smile grew wider, and he stepped in, slipping his other hand around her waist. "Well then… a waltz. Very simple, I promise." His position was, Anna realized, a bit of an intimate thing, even if it was only his hands. The prickle of uncertainty rose.

Let me remind you of the time you tripped and knocked five people over on the tram, her anxiety tittered.

"Right," she mumbled. "Are you sure? That sounds fancy." To herself, she thought: *settle down.*

"You're smart; you'll get it in no time," he reassured. She struggled to focus anyway. "Put your other hand on my shoulder... good."

"Okay."

"Then, I'll lead." His head was held high. "And when you feel me press your hand..." He gave her grip a subtle push. "...That means you step back with your left—your *left*—foot." Anna switched her stance, her breath hitching with embarrassment. "Right, then I step forward as you do, and we draw our feet together." His knee brushed hers as she jerked her heels to comply. "That's step one. And we can take that in any direction." He tugged her hand subtly to the left. Piecing the instruction together, she stepped that way, matching his movement.

Slowly, her breathing eased. Okay! Actually, it was an easy pattern. Forward, right, back, and left. They moved through it over and over until it came even easier, a square over the freshly upturned earth, the smell of rain and life and fire in her nose. Her hands stopped trembling. She smiled. "Wow, okay, I might actually get the hang of this." She stepped on his toes. "Sorry! But, this is all it is? Waltzing?"

Jackson laughed off his wince. "Basically. It gets fancier with practice."

"I can't believe I thought this was... oops! Sorry! Again..."

He flinched for only a moment. "It's okay!" They kept drifting through the simple motions, slow, easy, and Anna saw a couple raiders looking on, shrugging as if to say, *weird city types*. A burn of self-consciousness lit on her ears, but Jackson kept stepping as if no one was watching at all. This braced her nerves.

"Thank you." She was starting to feel comfortable with his proximity again.

"Of course."

"How'd you learn?" He moved with an agile, lanky sort of grace, confident and easy. She wondered if, back in the city, there was someone in his life who would be very jealous of her right now. He'd never said.

"For a while I think my father was trying to make something stick that wasn't pining after magic practice. Sent me to lessons!"

There was a turn in Anna's stomach, this time not pleasant. "After the Order voted you out?"

"Yeah." He shook his head. "But all that's a grim subject when spending the time with lovely company, you know?"

The words blindsided her. *Flirting?* Her chest fluttered. Skidding to a stop, her brain deployed evasive maneuvers. "...Yeah. The Order. Their Archmage is pretty awful, isn't he?"

"Their leader? You met him?" Now he faltered.

She grimaced, somewhat regretting her panic-topic. "Yeah. He was... cruel. Cold. Rifled around in my memories from before." *When I died*, she silently added. But she didn't want to talk about death, which meant there was nothing left but to ramble, voice falsely high. "He was some evil British guy with a crazy, dumb beard—he had letters shaved in it! I mean, really? Beard letters? What's up with that? Ha." She couldn't even force a smile into her weak tone.

"Wait, *beard*—the *Archmage*, he's the one with—"

"Those awful, cold blue eyes..." she whispered, remembering.

Jackson's Adam's apple bobbed in a hard swallow. *He knows who I'm talking about.*

It was then that Anna's conversational rescuer burst out of the dark: Shark. He was a bounding force of nature, clearly drunk and smiling for days. "NAKED BABY MAN! I DANCE AFTER YOU, YEAH? *HAHAHA!*"

And he was gone, a cackling, heedless locomotive into the night.

Jackson paled. His tongue twisted up anything he might have been about to say. "Oh! Oh... gods... I... Huh. I wonder who *he* was shouting at?"

Anna couldn't help it. The snorting burst out of her nose, undignified as everything, and the giggles tumbled after. Somehow, she managed to keep dancing, but barely. And after a minute of Jackson looking at his feet and getting redder, grace a little broken, she tried to stop. "Okay. Okay! I swear I won't ask. So. Um. How about we talk about something a little less, uh, terrible than the Archmage?"

"Of course." He brightened, looking so, so relieved in taking what seemed like a save for his pride. "How about... are there any questions about this time that I can help answer?"

Anna thought. "Well, when you speak... you say the *gods* a lot?"

"Just what I heard growing up." He smiled self-consciously. "Probably from Huxley. I don't even know if other mages really believe that! That there are beings who protect and guide us." He shook his head. "Maybe it makes some people feel better, to hope there are." His eyes spoke of an internal question he'd been kicking around for a long time. This intrigued Anna.

"What do *you* believe?" she pressed.

His response was slow, thoughtful. "I know I believe in *something*. Too many things have happened for me not to. I guess if there are gods... I'll accept their help." He shrugged. "But maybe they're full of secrets. Maybe they don't make life any easier. I suspect it's best to trust and help those in front of you instead. People you can touch and see." His guide hand gave hers a light squeeze.

Anna licked her lips, feeling the warmth in her chest light up again, unable to stop a small smile. "You know, I always called myself an atheist... but I like that. Everyone should take care of each other. We're all we've got." She sighed. "Especially in a time like this."

"What, you mean there might be a couple problems around here?" Jackson rolled his eyes. "Preposterous."

She snorted. "You know, I think the best thing I've experienced all month is having a bathroom to myself." His face grew serious. "I don't know. I've been a prisoner in two different cages. I've been in a ratty, roach-infested safe house, and I've been in a run-down building where an audience was paying money to watch other people kill each other. And now, I'm out here, and there's slavery and guns and…" Her voice caught. "This is a really ugly world, isn't it?"

Jackson shook his head. "No! No. I swear, it's not all like that. You haven't seen it like I have yet. You haven't had the chance to."

"What is there, then?" The deep-rooted exhaustion from two days worth of running and fighting and healing seeped from her bones and into her words. "Honestly, what can make anyone forget about all this?"

He licked his lips, swallowing hard. "Forget? Nothing. But make it easier? Well… you haven't seen the park."

"The park. Central Park?"

"Yes."

"This better be a pretty amazing park."

He shook his head. "I know it doesn't sound like much, but you haven't *seen* it. Most beautiful place in New York. You can walk through the berry farm patches, buy them right off the vine—so fresh, when you eat them, you can see colors. And there are flowers and trees, and in the autumn, when the sun hits it all just right, the way the light plays off the Barrier makes the whole place glow like it's on fire."

Anna paused. "That… maybe…"

"And the summer parade in Brooklyn. I swear, half the city turns out for it. People wear every color of the rainbow, and they sing, and they go through the streets, thousands of us, just to celebrate that we're alive, that the city will make it year after year. They raise money, donate it to families that need it, because we all know we need to be there for each other."

Anna squeezed his hand tighter. She closed her eyes, trying to capture a little of the song in his voice, the honest enthusiasm.

"Or the animal pavilion at Prospect! They've been keeping dozens of kinds of butterflies alive there for over a sixty years. Butterflies can't live outside the Barrier in this environment, not any more. So they get taken care of, and you can walk with them, let them land on you. They love people for some reason. It's like being surrounded by a swarm of fluttering gemstones, light as a feather."

"Do you think…" Anna smiled, feeling her mood lift on the thoughts of a hundred butterfly wings. "…that one day, the butterflies will be able to go free? That the world will heal?"

"That's the idea. And Anna, that's not even talking about the lantern festival, or the ferries, or the markets, or, just, well. Look. There are a million beautiful things here. There are things worth waking up for, and good people too. They're waiting for you to go see them for yourself. And all of this? It'll seem like a bad dream when you do. I promise."

The drums were dwindling, and he swayed them to a stop. A little overcome, Anna kept holding his hands, latching onto the faint outline of good dreams on the horizon.

Life from death.

"Maybe," he whispered. "Maybe we'll go together to see. If you like."

His warm eyes and grin had really grown on her. There was weariness and pain there, just like in her own chest, but there was joy. There was hope.

It was a feeling of safety, of togetherness. If they just believed everything would work out, then it would come true.

She came closer and rested her chin on his shoulder, wrapped her arms around his waist. Very slowly, he reciprocated, like a man unused to being hugged. But he didn't pull away.

It was companionable. Warm. Solid. Somehow, he'd even managed to smell good—there was a brush under her nose of lavender, pleasant, soothing, and almost out of place. His arms were quiet and sure. And perhaps she stayed there a little longer than necessary, but this was an anchor in her storm, and she was grateful.

Eventually, however, she pulled back. "I'd like that. Thank—"

His eyes had become dark, his neck flushed. His gaze flickered to her lips.

She froze, realizing she'd been ignoring his signals rather spectacularly, and probably on purpose.

Oh. Go and see the things… together.

The dreamlike lull faded. She was back in the real world, and she hadn't thought this far ahead.

Slowly, he stepped back in, his forehead coming to rest on hers, nose a soft brush against her own. In a warm rush of surprise and indecision, she froze. His thumb came up to trace the side of her cheek, lingering. He looked like he was searching for a secret in her eyes. For permission. The spot in the middle of her chest was pounding and insistent and…

"Uh!" Her brain finally engaged, and she scrambled back a foot.

"Hm?" The sound came from deep in his chest, throaty, confused.

Click click, the Geiger counter said from her pocket.

"I," she began, stepping back another foot. "I'm so sorry! Signals are… didn't mean… I, I'm very bad at them. I don't think…" He blinked, clearly in a heat-fog. "Friends! We are friends. Friendly friends. But, just, not *that* friendly yet, you know?"

"I—?"

The Geiger counter's whine grew louder. Feeling the edges of panic, Anna wrung her hands, trying to make sense. "I'm trying to say… I really like you. I do. You've helped me more than I can ever pay back, but… look, my entire world is, is *gone*, and I don't know what I'm doing, and, and—I'm not even safe to be around! I'm *irradiating* things, and putting people in danger, and…" She didn't even know what else to explain. Her stomach was quivering and hot and sad… and even angry. It was full of all of the horrors and questions she'd been trying to bury: the *What am I?* and *What does it mean to be this dangerous?* and *What life IS there for me now?*

She was barely coping. And here her one spot of stability and companionship was shifting, was standing there in the darkness, full of breath and warmth and heartbeats and *questions.*

Jackson's hands came together in a nervy steeple as he processed. "Anna…" he whispered, almost supplicating. "It's… it's okay. I've been living in what you call the end of the world for a long time. Maybe I'm just used to it. And when things *finally* start to go right, I…" He sighed. "I can't understand everything that's happened to me or you. I can't really explain this thing between us… but I *like* it. I like *you.* You're so kind, and *brave,* and…" He bit his lip like he was forcing down so many things. "I don't care that you're still figuring out your radiation. I have Quarantine. Everything else… I could figure out. If you want."

Anna had no idea what Quarantine was. Her voice was weak, brain still whirling.

"When you say… we have a *thing…*" she mumbled.

A spark of determination lit on Jackson's face. "I've felt something since the day I met you. Something familiar. And since you healed me, I've felt it so much more strongly, right here." He tapped his chest, dead center over his scar. Anna's heart pounded, lighting up over the same spot. "It's like… like a line right to you. I'm sorry, I know that sounds… just, tell me I'm not *crazy.* Tell me you've felt it too."

There was another dip in her stomach. Yes. In retrospect… there was an uncommon familiarity there, a strange tug that hadn't been before. "Maybe," she whispered, fighting the redness she knew was traveling up her neck.

"When I'm with you…" He sighed softly, closing his eyes. Anna understood what he meant, her defensiveness softening, just a little. It was a connection. It had started to have weight and meaning. And that, especially in this time and place, she cherished.

"But…" she said. "I don't think… Maybe when all this is done and over, maybe… we could… I just… no, I can't say that. I might never be *right.* I can't make any promises. I can't even tell you I can think about it. I want you as my friend. But for now, for anything else, until I know

I even have a future at all… no. I can't."

For just a moment, there was something in his eyes that was frightened. Alone. It took her breath away. "Of course, anything you…" He trailed off. A pulse radiated in her center: a sinking feeling. Jackson's face pulled into neutral wall. "I'm… I'm sorry if I overstepped. That's not what I… I'm sorry."

"I'm sorry too." Her emotions flared, churned in her stomach like a storm. All of the demons in her way were too many to fathom, to talk about.

The feeling between them in her core began skipping faster, shame and disappointment. Now that he'd called attention to the line between them, it was painfully apparent, and she couldn't look away. She didn't know what to say, how to make it better.

The terrible thing was that what she really wanted to do to ground them both was pull him close into another hug. All she let herself do was reach out, touch his shoulder.

"It's okay." He began to back away, offering a smile like a peace treaty. "I'm, ah, going to go back to the apartment. Enjoy the party, Anna. And… thank you for the dance. Really. I mean that. I had fun. And we're okay. I'm still here for you. Anything you need. I promise." He spun, looking like a pack of seething, messy thoughts, and she couldn't understand half of it, couldn't process it all. She didn't want him to go now, but knew it would be worse if he stayed.

So she stared off into the dark, alone, no idea at all about what she needed. Her breathing was shallow, like she'd been kicked in the ribs.

Click click click. The Geiger counter tapped out a nervous rhythm. Here was the distress, the fear. She'd tried to stamp down all the horror and the sadness of her past, all of the emotions she didn't know how to handle.

I can't… I'm not…

It was all bubbling up inside now again, sick and messy and grieving.

How much radiation was it bringing with it…?

Partygoers jogged by. People were gathering closer.

Anna's breath heaved faster and faster.

She was going to hurt someone. A lot of someones.

Click click click.

Leave, Maya had said. *Run, whatever you are.*

Anna stepped into the dark, not knowing what else to do.

Her demons were out there.

And she had to face them eventually, she knew, or she would always be standing still.

CHAPTER EIGHT
Wanderer

Jackson's shoes picked their way through the rubble and cement. The minutes passed. He found he was starting to get used to this decay, and it almost didn't bother him anymore.

What did bother him was that something inside hurt, something crushing, fearful, radiating out and out, and it wasn't just his broken dignity.

Anna had said *no*. But he barely understood what he'd been asking in the first place. Whatever it was, it was so, *so* important. He didn't know what to call it, but it was new and fresh and raw, leaving him feeling stupefied and burned.

He was reasonably certain he'd been about to kiss her. It was the only way he'd known to speak his truth. He wasn't even sure when he'd made that choice. They'd danced... they were together... they were happy... it had felt simple.

Why did I have to... we just met, and she's grieving, and of course she's not...!

The haze in his head, it had made him impatient. Made him stupid.

Someday, she'd said. Maybe then.

Or maybe never.

Everything Anna was had gotten under his skin, burrowed into all of the crevices he thought guarded and safe. She'd been there when he needed her most, when his life was on the line. It had *killed* him to sit helpless when she was sick.

And she knew what it was like to be alone—to have unexplained, uncontrolled powers. She was clever, hopeful, and fierce—and also adrift, vulnerable, and frightened to her bones. She'd fallen out of the sky into his life like a comet, called him *friend*, forged a connection he'd never felt before.

After all these long, isolated years, he'd looked into someone's eyes, and for the first time saw himself reflected back. She'd glowed in that soft firelight, smiled, and held him close with her chin on his shoulder, heartbeat to his. All those half-formed wishes and unexamined thoughts he'd set to the side for over a decade, they just...

He realized he'd stopped breathing, and manually restarted.

Idiot.

Now his one friend would forever know something he should have kept secret.

Idiot! You have no idea what you're doing.

He never longed for his missing whiskey flask so much. But by now, he bet the beer he'd found was probably gone.

What he wouldn't have given to talk to a familiar face to ease his restlessness. He did have the long-range communicator, he supposed. Frank was but a few buttons away. But he also knew just what his advisor would say: "Goddamn, you want some warm milk and a frickin' bedtime story? This line is for emergencies *only*, boss!"

He supposed he had to content himself with his own thoughts.

At the end of the road, Jackson ducked inside the open door to the apartment rathole. He leaned against a wall and mentally stepped back, trying to see himself as Anna might. He was poorly shaven. Malnourished. Dirty. He was a smiler and talker, sure, a person with nice promises—ah, yes, I'll take you to your home city, and I'll get you identification, and everything will work out! But he was a *liar*, and he knew it, and was in no position to promise anything. Even though he would gladly do everything he said, he didn't know when he was even returning to his normal life. He didn't know what he was or his path forward.

I just wanted to make her feel better.

Maybe she had. Just a little. She'd smiled. She'd enjoyed the dance.

But who on earth would look at him, this broken shell of a smuggler in this backwoods camp full of hunger and desperation, and see... a future...?

Gods, when had he started concerning himself with *futures?*

Perhaps, in time, she'd forgive him. He could learn to ignore that whisper in his mind that they were connected. He could forget this confused and lonely heartsickness.

He could be what she actually needed.

Right?

The book in his bag thrummed into his side.

He looked down in alarm. The pulsing turned faster. *Faster.* It was frantic, like the book was squirming.

Disturbed, Jackson fished the tome out, unsure of what to do. Was it reacting to his distress? "It's okay?" he spoke at it. "This is about... well. Someone I care about. But it's not a problem for you to fret over."

The book didn't stop buzzing in his hands. In retrospect, he wondered why he thought that verbally soothing it might help. It wasn't a pet or a toddler; it was some gods-damned magical... artifact... thing.

But it was also a puzzle. A distraction. Thinking about something else... perhaps that would be for the best. Feeling sorry for himself never got him anywhere, and throwing himself into his work always let him cope. It could be time to try and understand the road in front of him. Not even Anna could show him that: only this book, this strange thing a grinning god placed in his hands.

"Right. You want me to read you? Is that it?"

The old leather warmed under his touch, a feeling like a summer breeze. Jackson took that as an answer and braced himself as he flipped open the cover. Belatedly, he considered that he might go careening off into some nightmare wasteland full of wolves again… but… well…

How different was that, precisely, from his current reality?

But nothing of the sort happened.

There was only a page.

It had been blank. Now, it held a spot of ink in the moonlight. The splatter was blossoming there, bleeding from the vellum itself, trickling down in a line. Magic! The ink pooled and spread, pulsating with power. It was a dance under Jackson's fingers that his heartbeat answered, a song of *welcome*.

Delicate letters began to articulate themselves into existence, ornate and graceful.

The Book of Inoki's Chosen, it read. *Wanderer, young storyteller: look unto the stars, learn my wisdom, and walk unto your destiny.*

A deep sense of peace welled up in Jackson's chest despite all of the other messy feelings calling that place home. It was as it had been the night before, when he'd first clutched the tome to his body. It took root over his embarrassment and longing. He smiled, brushing the words with his fingers, the ink dry to the touch. Slowly, he turned the page, curious, tingling with anticipation.

Blank. No ink.

Brow furrowed, he turned back to the title.

His mind seized on something in the words. *You keep calling out to me… but only at night. And you tell me to look unto the stars.* He paced out of the ruined tenement. He knew it was the right thing to do, all the way down to his core.

For the first time since night had fallen, he looked up.

Overhead hung thousands of sparkling lights. It was a cosmic waterfall, dangerously close without the Barrier blue. For a moment, Jackson was struck with a deep fear of the open sky, a need to duck back into safety. This was why he hadn't looked upwards out here before, not *really* looked. Now he had the irrational paranoia that he might trip and fall away forever into that oblivion sky, only a speck in the vast, glittering void.

After some moments, the fear quieted. There he stared, jaw hanging, his shoes dragging against the asphalt. *It... it's beautiful.*

He remembered the stars in Inoki's eyes looking into his soul, the being laughing in his melodic, haunting way. He remembered the sensation that he might fall into that stare then, too.

Jackson tore away, breathing hard, the night air cool in his lungs. Sure enough, under the moonlight—no, *starlight*—the ink had begun to write itself afresh. It was positively soaking the vellum, pooling into lines and eddies of grays and black. It was making an image... it was writing a *face!* Broad strokes and crosshatches whittled down to shining eyes, young cheeks, and smirking lips: a boy, dark-haired. Perhaps... ten years old.

Jackson stared at this strange child.

There was something familiar there.

Chosen, the book wrote under the portrait in a flourish of calligraphy.

"That's me," he whispered in sudden recognition, smiling again, brushing at the boy's face. This picture held the same brow, the same dark eyes, and the same inky hair that refused to be tamed in the back. His face was full. His gaze unafraid. This was before he'd met the harsh reality of New York's streets, before hunger, cold, and hard concrete.

And to his astonishment, the boy blinked. The child's mouth moved. His eyes focused off into the margins. It was like his child-self was addressing someone beyond the portrait's frame. Words wrote over his head in time with his lips.

"Don't worry father," the boy said. "I'll make you proud. I'll change the world." He gave a clever, bright-eyed grin, innocent and full of life.

"Father?" Jackson said. "*Father?* Can you show me him? Did he know I was Chosen?"

The boy just kept staring off beyond the margins, his eyes full of security and… and love. So much love that it made Jackson's heart hurt. His biological parents… well, they'd never seemed that important. He'd never *let* them be that important. After all, what good were they? What had they done for him besides *leave?* Peter Dovetail was the only father that had mattered.

But… he'd looked to another once… with love…?

The words beneath the portrait shifted.

The Last Chosen, it now read.

"What do you mean?" Jackson demanded, ashamed for the desperation in his voice.

But the scene was frozen. If he wanted answers, he could do nothing but turn the page.

Here was another portrait of himself when young, but this time only a rough sketch, the lines faded. The detail lay in a swirling ball of ink over his heart, one that thrummed and spun.

Is that my magic? Slowly, the ink ball pooled outwards and upwards, obscuring his smiling face until the whole page was drenched.

The Chosen receive the gifts of the Shadowlands, a caption wrote on the page opposite.

"The… Shadowlands." The syllables rolled on his tongue. They rang in his head like a song he'd heard long ago. And as he whispered them, the image shifted, the ink streaming into a shiny whirlpool. At the top, thin spiderwebs separated from the darkness, transforming into fingers dark, slender, and clever. Jackson knew those articulate hands. They were shaping the void like a craftsman's might, delicate, careful—though what they were making looked like it might never come to be. At the bottom, the ink seemed to be fading. Decaying. There were two hands forming there too, clawing, angry hands. They were scarred, calloused, and careworn, with nails sharp and vengeful. They tore at the pool of shadow, unwinding and shredding it to pieces, and it seemed like they were doing it so much faster than the hands up top could create.

Another caption wrote itself on the page opposite.

In the beginning, there were two in the darkness.

In the end, there will be one.

The cradle of creation. The cradle of destruction. The place from which all our stories spring, and where they all come to rest: The Shadowlands.

—Atropos of the Watching Stars, 56th Year of the Rampant Lion

The decay from the hands below was working its way higher. The vortex of inky darkness was starting to look... thin.

Jackson bit his lip, feeling inexplicably nervous at this magical illustration.

The Fear in the Dark, Inoki's remembered voice rang.

Jackson turned the page.

Letters had already begun to write themselves on the next stretch of blank vellum, nearly done by the time he laid eyes on them.

The First Lesson for the Last Chosen.

Only one ornate word remained, so huge it spanned both pages, bold and shouting.

LISTEN.

That was all. Jackson turned the page. Blank. He waited patiently for the book to continue. It did not. He turned the page back.

LISTEN. The word faded. It wrote itself again, insistent, over and over.

"To... what?" Jackson sat on the curb, book on his knees, looking about warily. He flipped back and forth through the pages. The welcoming title. The boy. The hands of the Shadowlands weaving and unweaving. And, *LISTEN.*

His mouth dry, his tongue heavy, Jackson tried as the book asked. He shut his eyes to the beautiful, thrilling sky and the rot of the earth. He let the night hang in his lungs, campfire smoke and dust. There he sat, quiet, listening, for several, long minutes.

Perhaps it was just his imagination, but... the air, it was headier than he'd been thinking. Thick. There was a texture to it. He thought of Tony's magical aura. He remembered how sick it was, how it contorted and buzzed. This wasn't *entirely* like that, but there was something to it, something not like the rest of this wasteland. It was foreign, sticking to the roof of his mouth.

The line to Anna in his chest… he sensed that again too. It ached.

The chatter of raiders still awake felt far away now. Somewhere, one of their dogs bayed.

And there was a tingle in his mind. An itch.

Strange. He'd never thought of it before… but this itch had been there for a while, hadn't it? It was so tightly woven into this place's general discomfort that he never singled it out. But the more he turned his attention to it, the more unnatural the sensation was.

"I might actually feel something," he said aloud, surprised.

But what was it?

Unsure, he closed the book. The pages weren't changing, and he suspected they might not until he'd untangled this "First Lesson." Tucking the tome back into his bag, he stood, swinging his head this way and that, feeling the itch slide back and forth in his skull. He began to step forward. There was something out there. Something magical.

This was the way to it.

His former mentor, Huxley, had never tried teaching him anything like this—had never even mentioned it. Whatever he was doing felt like magical *tracking*. And The Order said he couldn't learn! He wasn't even using their precious Mage Language. He smiled to himself, vindicated.

There's hope for me yet.

Jackson began to walk. He wended in and out of alleys, through streets and empty lots. He felt like a dog snuffling along in its hunt, knowing where to go on pure instinct. His mind was clear. He strode with purpose.

The camp thinned. He passed darkening fires. He passed tents, broken windows, and walkways. One such path had little shrines and tokens of affection littered all the way up to the building beyond—small carvings, stones, beads, and bones, all clustered in colorful bursts. It wasn't much, but still, Jackson stopped, taking note. For those that had so little, this seemed an elaborate dedication.

At the fore of this collection was a flat stone, propped above all the rest. Fresh paint shone on its smooth surface.

BLOOD AND VENGEANCE

FOR THE LOST

Against this leaned a tiny cat carved out of wood, like a child's toy: a tiger.

Jackson shifted under a brush of guilt. An odd, cold feeling hung in the air here, though the busy magical signature he'd been tracking lay further on. He had some guesses regarding what this place was, but no clear answers. Perhaps they'd made this while he was so focused on dancing: a token to celebrate the victory against the slavers, an offering for the dead.

An electric lantern light shone from the window beyond. Jackson peered through the dark, seeing motion in the window frames—and just barely, he caught the halo of a large man, one arm made of metal and twine. He was holding his deer-skull helm aloft at face-level.

There the Warlord stood, staring deep into those skull eyes.

His mouth was moving like he was whispering to it.

Uneasy, Jackson kept walking. He did not want to be noticed by a Tiger's father on this dark and lonely night.

Nearby there were strong bodies moving in the black, strong arms with rifles pacing, watching. Jackson realized he was skirting a perimeter, recognizing a patrol's walking pattern. "Where you going?" a voice called, suspicious. A man no older than he paused in his march, adjusting his bandanna as he peered through the moonlight.

"Just for a walk," Jackson said. He wondered... could he leave?

The guard spit on the earth. "You want a place to piss where no one's watching, eh city boy? Ha. Wouldn't go far, aye no. Wolves are thick 'round here. More than I've ever seen."

"The *what?* Wolves?" The itching in Jackson's mind grew louder, making it hard to focus.

The man shrugged, grimacing, missing teeth on display. "What Warlord calls 'em. Guess they were dogs once. You got protection? They aren't real friendly."

"Yes." Jackson felt the shadows, felt the night. For once, he was secure in this darkness in a way that was hard to explain. And this pull, this feeling… it wasn't far now, not at all.

With a final shrug, the guard waved him on. Jackson could sense that any concern was cursory. No one here would lift a finger to help if the feral mutants did come, not for a citizen of the city. Maybe Shark might. But who knew where he'd gotten to?

Jackson breathed in the crisp breeze, full of wild things and promise, and he stepped over the perimeter line. His ears were perked for sound, and he was glad for the gift of being able to see well in the dark. Inoki had at least done that right by him. The itch, it pulled him further, onward, ever onward.

One block passed, then two. The last trace of the camp disappeared from sight. It was just far enough that he began to feel misgivings. He would be able to find his way back, right?

And then, he reached a barren lot, concrete and buildings long torn up and gone.

As he stepped onto the open earth, the itch burst open like an angry sore, flooding over his skin. His arm hairs stood on end, his teeth grinding in an unseen electric charge. *Something's here.*

This expanse of dust and weeds was unusually vast for what used to be civilization. So much space would never go unused within the Barrier. Had this barren site been leveled in one of the coups? Was it a site of battle no one wanted to touch anymore? There were no fences, no landmarks, no *nothing.*

The land dropped down into a little valley, the bottom not even visible until he drew near. He spun, looking, searching, hoping for an answer.

As he traced every path his eyes could seize, he realized… he *knew* this place, this nothing-space in the middle of nowhere! It was a different approach angle, yes, but…

Frantically, he retraced his mental maps to be sure. Yes, yes, the road up towards Yonkers, past the Old Bronx, off the beaten path… not a hot spot for radiation, not until she'd gotten there, alerted the Coalition… and…!

This was where he'd first met Anna, asleep in her box, naked and alone, a survivor out of time. The Warlord had been right. This was where Tony had been. Where'd they'd met, destinies colliding.

The field wasn't covered in blood, not anymore. No ravens tussled here over the feast a killer left them. No agents crept behind concrete ruins. Only the wind whistled over the unmarked graves. Green had even sprouted. Flowers were weeding up, burying what remained of the horror.

Furious sweats erupted down Jackson's neck and back. His hands shook. Old nausea flickered vengefully at his memories.

A haunting, manic lilt whispered in his ear then: Tony's voice. *The sky opened up, Jack. It opened up, and out she came, and I heard the singing, so I came to see.*

Jackson considered, for only a moment, that this place had been highly radioactive when Anna had appeared. But, he knew also that she might have been the entire source. The Warlord's people had Geiger counters, after all. Even for a leader's son, no one would have remained there if it would have killed them.

The earth was upturned in little mounds all over. Where the agents had been slaughtered, it seemed there even had been *planting*. Sunflowers.

Their harvest was growing quickly. The stalks were higher than his shins. Had it really been only three weeks since…?

Jackson swallowed his fear, trying not to consider that the dead made quality fertilizer. His wobbly knees told him to leave, but the book was still warm in his hands. There was something important here just out of reach, something he wanted, no, *needed* to understand. The crux of all of the tapestry was in this ugly field, and he had to know why.

He pressed on, kicking up patches of the freshly disturbed dust. The magic was so thick, it felt like he could squeeze it through his fingers.

Someone had gone to great lengths to clean up after Tony's killing spree: the bones, the debris, the box. All gone. He wagered it probably all now lived with other secrets behind the Coalition's brown walls and barbed wire on Staten Island.

They must have been very occupied indeed if they hadn't noticed the band of bandits just blocks away. Perhaps the Warlord just decided to hide and keep his peace.

Kneeling, Jackson pressed a palm into the soil. It was dark and damp. The fresh life was springy and good on his hand. Soothing.

And a raven called in the night. Jackson jerked his head up, though he didn't find the bird.

What he saw was a silent, prowling wolf of the wastes, just beyond the field. As he met its eyes, caught it in its hunt, it bared its teeth in a growl.

Jackson snarled back. A dog *once*, the guard had said—he'd been right. This creature's domestic bloodline had long since soured. It was a pitiable, tumor-riddled wreck, its patchy, gray-streaked fur curling back around its lips, framing wet yellow fangs. It skulked back and forth on the barren earth, ears flat on its thick head, paws light.

For once, Jackson was grateful for the raven's presence in his life alerting him. Still, now that he had the beast in his sights, he was more exasperated than anything else. *Can't believe I growled back.* Two decades later, and all it took was one mean-looking mongrel to summon up the feral boy he'd once been.

Another rumbling breath suddenly rattled the air. Jackson whipped his head to the left.

A second mutt. Of course there was. There was *never* just one. This one looked younger and stronger than the first. Its fur was russet and black, the mad lights of mutation dancing in its eyes. A second vestigial tail hung limply by its side.

The shadows were cool under Jackson's hands as he watched the canines flank him from either side. They might have been about forty feet away, but it was clear they weren't leaving. And there were likely more, just waiting for the call of the hunt. He reached out for the magic. The darkness was his friend. The stars were shining on him. He was *Chosen*, and some damned wasteland rejects weren't going to get the best of him.

After all, he'd shared tea with far more frightening creatures than these.

The first of the dogs began to step forward, pressing a paw to the barren lot, tongue lolling, hungry.

But it shuddered. A whine curdled from its throat. Its ears twitched. Finally, it yanked the paw back, baring its teeth wider.

The second dog stepped forward as well. It too pulled back, distressed, keening.

They see something they don't like. Jackson slowly rose, sharing his attention between the two prowlers. *Can they feel the magic too?*

It was then a man's voice snapped through the air, rich, fierce, *angry.* "Begone."

Jackson's head followed to the sound, startled, searching. No one. No one was there.

The dogs were whining louder now. The bigger of the two bayed with frustration.

"I said: BEGONE!" The roar was the powerful roll of thunder, raging and absolute. Magical power lanced the air. Jackson tried to

block it from his mind, holding his hands over his ears, but he couldn't. Ringing shuddered through his skull. The dogs turned into flashes of oversized paws and dust in their retreat, eyes rolling, spit flying.

And in the shadows, where there was not a man, suddenly, there was. It was like reality decided to step aside just a little to make room. His skin shone pale in the moonlight. Dressed in his archaic, pre-Bombings suit, his angular body was all sharp edges and aggression, just like his face, like his eyes. Jackson's hackles raised. The shaved runes in this man's beard seemed freshly wrought. He paced forward until he was only ten feet away, walking cane tapping the earth.

This, Jackson now knew, was the Archmage of the Order: a man who had nearly murdered him twice.

The circle was complete, then. The entire ring of destiny had come back to the beginning.

"I've been waiting," the mage growled. "And you're late."

CHAPTER NINE
Earthbound Misfit

Anna's path was a straight line down the main road. But it wasn't fast enough. Before she realized it, her jog became frantic and her breath began catching in her throat, sparks of adrenaline warning her of the Geiger counter's clicks. She stopped thinking. Her feet flew over the rubble. She saw a fence, turned right, and ran along it. She couldn't stop.

She tore through the littered alleyways between the empty remains of apartment towers. Though she'd never run so far or fast, she didn't lose her breath.

The minutes passed. Finally, the furious thrumming of fear eased in her mind, and she jogged slowly to a halt, dizzy. *What am I doing?* She slumped against a stone wall tagged with black graffiti bubbles, sinking to the ground. Her head fell to her knees. *Stop. Stop. Breathe.*

The frantic clicking and whining from the Geiger counter began to slow, but it didn't vanish, not even close. She hiccuped, forcing herself to look at the screen and note the measurements as her radiation leaked. Was she still dangerous? *Maybe. If there was just short-term exposure… it could be fine…*

Not that this would do Jackson any good if she'd been worse when—

The clicking sounded faster.

What was I doing?! Just standing there, babbling!

She didn't even know if she'd made sense.

As soon as she was under control, she had go find him and make sure he was alright, get readings from his clothes, then make sure he wasn't carrying around any harmful particulates—she barely even knew where to start with that, or how her thrashing, floundering powers worked.

What if I never figure this out...?

Anna slammed that thought into a mental box and shuffled it out of sight, next to the other things that she was shying from.

She tried closing her eyes. She tried slipping into the meditation Jackson had taught her to help.

It didn't work, because all of that was tied to him.

The clicking grew worse.

His crooked smile... his wry optimism... that fierce loyalty and bravery she scarcely felt she deserved...

Yes. Those were things she needed.

But he'd changed where he stood, and it was a reminder that nothing ever really stayed the same. And that *hurt.* The longer she was here, the more her entire life, her career, her plans—it all got faded at the edges, like her world was someone else's, just a piece of a dream. Mental touchstones like a peaceful childhood beach, or the triumph of a calculation well-solved, or even the smell of her roommate's fresh-baked bread...

...It was slipping away.

She wasn't ready to let it go. Doing that, committing to a life here, felt like destroying everything she was—felt like letting the man succeed who'd killed her.

But in the wreckage of old Anna, a new woman was already growing, whether she wanted it or not. She was someone freakish enough that the Coalition had locked her in a hole in the ground for study. She was someone who'd torn open a steel cage and ran through the streets of New York, tackling a madman, pulling bystanders out of the way, using some kind of mystical light *weirdness* to save people. Here was the woman that was now exiled to a burned-out, abandoned land beyond civilization, tugging along the one friend she'd saved, the one who'd saved her, too.

The friend who was starting to care for her in more ways than she'd known.

She pulled at her hair. It was wound up around her fingers, an old, nervous habit her mother had failed to break her of. When had the locks grown back so much...?

"Hey." A woman's voice made her leap to her feet.

She hadn't even heard anyone approach. But, there was Nyx. She was sitting on a cracked old bench, legs criss-crossed and eyes wary. Her head was cocked in curiosity, her long and unwashed dark ponytail tied up with a strip of leather. Thankfully, her burns were so faded now that they could have been mistaken for a minor rash.

"Nyx!" Anna breathed, making to turn and leave again. "I'm sorry, I'm not safe to be around right now, I'm kicking off radiation—"

"You're flaring like a bitch," Nyx said, tone flat. "And not the good kind of bitch, you know?"

Anna stared. "Uh."

"It's okay," Nyx continued. Her fingers drummed together. "I've got a Quarantine dose still kinda active from when I left the city. I was just resting, but... I saw you running. So I followed you. Girl, you make a woman happy she never skipped physical training. Something set you off?"

Anna tried to say no, that she didn't know what Nyx meant. Her throat refused to work. Her eyes stung.

"...Did someone try to hurt you?"

Anna shook her head, not trusting her voice.

"You don't have to talk about it if you don't want to. But let me help?"

Anna quaked under that gaze. "Jackson taught me an exercise." She heard the counter climb again, whining with distress. "But the meditation isn't working now."

"Of course it isn't." Nyx made a lithe jump to her feet. She reached out, seeming hesitant, a question of permission in her eyes. Anna didn't move away. A hand softly came to rest on her shoulder, giving it a comforting squeeze. "Tall, dark, and legally questionable probably only knows the Magic 101 stuff. You've got some serious potential in there. And you can only dam a river with a piece of cardboard for so long."

Anna pushed back her sadness, a speck of hope surging. "Do you know something I can do to stop all of this? Be safe and… and… normal?"

Nyx sighed. "No. I'm sorry. To control your magic, you need to learn how to use it."

Anna's back stiffened. "What? No! I'm really dangerous! How can I ever just be around people if…" She shook her head. "I don't want to kick off radiation at *all*."

"I didn't want to burn down my school, but there we go."

Anna stared.

"Yeah… bullies set me off. Twenty-one kids were hospitalized. Lucky no one died."

The wind whistled down an alley. A noise clipped out of Anna's throat, but that was all. There was nothing anyone *could* say to that.

"So I learned to control myself, and my unexpected arson rate is now 0% unless someone *really* deserves it." Nyx smiled, tugging Anna's body forward. Her hug was awkward at first, but eventually, Anna relaxed. There was a circle getting rubbed into her back, and it was… soothing. "I'm going to pay you back by teaching you how to be okay too. Alright? So stop looking like you're going to cry. It's going to be fine."

Anna let her rub that circle, not knowing what to say. The

emotional flailing left an empty hole behind, as it was wont to do, but for some reason, this emptiness didn't feel quite as vacant as before. It was strange how something as simple as a hug and being told things would be alright could be so comforting.

If even one of her problems could be fixed…

The other woman pulled back, keeping a hand on her shoulder. "Anyway, you ever want to talk about what brought you out here, I can listen. We jailbroke each other once each. Pretty sure that means we're friends now."

There was nothing for Anna to do but respond to that wide, laughing grin with one of her own, even if it was weak. "Thanks."

Nyx snapped her fingers under Anna's nose. A flame lit between them, the heat puffing their skin. "So, Miss Healer. Why don't we get started, huh? No time like the present." The fire in her hands seemed to light in her eyes, making her look wild. "Let's learn some magic!"

"I don't… I'm not…" Anna swallowed back years of skepticism. "Can I do that? I don't think I'm a mage, exactly, and…"

"Not a mage? Er… I don't know. You've got some next-level power on you. Healing is very, very rare. I'm shocked the Archmage didn't try to snap you up when you first came onto the scene."

Anna's tension coiled up her back again. Her mouth dried.

The fire in Nyx's hands went out. "I know that look."

Anna nodded.

"You met him."

For a moment, Anna was back in that room, that office with its burning hearth. Eyes reflected the firelight in the dark, pinned her in place like an insect. A cold smile. A cold smell.

"*Shit*. What did he do to you?"

"He said I wasn't a mage. But he got in my head." For a moment, she could still smell the coppery stench of her own blood, see the murderous soldier killing her friend and mentor.

"He *got in your head?*" Nyx's nostrils flared, her hands clenching into fists.

"He…" Anna struggled with the words. It felt like such a deep violation, and the Archmage had *laughed* at her after it was all over, had sent her packing into the gulag under the city for use in some plan she still didn't understand. "He made me watch everyone die, back then, back before… I watched myself bleed out…"

"That son of a bitch." Nyx's eyes were glowing as if embers were at their cores.

They stared at each other for a long moment. Anna reached out, put a hand on Nyx's shoulder, just as this woman had done for her not so long ago. "So I guess you know him too," she found the courage to ask.

"Yeah. Yeah, I do."

"Did he do something to *you?*"

Nyx took a deep breath, pulling back her hair.

"What happened?"

"Look… Anna…" White teeth bit chapped lips. "Maybe now's not the time for that one."

"No. I want to know." Anna steeled herself. "I need to know who that man is. I need to know about mages. If I don't, and he comes after me again…"

"…I…" Nyx winced. "It's just, I used to… *be* in his Order."

Anna stared. She almost flinched back, but stopped herself.

Shaking her head, Nyx gave her an apologetic look. "It was a *while* ago, I swear. I didn't have anything to do with what he did to you."

"Tell me?"

She paused, then rubbed the palms of her hands in contemplation. Her eyes fixed on a rock on the ground. And when she started to speak, it was like she was dragging words out of her depths she didn't truly want to touch. "Back when that thing happened. With my school. A stranger walked through the door when my parents were at work, told me he knew about… well, the fire that I started. He said he *knew* it was me, and that I hadn't *meant* to do anything wrong. The militia was looking for suspects, though. I was terrified."

"I'm sorry. A flare, right?" Anna remembered the word Huxley had used.

"Yeah. A bunch of kids were trying to hurt a girl that was important to me..." Nyx swallowed. "Anyway. This person that came to find me told me I was special, that I could use magic, but if I didn't learn how to control it... well. He said I needed to go to a special school. And I was totally on board—always read about princesses and magic and stuff. They told my parents I'd been selected for special classes. That I was a 'gifted' student." Nyx shook her head, smiling softly. "Mom thought I'd been secretly smart this whole time. Next thing I know, this nice old chubby guy with a huge mustache was making me do all these silly tasks, seeing if I could learn to set fires on purpose." She chuckled, her eyes less angry and sad at the remembering. "I almost burned down his study. Heh. But he was nice about it. I miss Professor Huxley. I miss a lot of the people there." A dark look began to brew again. "I do not miss the Grand Master Asshole."

Anna struggled to find words. "So they aren't all bad?"

Her companion shifted like she was standing on ants. "No, not by themselves. It's just, there was always something a little *wrong* with the Order? Not something you notice at first. They're *really* intense about keeping themselves a secret. You can't use magic that can be seen or traced on the outside. Not even if it's a matter of life and death. Frick, some literally take it as a commandment of their gods. But being a secret makes sure people don't attack us, don't exploit us, since there's not many of us left, you know? And they're right, in a way—you saw what the Coalition tried doing to *you*. The way the Order says it, it makes a lot of sense: magic must be protected, and we're the chosen guardians. You start to feel like you're part of something exclusive and amazing, something special. You also start getting a little immune to noticing weird things... because weird gets relative."

Anna nodded. She remembered feeling nothing but awe at seeing Jackson lift his keys with shadows, tricks of light that had no business being solid. *Yeah. Weird gets relative.*

"The Archmage was always this mystery guy at the top of it all, been there for ages. He didn't come out much, but when he did, everyone would go quiet. You could almost *smell* the power on him. And he's got those eyes… they're a spooky sort of dead, you know? Like you could kill yourself in front of him and he just wouldn't care."

Anna swallowed. "Yeah."

"I didn't like him. No one *liked* him. But for some reason, he was in charge and we lived with it, kept our heads down." Her hands clenched into fists again. "Anna… I wish I could say it in a way that would make sense. *No one* questions the Archmage. Everyone is scared of him. It was like we were keeping a viper in our handbags that could bite us anytime it wanted. But you have to understand, no one ever *tried* removing him. The son of a bitch is so damned magically powerful, has everyone so cowed, that he can do anything. If he doesn't like you, then at best, the rumors are you get cut off. For most of the mages, the Order is the only place they have friends or family. It's hard to connect with other people once you've seen a couple of the secrets of the universe. Most decide that maybe, even if he's a creep, at least he's *our* creep, protecting us. And who would want to go against the guy that's apparently been there for over a hundred years and still looks like he's in his thirties?"

"Wait, what? But that's—" Anna really wanted to say the word 'impossible.'

Nyx gave her a look, and she bit her tongue. "They say magic was different way back… well, *before*, when he's from, like you, Anna. There were more of us. The power was easier to channel somehow." Her tone drooped. "Mages could master more than one or two disciplines of magic. But the world got all crumpled up, and so did we. Good job, humanity." She chuckled, though it wasn't with humor. "Now, because of the Archmage's strength, most of the Order just keeps to themselves and ignores him. Except… except me. Because I couldn't."

The words stopped for a while. Anna shifted with discomfort, feeling the cold of night start to press on her skin.

"The year the Order found me," Nyx eventually continued, "there was one other girl they found too. Her name was…" Her eyes clouded. "*A'laria*. She was quiet, didn't make a lot of friends. And she had magic, that was for sure, but she wasn't, well, good at it. I think she was kinda dyslexic. A lot of the older members used to tease that she only got in because Huxley's eyesight was going. The Archmage didn't like weakness, they said. And this girl, we weren't very close, you know?" Nyx's voice cracked a little. Anna sensed that was a lie. "But I agreed to help her out. Solidarity since we came in together. Two people in one year is rare. I taught her how to summon fire. We thought a teacher would see how hard she was working and make sure she stayed."

"Did it work?" Anna sensed the answer to her question was *no* already.

"She was called to the Archmage's office. Everyone started telling her this was when she'd get kicked out. So, I ditched my lecture and kept her company, told her I'd wait outside the door for her, that she'd definitely show her worth with that spell.

"She went in, and it was quiet for a *long* time. Probably some silence ward, but I was getting worried. So, I tried the door, figured I'd say some bullshit like 'so sorry to interrupt, the librarian really wanted me to deliver this message to A'laria, blah blah.' Just to see how she was. Archmage didn't have the door locked. I guess no one ever just burst in.

"I… I opened the door a crack, and I… I saw him… and… I…" She shuddered, breathing. "A'laria was slumped over in her chair. Her eyes were open, but there was *nothing* in them. She was *gone*. He was standing over her, and had this stone with this light coming out of it… and for a second, I saw her *face* inside…!" Nyx was trembling now, her fists clenching and unclenching. "I pulled the door back shut, and I ran. Like a coward. I ran. I saw her face *inside* that stone, and she was screaming. But I knew if he caught me, he'd need to shut me up just the same way. He took her soul, Anna. He took it right out, put it in some rock, and… and… soul magic is *evil*. Dark, dark shit. I think it's what's keeping him alive. He's charging artifacts up with it, and… I *left* her. I left the Order because no one believed me. Even the people that could have helped *wouldn't*. They wanted to keep their heads down." She swallowed. "Well, then I tried to burn the place down. They set wards against me. That was that."

There was bile and fear in Anna's throat. "I'm sorry. I'm… I'm so sorry."

Nyx's look hardened. "It's… well, it's not okay. But it got me started looking for kids with talent too. I knew that the fewer mages *he* got his nasty grip on, the better." She grew more resolute as she spoke, swallowing, giving a final nod. "Even if that didn't always work out. But. You want to keep burning things down? You want to keep being a target for the Grand Master Asshole? Or do you want to get ahold of this?"

Startled at the shift, Anna saw the look in her eyes. Not poking at the hurt was the best thing she could do. For Nyx's comfort as much as her own, she let the subject change. "Yeah. Okay. I'd like to try."

"Good. So, here's the thing." Her companion drew herself up, easing into a teacher's tone.

But Anna couldn't shake the thought of a girl's face trapped inside a stone, screaming. She regretted pressing for the story a little.

"First, you need to stop hating yourself and fearing whatever it is that's setting you off. It's like a feedback loop. You're scared. Your magic is trying to defend you, and it's going about it all wrong because you're not telling it what to do."

"What? It's trying to *defend* me? How do I tell it to *stop?*" Anna stared at her hands, looking at the glow faintly rising under her skin, realizing that no matter how hard she thought, she couldn't turn it off.

Click click click.

"Well, getting it to do exactly what you want would mean you need to learn the Language, but that can come later, alright? Now you just need to feel it on a big picture level, get it to stabilize. Usually a teeny *tiny* pinch of witchbane once a month will make flares like this calm for a little while, but you're *really* worked up, and I don't have any. So we need to do something more drastic."

"Like what?"

Nyx gave her a contemplative stare, wiping her gaze up and down. "Got a few ideas. Saw a couple video feeds of you when they locked me up, questioned me, ha." She shuddered. "Learning control is different for everyone. What I want you to do is climb that." She pointed behind them. The crumbling ruin they'd been leaning against was that of a building long since collapsed, a ragged chunk of wall all that remained. It was at least forty feet to the top.

"How…?"

"There's an edge over there low to the ground." Nyx pointed to the wall's corner. "Pull yourself up, then keep pulling yourself up until you can't do it anymore."

Anna stared. Her stomach was already dropping. "I don't think I want to go that high."

"OK, then you better like sleeping under the stars, because Dr. Anna Matthews knows better than to go back to the camp blasting radiation out of her eyeballs."

Anna bit her lip, not ready for pushback, nor her full name and title coming out of nowhere. "You knew Agent Jaden Walker, right? He kind of implied you know who I was back in 2022…"

"Yep. You were a damned hero. I read the records he dug up. So do what you gotta do now and climb."

"O-okay." Anna felt the scrape of dirt under her tennis shoes as she dragged her feet. *This looks like a death trap.* The "low to the ground" edge Nyx had pointed out was still a few inches above her head. She hooked her palms and scrabbled her shoes against the wall, pulling herself up, smashing her knees and scraping her hands in the process. Now on the narrow ledge, she breathed hard, woozy, clutching the stone for dear life. "Okay, I'm up."

"No you're not. Keep going!" Nyx clapped her hands and pumped a fist in the air, smiling like a cheerleader. There was another ragged ledge, barely in reach, one with *just* enough space to stand on. Above that, there was another. It was a staircase, up, up into the moon.

Anna gulped. *Oh no no.*

But she grasped the ledge, feeling the cuts in her hands closing already, and she pulled anyway. That's all anyone could do when backed in a corner, right? Fight to get out. With an *eep* and a grunt, she struggled up. Each pull was harder than the last.

Ten minutes later, gasping, dizzy, and refusing to look down, Anna was hugging the ledge with her entire body, forty feet in the air. Nyx let out a whoop from down below, applauding again. "Can I come down now?" she called, voice tight. Her head was swaying. She hadn't been afraid of heights before, but this platform was narrow, and she didn't trust the structural integrity of the wall beneath her, not one bit. Some of the bricks were loose underfoot.

Maybe she could charge a rampaging truck, but she hadn't put a lot of forethought into that, and this, she had all the time in the world to think about the consequences.

"Yeah, you're gonna get down alright! You're gonna jump!"

"*What?* I'll break my legs!"

"Don't be *loca*, you're gonna fly!" Nyx pumped both fists in the air again.

She's calling me *crazy?* "It…! It doesn't work like that!"

"Sure it does! Do you know what they've named you in the dome right now?"

"…Wanted?"

"The Angel of New York! They got you on video, diving into a crowd, pulling those two women out of the way of that car!"

Anna gripped the wall harder. "They're calling me *what?* They saw me do that?"

"The Coalition's so pissed, you have no idea. Can't keep the lid on you now—man, I bet the Archmage is pissed too. But that video spread like wildfire, and those women are calling you an angel! A real angel. You're on every news site, every feed, every network. They saw you, and you saved people from something they didn't understand, something really scary that now they're asking questions about."

Anna swallowed, the night air dancing in her throat. *Click click click click.* Her Geiger counter peppered her ears.

"Then you turn up and get me out of that slaver caravan. Just can't stop being a hero, huh? Anna, you gave a lot of people a chance back in 2022. And now you're here again. Who knows why? But you're giving people hope that maybe there's something better out there, something that's protecting them. So missy, you're gonna master your magic, and you're gonna fly, because I've seen you do it. Now *do it!*"

Anna didn't know what to tell Nyx, didn't know how to feel. She was stunned, her heart warming and rising. "I don't know how I did it! It just happened!"

"You saw them in danger, and you wanted to protect them, so you *made* it happen. Now you're protecting yourself, making sure you're in control. *Make it happen again.* Fly."

Anna looked forty feet down. Her fingers were starting to go numb from clutching the ledge. "Can you catch me? If it doesn't work?" Her throat hurt from breathing so hard.

"This isn't a world that catches you if you fall," Nyx said. "And I think you know that."

Anna came to a shaky crouch. *Okay.* She'd done it before. She didn't know why it worked, knew it shouldn't work by any known laws of physics.

But that awful clicking from that stupid Geiger counter… it had to stop.

Anna teetered over the precipice.

I'm gonna fly. She closed her eyes. *It's okay. I've done it before. She's right. I can do this. I'm gonna fly.*

Anna jumped.

She shrieked.

She fell.

CHAPTER TEN
Burn

In a dark field blocks away, Jackson trembled.

The Archmage scowled and tightened his grip on his walking cane. A dusky red glow from the pommel shone between thin fingers. The magic of this place resonated with his commanding aura, roiling together into a thunderous, oppressive weight.

Jackson's brain sang to him of when this man's knife had kissed a cold wind across his throat, when he'd been promised a quick death. "What are you doing here?"

"Don't waste time with stupid questions. You're here to join me for a drink."

The Archmage made an imperious wave with one hand. Where before there had been nothing but earth, Jackson blinked, and suddenly, there were two white chairs. He blinked again, and a table joined them. The Archmage was taking a seat. The magic in the air billowed and tingled.

Shaking, Jackson thrust his hand in his pocket. He wished for his knife, but for all he knew, that was still buried in Tony's chest back in Midtown. Squinting, concentrating, he tried touching the shadows. Something made them flinch away. This man was somehow blocking his tenuous magic.

I'm defenseless.

The Archmage's blue eyes were clever and cold, a strange light just past the pupils. He reached into his jacket and extracted a two drinking glasses, crystal clear and familiar.

With a sudden snap of realization, Jackson knew this kitchen table. He knew these chairs. He knew the glassware, his *favorites* for whiskey after a long day, now all out in this damned field. Anxiety and indignity squeezed his breath tight. *What the hell?*

It was then the man drew a final item from the depths of his coat. A *bottle. That* bottle. Jackson had been saving it. Hell, his *father* had been saving it. It was easily worth hundreds and hundreds of credits— genuine Scotch, sealed before the Bombings, before Scotland fell into oblivion. He'd not yet found the celebration that would warrant its opening.

It almost sighed as the Archmage released the seal, the liquid gold tipping into the glass.

"I was considering whether or not to try and kill you again," the man spoke. His voice was a silky whisper in the dark, his accent so strange on the ear. British, Anna had said? That should have been impossible. Like Scotland, nothing on that old isle was habitable, not for a long time. "I think of whether to kill you often. Sometimes, I decide, *not yet.* There are still uses for you. Not... yet." He inhaled the Scotch's scent and drank, exhaling deeply with appreciation. "Tonight I found this bottle in your home, and I decided *not yet,* because at the very least, you do have good taste."

Jackson clutched his book tightly to his side. Suddenly, he felt *carpet* under his shoes instead of dirt, an old red rug his father had loved. His entire house was leaking through into this wasteland nowhere, bit by bit. "How are you doing this?" he hissed.

"Don't you feel more at ease with a bit of the familiar?" The Archmage's eyes shone with command, and Jackson knew this wasn't about being at ease. This was about being terrified at magic leagues beyond his own, magic able to warp reality however it saw fit.

This was about obedience.

He dug his heels in. "What do you want with me?"

The mage poured another finger of Scotch. "I come here often, now. Planning. Thinking. See, this is where *she* intruded in on the world for the first time in oh so long, where the old magic has been collecting and seething."

"Who?"

"You don't know her yet?" He chuckled. "You *will*. This place calls to you as it does to me, over and over again. So the threads of fate say. So they are." Glittering, stern eyes glared. "You've grown a little extra spine though, haven't you? I'm not joking. Sit. Or has that wretched book been filling your head with so much Chosen nonsense that you think yourself too special to listen? Even though I could kill you where you stand?"

Jackson was surprised to realize that he didn't feel inclined to obey, threats or not. He was trapped. He was outmatched. But, he was alive for *some* reason. This man could have killed him… but hadn't. So, he strangled the fear from his voice, fishing. "…You know about the book."

"Of course. I've known everything about you since the day of your birth. I grew the cage you still live in. Yes, I know all about…" The Archmage's mouth twisted in disdain. "…the *book*."

The look of surprise reached Jackson's face before he could stop it. *My birth? My cage?* His chest constricted. But he knew asking the questions he so desperately wanted answers to would be tantamount to admitting how very ignorant and disadvantaged he was. He finally sat at the table to mask the quake in his limbs, stretching his calm mask tight over his face. "What do you mean my *kind?* What have I ever done to you?"

The Archmage raised an eyebrow, lifting the bottle over a second glass. Liquor fell in an amber waterfall. The glass was shoved forward.

Jackson's nerves wanted that Scotch so, so badly. "The last time

I drank something you assholes prescribed," he snarled instead, "I almost died."

A shrug. "I wouldn't waste such excellent stock on poison. Goodness knows, they're not making any more." He set the bottle down, reclining in the chair, seemingly at ease, revoltingly so. "Besides, it's too late for your easy death now. The problem is no longer you. It's your master. You've moved to the next stage, and he's digging his claws in."

"The hell do you mean, my *master*—"

"Here's my offer. You've figured out the book's properties?"

Jackson's mouth was dry. "Which ones?"

"Don't play stupid. I ordered that thing hidden from you..." His lip curled. "...To prevent you from *linking* with it. But you have. I can just... smell it. You understand the book is connected to him. The man with the stars in his eyes. I will not speak his name to call his attention. And neither will you." A threatening finger pressed forward. The bending of reality continued. A tea kettle and cups appeared in a patch of mud to the left. "It would have been better for you to stay forever ignorant. But if you must join the game, then it will be to *my* benefit. You're going to give me a shot at him. I'll even leave you alone if you use your new artifact to let me have it."

Jackson swallowed past the cotton on his tongue. "You're the one that's been killing us all, aren't you? The Fear in the Dark."

The Archmage's once-dead expression stretched into a poisonous sneer. Slowly, pure loathing and fury blossomed there, his teeth baring. "If you ever put that title at my feet again, I will personally tear your heart out through your ribcage."

"But... aren't you...?"

The look of rage burned brighter. "I *am* killing quite a lot of you. But you are far, far too ignorant to even *talk* about the Fear in the Dark." His fingers entwined, and he leaned forward, the kind of stance that meant he was either about to try and rip a throat out with his teeth or begin negotiations. Jackson was glad when it was the latter. "I offer a trade. Your fate was to be used and sacrificed and broken. Like all Chosen! But I *might* refrain from adding your head to the pile. I *might* help you find a different path."

"After everything you've done to Anna, done to me, you think I'm just going to buy that you've decided to help?"

Part of a kitchen wall suddenly existed to Jackson's left. A haunting strain of sandalwood and familiarity caressed his nose, spoke to him of a sanctuary he deeply missed. The Archmage's laugh was the rustle of dead things. "Come now. I just needed to test some boundaries. Besides, Tony's dead, isn't he, the one creature who might have had the raw power to help you otherwise. There's no one left who knows your plight, could even think of aiding you... except me. And if you think you don't need my help, why don't you consider *Anna?*" The look of disgust inched wider. "You're certainly not strong enough to help her when she'll need it. Would you like to know what I've seen in her future?"

"No." The crack could not be kept from Jackson's voice.

"War is coming." The mystical spark in the depths of the Archmage's eyes grew hypnotic and frightening. "I see the bodies. I see fire. It will burn your camp to ashes, the Warlord's people to bones, for they're just the tinder. It is coming. And Anna!" Alarm flared in Jackson's chest. "She will be consumed by the flames. There is *nothing* you can do to save her."

Jackson's blood was frigid. He shook. All he could see now was Anna in his dream, falling into the fire, yanked from his grasp. "Leave her out of this."

"But don't you want to help her? I know your mind... there's no world in which you wouldn't be *smitten* with her. You're too sentimental and lonely not to be utterly taken in. And I've seen the fire burning her body until she is nothing but atoms!"

Jackson's chest clenched tighter, and he had no retorts, no defenses left.

"All I want in exchange for my aid is…" The man smiled, all menace and mockery. "A page."

"… A *what?*"

"A page. From your book. It can be any one you like. Give it to me, and you will avoid the fires of war for another day."

Jackson stalled. "Why?"

The Archmage's smirk turned into annoyance. "I have no answer you would understand."

"But you can't just take it, can you?"

"Has the book told you what the price is for just *taking* its knowledge?" He winced a smile as Jackson hesitated. "No? Oh, you *really* should ask sometime."

Balking, Jackson glimpsed the bars of his cage, frantic, but he couldn't see them all, couldn't say what was truth or lie. And so help him, he could almost hear the gentle hum of the Barrier on the wind alongside this scent of home, like a hundred butterfly wings, the promise of protection, of peace.

But the book was all he had to tie him to whatever destiny he was meant for.

He needed bargaining room. Answers. *Time.* If finding the artifact had been enough to get the Archmage to try and merely intimidate instead of murder, there might be more inside of its pages that would give him… something. Anything.

He needs me more than he needs to kill me, Jackson thought. *But I'm not here to be* useful *to you, you murderous prick.* Aloud, he said, "I'll think about it."

The Archmage scowled, as if he could hear Jackson's inner voice perfectly well. He rose, leaning on the cane with the glowing pommel. Abruptly, the traces of home, the furniture, the walls… they didn't even fade. They simply *weren't.* Jackson collapsed back into the dirt and rocks and wet, back thudding, the smell of his prized Scotch still in his nose, the ache for the familiar in his chest. He stared up at the looming mage, horrified, the unforgiving wastes crystal clear as if he'd awoken from a dream.

"You will see," the Archmage hissed. Slowly, he pressed the cane into Jackson's chest scar, eliciting a bright snap of pain. "Very soon. And when you do, I'll find you. I *always* have."

Then there was only shadows and empty air. Jackson's ears popped as if the world was depressurizing. Decay and dust blew through the field. The magic of the land settled on him like a thick blanket.

He didn't move for a long minute, sitting in his cold sweat. The darkness seemed welcoming again now that the Archmage had gone. There was a tingle in his fingers. A brush of shadows. They almost felt like they were comforting him in a strange way, like disloyal pets ashamed at leaving him all alone. Jackson pushed away the sensation, angry.

His adrenaline just wouldn't slow. A warring tug of emotions yanked his focus—involuntarily, he turned his head back to where the camp lay, and he thought of Anna. He was seized with the desire to check on her, to make sure she was okay.

She's fine, he told himself. *You're rattled. He got under your skin. She's fine, and if you go to talk to her now, you'll make things worse between you. Besides, you're not done out here.*

Now was no time for fear. It was time to find a way out of this maze.

But the feeling in his chest wouldn't shake. His heart was in his throat.

And the book began to thrum once again. Jackson sat up, alarmed, feeling the aura of this place sizzle around him, building like an electric surge, coursing along his skin. It was in his fingers, his hands, and he shook, suddenly feeling like a conduit in a storm.

"What's happening…?"

In some deep, instinctive place, he realized the book was doing something. Now, without the Archmage's interference, it felt like... like it was *harmonizing* with the air.

And then, it was as if everything in Jackson's senses clicked, fell into place.

The movement of the breeze, the buzzing in the book, the growing of the sunflowers, the questions in his heart—they became one, like the notes in an aria.

It's all connected...!

Jackson seized the tome with both hands, not knowing what else to do—and the powerful, ancient, massive pool of magic in the air responded. It surged through him, his muscles seizing, his eyes rolling back in his head. A song rode the current through his brain. It was achingly familiar.

And then, it was gone. Done. The air was light and empty.

The book was not. It weighed in his hands like it carried the world. Jackson gasped for breath.

He looked around, but...

...The land here, it was no longer special, no longer setting his teeth on edge. It was just a dark place in a dark waste.

The book took it all in. All of it.

How? Why?

He shakily got to his feet. What was he to do now? Try to coax the book? Consult his dreams? Hell, ask the Nyx woman?

Then, he heard something new. It robbed him of the time to ponder this new puzzle.

Mad sounds were bursting from the camp, just a few blocks away.

CRACK CRACK CRACK!

Are those...?

They were.

Gunshots!

⸻ ✦ ⸻

Anna leaped.

The moon was bright in her eyes, the blood pounding in her ears.

Anna fell.

She realized that she was about to crash into the pavement only a quarter-second later. She was about to break every bone in her body. She was a stupid physicist that thought she could cheat physics. A shriek tore out of her throat.

But as the moon shone, so did the light under her skin, growing brighter. Brighter!

An invisible caress, the gentle fingers of air slowed her descent. The terror in her throat morphed into an adrenaline-spiked yelp of surprise and elation.

She hit the ground, but she did it softly and on both feet. The bright glow continued to surge, bubbling brighter as she smiled, and she began to giggle, uncontrollable laughter and relief surging up and out. She stumbled and fell to her knees.

She was safe.

She'd dropped forty feet and *floated* on down.

"Did you see what I just did?! Oh my God! Oh my God! Oh wow!"

"YEAH!" Nyx belted. She socked Anna in the shoulder. "That's how you do it!"

"Ow. Oh wait wait wait!" Anna cried again, excitement cresting as she felt the warmth in her blood. "I think I can do this too!" She sprung up, casting her mind back to her descent. Something was unlocking deep inside of her, and she rose once more, straight off the ground. She drifted as she had in the wasteland when she'd first woken to this world, as she had when she'd dived forward to save lives, not thinking twice. Her toes touched nothing at all, hovering six inches over the earth. "I'm flying. I'M FLYING!"

Nyx was peering at her, mouth open. "Oh damn! I'd think that'd need the Language but... well, who cares? What's that I hear?" She brought her hand to her ear.

"I don't hear anything," Anna snorted, smiling so hard her face hurt. She'd been despairing, and now, she was *flying!* She could do what she'd only done in dreams.

Her mind snagged onto a detail.

"I'm not hearing anything!" She tore the Geiger counter from her back pocket. The device wasn't showing *normal* levels of radiation in the air, per se, but they were very safe. At long last, she'd dropped her levels suddenly, decisively.

Because she'd jumped. Because she'd decided not to be afraid.

"Alrighty," Nyx said. "Better come on down now."

Anna wobbled in the air, struggling to hold her focus. She stumbled back to her feet. "Oh wow. Oh wow. Okay. How long do you think I can do this? How high can I go? Can I propel myself? How fast?"

Nyx giggled. "Easy there," she said. "Ease into it."

"But I was flying." Anna couldn't help herself. She started to dance in a circle like a kid on Christmas—it was just like, well...! Magic!

"Better learn the Language too, ha. Don't get carried away. Or, uh, things might not happen as you expect."

"I need to experiment," Anna whispered, her love of the scientific method brushing against what was now one of the greatest mysteries in her universe.

A chortle. "Oh man, you're cute. If I were ten years younger, I swear... wait, you're technically over a hundred, right? I'm not robbing the cradle if I flirt with ya a little?"

Anna looked up with a start, not expecting any of that—and yet, somehow, it didn't completely upend her world, not like she'd expected it to, not like the same had done not twenty minutes ago. "Uh."

The chortle turned into a cackle, Nyx winking. "Sorry, sorry! I can't help it. Don't you worry; I already have a gent on my plate that I'd need to talk to before I try and sweep some cute scientist hero off her feet."

Flushing and smiling, Anna straightened out her shirt. "Heh. I'm flattered. Not sure if I swing that way."

Nyx stuck out her tongue. "Not *sure*, eh?"

Anna laughed. "I don't even know anymore… maybe there's a 'gent on my plate' too. Geez. I'm messing everything up. I don't even know if I…" She bit her lip as Nyx's expression grew more serious and interested. "Hey, I know, let's talk about 'magic' and its relation to the space-time continuum, specifically in regards to moving living beings over a century in the future. *That* is what's totally worth talking about. Everything else can figure itself out."

A dark amusement lit Nyx's eyes. "Why don't we start heading back? I don't know a lot about magic and *time*, but—" She suddenly froze.

"What?" And then, Anna felt a burn in her eyes, the direction of the wind changing, a tang of smoke flooding her nose. The night had been so dark. And now, there was the faintest impression of a glowing ember behind the buildings before her.

Something was on fire.

The crack of gunshots lit up the night, sudden, without warning, just a couple blocks away. Anna's teeth went on edge, panic already starting to brew.

"Are… are they under attack?" Nyx went ramrod straight, fists balling. "Shit! That can't be… it's too…! What do we do?"

"We gotta help them!" Anna didn't think twice about it. She was already running.

"No! Wait!" Nyx called, but whatever she was going to say, it was brutally cut off by the squeal of microphone feedback resounding through the empty streets.

"RAIDER SCUM!" A man's voice barreled through the shrill whine. *"SURRENDER OR DIE!"*

"Anna! Stop!" A hand yanked Anna forcefully to a halt, heart hammering in her throat. Nyx's eyes were filled with dread, her head shaking fiercely. "No! That is a Coalition cleanup! This band you found yourself with, they are *way* too close to the city. A patrol probably found them and was sent here to run them off!"

"And?!" Anna saw gentle brown eyes in her mind, Jackson's kind smile. She saw a towering, grinning Shark who had stuck his neck out for her more than once too, saw a one-eyed doctor's grudging gratitude, saw faces she'd fought alongside, faces she'd helped save from slavery. She struggled out of Nyx's grip. It wasn't hard with her new strength.

"Anna, what the hell do you think they'll do to us if they see us out there? Me, I *know* they'll kill me on sight!"

This gave Anna pause. "Why?"

Nyx winced. "Because… Jaden helped me escape. But I had to go through a lot of agents to do it! I'm on their shit list like you wouldn't believe! And… and I have a kill chip. If they see me in range, they'll detonate it."

"*What?!*"

"Yeah." Nyx gave a hollow chuckle. "Sort of the reason why I let myself get captured out here… I was desperate to hitch a ride to where there wasn't enough infrastructure to send a signal properly to my chip. Not like I couldn't eventually get free, being that I am what I am. But if I get in range of agents… all bets are off." She bit her lip. "If I hadn't gotten to you in the facility back before… well. You'd probably have a chip too."

Anna whipped her head back to the fire. The flames were growing clearer now. Two more buildings were lighting up. The line in her chest thudded, and she knew Jackson was there, somewhere near that inferno. "Then stay here, out of sight! *I'll* go help!"

"Wait…!" Nyx called, but Anna was already running again. She had no idea how she was managing it, being as pants-wettingly terrified as she was of getting shot. But there was something speaking inside of her that was stronger than that, that had been growing in volume since she'd remembered her past. It was something that insisted no one else had to die. Not on her watch.

Whoever she was now, whoever she'd been reborn to be, she decided she was going to be a force to be reckoned with.

And the Coalition can… can go right to heck!

⁕

Smoke choked Jackson's throat closed. His eyes stung, and he reeled away from the burning apartments, their temporary home that was now just a tinder box. The fires hadn't started until he crossed back over the perimeter line. Then, there was a stomach-dropping *whoosh* in the night, the sound of something being launched, and the conflagration roared up before him like a demon from hell, sending him sprawling back, ears shrieking.

"Anna!" he called helplessly at the place where they'd slept. If she'd been in there…

He struggled to his feet, just in time to see two of the Warlord's clan break a window and dart out onto the fire escape. They were yelping with pain and coughing up the toxic air. He frantically looked behind them for signs of more life, and didn't find it.

He could sense her in this direction, sense her fear and adrenaline. He warred with himself, unable to tell if she was inside, trapped, or outside, witnessing this sudden horror.

The two people up the fire escape bounded down, dropping and rolling as soon as they hit concrete, crying out from burns and smoldering clothes.

He'd heard the screeches on the megaphone as he'd run from the field, so he knew just who was responsible. The Coalition was going to kill everyone here, decimate this place, and salt the earth in their wake—just like his taxes demanded.

He saw no soldiers yet, but he suspected they were moving in fast. Running, he made it to the two on the ground, hooking his hands under their arms and helping them drag themselves further away. He'd seen them both, a man and woman, dancing together earlier that night, celebrating, laughing. "Are… are you okay?" he heard himself ask, realizing the extent of their burns. They looked weakly up at him, dazed. "Did you see Anna in there? The blond woman?"

The man responded with a new hacking fit. The woman shook her head.

Jackson's heart was punching a hole into his ribcage now.

A second *whoosh* hummed through the sky, a second unearthly whine shrieking after. Instinctively, he crouched, and this time, the building next to his once-apartment ignited, windows blowing out. Heat swelled over his skin. His lungs seized and choked. *What the hell are they shooting at us?!* The two fires were catching everything they touched, the blaze licking up the sides of a third building.

"Anna!" he yelled, his throat stinging, feeling out the line in his chest. It pulled him forward.

⁂

Anna saw a rocket light up the night well before it struck the tenements. The concussive heat wave shattered the windows, sending her hair floating off her shoulders. A whimper tore from her throat. "Jackson…!"

I'm going back to the apartments, he'd said, right? All hurt and shame, but even through the rejection, warmth and smiles.

That conversation was not the last thing she wanted to have said to him.

She kept running, the only comfort the fact that wherever he was… she felt him. He *couldn't* be dead, because his heart was beating somewhere at the end of that line they shared. Still, what she felt in her chest was nothing but cold fear, and if it was his as much as hers…

A zippy buzz whirred overhead, then from her left, then from her right. The growing flames illuminated tiny, dark drones. Little red camera lights blinkered on their fronts. They skipped after her. They darted down side streets. The Coalition's eyes!

She slipped down a narrow alley, and the drone on her tail passed her by. The sting of smoke was starting to make her wheeze. Her eyes watered.

Jackson.

She burst back onto the main street, the conflagration that used to be a tenement block towering overhead.

And she saw him.

Oh thank God. Her heart almost burst with relief. There he was, racing in her direction. Black ash was smeared on his face from sweat and wind.

"Anna!" he yelled, his eyes bright, wet, his hand outstretched. A man and a woman were staggering after him, the man coughing furiously. Their clothes were torn, angry red burns peeking through.

"This way!" the woman cried, waving them to the left, insistent. She tugged at the shoulder of her staggering companion, keeping him in a straight line as his head bowed, his lungs working against him. Anna reached them and they pivoted as one. The whine of drones was growing louder. Jackson's hand briefly brushed her shoulder, untold relief flickering across his face. She touched her hand to his, acknowledging it, just as glad that he was safe too.

The woman guided them down a zigzag of streets, away from the flames. Dogs bayed in the dark. Rifle reports snapped the air from the east, getting closer and more furious with each step.

"I hate the Coalition," Jackson muttered.

"Aye yeah," the woman rasped. "We cannot fight them. *Never* can." Her eyes were welling with a thousand emotions. "But we are near the escape. We *always* have an escape." She staggered into another narrow alleyway, and Anna finally saw the shine of more eyes. A group of thick-armed men, almost staggering under the weight of carried crates, were unloading cargo into the earth, an open manhole before them. Between crates, a handful of people skittered down the ladder. *A hiding hole.*

An ungodly stench of stagnancy and mildew drifted to Anna's nose.

"In, in!" a familiar voice roared. Shark! His arms were trembling under a stack of boxes three high.

Clearly, Jackson didn't need to be told twice. He grabbed the ladder and clambered down, the pit swallowing him. Anna held her breath and followed, passing into the earth.

Light! It suddenly beamed into her eyes before she could even consider pleading with her so-called magic to come to her aid. The Warlord's keen stare watched her from below, helm proud and high on his head. The light came from an electric lantern resting on his prosthetic hand. In his other hand, he clutched a tiny, carved tiger.

"Always have a tunnel," he whispered.

The burned man and woman were following down the ladder quickly too, uncomplaining of their injuries. Anna got out of the way, trying to get her bearings, feet scrambling to find purchase on the damp and slimy stones of the aqueduct.

There had to be twenty people down here. Two had arms flung around panting, straining dogs. The big man that had been in the slave train was here too, rubbing the red marks still around his neck... but most of the other former slaves were missing.

Were they all back in the camp's center? Were they safe in their own hiding holes?

Nyx...

A black river of sludge and ancient garbage lapped against the walkway, kissing the edges of about fifteen crates. These, unlike the ones Shark was loading from above, were damp and dirty, as if they'd been here for some time. Perhaps the Warlord had always known that one day they'd be forced to leave.

A cockroach the size of her fist darted from the lantern light. She shuddered and turned back to the ladder. Shark looked to be done and was clambering down with the rest of the cargo loaders. The violent scrape of metal on concrete sounded overhead as he dragged the manhole back and re-concealed their tunnel.

Silence reigned, save for a muted gunshot above.

The Warlord's voice creaked through the air, a blanket of sorrow and rage. "We cannot fight them head-on. We know this. If any others escape, they know the plan, where to go. If they do not… we will honor them. Now get what you can carry. We move now, before the patrols realize what they've missed."

He turned, and he walked.

But… that's it? Anna wanted to call out. *We just… run?*

The lantern pulsed light down the miserable and dank corridor ahead. No one cried. They just picked up what little they had and started to walk after their leader, like this was a note in a song they all knew. Anna stayed frozen in the dark until they'd nearly all passed, thinking of Nyx in hiding somewhere in the ruins, of the other rescued slave boy, of all the faces she'd seen today that were not here.

At least fifty people were missing. At *least*.

She hadn't been able to help anyone. Her newfound resolve struggled, impotent, nowhere to go.

If I go back, if things are really overrun… I'll get caught. But I… I want to help… I came here to… She sighed, trying to corral herself with reason. *If I get caught, I can't help, and I can't go back for Nyx. I have to… I just have to get these people to safety and hope everyone else will make it for now, and go back when it's safe.*

Biting her lip, she dug in her feet and lifted two of the stacked supply crates into her arms, twice as many as anyone else. It was unwieldy, heavy, but she was strong now. She could handle it.

It tore at her heart. But she walked too.

CHAPTER ELEVEN
The Courtship of the Sun

Each step down the sewer corridor was more suffocating than the last. The pained gasps of the wounded echoed drearily off the bricks.

Jackson struggled with his crate. Still, he hefted the supplies without complaint, book bag hanging from one shoulder. After twenty or so minutes, his gag reflex no longer fired against the wet, rank air, but his lungs wheezed, trying to find more oxygen. His head fuzzed. Humans weren't meant to be down in these tunnels and hadn't been for a long time. It was shocking these underground paths were clear at all this far beyond the Barrier.

At least it wasn't raining. This backed up sludge of a waterway might flood at any moment.

After many long minutes, the Warlord finally stopped them all. There was another ladder. Shark paced forward, setting down his crate, and darted up. A throaty scraping of a manhole could be heard... the barest kiss of fresh air floated past Jackson's nose. This did more to revive his hope than anything else ever could.

Moving the supplies up and out was backbreaking work, and he found he envied Anna's ease of lifting. But the quiet determination in her eyes gave him strength as each crate passed her hands. The Warlord seemed to be taking a whispered inventory as each box went up the ladder—and strain marred his expression. This was not the look of a man who found his rations well accounted for.

What are we going to do?

Finally, *finally*, it was time for the people themselves to go back to the surface. Jackson welcomed the oxygen and the moonlight like he'd been slowly getting strangled to death. For a moment, his legs gave out, and he simply rolled back on the concrete, aching, looking up at the stars.

The night was tranquil, despite what had happened not so far away.

He was starting to distrust such a quiet.

There was a whisper of tires on the road. A cargo van pulled up alongside them, a faded logo out of view—unarmored, not one of the former Foxhole train. It must have been hidden nearby in the event of such an escape being needed. Jackson dragged himself up. He tried to forget about his forming blisters and resigned himself to the task of loading the boxes into the transports.

When he got close to the van, however, he saw it fully, and he couldn't help but put up a hand to caress the decayed logo. A dove. Of *course* it was a dove. How long ago had this vehicle been stolen, written off in his company's inventory? Had his father been the one to get the news? Had the driver lived, or had he been executed?

He hoped the van had fallen into this clan's hands long after the robbery had been carried out.

At least the dove was a sign he'd be safe for one more night.

A gentle hand fell between his shoulder blades: Anna. She was giving him a sad, sympathetic gaze.

They didn't stay for long. Eventually, two other vans joined them. They carried only ten souls combined, eyes haggard, throats raw with smoke—a group of nothing but gray-haired stragglers with a teenaged boy and girl driving them on.

Gods.

Eventually, the decimated band had to stumble on its way, for they all knew staying wasn't safe. The wounded and eldest were given priority in what little passenger space was left in the vehicles. The exhausted sat on the roofs or trailed alongside.

The moon rose higher.

Eventually it began to sink.

Still, they walked.

Jackson's feet split open, his back and legs throbbing at each step. How many miles did they need to go?

Anna had been allowed a place in a van—her hands were glowing with soft light, her eyes with determination. She was going to heal those she could. Jackson worried she'd sink right back into a magical coma for her troubles. When she wore an expression like that, she didn't seem like the kind of woman who understood what it meant to "pace yourself".

She wants to help, make everything better. She's so… kind. Selfless.

Every few minutes, flashes of light could be seen from the nearest van's windows. He shook his head, dizzy, distracted, hurting. He'd long begun to stagger when they all drifted to a halt. The Warlord and Shark both exited their vehicle, talking in hushed voices, brows furrowed. They spoke in a frustrated, foreign tongue, one of many Jackson heard tonight. Finally, Shark scowled and stomped off. The Warlord turned to the weary. "We camp here for a little while," he said. "Find shelter. Rest. Recover. I am hiding our supplies."

With that, people just stopped their march, fanned out, found places moderately covered from the sky, and settled down on the cement. Their exhaustion was a heavy fog. The Warlord got back in the van and wheeled it behind a building, the other two vehicles following. Jackson stared, then sat. The sidewalk's chill leached into his bones almost immediately. A memory: it was fleeting, but for a moment, he was a boy crouched under an awning, stomach empty, hands dirty, watching people walk right on by. He'd been invisible to all of New York's citizens. Just another face without a home.

Jackson the man reclined against a brownstone wall, feeling like he was treading over one too many old paths lately. Once again, he'd sleep until it was no longer safe to, or until someone told him it was time to move on.

At least one thing was different.

Discreetly, he rummaged in his bag, finding his handful of ration bars. The crunchy, tasteless mass didn't exactly give comfort to the soul, but it most certainly did for the body. He ate while thinking about how Anna probably would have started passing the food out to anyone she could. Perhaps he was fundamentally less *good* than she was.

But Frank hadn't given him that food to give away. In the back of his mind, his advisor's threatening stare made him freeze the good Samaritan thoughts, like he'd been caught sneaking out of the house.

Thinking of needs... he had maybe twelve hours, at most, before he was due for his next dose of Quarantine. There was an off-chance Anna wouldn't actually require it, given that her magic was what it was. But *he* certainly would. And how would he hide his injectors with no apartment walls, hungry eyes clustered all around? How likely would it be for the drugs to be seized? Clearly, these people had been beyond the Barrier all of their lives without regular Quarantine access, but... they probably didn't live that long. They seemed riddled with health problems: coughs, tumors, sores.

Too many things he didn't want to consider.

Reaching in his bag again, he pulled his book free and cradled it in one arm, letting the cover fall open. His work always helped him cope when nervous.

The tome still felt oddly heavy from the field. The dim moonlight beamed over the pages, and though there was a buzz of heightened magic laced within, all was written as it was before. *LISTEN*, it said.

"Yeah," Jackson grumbled, quietly so no one else would hear. "Did that. Got into some trouble for it too." He turned the page, taking a bite, looking at the blank vellum.

And then, something *changed*. He felt the tide of new magic under his hands.

Fresh letters began to write themselves. They were foreign this time, angular, strange. In his ears, whispers were growing. Jackson winced. But as he moved his fingers to brush the alien script, the texture of the whispers altered. Some became louder and clearer, some softer. He could swear he could pick out words now… what were they…?

"I am. I am. I am," one said.

"I am Balthazar, a first, and a witness to the last," another called.

"I am Josephine, and I fought until the end. Listen—"

"Listen to my story, for I am Akia, and I—"

"My story, Chosen, listen—"

Jackson had to yank his hand away from the vellum, overwhelmed, a wetness in the corners of his eyes.

The book of stories, this was called.

Chosen stories. He understood now. They were… speaking. It was as if a hundred thousand ghosts were walking past, brushing him with their words.

No wonder the Archmage had thought keeping the book from him would keep him ignorant.

Taking a breath, bracing himself, he once more traced the strange letters. The whispers began to peel away, whittling down, clarifying.

"My story…"

"Listen…"

And finally, one came forward, clear as if a woman was sitting beside him, voice earthy and deep. "Ah… finally. Greetings, young one. Not many can channel the power to reach me. I've been waiting for you for a very long time!" The way her words rang in Jackson's mind, he knew that she spoke in another language, something long buried and gone. He understood the words as English, but it *wasn't* English, and madness dwelt somewhere in the thinking of it.

"Who are you?" he asked, hushed, aware of the Warlord's people all around.

"You may call me Atropos." The voice was laced with a smile. It buoyed his flagging spirits. "Jackson, yes? I foresaw you would come."

"You foresaw…? Wait. 'Atropos of the Watching Stars'. I saw your name…!"

"Ah, did you?" The smile in the voice seemed to grow. "But… not all is as it should be, is it? Your voice. You're not a child?" Suspicion and dismay were creeping in.

"No. This book was kept from me. But it doesn't matter, right? I'm here now."

There was a silence for a moment too long, the sort that said yes, it *did* matter. When Atropos spoke again, the cheer in her voice was gone. "We must begin. Now. There isn't much time."

"What?"

"I might have taught you so many things…" Regret seemed to wind her words tight. "Magic. The mysteries. The Sight that would let you scry the future and past. But now… we must speak of war, young Chosen. Of the first light, of the accursed *game.* Or you will die."

The book was growing hot in his hands. The letters swam. Gasping, he shook his head, feeling a dreamlike trance taking hold. The outside world blurred at the edges, fading.

Jackson recoiled. "I'm not in a situation where I can go into a trance right now, I—" He would not admit he was afraid.

"You must. I'm sorry. You *must.*"

And the weight of the book was gone. He was simply alone in the dark. He saw no one. He heard nothing.

The crumbled city had disappeared.

Here he drifted, weightless in the silent void. "What are—"

"Tell me: what do you see?"

"I…" Jackson whispered, breathless. Was he falling? Was he flying? He couldn't tell, had nothing to orient himself to. No sound. No wind. *Nothing.* Infinity consumed him. "I can't see anything," he said, and it was as if his words were smothered in the fathomless vacuum the moment they left his lungs.

Her chuckles curled around his ears, warm, if likewise strained. "But do you understand what this darkness really is?"

"I don't see anything to understand!"

"No, no!" She laughed again. "In the darkness, there is *everything!* I suspect Inoki's stories may not have survived into your time. But the truth of them never really dies. So many of your creation tales—what do they say? That at the beginning, there was darkness." Jackson felt his stomach flip, like he was gently rocking on the nothing-sea. "Perhaps it was a void or a pit or an abyss or an empty universe, but it is the same. It was a cradle, and it was full of the infinite possibilities for life."

"Life…?"

"It still is! The darkness of a womb, the seeding ground of a dream— secrets lie waiting in the darkness, waiting for their story to be told. And young Chosen: this creation-darkness is, what in my time, we called *Inoki.*"

Jackson drifted, feeling so utterly small. "…Oh."

"And from this cradle came our world."

The darkness was no longer so empty. Under his feet, Jackson felt a tug of gravity, then something solid. Earth: soft soil. He reached out. A tree bloomed under his palm, the bark rough. He could have hugged it in relief. In this utter blackness, he could barely see, but the faintest outlines of trees were coming into focus, their tangy, musky scent filling the once-emptiness.

A forest. A wood at the dawn of time.

"Also from this darkness came all of us! So many new stories, new possibilities! Inoki was delighted when we came. We humans were his favorite beings of all."

Jackson tried to ground himself, searching for others. "That's… good. Right?"

"Well, here is the riddle I must give. Inoki saw to it that we came into being, yes? He is proud of all the secrets held in his shadows. He loves them. He cherishes them even more when they are born. But he is not all there is in the darkness… no. Something else lives there too. And what might that be?"

Jackson's breath caught, and he wasn't sure why. His neck prickled. A shudder ran from the base of his skull all the way down his spine, causing him to whip his head around, peer farther into the black.

Am I being watched?

There was something primal in the feeling. It forced his breath low, quiet. He slipped behind a tree. The crackling of his shoes on the brush made him flinch.

A low whisper of breathing answered him: a long, throaty *whoosh*, the soft crunching of plant life underfoot.

Jackson's heart began to pound.

Whatever was out there, it began to snuffle. To scent.

A rumbling, hungry growl vibrated the very trees under Jackson's hand.

The Fear, he thought.

The woman's voice hissed. "Yes. The hunter. The killer. The balancing force to creation: un-maker, destroyer, the tester of our *worth* to live. He who we did not name, for we did not want his eyes. He who made us his favorites too, though this was no honor. Inoki's dear brother: the Fear." The voice in Jackson's ear made a nervous, trembling keen. "I'm sorry you must be here. A wise Chosen would hide. For in this time, he unleashed upon us *monsters*. And they were very good at hunting us down."

The thing in the dark crackled against twigs, slid against leaves.

It was closer.

It knows I'm here.

"Take me out of here." Jackson searched the tree with his hands. No branches were low or sturdy enough to take hold of and climb to safety.

"No," the woman said.

Jackson sputtered, shocked.

"You need to know why my ancestors lived in terror, and how they were delivered. You must face the darkness yourself. Are you as clever as they were, they who were slaughtered endlessly?"

"*What?* I don't know!"

"Then find your cleverness, boy. Inoki gave us the means to live—magic. Insight. We passed the tests. We grew strong. Will you?"

Her teasing laughter rang in the dark, loud and clear.

A fetid stink rose in Jackson's nose. A light, airy rush sounded nearby. In. Out. In. Out. His hair softly lifted from his shoulders in the wind.

A raven cawed.

Monstrous, stained fangs were a foot from his throat a bare second after the bird's warning, erupting from the left in a spray of leaves. Jackson screamed. But the darkness moved under his hand. It slipped under the black thing's feet, sending it careening just a few inches away. Its snout collided with a branch. A pained yip tore from its throat as it danced backwards.

When it reared up again, Jackson almost felt his knees give way.

It was a wolf, just as he'd seen in his dreams. But it loomed so high it might have been able to crunch his skull in its teeth without even stretching. The thing's furious golden eyes glimmered in the darkness as it bayed. Jackson heard more snarls in the dark, more shifting of leaves. Beasts hissed. Some roared. Some yowled.

Monsters were coming for him of a hundred kinds and forms.

Jackson tried to run away—but he'd already put his back to a tree. He ducked. A rock! He tore it up into his hands. His attacker pranced to the left, an agile, furious intelligence in its gaze.

Jackson gripped at the shadows again.

The thing skipped lightly to the right, feinting away from the magic—clearly too smart to fall for the same trick twice. Its teeth snapped an inch from Jackson's face. He gasped, throwing himself low, rolling to the side, bruising his shoulder. The monster spun again. It gathered its powerful hind legs to spring.

Jackson's foot slipped on a patch of muck. His knee twisted.

"Help!" he gasped on instinct, trying to fight back up.

Suddenly, without warning, the pitch wood flooded with brightness, harsh and burning. Jackson cried out. His head spun in pain. A frantic chorus of snarls answered. There was a flash of a tail—the black wolf was running! Blinded, surprised, it tore up tree roots and grass. Its unseen followers were lumbering, crashing away too.

Sagging in relief, spared, Jackson breathed raggedly against a tree. He painfully clutched the rock he'd picked up for defense.

Where had the light come from so suddenly?

The sky told him all he needed to know.

It was a gorgeous dawn. The sun bloomed over the wood, vibrant and unreal. Flowers burst from the ground. Tendrils of green snaked up the trees, and the wind carried a song to his ears. It was a song he'd heard before, deeply warm and reassuring.

You're safe now, it told him.

"RAWWWK!" The disgruntled raven above that had warned him of the wolf's attack was now prancing in the branches.

"You passed the test," Atropos's voice came again to his mind, pleased.

"*Test?*"

"You knew you could not win. So with all of your magic, you called out. You prayed. And like my ancestor's cries, yours were answered: the first dawn." Atropos breathed a contented noise. "Was it not magnificent?"

Jackson simply stared, stunned, breathing.

"I wonder what Inoki's little friends thought, as this new age began." Atropos spoke with a reverent hush. "I wonder what it was like, to see the Fear's monsters scattered for the very first time."

The bird in the tree launched into the air, fluttering to parts unknown. Jackson began to stumble forward, fingers brushing bark, still panting, still wary. He wanted out of this forest.

Eventually, however, the tree line came to an end, and he emerged into a clearing.

Wind whistled through a valley, bright and strong, turning the heads of radiant wildflowers. Sapphire waves crashed against glimmering white sand far below. It buoyed his spirits.

"Hello, young Chosen."

The voice startled him, no longer in his mind—Jackson whipped his head to track it.

There sat a woman in an outcropping of grass, a beautiful, close-lipped smile on her round, umber face. Her black hair was wound into many braids, wrapped and piled on her head in a winding cascade. Her clothes flowed much the same, bright red studded with silver. She curled her fingers into an articulate gesture, three fingers in the air. Perhaps it was a greeting.

"There he is," she said. "Finally in the light. I see you, Jackson!" Her eyes sparkled. "Not a boy, maybe, but a fine, handsome man, emerging from the woods for the first time."

Jackson shuffled in his shoes. "Hello? Atropos?"

"Yes." She patted the blooming earth beside her. Recognizing the invitation, Jackson sat. The plant life was plush under his fingers—and it felt good, very good. There were no old bones and decay. A satisfied instinct that he never knew he had thrummed in this natural life, one that was banishing the fear like the darkness was a lifetime ago. He just wanted to lie back and *smell* everything, the dew and the flowers, clean and fragrant.

Anna... it was no wonder she missed her world so much.

"A question I have for you," Atropos continued, voice grave. Jackson tore his attention away from the riot of colors and life. "Having truly seen it now, are you afraid of the dark?"

He considered that carefully. "...No," he said. "I think I'm more afraid of what's in it."

She nodded, chuckling. "Wisdom. But our ancestors... they were not quite as wise. They *only* wished to live in the light after the first dawn, to leave the dark and monsters behind them forever."

The air was getting uncomfortably hot. The tips of Jackson's ears tingled, his skin starting to burn. Tugging at his collar, he started to sweat. The plants of the field began to droop, wither.

And something almost unreal caught his eye, something that made him squint, unsure if he was seeing things correctly. The world was... oddly flat. Almost like a strange painting.

"Why... why doesn't anything have a shadow?"

Atropos shook her head, sweat beading on her brow. "Such is a world in which there is only light." She smiled. "Inoki's loyal friends saw this too. The ravens: clever creatures. They see truths that most do not. And what they told their master was that a beautiful woman had come to answer his human's fervent prayers. She was cloaked in light, dancing up in the sky, basking the world in her warmth and glow. They said she was keeping the monsters at bay, but was refusing to leave. She was disrupting the earth and stealing his people's hearts rather entirely."

Jackson squinted upwards, face flushing in the heat, a thudding in his chest. *A woman... wreathed in light...?*

"Inoki, of course, came to investigate. He took up his walking stick and his favorite song, dancing out of what remained of the Shadow. And he was almost blinded as you were: for there she was in the dawn. Her dance burned with such passion and joy that he was near overwhelmed. But her song... that was what enraptured him the most."

Jackson still had his neck craned in the oppressive heat, thinking of a blue gaze, of another. "....The sun is a woman? How...?"

Atropos snorted, rolling her rich, brown eyes. "Is it that hard? Two things being true at once? She is both Sun and a woman. You are Chosen and a man. Inoki was a boy, a god, and the part of the darkness from which magic and dreams are born. Everything has many truths, and a few lies too—so Inoki teaches."

Jackson cocked his head. He laid back on the earth, flustered, getting a sunburn, and just accepted it.

She continued, "Of course, the moment Inoki saw the Sun, I suppose he was a boy no longer. His walking stick fell useless from his hands. He would *gladly* give this woman the heavens. His cherished humans were so happy! So carefree in her light! So he covered himself in feathers and took to the skies."

A dark shape emerged from the forest—another soaring raven. "Is that...?" Jackson sat straight up. The bird beat its wings with no uncertain power, shooting into the air like a dart, until it became nothing but a pinprick against the eternal morning.

"Maybe." Atropos flashed a mysterious smile. As she tossed her head, black feathers swayed there, woven into her braids. "Sun danced so high that he had to chase her for a very long time, and she blazed so hot that his wings almost caught fire. But finally, he called to her, shedding his raven form. She ran, but he begged her to stay. He said he was the riddles, the mysteries, and the magic of the world! He was *Inoki*, and he promised her stories and secrets in welcome. Won over, she said she'd like to tell him in turn of wonders of life new and glorious. They even agreed to meet every day." Her lips pulled back in a gleeful laugh, like she was about to share a good chunk of gossip, just for the two of them. "Inoki, he was a charmer, you see!"

Jackson fought with his dry throat, trying to hold it all in his mind.

"One day," Atropos continued, "Sun's and Inoki's words turned to his home. He grew sad, distant. She grasped his hand, asking what could be wrong in his heart.

"He told her why he'd first come: that her presence caused the humans to shun his shadows. They abandoned the quest for the unknown in their souls. The world may have looked more alive than ever, but part of it was dying." Atropos's voice took a rueful downturn.

"So Sun offered to leave. Perhaps if she had, things would have been different. You see, Chosen: you were born under the Sun. You cherish her daylight. But when we invited her to our world in our prayers, we also called down a much greater doom—something not even Inoki or her, gods both, could see coming."

A queasy pit of alarm bloomed in Jackson's stomach.

"And Inoki would not let her just *go*. He knew neither he nor his humans would be content without her again. So, he offered her a different agreement: for half of the hours, the Shadowlands would reign, and his people would dream, discover, and look into themselves in wonder. For the other half, Sun would dance, washing the world in light and life, keeping the monsters at bay. She could stay forever at his side. And you see: she agreed." Atropos's voice swelled. "For they had fallen in love."

Jackson's arm hairs stood, electricity suffusing the air. A form dark and immense moved before the sun, engulfing it. For a long, terrible moment, the world fell into shade. A cold wind rattled the land. The sun's fire emerged around the black orb in a bursting halo of light.

Jackson's heart pounded wildly with awe and horror.

Then the sun began to do what it had never done. It *moved*. It danced lazily towards the horizon, where finally, it set.

Twilight fell.

Now, hundreds of tiny stars glittered in the night, pieces of the Sun's passing. Proud and bright, another orb stood among them too, another promise of her eventual return: the moon.

Jackson shifted, restless, grappling an odd sense of longing, as if the story was dusting off forgotten things in his bones. The stars seemed more primal in this time. They were fresher and brighter than even the galaxy he'd witnessed outside New York.

Time passed quickly in the silence, like it was compressing. When the sun did rise, its glow was pleasant, no longer harsh and burning. It cast long shadows along the ground as it reached its zenith, small, cool kisses of night.

"They have entwined." Atropos stood on sandaled feet. "So you know the story. You know the agreement that made our world. And you know who gives you your powers, who gave *all* of us magic—who you serve."

"...About that." Jackson found it hard to speak in more than a whisper. This place was now charged with wild energy, electric and bright, like Anna's field had been. "Inoki gave people magic and inspiration, and joined with the Sun, kept his brother's monsters back... but what does being a Chosen mean? What *exactly* am I supposed to do?"

His guide's eyes narrowed as she crossed her arms. "Tell me. What do you think Inoki said to his brother when he returned to the Shadowlands, the Sun's fire leaching into his heart? That he'd just given away half the world's hours to an interloper? That his brother's empire of horror and blood was destroyed by a woman's dance, by the love it inspired? That humans were now forever beyond the Fear's full reach, he himself consigned to the edge of nightmares?"

Jackson swallowed. "Oh."

"Do you not think the cheated one might try to take back what was his? Do you not think *destruction and terror incarnate* may plan vengeance?"

"...Oh."

Her teeth bared. "*Oh.* We are Inoki's Chosen. Our bloodline made the pact to bring magic to our people, *to defend humanity in the first place.* It was we who prayed, we who brought Sun among us. Others may *use* magic! But we are its anchorstones! And if we should fall, all we brought..." She gave him a warning scowl.

"The Chosen *anchor* magic? Are you serious? Are you saying that if all the Chosen died, magic might just...?"

"The great unraveling of this world would begin, dear one. It would be as terrible and bloody as you can possibly imagine. The Sun would fade. The Fear would come back among us. And all of us would fall, back into the darkness from which we came. He would make us suffer. He would make us bleed for daring to rise above him."

Jackson stared. "But…" The weight of Atropos's pronouncement settled on him, weighing down to his bones. "Am I… am I really the last…?"

Her frown wound deeper. "Yes. I am afraid so. Something changed… something terrible. It is closed to my scrying, but something is hunting us down. When I lived, I saw your future, your broken world. I saw magic hanging by a thread. I saw dwindling mages pawing over access to withering domains. I saw decay, hunger, and fire, and…" Her nose wrinkled, eyes shining and sad. "I saw your survivors hiding under bubbles of light, the air and the water and the soil rotting. I saw them cower there, hoarding the scraps of old glories, turning a blind eye to all else. And I saw war coming for them too."

"War… everyone keeps talking about *war*. But I don't understand. Believe me, no one thinks the Coalition is good and perfect, but there's been *no* talk of anyone turning on each other. If any one of our city-states tried to revolt, they'd be decimated. Their Barriers would be deactivated remotely. And with that threat? Well, we all might make each other angry now and again, but gods, we *won't* have another Bombings."

She bowed her head. "The Fear in the Dark whispers to the hearts of the desperate. Believe me, anywhere there is suffering, where there is pain, he will take root." Her voice turned arch. "Those who put knives at each other's throats for some imagined noble peace… I think you've turned on each other already. Don't you?"

Jackson considered. He thought of the Coalition's search-and-seizures setting off furors in Moscow. He thought of Rio, controlling untainted farmland for nearly a quarter of the world, eternally simmering that they were taxed the same as everyone else too. He thought of Johannesburg and Brazzaville and Abuja. These were only a handful of the powerful cities in the African Union. They never did let everyone forget they'd been spared the worst of the bombs, or that they'd led much of civilization out of the dark ages with their resources.

"The world," their most recent council was quoted as saying, "Is a very expensive and ungrateful project."

"I see you are troubled, Chosen. As you should be."

While Atropos spoke, the sun was setting again. The stars gleamed overhead, but something about them seemed… colder. Far away.

"No pressure," Jackson uttered weakly.

She smiled.

"It's just… how would someone like *me* prevent a war?"

"Prevent? You're ambitious. No. It will happen, whether you want it or no."

Jackson stared.

"But, you can help us all survive it, by listening, by becoming who you were meant to be." Atropos turned, spreading her arms wide. "As I did. As did all after me. So give yourself over to Inoki. Learn quickly to make up for your missed boyhood. Embrace your destiny. Because I give you despair today, but I give you this hope too: if you master yourself, if you survive, there is still a chance for us to win."

Shadows began to creep over her form. She fell to her knees, a smile on her face still—and the darkness took her, flooding over her body. She was gone.

In her place, there was only a raven. It let out a cry, bold, piercing, then flew off into the black.

"…Wait!" Jackson stared at the spot where the woman had been. Two taloned imprints rested inside one human heel.

No one answered him.

But a thick, throaty growl punctured the darkness instead.

Jackson scrambled up, reaching for the heavy rock he'd been carrying. It was nowhere to be found, forgotten as he'd listened to Atropos's stories.

The monsters were back.

Heart pounding, primal terror flooding him, Jackson turned to run for the shoreline.

Scores of eyes gleamed in the night before him, blocking his way.

One by one, yowls and baying rose in the dark, the song of a hunter that had brought its friends. One of the monsters stepped forward. It was patchy and half-starved, its milky, tumor-ridden stare burning. Unlike the giant wolf from before, this was one of the wild dogs of his own time—but it was the biggest he'd ever seen. It charged. Its paws thudded against the earth, claws skittering, tongue lolling.

It leapt.

"No!" Jackson tried to scrabble back, flinging his arm up to guard his throat.

A lancing, burning pain shot through his arm. Teeth sunk into his flesh. The limb wrenched wildly to one side.

Suddenly he was gone from that place—there was no grass, only decayed asphalt and cement. There was no shore, only the Warlord's exhausted band.

But the beast remained.

All of its teeth sunk deep in his bone. Its breath was foul and tinged with copper, and it snarled, it's strong paws smacking him, its iron jaws swinging until it felt like it would tear his arm clean from its socket.

He screamed, hitting it uselessly, seeing his death in its triumphant eyes.

And he called to the shadows to save him, but he knew it might be too late.

CHAPTER TWELVE
A Light Against the Dark

Anna's head spun, her joints aching, her fingers tingling.

Take a break, her mind told her.

No, her heart said.

As she drew her hands away from Maya's skin—the flesh no longer burned and blistered—she closed her eyes. Her feet were cold and numb. Her strength was sapping. So she made sure to only heal small things, nothing like Jackson's injury in New York.

It still took its toll.

And there were so many people in this van who needed help.

"Who's the doctor here, eh?" Maya sighed, rubbing her hands ruefully. "Thank you."

Then the shouting started. Anna tore herself away, shaking.

"What the hell…?" Maya staggered to a crouch. Her eye narrowed in suspicion. "What *now?*"

Several others were reaching for guns. Anna's stomach roiled.

"No shooting," another man hissed. "Can't have the Coalition hearing and tracking us again!"

An animalistic howl of pain raged through the air. "Might be too late for that!" Maya slammed open the van door and dove into the night.

"Wait!" Anna called, running after. As she entered the street, she met chaos: screeches, yips, snarls. A furred, mangy body flashed through the darkness, all blood and spit and moon-eyed anger. There were easily a half-dozen of the beasts.

"Damn it! Those strays!" someone cried out.

Anna, fear in her throat, ran towards a cluster of warriors. Shark was one of them. He hollered vengefully, stance wide on a chipped sidewalk, swinging rebar like a baseball bat. Someone was down against the wall; she saw a prone leg, a shoe—wait. *Jackson?!*

His unmoving form made her reel.

What if his lungs gave out? What if I didn't really fix him?

She stumbled up behind Shark. "Get him to the van!" the big man roared, brandishing his weapon and snarling. A dog skittered before him, vibrating with fury. "He's not waking up…!"

Three dogs on the street spun to face her. They charged. The pack split and tried to flank the group from the front and the sides: circling, frighteningly strategic. Anna didn't even think. She remembered something, a lost memory from a dream, and her skin flared bright. The wild dogs broke their formation, deterred by the sudden burst to their vision, snorting and shaking their heads.

Then one overcame its daze and surged forward again. It's sharp fangs were around Jackson's arm before Anna could move. It whipped its head back and forth, worrying the limb like it was trying tear it off.

Jackson flailed—*he's awake!* He yelped and began beating the beast on the nose, kicking at it, eyes confused and terrified. The dog yanked his arm harder, ignoring his attacks, drooling and bloodthirsty.

Then, out of nowhere, a furious roar rumbled through the streets like a vengeful spirit coming home.

Fire fell from the sky.

A brief, blazing ball of embers exploded in the dog's face. Its fur singed, the rabid creature scurried back with a startled yip of pain. Nyx was running up a side path, a small beacon burning in her hands. The

Warlord strode out of the dark in the fire's wake beside her, bellowing. He swung his prosthetic arm like a club. The dog went flying.

"*Not! Yours!*" He spat each word as he swung again and again. The dog scrabbled back to its feet, dodging, frantic. More orbs of fire kissed its flanks, Nyx shouting a war cry with each pitch. The beast howled, dancing to the right, then to the left.

Finally, the pack turned tail and ran. They loped down the side streets, and fire lit up the trail behind them. Slowly, their growls faded into the night.

Anna sagged in relief. Wordless, she stared down the road, one less weight crushing her shoulders.

"Found you." Nyx smiled weakly.

Her left shoulder and arm were covered in blood.

"Oh my God." Anna stiffened. "Are you okay? Are you—"

"I'm fine, don't worry. I just fired up a locator spell. And this, it's not as bad as it looks." Her friend chuckled, then flinched. "Hey Jackson? You okay, man?"

Anna turned. Her friend's gaze flickered, his eyes wide with shock. Over him, the Warlord was panting, fierce, teeth bared in a warrior's rage. He looked half a step from crushing *anything* within reach. Jackson gingerly clutched his shaking arm to his side and stared. "Come on." Anna offered him a shoulder. "Let's get you to the van where it's safe. I'm going to look at that arm." He looked at her like he was half-delirious. "Come on," she insisted.

"Better do what she says," Shark rumbled softly, one uneasy eye to his king. "She's really strong, yeah?"

"Yeah," Jackson finally said. "She r-really is." The words settled into a pleased, warm spot in Anna's solar plexus. He braced himself against her, gathered up his book and bag, and stood. His game face was decent, she had to admit. If she hadn't been holding him up, she might never have noticed how much his legs shook, how much weight he was putting on her.

"Catch up with me when you can, okay?" Nyx whispered as they hurried off.

"I will!" Anna said. "Maybe you should come with us though… That's a lot of blood…"

"Yeah, but… don't worry about it. I'm fine. Trust me."

"If you're sure…" Anna's eyes stung with guilt. "I'm sorry I ran off and I couldn't come back, and…"

"Oh no, no! I'm fine. You're fine. It worked out. Do what you need to do." The grin Nyx gave her was genuine.

Anna bowed her head. "Thank you."

"Yes. Thank you," Jackson echoed, almost too soft to hear.

Their cargo van was squeezed between a handful of dusty auto skeletons rotted on the asphalt, ivy wound round their tires. It wasn't the best camouflage—anything here with all of its windows intact would look suspicious. But it was the best they had. Several of the wounded patients Anna had worked with appeared to be "walking it off". No matter their situation, she had to say, this was the most resilient people she'd ever met.

"Thanks," Jackson whispered again as he crawled in the vehicle, settling himself into a pile of blankets near the supply crates

"Do you need…?" She offered her hands, palms up, the healing yellow light still there.

"It's probably not…"

"It probably *is*. Let me see." She pried at his elbow, forcing his forearm forward. The hide shirt around his wrists was shredded. Fresh blood dotted the leather. She could tell that if the material hadn't been so tough, the dog's iron jaws would have done *far* more damage.

"They don't have any more antibiotics," she lamented. "And you really should have those. But…" She closed her eyes, tapping into that warm well of power at her core. In seconds, she felt that strange line they shared, pulsing, making her squeeze his hand tighter. She pushed her power along it just as she'd done the first time. Her legs went even colder, tingling with pins and needles.

The punctured skin began to close. The bleeding stopped.

The exhaustion hit her like a truck. She was forced to drop his hand, breathing hard.

"Anna?"

"I'm… I'm okay." She closed her eyes, trying not to sway. "I've just been healing a lot of people. What about *you*? Shark said you passed out before the dogs came…"

"I… it might have just been low blood sugar. Thank you. For healing me."

"You've barely eaten anything since this whole mess started, so I'm going to say you should try. There's some rations in the back." She curled her legs up under her body, trying to breathe and stay in the present.

Take a break, her mind insisted again. *Do it. Before you drop.*

Jackson looked around as if confirming no one else was there. He snuck a hand into his tote, pulling out two ration bars like the ones she'd seen in the safe house in New York. Slowly, he offered her one.

"We brought food?" she asked.

"Yeah."

"How much? We could pass it out—"

"Not a lot. There was just enough for us both, and not for long. A gift from Frank."

"…Oh." She took the bar. Her stomach growled. "It's just… I've been back here with the supplies all night. No one wants to say it, but I think they're running low. They're protecting us… we should share."

Jackson peeled back his ration wrapper, crunching the bar between his teeth. "You're one of the most generous people I've ever met."

A trembling sadness bloomed in her chest. "Gotta do what I can. I mean, I lived, you know, when everyone else died. Gotta make sure it means something."

Jackson's eyes widened. He swallowed his food. "I'm so sorry. I… I keep putting my foot in my mouth." He offered a weak smile. "Usually people say I'm charming and that I don't constantly remind them of death."

Anna chuckled. "Don't worry. It's not your fault I'm being morbid." This earned her a widened grin. She bundled her knees to her chest, recognizing the empty feeling still bothering her. "Please take care of yourself though, alright? When I saw you on the ground… look, I saw you like that only a day ago, covered in blood, barely breathing. For a second, I thought you were dying. Again. Like maybe I'd only fixed you for a little while."

A silence stretched between them. Anna reached out her hand, drawn to touch, to maintain that link with her friend, even if it was confusing, even if it hurt a little. So far, she hadn't felt this connection with anyone else, no matter how many people she healed. She didn't understand it. But she pressed two fingers to the center of his chest, to where she knew the scar lay under his shirt. He froze, and she felt the warmth in her ribcage answer his, pulsing stronger.

For a moment, she felt peaceful in their companionship, no matter the rest.

"Just stay safe," she said, and let her hand fall.

"I will." His Adam's apple bobbed as he ducked his head. "I promise. I can stay here and rest. And help you when you think I'm ready. Anything if it'll take some worry off your plate."

"Okay. Then finish eating and get some sleep. I'm totally a doctor, and those are my orders." She swung her feet out, making to leave, but another wave of exhaustion rocked her. "When you feel better, maybe you can think about putting our food in the community pile." A yawn cracked her jaw. "Then… um. If it's not too much to ask. I… I think I could use some company. Someone to talk with. Some of what's going on… it's just, it's *really* hard to…"

His hand, hesitating, came to rest on her shoulder. There was such a delicate fondness in that touch that she couldn't help but lean into it.

"I will." The hand braced her, warm, reassuring. *Not alone*, it said. "Are... are you sure you shouldn't rest a moment though? You seem very..."

Anna yawned again. Her eyelids drooped. Her hands still shook. "I think I used my healing too much again."

"You've done everything you can."

Anna knew he was right. Wordlessly, she scooted into the cramped space, leaning back on the blankets and boxes. He seemed to reflexively put an arm around her, and she realized she was fine with that for now.

"Can you wake me up in five minutes?" she whispered.

"Of course."

And she was gone.

...

Her eyes opened. She was warm, Jackson's arm still around her, though her back was complaining about the van floor. The exhaustion remained, but... it was less. In her bones, she knew she'd been out for much longer than five minutes.

Jackson's eyelids were fluttering, his mouth twitching—asleep too. Well, no wonder he hadn't woken her up.

Anna extricated herself, regretting the loss of warmth, gently laying his arm back onto his side. There was an unconscious, pleasant smile on his face that made her heart rest easy. For a moment, none of this was complicated. It was what it was. *I'm glad you're okay.* Deciding not to think better of it, she smoothed his hair into place, hoping his rest was a peaceful one. His skin was smooth and calming under her fingers.

She opened the van door as quietly as she could and left, feeling a little warm and wobbly.

I'm okay, she told herself. *I took a break. I'm fine now.* It was time to move on. She'd promised the Warlord she'd help, so she would.

She found the chieftain by what seemed to have been a restaurant, looking ponderous now instead of tense and battle-ready. The windows were caked with grime. His lantern illuminated a checkerboard sign dangling and creaking overhead, an illustrated slice of pizza in the center. Her stomach growled.

It had to be pizza, didn't it?

The Warlord peered off into the dark. "Anna," he greeted as she came up, hugging herself in the predawn chill. The skull crown was high on his head. She was starting to wonder if he ever took it off.

"How can I help?" she asked.

A soft chuckle. "You've done so much. I see how easily Lupe moves. Maya can lift with both hands. You're what my mother would have called… a miracle." He paused, a distinct coldness entering his tone. "How is the city man?"

Anna shivered. "Jackson's okay. He just needs to rest. He hasn't been eating enough." Of course, the same could have been said about most people here.

"Hunger and thirst will kill you quicker than anything else. Did he take food?"

"Yeah."

"Good." The chieftain's voice was fretful, strange, and dark. "We will need him."

"…Is there something going on?"

He turned his lantern to fully face her. "Perhaps."

A rough voice cut in. "You needed me?" Anna turned. There was Shark, moving quietly despite his mass.

"Perimeter checks," the Warlord spoke. "Ongoing fires may alert our enemies, so we keep it dark. But two small lights, they will not notice. And two lights, I am told, we have." He lifted his lantern high.

Shark grinned at Anna. "Aye yeah." Anna couldn't help but smile back. "You keep yours. Send her with me."

"Aye." The Warlord nodded her way. "He will explain." With that, he strode off, steps long and confident.

Shark waved Anna on. "Come on. Make yourself the glow-witch I know and love, yeah?" Sighing, Anna called the warmth inside. She was only able to linger for a second on how easily the power of light came to her now, because as soon as it occurred to her, she had to start trotting to keep up with her giant companion. They passed hastily assembled tents and open doors where exhausted clanmates had taken refuge in the ruins.

Finally, Shark came to a halt at what Anna sensed was the unofficial perimeter. "We are still followed, that much, I know," he said, words hushed.

"What? Did you see them?"

"Listen," he said.

Feeling nervy, Anna closed her eyes and did. It was silent, and she didn't like it. Her skin crawled in the unfamiliar and hostile darkness.

"You feel the way you prickle and want to fight?"

She grimaced. It was more like *run and hide* rather than *fight*, but she nodded.

"Trust that feeling. Might be Foxhole. Might be more dogs. Eh, might even be Coalition, just hunting for us so they can finish the job."

Anna winced. More Coalition. Always Coalition.

A clatter resounded out in the dark, snapping the tension in her muscles. Shark pointed, and she understood. The sunny brightness spilled even further around her. She caught a glimpse of two mange-ridden tails darting back into the shadows.

Shark frowned, and she dimmed herself, four more sets of eyes blinkering pale yellow in the night before they vanished. "They've been following us for months. First just one or two. Now... the farther we go... there's so *many*. But they never attacked." He sighed. "They finally remembered we are meat too, I guess."

Anna wrung her hands, glad Jackson had been protected.

Shark's eyes shone anger and suspicion. He spit on the ground. "Too bad I couldn't kill them. That is always my problem these days."

"But what if there's Coalition out there too?"

In answer, she got a *growl*. "If it is, they wait for something. But if it is, I will fight. They took my home. My family. My Father. Warlord says they will never stop coming for us. He knows. Can you hear it when he talks? He still sounds like you."

Anna bit her lip. She was in no position to evaluate that. But it was true enough that the man sounded little like Shark. "Yeah. I guess so."

"Never did stop getting books when he could. Even taught Mother Echo to read too, I think."

"How'd he come to be with your people?"

"Back in his old home, Coalition needed the rocks there for those 'datapad' things you city types like? His father said no. His family was killed."

Anna gaped. "Killed? Over minerals?"

"Aye yeah. Of course. Datapads are worth many, *many* credits! More credits than settlement. He found his way to us, almost dead, arm all cold-eaten. But my mama's sister became his new mother. He married Mother Echo, yeah? Strong lady. Best leader." He swallowed. "Wise. Died fighting. Never would bow to city! But Coalition took her. Took Tiger. Took everything."

Anna shivered, a pang of sympathy swelling for the crowned man at the other end of the camp. Perhaps his war-face was a little frightening, but otherwise, he seemed so stony. Placid. From his unbending stature, if she hadn't known better, she would have thought nothing was wrong. Perhaps that was the point. "And that's when you were forced to settle out here, right?"

Shark bit off a grunt. "I… We all… Agh." He shook his head. "No one settles here. This land is *garbage*. Even Foxhole knows not to stay. But… we had to come here. It is our way."

Anna squinted, not understanding. "Your way? Why?"

"At first, we were going to find a new home. But things kept changing. *He* kept changing. Even now, he is… different from when I left…" An unsettled look fell on Shark's face. "But he is right. All we have now are sunflowers." His hand reached up, reflexively squeezing a little pouch strung around his neck. Anna wondered if it was filled with seeds. "We could not find food. Water. He saw it first, that we never could make something like before. He has many dreams, yes? And plans come to him in them. It's why we are alive, even through everything. I do not understand, but I will follow him with all I have if it helps us find our way again."

Anna mulled it over. Perhaps, closer to a city, there was more to scrounge—more for a suffering community to take. "What will you do now?"

Shark smiled. "As long as we live, we keep walking. And when we get to the end, it will be beautiful! That is what he promised. Sunflowers will grow on the road we came down. One day, maybe, the land will grow good things because of us!" He laughed and rubbed his head. "Big Shark can't count so high, you know? But I see there are not many of us anymore. Maybe we will not make it to anything better. But if we leave sunflowers on the way, it is not so bad."

Her stomach making a sick twist, Anna struggled to reply.

Shark kept rumbling. "Stop with the pity-look, yeah? We are not in chains. We do not bow. Our mothers and fathers would be proud. We walk and die in honor."

Anna could only keep looking out into the dark, feeling awkward and sick.

No wonder no one was talking about their current losses. Loss was the order of the day. All they knew was to walk forward, and she had no solutions to offer, no false hopes.

Maya had invited her to stay until the end. In retrospect, it had been such a strange way to phrase the invitation, for someone that would have thought she had many years ahead.

Then she heard a humming. It was soft but full, a rolling baritone.

Alarmed, she looked over, and she realized—it was Shark. The music vibrated up from his chest, and on his cheeks, tears were falling, slowly, uninhibited. He stared off into the night, hummed the throaty melody, and wept.

What…? What do I do?

Anna shifted, unsure, used to the loud, laughing giant, not the crying one. Perhaps he mourned his companions—those he'd left behind in that place called "Sunrise", or the brother named Rat back in the city, or those he lost tonight. Perhaps he cried for himself. But such an open display of grief called to her own sadness and loss. Her breathing hitched.

Shark's humming stopped. "Sing with me," he said.

"Wha… what?" she managed.

"Don't you city people sing for your dead?"

Anna sucked in a long breath, letting it fill the hollow space, stabilizing. "I just… everyone I knew… they're gone. I didn't even get to say goodbye. And they've been dead for so long, but I'm *here*, and… I'm sorry, I shouldn't cry." It was starting to happen anyway. "You've lost so many people too, and I…"

A giant, meaty hand thwacked her in the back, startling her so badly that she had to stop. It forced her to regain her breath. "Easy, easy," Shark replied, the dampness still on his cheeks. "No sorries. It is the ghosts."

The ghosts. Anna bit her lip, voice cracking, almost wishing for more perimeter distractions so she wouldn't have to talk. "I don't understand."

"Tch! City teaching is no good…" Those giant hands came to rest on her shoulders, and he leaned down so they were eye to eye. "You feel this, yeah?" His thick finger prodded her sternum. Anna realized from the look he gave her that he wasn't referring to the poke. It was the awful, ruptured feeling that lay just beyond it, the one that had settled in her chest ever since she'd found out where and when she was.

The last horror she didn't know how to face.

"Yes," she whispered.

"Okay, that is the ghosts. How they speak. How they make sure we remember them. They follow us, yeah? And we should never forget them. But if we keep crying out to them, they don't get to rest. They keep coming back. Sometimes, they have things we need to hear. But mostly? They need to go down their road, and we need to keep walking down ours. Yeah? You understand? You let them go."

Anna's face crumpled a little, almost threatening tears again. "Just... just like that?"

"You have to." Shark shook his head. "You *have* to. Like me. Or you don't see where you're walking, and you join the ghosts sooner than you should."

"But how—"

"We sing," Shark interrupted. "We sing that we remember them and always will. They hear the song, and they know that they do not have to follow. I felt my ghosts right now, yeah? So I sang. And I keep walking, so I can do what I must."

Anna made a burbly noise. "O-okay."

"Come on." Shark let go of her shoulders and faced the dark again. "I show you. Tell me about them."

Anna struggled in the silence of the night.

"Tell me," he prodded.

Finally, after a long wrestling with her throat, the word that fell out was, "Mom."

Shark nodded. His wrists began to strike each other, a soft, tapping rhythm. "My mother too. She was good and kind, yeah? Not like big Shark, no."

"She was... she was smart. She was more than what my father made her." Her voice cracked. "She always believed in me, even when she had to whisper it so no one else could hear." The tears fell freely, but Anna's throat wasn't constricting like before. The words began to come easier. "And she didn't deserve to die."

"She didn't," Shark intoned, the rhythm of his wrists keeping on. "But she'd want you to live, right?"

Anna almost stopped breathing. "Yes... I... I guess so." But the tidal wave of emotions wasn't done with her yet. "And dad! I don't know what I thought of him. I can't hate him. I don't think I loved him either. I can't cry about him being dead, just the fact that I… I…" The rest piled out in a shameful whisper. "I don't think I care."

"Is that so bad? Who says you have to cry over him, eh?"

"I… I don't know… it's just, he's my *dad*, and…"

"My father was a big, ugly thief, and he hurt my mother when he came to rob Sunrise. I look like him, I bet. But old Baldur… eh, the Warlord killed him, and that's okay."

Anna blanched.

"Keep going," Shark encouraged. "It's okay not to cry over all of 'em, yeah?"

Rolling on, still unsure, Anna seized on the next ghost in her mind, seeing Shark seemed to be at peace. "Dr. Appleby. He gave me so much advice. I was afraid it was just because I was a girl, but it wasn't. He saved my life. I had to watch him die, lying to that soldier so I could stay hidden. Why would he just… just do that? For *me?*"

"Some people are brave," Shark intoned. "Like you. Maybe you learned it from him, eh? Maybe that is how you honor him." His foot began to tap in time with his wrists. The fabric on his body started to rustle, almost musical.

Anna took a deep breath, trying to nod, to acknowledge it and make it part of herself. "And my roommate, Rebecca. We were friends, and she's dead. What happened to her? Did they tell her, when I didn't come home, that I got shot by some terrorist in the desert? Did she take care of my cat? God, Checkers… she needed me. My cat needed me, needed me to feed her and love her, and I *left*. I just *left*."

"You choose to leave?" Shark tossed his head.

"I…" Anna's heart quieted. "No. I never would have chosen to leave."

"Then it's not your fault, aye yeah. I left brothers and sisters in Coalition chains back in the city too. Didn't want to. Did anyway."

"But…"

"There more ghosts?"

Anna quivered. The enormity of the question hit her, *really* hit her. "A whole world of them."

"Then we sing and we tell them we remember them, yeah?"

Her voice broke. "I don't know how to…"

"Here." Shark began to thrum in his throat again, the same mournful tune he'd hummed the first time. It had a peculiar bent in the dark, something that spoke to all the loneliness weighing on Anna's soul. Yet, it was too full, too rich, to be small and afraid like she was. It was simple, just one beat after another. One moment at a time.

It's a song to keep walking to, she thought, feeling like she was starting to understand.

Shark was nodding at her now, eyes encouraging. Her cheeks heated with embarrassment and tears. She could barely pin down the wending of his melody, and certainly couldn't just join in. She'd screw it up.

I can't….

And then, there was a song in her chest too, and she stopped worrying about it.

It was startling, the humming beginning to pour out of her, something she could barely control. The melody soothed her, moved her, vibrated through her tense muscles and aching heart. It was the song she'd heard in her delirium, in her dreams, by the fire when she'd danced with Jackson. It harmonized in a friendly way with Shark's dirge, and he smiled with approval.

She realized the soft glow under her skin was growing brighter, and somehow that made her feel even less alone.

They hummed together, a minute passing until the tune possessing her suddenly just ran out. Her light flickered off. Shark trailed off too, and they were quiet.

Anna breathed, stunned. She wasn't sure what she'd just done.

But the dark hole in her chest...

Something deep inside told her that this was the end of it, that she couldn't dig it any deeper.

It was time to climb out now.

Shark shrugged, like he understood. "Ghosts." Smiling in his sharp-toothed way, he gave her a salute. "Tomorrow morning, first light, you get the fire-lady, yeah? Warlord wants us to go back through the tunnels to the old camp, get more supplies, and look for more survivors. We keep walking and we keep everyone alive." Not waiting for a response, he turned and trudged back to the vans, still grinning.

Anna smiled, wiping the tears away one last time.

Keep walking.

It hurt, but that was okay. She was okay.

She made it back.

There were no fires in the temporary camp, but there was another light, a faint ember-like glow wrapped inside a blanket: Nyx. Anna felt an unexpected bubble of happiness at seeing someone else light up with magic for a change. Nyx waved. "Hey. What's up?"

Anna trotted to a stop. "Hey."

The two stared at each other for a long moment. Anna wanted to hug her, still glad she was alright, but she was full of so many emotions that it was hard to breathe. And because of that, a far more absurd thing simply fell out of her face. "Hey, want to go on a secret mission with me?"

"Okay."

The answer was so immediate, so devoid of jest, that she almost didn't know how to continue. "...I! Um." She finally smiled, bowing her head, grateful. "Thank you. We're going to help Shark find supplies and survivors. Apparently we're going to use the tunnels."

Nyx grimaced. "We're going... into the sewers...?"

"Yeah." Anna tried to quash the nerves from her voice.

Nyx made an *euuggh.* "Well, alright. There's goes my sleep tonight, secret mission nerves and all. I guess I'll enjoy being nice and snug for now." She cozied deeper into her blanket. "I'm not used to being able to warm myself with magic in public. I mean, I got some stares, but who's gonna rat me out to the Order?" She smiled. "Oh yeah, how's Jackson doing?"

"Oh. He just got kinda hungry, and he fell—"

"He was doing a spell."

"…How do you know?"

"Felt it. I don't know what the hell it was. But it knocked him on his ass. And… he's doing it again. Right now."

"What?" Anna jerked her head back towards the van. "I thought he was sleeping!"

"Well, I guess so if it knocked him out. Again. Buuuut—and this is just my expert opinion—it probably isn't safe, casting spells that do that to you? And not setting up wards or protection before a ritual… not good. You know anything about that spellbook he's got?"

"His *what?*"

"…Guess not. Well whatever it is, it's packing some serious mojo. Can't believe I missed him when he was a kid. Tony Bertinelli's magic masked him right over." She gave the darkness a contemplative stare. "Helped him dodge Project Esper, I guess."

Anna made an exasperated wave of her hands. "But *spellbook?* Look, tell me right now: am I going to wake up tomorrow and find out he's been hiding a pet dragon? Or that I've got a letter from an owl?"

Nyx laughed, full from the belly. "Oh gods no. Dragons aren't real." She kept giggling. "And I'm pretty certain Atlantis, elves, and fairies are all crap too. I mean, the Order has some different opinions, buuut…"

"…Different opinions? About *elves?*"

"Ugh. No. Atlantis. They never shut up about *Atlantis*. Got some massive painting of this Gandalf guy in their libraries, 'High Mage Balthazar, Preserver of the Lost City's Secrets'… *yech*. He looks out at his students, beard flowing, eyes twinkling, granting us all the privilege of his old-white-dude magic secrets. It's such crap."

Anna crossed her arms, chuckling in spite of herself. "Wow. Huh."

"Yep."

"What about… um…" She grimaced. "…Gods?"

Nyx chuckled. "If you're gonna ask, you gotta make eye contact."

Her face heated. "It's just… Jackson, he said… look, do I hafta, you know, start *praying* or something?"

"Oh lady, do not even get me started. No. Most of us don't have religion, and that's fine." She sparked a flame between two fingernails. "They're good for visualization, I guess? Sometimes I think of Hephaestus—Greek dude who forged weapons of war in his volcano. I think of lava, of battle-things, and…" The fire in her hand shifted, kicking off more heat, turning a brilliant blue. "Oops!" She snuffed out the light, then popped her fingers in her mouth like she'd almost burnt them. "Mmhmm. You get the idea."

Anna sighed in relief.

Shaking her head, Nyx continued, "If gods were *real*, they wouldn't have let the Bombings happen. One of 'em might have bothered to pull a miracle or two out of their ass and save their so-called faithful. So they're either fake or they're dead, and we just gotta take care of each other, right?"

Anna nudged her friend's shoulder with her own in agreement. "Jackson said something like that too."

"Oh yeah?" Nyx laughed. "He grew up alright I guess. Eh, look at us being philosophical. Magic. Geez."

Anna snorted. "Do you think he's putting himself in danger with that spell thing?"

"…Hrm. Hard to say."

"I don't think he knows how to talk to me about this kind of stuff. But, maybe you could…?"

What looked like cinders flickered in the air again around her friend's fingers. "Hmmm. Yeah, okay. The Order didn't teach him for long. He probably doesn't know any better." She bit her lip. "Probably." Sighing, she settled down on the curb again. "Saved a blanket." The scratchy bit of wool came up in her other hand.

Anna took it. "Thanks!" She wrapped it around herself.

"Thank you for talking. Calms the nerves."

"Yeah." Anna sat as well, just as another huge yawn cracked her jaw. Her eyes blurred and her head fogged. "I'm so sleepy. But I *just* slept."

"You're welcome to crash here some more if you need. Air will be warmer around me anyway. I'm gonna keep watch."

"Right on the ground?" Anna looked around, saw several other blanketed bundles, then laid back as Nyx said. It wasn't comfortable. In moments, her hips ached. This was far worse than the van.

It was then she noticed a small patch of blood again on Nyx's collar, seeping through the blanket.

"You're still hurt."

Nyx started. "No, no. It's fine."

Anna tried to struggle up. "Let me help."

"No!" The snap made Anna jerk back. "I mean... sorry. It's just, you should recharge. Healing magic... that's not easy. Can't believe you can do it. Really, I don't think you should. You don't pace yourself, it *will* kill you."

Anna shivered. "...Really?"

"Yeah. No joke. That life force has to come from somewhere. Don't tell me you haven't been feeling it."

"...I didn't... I mean... oh."

"Yeah. *Oh.* So stop wasting it on the small stuff."

Anna rolled over, shaken, sinking with tiredness. She lay there for a minute longer, struggling. And in the end, she still wasn't quite able to overcome her concern for a friend. "Nyx, maybe after I sleep, you can let me take a look at it, at least...?"

She didn't finish, nor did she hear the answer. Despite the rough concrete, her exhaustion was greater.

CHAPTER THIRTEEN
The Fate of All Chosen

When Jackson did drift off, it was with Anna's even breaths puffing against his shoulder, warming him, a welcome feeling in this journey through hell. He was happy in her companionship. And if she was okay with being there, then so was he—yes, his heart ached, but just as much, it was relieved.

I have so much to tell you.

But before he slept, with his free hand, he let his book fall open again. With one thumb, he flipped through what was once endless empty pages. Several now held strange, ancient script, and he knew—didn't know how, but he did—that this was the story of the Sun and Inoki, perhaps as Atropos had written it.

Beyond it, matters were blank, as per usual.

Then, suddenly, a riot of ink leapt out at him from between hundreds of empty spaces. He stopped, flipping back. *What is…?*

When he uncovered the page once more, it made his blood freeze, regardless of the warm woman at his side.

There was a man burned into the vellum, face contorted in a scream.

He was a man Jackson knew. *Huxley*—his old teacher from the Order. The mage had always been a creature of grandfatherly smiles and twinkling eyes, always fiddling with the golden buttons on his large waistcoat, pushing more dream tea, poisoning his former student, bit by bit...

Here, his eyes were screwed shut as if he were being tortured. His sketched skin was drenched in sweat. Exhausted rings sagged under his eyes.

"What the hell...?" Jackson touched the illustration. In the back of his mind, a scream echoed. He yanked his hand back. "What is this?"

Words wrote themselves on the page opposite, as if the book was endeavoring to answer.

No secrets are free.

That was all.

Cold sweat beading on his neck, Jackson thought of the Archmage's cryptic words. What, exactly, was the price for taking the book's knowledge? Had Huxley once tried paying it?

Disturbed, he turned the page. He tried to turn his mind instead to meadows and flowers, to the green and dew of the world before. If something had happened to some old murderer, well, why should anyone care?

After many minutes of focusing on happier things, Jackson put the tortured imprint from his mind.

That was how he fell asleep, book open on his lap.

And when he opened his eyes, he saw the ancient world he'd been daydreaming of, no dome of safety, and no crumbling rot either. Here was a bubbling stream lined with trees covered in puffy pink bursts. Here was a ridge blanketed with gently swaying grass.

Listen, Chosen. Listen to my stories, the soundless voices beseeched from the book.

Jackson listened.

And he was no longer himself.

He walked the ridge by the stream, the breeze gently lifting his hair, now long and flowing. His hands flashed in his peripheral vision, but they were tan in color and graceful in manner. Nothing felt natural, not the sway of his legs nor his center of balance. This wasn't his body, and yet, it was.

Another's consciousness kissed up against his own.

My name is Xīng, a woman's voice whispered in his ear. *And you will see what I saw.*

Like with Atropos, her words weren't English, but Jackson understood them anyway.

Xīng turned her head, catching a flutter in the sweet-smelling forest. A dark bird was perched in the branches above, eyes beady and watchful. Her face pulled into a frown.

She wore a drab, brown robe, but her mind was anything but subdued. Jackson felt a rush of knowing, of memories crowding to be heard: packed firesides, delighted children, clever wit, and always a mission, always a reason to press forward. Xīng was a traveler who shared stories of the past and future that had been revealed to her. Sometimes she was derided for her ways and her gender; sometimes she was treated as a strange novelty. Always, though, she lingered to help those who needed her wisdom—and her powers—most.

He saw that she learned what she was when a dark-winged creature fluttered into her family's farm. It had settled down on her lap like an old friend, a bird with three legs. When it caught the sunlight, its dark coat burned a heaven-sent red.

Her mother and father had screamed. But Xīng loved the divine creature as much as she'd feared it.

A scroll of stories appeared in her house the next morning, beautiful and gilded, something she thought stolen from royalty. It spoke her name, and when she told it she was just a lowly farmer's child who couldn't even read, it proceeded to teach her.

Her parents were unwilling to put up with either this parade of omens or her notions about herself and her destiny. Her younger sister and older brother were enough mouths to feed.

They threw her out; threw her *away*.

But a traveling monk took her in, believing her a boy. He'd put her unusual literacy to work.

In the end, she'd found herself a new path, chosen a new name: one that spoke of the guiding lights in the night above.

Xīng listened to the scroll and heard the words of spirits and the songs of the divine. She peered into the unknown realms. Even the elements came to her aid. And so she wandered, blessed, lucky, and with a knack for finding those that needed her gifts.

Now, her holy feathered friend was croaking up in the tree branches. Its unhappy cries were the only sounds in this riverside glen full of nothing but dead air, a place that should have been bursting with life.

So the problem she sought was here.

She hefted her walking staff. It was a heavy, chipped thing. A ceremonial sword hung by her side, her symbol of battle and resolve.

In her other hand, she bore a torch, despite the sun. It too was a symbol, one of purifying life and hope.

"Why do you curse this place?" she whispered to the silent trees. "The villagers near here cry out from the nightmares you send. They grow sick, some turning into rabid beasts. Why? What pains you so?"

Typically, such a question would end with an aggrieved spirit bending to her will, perhaps demanding some small tribute to right a perceived wrong. A simple exorcism and a little shouting would solve a more stubborn problem.

But something felt... off... here. As she stepped through the shin-high grass, a chilly slither crept down her spine. The burn of eyes was on her. Her neck hair rose.

And the glen went dark, as if the sun forgot to exist.

Sudden cold blasted her! Xīng froze, her fingers going rigid, fumbling her torch. The grass rippled and shriveled in a ring around her, desiccating into strips of ash.

"Who are you?" she demanded. An evil paralysis locked her legs to the spot. "What do you want?"

From behind a tree slunk a creature. It might have been a fox once, but its flesh and fur quivered and seethed as if it were roiling with insects beneath.

"*Yaoguai*," she cursed.

A shrill scream of wind-words stabbed her ears. ***They are mine. All of them. All of you pitiful beasts! I will devour you all!***

The fox stretched its mouth wider and wider to smile, like a snake unhinging its jaw. The wind howled louder. It drilled into her skull like the frost. The trees began to groan and crack. The pressure in the air slammed down, dropping her to a knee.

Each of her bones felt as if it was getting wrenched to snapping point. She screamed, tears starting to stream down her face, and Jackson screamed with her.

But Xīng had long ago learned resolve, for the world had always been against her. "No!" she cried into the foul, smothering aura, to the thing that had overtaken this glen, had fooled her into thinking it blotted out the sun. Hands shaking, she thrust the staff into the earth at her feet, thrusting the torch out, then her sword. And from her throat poured a litany of exorcism, incantations, and scripture. There was a singing of magic and authority snapping up and down her skin. It was electric, crackling behind her eyes and under her fingernails.

She was every inch the mage Jackson had once hoped to be.

"Begone!" she shrieked, beating the air with the sacred fire. Smoke burned her eyes and she didn't care, the pain of the creature's presence far worse.

It resisted her at first. It was strong, its will seeped deep into this wood.

You DARE...! the voiceless voice roared in fury. ***You weak, worthless lump of blood and flesh! You DARE use my brother's magic against me!***

She could barely linger on its message, her will locked in the struggle to keep the aura from crushing her soul. Never had she seen a *yaoguai* with a presence so powerful. It was as if the dark energy filling it was only a tiny twig on a tree, and the true nature of it was vaster than she could ever know. How *old* was it? She was using every inch of what the dreams and scroll had taught her, and *still*, it held on!

I will slaughter you all, if I have to wait centuries! Millennia!

And as she screeched, "Begone!" one final time, plunged the fire into the darkness…

…The curse cracked. The fox collapsed, twitching, and the grove began to rise from shadow. The sky turned gray, then, slowly, the sun returned.

She felt the evil yet, but she fell to her knees. *Am I strong enough to cast it out?* A knife felt as if it was sawing into her solar plexus. The strain of magic against this power… it had…

She sagged, coughing up blood, throat raw. Her eyes watered, her nose streaming red, breathing short and labored.

"Begone," she whispered, rebellious to the last.

A grudging reply seeped inside, the sound of iron grinding against bones.

One day, you will remember why you fear me.

One day, you will beg for my mercy, and I will have NONE.

Slowly, the twisted, collapsed bag of bones and fur simply dissolved.

Xīng fell back into the grass as the presence vanished. Blood trickled down the side of her lips.

She had the distinct sense that the thing had only left because its weak vessel could no longer last. If it had wanted, it could have ground her into the dirt until she was only a stain.

All of my power… and I'm still nothing.

She hoped she'd saved the village. That would have to be enough.

As she slipped in and out of consciousness, Jackson slipped with her, each drop of dreaming a dip of vertigo. Time passed in spurts of minutes and hours without warning.

And then, in a blink, he was just Jackson, not Xīng at all. He was light, floating in the air, soaring above her prone form. The stars were above, the moon glittering.

The raven still sat in its tree, keeping its vigil, an ink spot in the night. It made a mournful noise.

Xīng's dark eyes opened and bore right into him, like she knew he was there. He trembled under that stare. Her pupils were waxy, the light almost gone.

"I should have seen… what it really was… how *strong…*" she rasped, throat destroyed. "I'm beyond its reach now. But you aren't… are you? Tell me… tell me the answer. What the scroll wouldn't say."

"I… I don't know. What are you asking?" Jackson's heart beat with a machine-gun patter.

Her bloody lips curved into a smile. She coughed. "The Fear. We Chosen… we live. We fight. We die. When will we win? It must end one day. It… it must… it…"

The smile sagged, the flicker of her pupils drifting up to the moon, freezing there.

She was gone.

A part of Jackson left with her.

But the night swallowed him, clouding his vision, and the river, the glen, and Xīng were no more.

The darkness cradled him close for long moments, and then, the world changed. A wintery breeze spiked his face. A cloud of tangy pine burst in his nose. Here was another wooded grove. Nothing bloomed in this new place—the towering evergreens were weighed down with mounds of dazzling white. Kisses of snow flurried against staggering cliffs and steel-gray mountainsides.

Jackson would have shuddered if he were in his own body. He'd never felt the bite of snow on his skin, just as he was still new to the rain. He still reeled from his vision of Xīng, mourning this woman he'd never even met.

But he was in the body of another, and there was power in his stride, thick, corded muscles in his arms and chest from years of use.

I am Magnus, a man's mind said, brushing his. *And you will see as I saw.*

Before him, staining the virgin snow, was a ring of blood and carnage.

A wolf kill, Magnus thought. *An omen.* He kneeled gingerly plucking a black feather from the ground, eyeing a severed wing. Canine prints dotted the thick powder. It was recent.

Strange. Ravens and wolves, Magnus knew, were two of a kind. They often hunted together, the birds calling the pack's attention to prey. In exchange, the beasts would tear open flesh for their winged companions to eat. Together, they followed battle. Together, they kept to Odin's side.

Wolves hunting ravens for just a nibble meant they were getting hungry this winter. It could be a problem for the town behind him.

He needed to think on this.

Magnus tightened his gloved grip on his sword hilt as he resumed his march, keeping a wary eye to the trees. Omens were serious. He, a friend of ravens and speaker to the gods, needed to exercise caution, lest they make him a fool.

But he reached his sacred cave untouched. Kneeling by the fire pit at the cavern's entrance, Magnus struck his flint and steel. Soon, a great blaze rose, fighting back the biting cold, letting him drop the heaviest of the furs from his shoulders. The cavern's walls were revealed.

Towering to the ceiling, all the way into the darkest depths, were carvings. Some were pictures, and some were a strange, angular language Jackson couldn't understand—but Magnus did. He'd stumbled into this place as a boy while learning to hunt with his older brother and father.

The wights here overwhelmed him, the weight of the divine pressing down on his mind. For a fleeting second, he felt as if he'd drunk from the well of prophecy. He'd seen things he couldn't have possibly known, heard voices telling him stories of times long ago and times to come. His family had found him crumpled, raving.

They couldn't see the carvings. None of them could.

But Magnus's strange visions and dreams kept coming true. It wasn't long before he was serving the village as an oracle and mouthpiece of the gods, considered wise and necessary.

He had a place. And for a moment, Jackson was snarled in a pang of envy.

But this cave was lonely, frigid. As memories poured in, Jackson witnessed the uneasy, mocking stares of the other men. He glimpsed the bloodletting, the uncertainty of the rituals, and the exhaustion, the endless exhaustion...

No secrets are free.

This man could never fully be part of the mortal realm alongside his brothers. He forever would have one eye to the spirits, and they were always shifting underfoot.

But that was just how fate wove. Today, he simply needed to work his magic, then get home in time to see his sons before they fell asleep. Perhaps he might lay with his wife a while and forget the cold.

Slowly, contemplatively, Magnus tossed the dark feather from the woods into the fire, then a fistful of dried herbs. The smoke filled his lungs. The whispers of the sacred filled his mind. He grew dizzy, his head sagging. The darkness seemed to loom tighter around him, a conduit for the cacophony of the spirits.

"*Beware,*" a whisper hissed.

"*The wolves,*" another beckoned.

"What does this mean?" Magnus mumbled back into the shadows.

He began to move through trances, but the whispers were jumbles struggling to be heard. He was unsettled, and his unsure intentions could not chart his path. Clenching his fists, he gathered his focus, pressing his mind out.

What makes the wolves hunt the ravens?

Suddenly, the crackle of rocks under boots wrecked his focus. Magnus, surprised, opened his eyes.

By his fire was another man, pale and huge. He had a frosty waterskin hanging by his side, a battle axe in his grip. "Mind if I join you?" Wary gray eyes betrayed no emotion, but the man laid the axe down. It seemed he came in peace.

Magnus only nodded, perplexed, irritated that his concentration had been broken. The men of the town knew better than to disturb him… but this was no man of the town, now was he?

The newcomer adjusted the furs on his shoulders as he settled by the flames, shuffling off his gloves. There he shivered off his cold and wet, warming his milk-white hands. "I'll not be long. The port's near, isn't it? I have business there."

"Yes," Magnus grumbled. "Though it's a poor season for travel, stranger. Ships won't be sailing through the ice."

"All the same: the signs were right, so here I am."

"Then you should kill your sign reader."

The man made a raucous, bellowing laugh that didn't quite meet his eyes. "I *am* the sign reader."

Magnus raised his eyebrows and said nothing.

"My dreams told me to come west when I next saw blood," the stranger continued to rumble, as if in explanation.

Magnus kept his silence.

"See, they said I'd find a man who weaves raven feathers into his cloak—that he was to blame. And here you are!"

Neck hairs prickling in warning, a spark of violence lit in the back of Magnus's mind. He didn't trust this man. And the omen he'd seen… "Blood? Blame? A dream?"

With a shake of his matted blond hair, the man only said: "So why did you kill them?"

Magnus's right hand settled on his sword hilt. He could draw it far faster than this stranger could pick up that axe. "I don't know what you mean. You should leave."

"He said it was your fault." A sneer curled the traveler's lips, his body starting to shake. "That you're the reason my village got sick, that they started raving about *war* and *blood* and *glory*. That you're why my brothers went mad and killed my wife and son, the reason I found them dead under the sky. And it was clear they had *suffered*." His voice cracked, hysteria leaching in. He rose, towering, tears mingling in his thick beard, and Magnus rose with him. "*Why?* What magic did you use? What did *we* do?" The stranger's hands clenched into accusing fists. "Was it your king that told you to curse us so you could take our land come spring? That's all I want to know! *Why?*"

"I don't even know you!" Magnus drew his sword. "I only listen to the signs. Nothing more!"

"The man in my dreams… night after night he told me of your kind." The man reached inside his furs. "Perhaps he was one of Odin's guises, the wolves by his side. Everything else he said was true. So I believe him."

With one brutally smooth, practiced movement, the stranger drew a throwing axe from his cloak and spiked it through the air. Magnus dove aside, but he was off-balance, realizing far too late that the larger axe by the fire was a ruse.

There was a horrific splitting in his neck, like the vertebrae were being ripped in two. Jackson screamed with Magnus, his vision going red.

The darkness swallowed him again, sudden and final. He was gone, vanished along with all of a man's unfinished intentions and hopes.

Though he was formless, Jackson wept again.

And again, the sun rose.

No. No no no.

This wasn't what he wanted—to live over and over, to die over and over. He wanted to wake up. He wanted to be in his own time, feel Anna against his side, fumble with his own fate.

But it wasn't to be. One, last time, he opened eyes that weren't his.

He was surrounded by white stone and wood, the scent of salt, fish, and spices on the balmy breeze. A metropolis engulfed him, scores of buildings and banners and faces, people hurrying along a dusty street, shouting in foreign tongues. They were well-fed, faces a thousand shades of umber, sepia, and earth, all bedecked in rich cloth and elegant jewels.

He had black hands now, sandaled feet, though he was small, so small. He was but a boy.

And everything in the air was teeming with power: magic that made his skin tingle.

I am Balthazar, the thoughts spoke, *and my mother's going to die if I don't ask the Raven-God to save her.*

The boy's heart was pounding so hard it was painful. Jackson saw a flash in his mind, a woman of full cheekbones and warm smiles, tightly curled hair woven with glass beads.

She was dressed in shabby rags, but there was no mistaking her.

Atropos?

There were tears stinging the boy's eyes. His cherished memory melted into a woman with a stare hollow. Her expression was dull and waxy. She kept fighting sleep and sending pained cries in the night when she failed.

Nightmares haunted her.

Nightmares from the Raven-God she'd offended.

Dizzy, Jackson let himself be thrown through the crowd as this boy hurtled forward, nauseous with frantic need.

He must have mercy, the boy insisted to himself, sick. *He must. He must.*

Rising before this boy, this Balthazar, was a smooth, elegant masterpiece of stone, something every bone in Jackson's body wanted to call a *cathedral.* The walls glittered with marble, opal, and mother-of-pearl, dazzling in the afternoon sun. People wandered past, heads bowed under headdresses as perfected as the architecture.

This place was sanctuary, and the boy's stomach lurched in both hope and horror at its door.

He ducked inside.

A tiered fountain rose before him, intricate mosaics glittering above. Around this was a ring of statues on pedestals—the gods—and at their feet were offerings of coins, bones, candles, and flowers. The closest statue, and every visitor's favorite, was a curvaceous dancer of polished marble, her form heartbreakingly elegant, her face alight with a brilliant smile. A golden orb was balanced on her head in the midst of a halo of hair. Her pure grin, it reminded Jackson of…

His stomach flipped, and Balthazar tore his gaze away. His calloused hands dug out his cleaning supplies, and he threw himself scrubbing Sun's feet, glancing around. *No one saw I was late.* He felt like he was going to break in half from relief. Old Bear, his grizzled taskmaster, was only just emerging from the scholasticate above, where the sons and daughters of the wealthy learned the kingdom's secrets. These students reveled in the arcane power that was their birthright. They would one day keep the kingdom prosperous and safe.

For this boy, however, he would only see Old Bear's cane. He couldn't even read. His mother usually fed the animals here in the mornings, before the students and worshipers arrived, and she too had the bruises to show for the High Teacher's temper.

Her sickness—no, her *curse*—had kept her at home this morning. Balthazar could only pray the old man or his students hadn't noticed. If anything, the pupils were as bad as the master: fiercely loyal, like little spies. Who knew what he'd promised them. But ruining a servant's life would, by most of them, be considered good sport.

Some of the other statue-scrubbers joked that if Bear ever wanted to overthrow the kingdom, he'd certainly drawn to himself an excellent and spiteful vanguard.

Swallowing fear, Balthazar tried to find focus and solace in the god-stories his mother had told him as a baby. On a normal day, he would whisper these dedications to each polished face. It was poetry even an illiterate boy could know. Usually, he would have grinned at Sun's vibrant smile as he polished her golden orb. He would have spent extra time cleaning the Man of the Wood's great antlers, dreaming of long legs darting through glens and magical springs.

Today the words fell meaningless from his tongue. He was consumed with keeping watch, waiting for an opportunity to commit a grave crime.

I must, Balthazar thought. *I have to.*

Old Bear was making his rounds. His voice snapped to Balthazar's left like a whip. "You! If Sun's statue doesn't shine like her presence in the sky…"

"Yes, sir." The boy bowed his head. He hoped the nervous bile in his throat couldn't be heard.

Old Bear grumbled and moved on. Even he couldn't complain at utter obedience.

The boy hazarded a glance over his shoulder to his true goal.

Far into the shadowy back lay the Secret Gods only the Highest Mages were allowed to petition. Knowing these gods' names was forbidden. Until recently, Balthazar had only known the Raven-God as The Storyteller, the Shadow Prince, and the Dreamwalker.

Sadly, he knew one other name now, and it was what was destroying his mother's life.

Inoki.

As the forbidden word welled through him, making his hands shake and his throat choke on the taboo, Jackson felt his heart grow cold, finally understanding what Balthazar intended to do and why.

His mother hadn't been careful one day. She'd stayed too long feeding the animals and overheard a Highest Mage's petition. When she'd come home that night, face sallow with fright, the forbidden name had just tumbled out of her lips over and over, damning them both.

That night, she'd been afflicted with the Shadow's Curse: the nightmares.

She wasted away. She began raving that she saw the city *burning* until nothing was left. She wandered the house, wringing her hands, refusing to sleep or eat. "The Fear is coming!" she wailed. That morning, Balthazar found her edging through the streets, trying to warn people of her visions, sounding half-crazed. He cried and begged, but she wouldn't come home.

Even if no one realized she'd broken taboo, if she was caught like this, they'd throw her out. Food would dry up, and she'd just get *sicker*...

"I am a *man* now," the boy whispered, voice cracking. "I must fix this."

His small hands ached as he scrubbed, and he felt no more a man than he had a week ago.

But despite his terror, he knew his path. He'd cleaned this temple every day since he could walk. He knew that when Sun's shadow touched the fountain, his overseer would trundle off on arthritic feet, fetching a small bowl of grain and fruit to start his day.

There would be exactly five minutes to petition the Secret Gods. Jackson's link with Balthazar converted the foreign measures of time as easily as language: there were five minutes before this boy could be caught and beheaded for his sins.

So Balthazar kept polishing Sun's golden orb, his gaze bowed. She always knew the truth of a man's heart, always brought secrets to light. He wondered, if he met her eyes, if he might be compelled to confess his family's crimes, the things they never should have known.

Even if he succeeded here, one day, he would answer for this.

Old Bear's feet began their shuffle just when predicted.

He was gone.

Five minutes.

Balthazar turned his dishonest back to Sun and ran. Clutching his mother's remembered smile to his heart, he skidded to a stop in the shadowed alcove, throat dry and tongue clumsy.

The carving here was pure basalt, black as night, ancient beyond memory. Two stone boys were crouched there, faces long since worn away. A birdlike lump rested on one's shoulder, a doglike mass around the feet of the other. Some said this mighty rock was a token of a much, much older world before the Sun rose, when the darkness and its monsters forced his people to learn magic so they could survive.

They called those stories the Dark Stories, and Jackson's heart shuddered that they were all true.

Balthazar considered that there was still a hint of a smile on the Raven Boy's face (*Inoki Inoki Inoki*, the forbidden name whispered in his head.) He prayed only Inoki was listening. The *other* stone boy could bring him much worse trouble.

"Please," his throat wrenched. Belatedly, he kneeled. Others had left long scrolls bursting with ink and expensive illustrations, or trinkets of solid gold, blessed bones and gems. Feeling feverish, the boy pulled his dull cooking knife from his side pouch and drew it across his palm, wincing, squeezing drops of blood into the offering well. "Blood's all I have. I'm poor. But my mother did not mean to hear your name. Please. Have mercy. Take back the nightmares you sent her. We only want to serve you. Please. I… I love her. Please don't let her die. Don't let us be thrown out. She didn't mean it…"

Gasping, Balthazar bowed his head, touching it to the bowl's rim, cradling his cut hand to his chest. Tears slipped free from his eyes, joining his blood.

Then, the hairs on his neck prickled. He had to go. He could only pray his pleas were heard, that no one noticed his hand, that Inoki would choose to spare them, that—

There was a ruffling, tinkling sound from above, the sound of doom.

A raven of the temple.

The sacred bird descended from on high, alighting on the Raven-God's head, its talons clicking the basalt. Peculiar white feathers around its neck spoke of the Sun's and Shadow's bond from ancient days. Its golden ankle chain strained, preventing it from landing on unclean floors.

It peered into Balthazar's eyes, though Jackson had the eerie feeling that he too was seen.

"SEEEECRETS," the raven croaked, wings in an agitated fluff. "SEEEECRETS."

Balthazar and Jackson fell back as one, hearts slamming into their ribcages.

Oh gods, no, no don't talk to me! They'll see! Balthazar flailed to his feet. The raven didn't seem to care that it was shattering the law, that the boy before it was no priest or magician. *Shouldn't have come here!*

His feet turned to run away.

"Chooooooosen," the bird warbled.

Balthazar stopped.

Or Jackson stopped him.

He couldn't tell anymore.

Eyes wet from fear, the boy turned again, feeling as if his legs were made of stones. "What did you say?" His voice was small and weak.

The raven tittered, the golden chain tinkling, the white ring around its neck flashing. "Not curse. *Giffft.* To saaave her. The magic! Steeeal it. War is coming. Waaaaar. All lost. Lost forever!"

Both Jackson's and the boy's hearts were paralyzed.

The warning was achingly familiar: war.

But to this boy, this city was eternal and glorious and so much bigger than he could ever hope to be. The idea of war was unthinkable.

None could ever bring the kingdom of Atlantis down.

Besides, the only thing Balthazar cared about was his mother.

The raven kept wrenching its simple vocal cords into noises nature never intended. "The Bear... the Bear has given his soul! He will take all! All for himself! Steal his seeecrets! The brother hunts! *The Fear comes!*"

Its head began to seize and twitch, its beak hanging open. Something cracked inside its tiny skull.

Once, twice, it staggered on its perch.

Its wings spread helplessly.

It fell.

Back and forth, the raven swung from its glittering chain, back and forth: dead.

Balthazar ran, unable to to stop the tears, the terror building in his throat.

He didn't see Old Bear until they collided. The man's knobbed cane fell, his arthritic hands suddenly precise and made of iron. One seized the boy's wrist painfully, wrenching him close. His eyes were full of rage and hunger, like a beast thinking its prey was about to be snatched. "*What did it say to you?*"

Balthazar screamed.

The cry erupted from Jackson, and he vaulted up, heart pounding. The boy, the city, it was all gone. So was Anna. There was only the book at his side, eerily warm. Three pairs of sleepy, irritated eyes glared back at him.

"Excuse me," he said, gathering up his things and scrambling for the vehicle door, for fresh air, gods, *he felt trapped…!*

His exhausted feet touched the ground, and he stumbled, slamming the van door behind him. He tried to bring himself down, panting, re-establishing what was real.

Of course, it was all real, the dreams, *everything*, but he needed *this* real right now, the one without dead ravens, dead Chosen, and the grinding sense of doom. Or, he was going to scream again, and he didn't know if he would be able to stop.

The enemy is sly! Silent! Blood-mad! The voices from the book whispered, a chorus rising and falling.

As Jackson blinked, he saw flashes: there were crowds fleeing, the ancient city burning. People savagely turned on each other.

The Fear is here! He is everywhere! the voices cried.

He saw the endless sand of an empty coastline now, a place that once held civilization. Fresh bones drifted on the tide. Glass scars scorched the earth.

His creations, they have your scent!

The fog cleared, and the tide of voices fell to nothing.

The light of dawn had wiped back the stars. Hours had passed. Everything hurt. Everything.

Anna was just a short distance away, speaking with Nyx. An electric nervousness seemed to surround them all. By her side stood the Warlord. His arms were crossed, his helm tall and proud on his head. Under it, his dark stare burned, like his eyes were lamps fueled by nothing but anger and loss.

They peered into Jackson as if they were peeling back all the layers of everything he'd ever been… and found him wanting.

Jackson looked away first, shaken. His forearm ached from the dog bite, even though it was healed.

Death. Nothing but visions of death and danger.

Here he was, Inoki's last Chosen, clearly meant to play some part in this fresh hell.

Maybe his father had been right. Maybe he really was cursed.

Jackson always assumed the destiny he was looking for would line up very neatly with some deep desire he'd been searching to fill his entire life. He'd thought it would give him meaning, put to rest the cold, empty questions of his soul. But this…?

For gods' sakes, he was a businessman! He'd only ever dedicated himself to paying back Peter Dovetail, who gave him a home, love, and a place in the world. How could all of that just *stop mattering?* If Inoki ordered him to do something, to become something new in this… this game, this war, whatever it was… could he accept it?

After all, the consequences if he *died...*

But the voices of the book were not the only ones he carried with him. As he spun his gears, his father's words rang too. These were clear, calm, and solid as a mountain.

Spit in the face of curses, son.

Jackson shut his eyes, dizzy. Silently, he asked his trembling heart to stand up, to make this destiny his own. He wanted to breathe. He didn't want just what the gods shoved on him; he wanted a good life to fight for, one he'd be proud of, with people he loved and memories he cherished.

Perhaps he couldn't walk away from this tapestry into which he was woven. If he was as important as they said, that would do no one any good.

But I won't live a cursed life either.

Deep in his bones, he felt the memory of home, of silence and peace. He thought of Anna's head coming to rest in the crook of his arm as it had in the night. Every fiber of his being ached for that simple thing, this show of *I am here, we are safe, and you're not alone.* He let himself imagine a time with her like it was before the Bombings, the air fresh in their lungs, just living and laughing in that impossibly beautiful world that could no longer be.

He imagined kissing her too, and felt guilty about it. Some things weren't meant to be his.

Still, he wanted that sanctuary more than any success or power. It was so small and fragile, and perhaps all of it was beyond his reach, but... if he could even just achieve the *semblance* of it all... solidarity, safety, beauty, and peace...

This was what might pull him through this grudge match between gods. Not just surviving. Living. Hoping.

He couldn't stop the war from arriving, as Atropos had said. Chosen of a god or not, he was one man. That didn't mean he couldn't anchor himself against the tide and change what was in front of him.

Make a difference, bit by bit.

Maybe that was what she was doing, too.

Maybe that was enough.

Resolved, with clarity, Jackson gathered up his bag and opened the back of the van, glancing at the caravan supply pile. He took out his ration bars and put them with the rest of the community food. *The right thing to do. What... what a hero does. We're all in this together.* Finally, he stuffed his bag tightly behind the supplies, where he decided it would stay until he spoke with Anna about their options and called Frank.

He didn't feel these people were thoughtless thieves. Not anymore. They'd defended him when he'd been unconscious, when the wolves had come. They'd earned some trust.

A break from carrying the book's weight... now and again, he knew, he would need it.

His shoulders felt lighter already. It was time to chart the road ahead.

CHAPTER FOURTEEN
The Roads Below

Anna was inwardly reviewing her day's mission when there was movement from the corner of her eye—a splash of dark hair against the faint dawn.

"Jackson! You're awake!" Her antsy feelings were all but gone. After the emotional rollercoaster of her night, her brave face was the first thing she reached for come morning—and shocked, she found she meant it. "Wanna come on a secret mission with me?"

He blinked, hollows under his eyes even darker than when she'd seen him last. Still, despite his look, there was an ease of resolve about him today. "Sure! Of course." He even gifted her a bright, warming smile, one that seemed quite genuine.

She smiled back. *We're okay.*

Jackson and Nyx were both ready and willing to follow her into danger when asked, no hesitation, just courage. She'd never had people who had her back no matter what, and it made her hands steady, stomach quivering with happiness. She couldn't totally shake the charge in the air, but... she could do this.

"There's tall, dark, and bookish." Nyx gave him a thumb's up. "Good man. We're gonna be secret scouts."

"Oh," he said. "That doesn't sound too bad."

"Secret sewer scouts."

His face became drawn. "Uh. These hides, though. They're dry-clean only."

A bark of laughter fell out of Anna's throat, surprising even her. Nyx slapped Jackson on the shoulder. "I think you and me are gonna get on just fine," she said.

"Actually," the Warlord intoned. "I require your friend of the city for a different task."

"Oh…!" Anna's mood sunk a little. "What's going on?"

The chieftain loomed, arms crossed, looking like a pensive lightning rod. "…I have questions about the Coalition's movements that only he can answer."

Jackson blinked.

Nyx shrugged. "Hey, not for nothing, but I know a bit about that kind of thing too."

The man shook his shaggy head. "One is enough. Your mission requires a powerful guard that would be difficult to predict for any soldiers left at the old camp. I need you, firebringer, to bring everyone back safely."

Anna frowned. There were clear lines of distaste in the Warlord's face, still an abject refusal to use Jackson's name. She had no doubt that he wouldn't ask this favor if it wasn't necessary. So she went up to her friend, giving him a hug. His return embrace was light, almost as if he was afraid of impeding her ability to break free. "Be careful," she whispered. "Great chance to get on everyone's good side, right?"

He nodded against her head. "We all have to prove ourselves."

She slowly pulled away. The sureness in his gaze definitely wasn't imagined. "Just don't get hurt, alright? No more spells that knock you unconscious?"

He at least had the good grace to look abashed. "You… uh…"

"Nyx."

"Oh." He bowed his head in what looked like a silent, awkward apology. "No. None of that. I won't get into any trouble that I can't get out of. I promise."

"Then… same. And when I get back, let's talk about all of that, okay?" She fidgeted. "And about where we're both going. After all of this is over."

A quizzical blink met her. "Oh! Yes. Okay." His smile turned heart-skippingly boyish, blinding white.

Anna wasn't sure if he should look all that hopeful, but still, she couldn't help but smile back. Even if the future was like a rampaging semi-truck gunning for her, she would face it head on now. That meant talking about what chances were *really* waiting for her back in New York, and how they'd even return at this point. That meant making solid plans: where she'd live, what she'd do.

It meant coming to terms with where she was needed, and what any connections could mean in the middle of that storm.

"Anyone else coming, Anna?" Nyx asked.

"Well, there's—"

A giant's shadow suddenly threw them into shade. "I am here, city friends!"

"—Shark. He's our guide."

The man in question flexed his tattoos in a dance and grinned like his face had never known any other way. "Muscle. Pathfinder. Shark got you. This is a hard job, but for us? I think we can do it. Small group! Smart group." The big man punched his knuckles together. "And don't worry. I know the way back to the old camp that soldiers won't see."

The Warlord loomed in the growing dawn. "Don't take any unnecessary risks." His dark-rimmed eyes seemed to bore down. "You're so much like Tiger. Ready to fight. Ready to prove. That is why the demon took him. *Do not share his fate.*"

What was left of Shark's smile deflated. "I… yes. You honor me."

"Good." With that, the Warlord turned and strode away, ostensibly done with the pep talk and ready to go cheer everyone else up too.

Jackson gave them all a little wave, then trotted after.

Anna tried to stamp down her new apprehension. It seemed that whenever they parted company, it didn't end well. But it was unrealistic to expect the world to make room for her irrational fear. *He'll be fine.* That line in her chest beat its rhythm, reassuring in its way. She would know where to find him if she needed to.

Their guide turned and made a subdued beckon to his group, adjusting a large rifle on his back. "Let's go."

"Hey, do *we* get guns?" Nyx piped in.

"I don't know how to shoot." Anna fidgeted. The last time she pointed a firearm, she'd forgotten to even turn off the safety.

Nyx cracked her neck. "I could give you a few pointers. I'm good with a pistol."

"But better with fire?" Shark prodded.

"Well…"

"Shouldn't use bullets when we don't have to. Most of our new guns were stolen last night. Come easy, go easy, yeah?" He shook his head. "But you have other things. So come on! The road below, it is long."

Without further chatter, he strutted his way through the street, coming to a stop at a manhole. It had been freed from the pavement already, just by an inch. Spreading his arms in an arc like he was greeting the sky, Shark's back extended, making an audible, satisfying pop. His huge biceps coiled as he kneeled and gripped the steel disc. The manhole scraped aside with a grunt of exertion.

There was a dank, musty gust from down below, right up into their noses. Anna knew it logically couldn't be any worse down there than the night before, but it seemed like it was anyway.

"You sure the air's breathable?" Nyx muttered. "I want to say the city sealed off the northern aqueducts to this Old Bronx area decades ago."

"Nah," Shark said. "Open now."

"Wait, *what?*" Nyx blinked. "Excuse me? Anyone can just walk *under* the Barrier?"

The huge man shrugged. "Ha, yeah. We blasted the old roads open to go looking for Tiger! Same ones the slaves escaped through, back in the old days! Big Shark, he is not dumb, no. Got a long look around down there."

Nyx's jaw was tightening.

But, the man was jutting his proud chest out. "Of course, you can't walk the whole way there from *here*—too many dangers. You must get closer first. Besides, we go the other way now, back to the edge of this Bronx place—to old camp, right? Maybe we find supplies soldiers didn't take. Maybe we find more survivors." He took a shuddering breath and chuckled. "Maybe they all just hid and couldn't follow, right?"

Nyx bit her lip.

Shark blinked away the worried gleam in his eyes. "Now, rules! Lots of trash here, okay? Lots of..." he rolled a hand on his wrist. "... Nasty things. Not like nice city tunnels. Forgotten." He pointed to Anna, who had to agree that, as far as abandoned mold-mazes went, things were somewhat more tolerable in inhabited New York. "You make light." He pointed at Nyx. "No fires. Do anything except fires. I won't even use my gun down here."

Nyx pursed her lips even tighter. "There's gas, isn't there?"

"Yeah, poison air." Shark shrugged. "Why no one lives beneath streets. And we don't stay long. Every now and again, we go up, we let fresh air in. You start feeling dizzy, dumb in the head, you let me know. Right away. Don't want to pass out into muck, yeah?"

"It's not so bad," Anna supplied. "You kinda... almost get used to it after a little while? Sort of."

"Yeah, yeah! And I have done this many times." Shark patted a meaty hand to his chest then gave Anna and Nyx a thumb's up. He sprung lightly into the pit, grabbing the ladder and descending.

"Hooray," Nyx said without enthusiasm.

"Guess me next," Anna whispered. "Being the light and all."

Fighting the urge just to hold her breath, she drew in her courage, beckoned to the glow under her skin, and forced herself down into the oppressive darkness. The rungs of the ladder were rusty and rough under her palms. The wet and stinking air wrapped around her like an unpleasant cloak she was getting tired of wearing.

Finally, her heels struck floor with an echoing click. Not a moment later, *something* whispered over her ankle, a skitter of insect life. She nearly screeched.

"Ha, yeah, it's awful down here." Shark laughed, teeth flashing in her illumination, equal parts friendly and unsettling.

Anna agreed. The stonework under her shoes was sending up squelches of wet garbage and rot. She gazed down the stilled black rivers alongside the corridor. How deep those streams ran, she couldn't tell. Something slimy and long and *alive* broke the water's surface, then fell away again into silence.

"Not a lot of mutants find their way here at least," Shark growled, seemingly reading her distress. "Except the big rats."

Anna hesitated, taking only shallow breaths while plugging her nose. "I thought big rats were normal New York stuff."

"No way, rats don't get this big without being skin-sick. I don't believe it."

The echoing clicks of shoes on ladder rungs let Anna know Nyx was on her way, too. "Oh gods, it smells like Hades," the other woman gasped.

"Good thing I didn't see rain in the sky," Shark mused. "Rain for an hour, whole place floods. Already gonna have to walk through some water if it's this high."

He wasn't wrong, and it was a poor note on which to begin their merry excursion. But, onwards they trudged.

At first, they were silent. It was easier that way, not needing to breathe so much. Anna kept just a step ahead of Shark, already accustomed to interpreting his grunts as indications of which way she needed to turn. Just as he'd been in the tunnels under New York, the man was an unerring pathfinder—it was clear from his complete lack of hesitation that he had a solid mental map of this place.

How many times have you been down here? It seemed like an awful hobby.

"You ever get lost?" Anna wondered aloud.

"Nah," Shark said. "Never. Is what I do best. Which is why you stay close."

Anna peered down the labyrinth. His words seemed to echo back like a threat.

"If we did get lost, it's not like we wouldn't be covered," Nyx chirped. "I've got my locator magic. Like how I found you last night." She reached into her pocket, taking out what looked like a flat stone and a grimy, bent paperclip. Balanced all together, it was quite the trash compass. "Ta-da."

"Uh," Anna said.

Nyx grumbled. "I know, I know, but I swear it works."

"Really…?" Anna kind of wanted to see these garbage-spells.

"Yeah! 'Like finds like' stuff. It sniffs out someone's essence, their *soul*, I guess you could call it. On my end, I just need a true name, maybe some item."

"Wait… you only need a name to find…?"

"You bet. It's why most mages don't give out their real ones left and right."

"Oh… okay… wait." Anna thought. "What about *Nyx?*"

The woman gave a mysterious smile. "That's what everyone calls me!"

Startled, Anna wasn't sure how to assimilate that she didn't know the real name of someone she was trusting with her life. It didn't change anything, and yet, it was *weird.* "Did you pick that?"

"Yeah… I wanted to get control of my fire. Nyx means night. Put that light out, you know?"

"Ah!" Anna forced a bright laugh, wringing her hands. "Can I be Nuclear Girl?"

"What? No. That is *not* a proper magic name."

"The Fabulous Flying Woman?"

"I don't think you're taking the conventions seriously."

Anna paused, feeling rather serious indeed, jokes or not. "So what if the Archmage tried using that to find me?"

Nyx stopped walking. So did the rest of the group. Shark threw his hands up in the air. "What is it?" he grumbled.

"Uh. Well, I warded myself, but…" Nyx paused. "Shit, I assumed Jackson would know how to ward… he doesn't, does he?"

"I don't even know what you're all talking about, but it's wasting the good air." Shark was twitching his thumbs, clearly irritated. "I'm gonna check where we are, yeah?"

With that, he sprung for a nearby ladder. Soon, there was a scraping of metal on stone. A tiny arc of sunlight bloomed down to their pit. It almost made Anna's whole body shudder. She breathed it in and desperately wanted to be the one to check the surface next.

Finally, there was more metallic grinding, and the sun was gone. Anna hugged herself. Shark skipped down. "Nothing up there yet. Silent. We are getting closer. Probably, we go up again soon, take the surface for another hour. Then back down here. Journey will be… maybe until sun is in highest place. We should be back before dark." He sighed like he was teasing, the irritated hostility from earlier bleeding out of his tone. "Lots of time to use up the good air talking about your *magic* and stuff I don't understand, yeah?"

Nyx's jaw looked a little tense. "Yeah… about you, Shark. And your people. I'm kind of surprised you're all just totally okay with *magic*. The Warlord even told me—just walked right up and said it!— to be mindful of where I cast fires. Everywhere else I've been… well, no one even *knows* about us, by design. So why is it so different with you?"

"Maybe we are just better than everyone else." Shark shrugged his big shoulders. "Yeah, that's probably it."

Anna chuckled. "Maya said there were some stories about a person like me who helped you all escape from slavery."

Shark laughed back. "Yeah! Yeah, there is. That's why, when I saw you, I knew I better stick close, because you'd help me escape New York too. Just like in the stories of our grandmamas, yeah?"

Anna's glow burned a little brighter as her heart warmed. "Aw, thanks Shark. I'd have helped either way, magic or not."

"Aye yeah. You're brave. Is what you do."

Together, they fell into a companionable quiet. The minutes rolled on, but the dark wasn't as oppressive as before. As Shark promised, at the next ladder, they all ascended. Anna stretched to the sky and breathed happily, recharging as the sun hit her skin and the dank smells fell away. This new place was a residential block of red brick, overgrown ivy, and rusting fire escapes.

They'd been underground for at least an hour. She hoped they'd be above it for that long too.

It took her almost a full minute to realize Shark was hunched and tense, eyes darting as he ushered them along the road.

"Is something wrong?" she asked in a hush. Nyx's stare snapped with interest to the question.

"Is very quiet," he whispered back.

Anna blinked. The wastes at rest generally seemed quiet. After all, this was a world emptied of so many cars and people, except in the safe Barriers. But now that he mentioned it… this was the slimy sort of silence she'd felt earlier when she'd been looking off into the dark. It was the kind where something was waiting, looking back. There wasn't even any birdsong.

She hunched her shoulders too, moving lower around a crumbled wall.

And then she saw them.

A hundred of them: wild dogs.

They were trotting down the road, coming their way. Grass tore up under their worn claws. Drool fell from their jowls.

Shark looked as if he wasn't even allowing his chest to rise and fall as he breathed. His hands eased towards the rifle on his back.

But the score of mangled, twisted canines, growling, nervous, trotted past them all. Only a few raised their heads. They snorted and smelled, and their shining eyes met the band of humans, flickering gems of blue and brown. Their lips curled and teeth bared. But they did not break their ranks. They came no closer.

A hundred sets of paws trampled the weeds, continuing down the road from which Anna had just come.

And when they were gone, Shark wheezed, "What the…?"

"That was spooky," Nyx laughed, nerves lancing her flippant tone.

Anna shuddered. Those dogs, looking hungry, looking *mean*, had been walking like a platoon with marching orders. She didn't believe in omens, but…

And even though they were gone, her adrenaline was spiking, winding tighter and tighter. Soon, she was fighting to keep her breathing controlled. It was like she couldn't get enough air, like someone had thrown a suffocating bag over her head.

"Easy." Nyx reached out, squeezed her forearm.

Anna nodded, but there was a feeling in her chest, and it was insistent. *Something's wrong,* it suddenly sang. It twisted her head back towards the camp. It constricted around her entire ribcage. *Something's wrong.*

She fought it down. She wasn't going to let feral dogs send her into an anxiety attack. The people at the camp, they had guns. They could handle the canines if they got out of control.

She shivered again, violently.

"We have to keep moving," Shark reminded, echoing her logic. "We have a job. Our people will be okay. And those wolves… they don't mess with the Warlord, eh?" He swallowed. "Usually."

Slowly, he coaxed Anna and Nyx on, even as Anna's heart refused to slow. *Something's wrong.* She put one foot in front of the other regardless, knowing she was needed.

"So how long have those things been following you?" Nyx finally whispered after twenty minutes distanced their group from the pack. "I've been outside the city on a bunch on missions, and I've never seen anything like that."

Shark winced. He made an uneasy chuckle. "Long time. Warlord, he says not to worry. He used to go out and feed some of them. But… I think there's now more than he can feed."

"He *fed* them?" Anna recoiled in surprise.

"Hasn't for a while," Shark muttered. "Not enough meat. But they stayed."

"Maybe he thought he could tame them," Nyx whispered. "Protection."

Shark shook his head vehemently. "They are too far gone. *Not good dogs.* I don't know why he still tells us not to shoot them."

Anna blinked. Shark *had* said he couldn't kill them, but she'd thought he meant they were too fast or something. He had orders…?

But before she could ask, another sound came down the street, a clatter of gravel around a bend—and a catch of a voice.

Shark signaled they follow. He ducked behind an old overturned Jeep. Nyx fell to her belly and crawled out of sight like she'd been trained. Anna, impressed, went low too.

After she settled, she peeked around the Jeep's edge. What she saw eased her thumping heart. Down the road, two people were walking—a man and woman. Both had a ring of healing skin around their necks. These were two former slaves, ones she'd helped to free.

Shark breathed a relieved sigh and cautiously waved from behind the Jeep. His hands made a three-finger salute to the sky.

The two stopped walking. They stared.

"Friend!" Shark said, clarion voice carrying in the silence. "You remember Shark? Helped you yesterday!"

Anna noticed the two were bearing handguns, but in an awkward way that showed just how unfamiliar the weights were. Slowly, the pistols lowered. They whispered between themselves.

"Friend," one of them finally managed back in a wary, parched croak.

Shark cautiously left cover, arms spread like he was embracing them from afar. Anna rose and followed, and Nyx slowly after. The former slave woman pointed at them excitedly. "You!" She said. "You're the glow-witch! The healer!"

Something inside Anna groaned. Glow-witch. Of all the nicknames that had to stick, it was *that* one.

"Help my friend!" the woman said, pleading in her eyes.

Anna's stare focused. The man's left arm was running red with blood both old and new. He looked at her in a daze. She sprung into action, dashing past Shark, taking stock of the problem. It was a bullet wound, a bad one. The shot had passed through his bicep. What was left behind was shredded and broken.

She settled, bringing her hands up, reaching inside herself for that familiar healing light.

"Did you find who led the Coalition to your camp?" the man hissed as his skin started to knit.

Shark made a confused, troubled grunt. "Led? No one led the soldiers. Just bad luck."

"Not what they said." The man grimaced. The blood was starting to stop.

Shark stiffened. "What?"

Anna tried not to be distracted as the shattered bits of bone creaked back to their rightful place under her fingers. Weariness welled up inside her core. The former slave woman's eyes were dark and sad as she placed a grateful hand on her shoulder.

But Anna knew she couldn't give any more, so she tore her hands away. Under them, the man's skin was mottled and red, twisted and scarred. "I…" She blinked, spots in her eyes, dizzy. "I, if you come with us, maybe I can do more when I rest…"

"Thank you," the man breathed, surprised. "Thank you so much. I didn't believe it when she said you could…"

Anna nodded, heart and head light.

The woman fidgeted. "Was a stray shot. They didn't catch us. We hid when they… I'm sorry, we couldn't help, and there were so many soldiers, rounding everyone up, and…"

"It's okay," Anna managed.

The woman's eyes were wet. "It's not. You freed us, and we couldn't help you. But… we did hear the soldiers talking. Mike and I, when they moved on, we started running, hoping to find a way back to the city if we couldn't find someone to help. I… I think we're the only ones that made it out."

"Who *led* the soldiers to us?" Shark's quiet growl raised the hairs on Anna's neck.

"I don't know," the woman continued. "I guess the Coalition was supposed to meet them at the camp. Called them a *sleeper* agent? But they couldn't find the person, and they were *really* mad about it. They didn't say a name. I'm sorry. I'm so sorry. Your people, the ones that got caught, the soldiers said they were taking them up north. They're long gone. They had these huge transport trucks—"

Shark's vocal cords vibrated, low and threatening. "…North?"

"Yeah. They were screaming over those speakers about how *lucky* we were that they just didn't shoot all of us. Said there was land they'd captured that needed people to work it. Farming or something, to send crops to the dome."

"What they said was that 'the work program would sort all us bandits out'," the man named Mike whispered. "There were already other people in those transports they'd picked up, too. Mean-looking guys. Maybe Foxhole scouts."

Shark's eyes drifted far away, unseeing.

Anna's hand drifted to her mouth, almost as if it could block her gasp of realization, stuff it back into that black pit in her stomach.

"They took my people to be *slaves* in the *north*." Shark's voice cracked, fists shaking with white-knuckled fury. The man and woman winced away. He seemed as if he barely noticed. "*The Coalition took them to their own stolen land to be slaves.* And they took you all too? To be slaves *again?!*" A small trickle of blood dripped from his clenched palms.

"Shark..." Anna whispered, reaching out to touch his shoulder.

He spun. His eyes were jagged diamonds of fury. "Whoever did this, whatever traitor brought them to us, I will *kill* them!"

Anna's heart hammered. *Something's wrong. Wrong!* it kept chanting, and it was getting louder.

"No one else made it out?" Nyx asked, voice strained. She too was sorrow-eyed and scowling.

"No." Both the man and woman shook their head with finality, the woman continuing to answer. "The soldiers were taking everything else that wasn't nailed down too, or burning whatever they didn't want. Even your seed crates. It's all gone."

Shark made a keening noise in his throat. He looked to the heavens.

"There's more of us down the road," Anna said, vision flickering a little. "Come back with us."

But the pair hesitated. They looked to each other. "Whoever you are, thank you," the woman said. "But... I think Mike and I just want to get home. Your people, well, they helped us so much, but they're..."

The look in her eyes, it seemed to utter the word *cursed*, even if her mouth wouldn't be so rude.

Anna nodded, understanding. "Stay safe, okay? Get a doctor for that arm?" The two began to pass, gazes full of sympathy and worry.

Then they were gone, rifles bobbing in their grips.

Shark was quiet, watching the clouds, tears running down the sides of his face.

Anna's gaze flickered in and out again. "We need to go back," she whispered. "There's nothing left for us ahead."

Yes, her heart hammered. *Please, we need to go back. Something's wrong.*

Nyx covered her face with her hands, then suddenly swore, loudly, vehemently. She breathed, collected herself, and then let her hands fall. Her voice dropped to a whisper. "I think we better give him a minute," she said. "It's gonna take us a least an hour to walk back, and…"

Anna's vision flickered black again. She fell to her knees.

"Hey…!" Nyx called.

Anna didn't see her. For just a moment, indeed, Nyx wasn't there at all. Anna looked up, heart in her throat. Her hands were suddenly pinioned behind her back. Black smoke filled the air.

She was struck with the utter certainty that she was about to die.

Her ears popped, her head tilting. There was the blank sky, Nyx, and Shark, none of what she'd just seen.

Her chest pounded with the insistence of *wrongness*.

It was *that* line that was pulsing, she suddenly knew. It was her connection to Jackson.

"We have to get back to the vans *now*," she said, shaking. "Now." She struggled to her feet. "If there's a traitor, the vans are a target!"

"Anna…?" Nyx was biting her lip.

"I can't explain it." Anna tasted bile. "I can't, and I know I probably sound crazy, but I just, I saw something, and maybe it's a magic thing, *I don't know, but we need to get back.*"

Nyx caught ahold of her shoulders. To Anna's surprise, in her eyes, there was no disbelief. "Are you sure? Absolutely, one-hundred-percent?"

She quavered, feeling her heart squeeze. "Yes," she whispered, shutting her eyes. "Yes…"

"Okay, well, this will take me a minute, but there's something I can do." Her friend settled on the road's shoulder where they'd been standing. She pulled a sharp, wrapped bit of metal from her belt, held it over her palm, and lit a flame, burning the pseudo-knife hot.

"How can I help?" Anna sank beside her, face in her hands, dizzy.

"Just get Shark and sit in front of me with him. We're gonna try a teleport."

"Okay." Just days ago, Anna had been desperately trying to grasp a world in which teleporting could happen to her, but right now, she'd happily just go with it.

And yet, Nyx seemed very serious—worried.

Nonetheless, Anna took Shark by the shoulder. He didn't respond.

"Hey," she whispered.

Nothing. His glassed eyes watched his feet.

"Shark," she tried again. "We're going back. We need to tell your people what happened. There's nothing left here. I think there's something wrong back at the vans. We gotta help them, okay?"

Finally, the man took a long intake of breath, and managed one word: "How...?"

"Nyx has got it. Going to do a magic thing. You're going to need to stay really still, alright?"

Stone-faced, he didn't move so much as let her guide him to the designated spot. There, he proceeded to stare at some middle-distance, the wheels of his mind looking like they were turning. Anna didn't offer condolences or cheap platitudes. Nothing was making this right, she knew. There weren't even the dead to sing for and let go—just the living, people he loved, consigned again to an awful fate. So she kneeled before Nyx, keeping quiet, watching.

Nyx had drawn a circle around herself with a stick. The sharp metal in her hand was glowing red-hot, though it was cooling as her eyes fluttered. She began rocking back and forth. Strange, rasping syllables poured from her lips. Then, her eyes opened again. "Air to the north," she said, puffing a breath between her lips, sending Anna's hair lifting past her cheeks. "Fire to the east." She tapped the earth just outside her drawn circle, and there, a tiny flame lit. "Earth to the south." She reached behind, bunched up the dust into a mound. "Water to the west." Finally, she labored to spit to her left, a difficult, dehydrated gesture. "Anna? Shark?"

Anna's head perked up.

"Again, you have to stay totally still unless I say otherwise, *no matter what*. If literally a single thing goes wrong here, you both could get *very hurt*. I don't have margin for error. This is emergency-only magic shit—especially when it's not in a person's domain. Like for me. Okay? It's gonna cost me. Like with your healing."

Nodding, Anna tried to understand. When Huxley had kidnapped her, taken her to the Order, there was no ritual like this, no warnings of danger. It certainly had been unpleasant, but…

"Whatever's going on when we get there," Nyx warned, "I'm probably not going to be able to help much. So, like, I don't know, drag me behind cover or something and bind any wounds that get too bad."

Now Anna started to fret, but the pull in her chest was stronger, more distressing by far. "Thank you. I promise we will."

Without any more preamble, Nyx lifted the cooled pseudo-knife. "I hate this part." And she drew it across her wrist. "Argh!" She cursed and winced, the blood pooling in a rapid well. Dabbing her fingers in it, she started to trace strange squiggles up her arms and on her cheeks. The words that must have been the Language flowed from her lips. The air started to tingle. Anna's ears popped. Her vision blurred, the depth of the world going flat. She barely forced herself to remain unmoving. "Frick! Frick! *Frick!*" Nyx was hissing, almost like it was part of her chant, taking the knife across each of her palms. More red started to flow. "Hands! Give hands!"

Anna thrust her arm into Nyx's circle, all of her hairs standing on end. When Shark didn't move, she grabbed his arm and did it for him. Electricity crackled up her skin. Nyx's eyes rolled back in her head, and she grasped them both, blood smearing their grips. The world went hollow and dark. The breath burst from Anna's lungs. What felt like a suffocating rubber tube squeezed her through a void. Stars exploded in her eyes.

Then suddenly, she could breathe again. The sun was shining.

The dust in the air was different in her nose. The world was eerily silent. To her left was a crumpled and dusty shell of a Mazda, and to the right was one of the clan's cargo vans, doors open, crates empty, unguarded.

A pyre of black smoke was billowing a column into the sky, not that far off, behind several buildings.

She fought herself up. Nyx was at her feet, eyes rolled up in her head, convulsing. Shark was on his back, blinking rapidly, coming out of his stupor. "What...?" he whispered.

"We're back," Anna said. She kneeled, grasped Nyx's sliced hands and wrist, and willed the wounds to close. Then she lifted her friend, fireman-carried her to the van, and propped her against the seat.

Nyx lolled her head at this final contact, blinking. "I'm awake..." It sounded like she was convincing herself more than anyone else.

Anna's heart rattled. The line in her chest was frantic and squirming.

"I have to go," she said. Nyx nodded weakly.

And suddenly, Anna's heart stopped entirely.

A man's scream pierced the air, long, in agony.

She knew whose it was from the way it punched her in the chest, didn't need any explanation. She took off running. Shark's heavy feet started to follow in her ears.

She was faster.

CHAPTER FIFTEEN
Highwayman

The Warlord was a grim companion. But Jackson didn't waver away.

Perhaps it was his lack of sleep or his new resolve in the face of looming omens. Perhaps it was Anna's parting, affectionate words. All the same, he was content to put one foot in front of the next, not needing to fill the silence with small talk. Chatting was a tool to make agitated parties think him charming, and here, that was pointless.

Just have to let my actions speak for me instead.

The space near the vans was bursting with activity. Supply crates were being opened and examined. Jackson craned his neck—Anna seemed to be right. He wasn't seeing a lot of food, though one or two people were eating the ration bars he'd donated. They seemed glad for them. He smiled.

More often than not in these crates, there were scores of wrapped orange bricks printed with symbols he couldn't determine. Maybe... soil nutrients?

After everything, did they still cling so firmly to a way of life they might never find again?

"You have dreams," the Warlord rumbled.

Jackson snapped his head away. "...Doesn't everybody?"

"You have ones that wake you in the night screaming. So tell me. Do you see wolves?"

Stopping in his tracks, Jackson stared. "Yes."

The Warlord's gaze was inscrutable. "And do you see what is to come?"

In his stomach, Jackson was roiling with indecision, caught off-guard. "Once or twice. You—you see things too, right?"

He received a stoic, simple, "Yes."

The chieftain kept walking, saying nothing more. Jackson scurried after, baffled, wondering why such an utterly groundbreaking commonality was being treated like discussing the weather. "Has it always happened to you? Do you have magic? Did Tiger?"

"No." The Warlord turned past the van with the Dovetail crest, padding down an empty street. It seemed he would speak in his own time. Jackson fell silent, though inside, he was bursting.

Together, they reached a tree line. Green overtook Jackson's jarred senses: pines, maples, elms, and crackling brush. Freestanding, ruined homes peeked between these trees, big wealthy ones of old that nature had consumed. Their silent roofs were washed with moss and thick leaf blankets. The sound of rushing water sang through the air, hidden somewhere nearby.

Before them, there was another street. It was wide and well-paved... relatively speaking. In fact, it seemed like a main transit. Jackson smiled in sudden recognition. Despite all the loops and bends in the night, he finally saw the familiar: this was the road that ran by the Bronx River. So *that* was the water noise! It was far from the main northerly thoroughfare, but for that very reason, it was a good route for those seeking less attention. His own trucks traveled these lanes now and again.

Sudden movement came from the left—Jackson whipped his head. There was a flash of tawny tail dashing into a grove.

Dogs are still following.

He shuddered, uneasy. The Warlord was stopping just a few meters away, and he hurried to catch up.

Together, they stood, listening to the wind in the leaves, watching the ancient asphalt. One of the Warlord's people was also at the side of this highway, not far off, digging at something with a shovel.

A straight shot to the south, Jackson realized, was Checkpoint E on the Barrier's edge.

His head turned, and there it was, that blue, shimmering rise. It was a lot closer than it had been.

This was a relief, to finally have his bearings. Frank would need that. And if worst came to worst, he might just be able to ignore his blistering feet, convince Anna, and walk to the checkpoint, maybe use his connections to weasel back in without papers. He might pay them to turn a blind eye to her too.

If a wayward patrol fell on this group again, a backup plan was crucial, even if it was dangerous.

The Warlord was settling on the ground. "This is where *my* dreams took me," he said. He waved an arm up and down the stretch. "Where the traders come and go, where the sign counts to three, after my shelter is consumed with fire. Here, where the river sings, where the trees remind me of home. This is where and when I was told to be." He smiled. "It's why we came, why we suffered for so long in this wasted hole. See? Even though we lost so many… we always make it."

His palm scooped up a bit of soil, turning it over and over, as if discerning qualities to it Jackson couldn't hope to fathom. Mulling over those words, Jackson stared down the skull's nose, following his gaze. There indeed was an ancient, repainted signpost. *Checkpoint E: 3 miles*, it said. "Is that what that person's digging for? For what you saw in your dream?" He settled down, pointing to the lone person on the road's shoulder.

"No. That is our offering to all that brought us here. Our thanks."

The woman examined her work, then drew something from her

bag. She placed and nestled it with the care of a new seedling. *One of those bricks?* After patting it gently, like a wish for it to grow strong, she began to fill in the hole.

The Warlord shifted his raw stare to his companion. "The soil is good. Good things are on the way for us. The dreams told me so—they are my gift, even if I listened too late to save what I loved."

In the distance, one of the wild dogs began to howl. It sent a prickling shiver up Jackson's spine.

"Are your gifts like mine?" the Warlord whispered, ignoring it. "Do you see him too?"

Jackson rubbed down his goosebumps. "I think if you're asking, you know I do. Us meeting like this... once I talked to someone who would call it destiny."

Slowly, the Warlord reached up, removing his crown. When it came free, it was as if it lifted away an entire cloak of anger, responsibility, and near-divinity from his shoulders. For a moment, he almost put it to the ground. But then he yanked it back, shuddering, holding it to his chest. The antlers circled around his head like an embrace.

And Jackson saw for the first time that he was *old*. His hair was washed with gray, his face lined with regrets. His spine curled into an exhausted slump. Gently, he pressed his lips to the bullet hole in the skull's brow. Then, he reached into his belt, taking up a wooden charm there—Jackson stiffened as he saw the little carved tiger that had once been at the memorial shrine.

The aged king rested his forehead on the charm and let out a great, shuddering sigh. "My name. It is Baldur."

"You carry your son with you," Jackson tried. The man's gaze softened a fraction. "Sometimes, I dreamed of him, before we met."

"I will always carry him." Sorrow laced the whisper. "He made me strong. He knew I would make it. And I did. We all did. For him."

Jackson remembered the gladiator's final statement of loathing, the only words he'd ever heard him speak: "*Will not die. Not to YOU.*"

He wondered if Tiger dreamed every night in captivity too… perhaps of his people. Maybe he'd prayed for their safety. Maybe he'd killed his opponents only for the chance to get free and find home again.

"I did everything I could." The Warlord's gaze shone with pain. "But I could not save him. He was the strongest of us, the fiercest—one day, if our road was different, he would have been a better leader than me. But when something bigger calls you… you must answer. For it, my wife lost her life. For it, I lost our son."

Jackson nodded numbly, feeling almost as if Inoki's words were choking him. "You needed to become something more than you were." *And what you were before couldn't matter.*

"The man in my dreams, he did not offer me what I wanted." A grief-wracked sob touched the Warlord's words. He sucked it in, held it in his chest. "That's not what they do. They give you what you *need*. We've all come to see our suffering means something greater. Tiger understood. If Tiger hadn't met you, perhaps Shark might not be here now. Perhaps we would have been too weak to go on without your friend's healing ways. The demon in red would still be out there, would kill us all for daring to get this close to his city." He paused. "Tiger, if his ghost is watching, would know he saved us in ways he couldn't have seen. What of you, city man? How did your people raise you? Did they make you loyal like him? Did they make you strong?"

Jackson wasn't sure what to say. "Just my father. And he's gone now."

"It is bad for sons to lose their fathers. It is worse the other way around."

Jackson bowed his head.

"So tell me: if you were given a choice to make his ghost proud, would you?"

"Yes. In a heartbeat."

"And what if…" the old man named Baldur sighed. "What if you could bring life and happiness from that death, as my people celebrate every year, sowing seeds to spite our enemies?"

Jackson blinked.

The Warlord stared. "Maybe you would give everything you are for that."

Unsure, Jackson nodded back.

The digger was walking away from the road, shovel over her shoulder. She bowed to her leader, then kept going.

"She and her friends, they dug our offerings all night," the chieftain sighed. "I can ask nothing more. I am so proud of my people, all looking death in the eye, always fighting."

"I'm sorry. I can't begin to imagine what you've been through. But..."

A silencing hand rose. "No. You cannot. But we have chosen our road. Both of us. Yes?"

Jackson tipped his head in agreement.

"Then onward. To our fates. Here, we wait for them." Baldur creaked his heavy shoulders, wincing as he lifted his crown, as if it were a great burden. The moment it touched his hair, his face fell neutral. He was powerful. He was still.

In the shade, it was as if the dark hollows of the deer's eyes had spread to his own.

"What are we waiting for?" Jackson hazarded.

"For the ones that would have killed us all in our sleep and told the world it was because they were righteous."

"Are you..." Jackson darted his eyes up and down the road. "Are you hunting Coalition supply trucks?"

"Mmm," the Warlord acknowledged. "Who knows what comes?"

"Sir," Jackson tried, sensing the situation shifting underfoot. "Am I meant to help attack *shipping* trucks here?"

Silent shoulders shrugged. Those eyes only stared keenly far down the street, away from the dome.

The remaining moisture in Jackson's mouth dried up, his hands starting to shake with adrenaline.

The solemn king barely even moved to breathe. "Are you scared? Do we disgust you?"

"No!" Jackson thought back to the hungry eyes, to the loss and desperation. "I… it's just…"

"You do not like stealing from… *your* people."

Jackson weighed his words. What if the next courier they saw bore the symbol of the dove…?

The Warlord waved a dismissive hand. "If you're still loyal to the Coalition, speak your truth. Get it over with."

"I've *never* been loyal to the Coalition. But it's not black and white like that. There could be people I care about on this road."

"Not loyal, you say?" That grim mouth twisted into something strange, fraught. It was as if someone entirely new was sitting there now. His dark eyes glimmered like a hunter's in the dark. "Then why do I hear you left the camp *just* before the soldiers attacked us, hmmm? And why did they find us the very day you arrived?"

Jackson balked. Blindsided, he hesitated, and he knew it was just a second too long. Uncertainty and bile rose in his throat. "I did leave the camp," he said. "But I haven't been in contact with anyone. I was on a walk."

"Maybe the man in my dreams, he says something different."

The familiar hum of tires on asphalt suddenly cut through the quiet morning. Jackson was keeping one eye to the chieftain, but he saw what was coming around the faraway bend nonetheless. It nearly stopped his heart a second time.

This was no mail courier.

No Foxhole slaver.

Nothing simple like that.

It was a procession. Ten Coalition-stamped combat rovers were coming this way, forming a ring, taking up every lane on this tree-lined path. At their center was an armored truck.

A grim smile was emerging from the king's accusing sneer.

"I'm not working against you," Jackson said, shaking, wanting to flee far into the trees. "We need to hide!"

The guns in the rovers pointed in every direction. It could have held a minimum of twenty-something agents and soldiers, probably many more.

The Warlord didn't even twitch. "No. I want you here, man of the city. Do not run. There's a gun sighted at the back of your head."

Jackson fell very, very still.

The procession was gaining ground.

The Warlord chuckled. "Again, he's sent what I needed. He expects me to pay the cost. So we will."

"Are you going to *attack* that…? That's suicide!"

The man snorted. "It's never *easy*. We took down a truck once before, too—paid for it with ten lives. And it didn't even have food." He leaned in, voice taut and angry. "But it was going where I lived when I was a boy. Before they made it a mine." The dark, fierce look burned. "And do you know how they *mine*, city man?"

He reached in his pouch. From it, he pulled a simple box. On that box was a little antenna, a dangerous red button.

Jackson's chest seized. Orange-wrapped blocks…!

The Coalition caravan, mighty and unstoppable, was rolling inexorably over where the woman had dug.

"I want you to know," the Warlord said, "just what I intend to do to you all."

He pressed the button.

The road detonated for two hundred feet, all the way up and back. A horrific screeching and roaring blew out the world. Jackson fell back, feeling the concussive wave even from this distance. Choking dust billowed out and up. The gunshot cracks of splintering tree trunks wracked the air. Tall pines toppled, fell.

A tire rolled by the Warlord's still form, smacking into a tree. He rose like it was his sign, this titan of anger and loss, the dark hollows of the skull staring down his quarry. Tired, dirty feet were emerging from the tree line now, guns and hollow eyes coming from the groves.

With them were dogs, a legion: dozens of half-starved and wild mongrels running *alongside* them, eyes lolling, spit flying in their hunger.

None of these people paused as if this was strange. Their gazes were filled with vengeful energy, a unity of purpose. The packdogs' hunger, their rage: it was their own, too.

"It is time for war," their leader whispered.

His expressive single hand rose, pointing to the thick black center of smokey carnage. Somewhere at its heart, soldiers were screaming.

Then, he made a separate signal, pointing to his side. Jackson shook off his disorientation, tried springing to his feet, but a thick, sharp cord around his neck took his breath. Hands grabbed him from behind. A bag fell over his head, and he lashed out, but his wrists were seized too, a finger almost broken. He was forced roughly to the ground, nearly knocking out his teeth. It took him only a half-second to be bound.

Too late, too slow, he truly understood his book's warning.

⁂

Anna's feet were a blur. She wheezed and gasped.

Nyx hadn't followed, but Shark had. He kept reaching out, trying to grab her, making protesting noises. On instinct, Anna wove out of the way and ran harder.

Sometimes, her feet left the ground far longer than they should have.

Her chest felt like it was going to burst. She wasn't fast enough. They'd come so far, but where was…? She couldn't… couldn't *run* all this way…!

The fear sapped deep into her heart.

Going to die, it said. There was sadness and regret, betrayal and impotent anger. None of it was hers.

Faster! Have to…!

Her feet left the ground again, and this time, they didn't come back down.

Jackson was dragged backwards over brush, rocks, and concrete. His back and sides were rubbed raw. He tried feeling out cool darkness to trip his captors, to tear the blinding bag from his head. Sometimes, he felt a whisper of shadow, heard a stumble or a curse, but he couldn't do more. He needed his fingertips to touch and feel his magic, and he couldn't move…!

He lost track of how many times he involuntarily cried out in pain, but no one cared.

At the end of the trip, he was braced against a cold wall. It soothed his burning skin.

For a long time, he simply waited. The slightest motion earned him a piercing kick to the ribs. He decided it was best not to move.

Under his blinds, his eyelids fluttered in concentration.

Minutes crept by. He could sense a bright afternoon on his arms. Perhaps a thin shadow lay here or there, but too weak, too *little*. The Warlord clearly had some idea of what his weapon of choice was.

Dreams. Probably those gods-damned dreams told him.

Jackson was starting to get the sense the Fear was a lot more direct with his instructions than Inoki.

Sometimes, he caught the sound of breathing, or hard, stolen boots rapping asphalt. Muted voices. There were at least three people guarding him.

The line in his chest pulsed. Anna was far, far away from here, wasn't she?

Good. He prayed they wouldn't turn on her too. After all, he was the one that represented everything they hated.

Blood and vengeance. The Warlord never wanted Frank's credits. I'm just his sacrificial sheep to bless their battles.

Perhaps the man had planned this from the day they met. Maybe he'd only bothered pretending to be a gracious host this long so as to get something out of it. Anna's help, perhaps?

Jackson wasn't even sure if he hated them all for it. He wanted to, *deeply*. But he just couldn't.

All the same, he bided his time, coiled and ready to get free. Minutes passed. Perhaps an hour. Then he began to hear more voices. A *lot* more.

Someone grabbed his shoulders, undid the cord around his neck. The sack lifted. His eyes were dazzled in the light.

Before him stood the king, antlers high. His eyes were viciously unforgiving and victorious, no more restraint remaining. An ancient bistro lay to Jackson's back, an old walking mall to his front. The Coalition-owned wreckage was nowhere in sight.

Behind the king, there was his crowd. In their stares was accusation and blazing white-eyed rage. What had he told them? Had he even needed to give them a good reason to bring him up for execution?

"I didn't sell you out," Jackson rasped.

This didn't seem to make any difference. A strange electricity was coiled in the air, like it was binding the crowd together. It clouded over their kindness, their reservation. In it, they seemed to seethe as one, a great mass of fury. Though they were hungry, were flagging, all they seemed to need was a little push to topple worlds.

Maybe they thought the story of his betrayal was true, and maybe they didn't.

But he'd have a difficult time getting them to *care*.

At the edges, dogs prowled. Blood stained their teeth already. Their starved eyes begged for more.

His executioner held out his good hand. A guard came forward, passed over a sharpened wooden pole—it seemed they wouldn't deign to waste bullets on this.

Jackson struggled against his bonds. The weak shadows flickered in the sun. "Wait," he said. "If you do something to me, what do you think Anna will do about healing all of you?" He wished he had any excuse better than that, but he would stall with what he had. "She's my friend. She won't help you if you do anything to me."

The Warlord blinked. He loomed. "She will not return from her work until nightfall. And she'll look upon your broken body, hear it is the Coalition's fault—because it is, in the end. Perhaps she will cry. Perhaps she will want vengeance. As we all do, for all we lost."

"I didn't help the Coalition find you!" Jackson strained against the ropes, speaking more to the crowd, to fight their mob-mind and whatever strange enchantment was driving it, frantic.

The audience murmured, disbelieving.

"Shark! He vouched for me! You all trust him, don't you? I swear, I haven't—"

The spear point lightly kissed his chest, right where his scar was, right where Tiger's spear had been not so long ago. It set off an ache deep in his lungs.

"I knew the moment it happened," the Warlord said. "The day my son died, I knew."

Jackson's words, for just a moment, stuttered.

"In dreams, I saw his blood. I saw your face!" His teeth bared. "And now you betray us, even after we offer you shelter. Just like I should have known you would, man of the *city*."

"No! Tiger's death was *not* my fault!"

"Your hand was in it. We don't care if it was your *choice*. Not when your people have always thought so little of our lives."

"Your dreams, the man with wolves—he's not telling you everything. You have to believe me. I swear it. Ask me anything. Tell me how I can prove that I mean to help you!"

The crowd regarded him. A few made questioning noises. "He

knows the man with wolves?" one uttered.

The Warlord pressed his weapon forward, seething. It pierced the hide shirt and drew a trickle of blood from the throbbing scar. Jackson gagged. "Very well. I have one question you can use to prove yourself. The *one* chance you have to atone for Tiger's death. And if you lie, I will know."

The spear withdrew, was thrust into the dirt. Slowly, from his pouch, the Warlord drew a rolled paper, unfurled it at their feet. It was covered in rough, charcoal sketches—a maze littered with symbols and arrows.

"This is what we know of your city," the chieftain said as he kneeled. "This is what Shark brought us." Jackson's stomach grew colder. "If you truly want to help us, then tell me: where are the wall-makers?"

Eyes darting, Jackson looked at the map. "I don't understand."

Keen eyes considered. The weapon was drawn again. Sharpened wood tapped Jackson's neck, leaving a burning, stinging trail in its wake. He winced, trying not to move.

"Where," the Warlord tried again. "Do they make the Barrier?"

Jackson's eyes went wide. That, he more than understood. "You want to do something to the *Barrier?* Blow it up like those trucks? Storm the city?" He barely had words for it. "That's even more suicide than the caravan. Do you know how many soldiers are in the checkpoints *alone?*"

The Warlord's grin was dead. "We know." It was like Jackson had told him there would be rain tomorrow. The crowd at his back seemed unimpressed. "But let us worry about bringing life from death. We're farmers, city man. It's why we were *chosen* for this."

The words shot right into his heart. "Chosen? *Life?* If that Barrier went down, you could kill *thousands*. People that don't have anything to do with you!" Even as Jackson said it, he knew no one here had any reason to care.

And the Coalition, the city... they'd never see this coming, eyes glued to the petty dramas overseas. They'd never dream that those they thought of as rabid, disorganized animals could ever breach their walls.

No one can threaten Atlantis, a remembered boy's voice whispered in his ear.

"It won't bring your home back," Jackson tried instead. "It won't avenge anyone. You'll be dead!"

"Ah, so I suppose we could instead just rob someone else's food, find a new home," the Warlord said. He turned to his people. Then, he balanced his spear articulately against his false wrist, wiggling a few of his real fingers as if to beckon his audience closer—like an invitation to come and hear. "Right? We could steal their seeds, try to start again."

Jackson realized he'd inadvertently given the man just what he wanted.

"But the Coalition would come steal that again too!" this king declared, voice loud and guttural. "On and on!" Angry, restless grumbles of agreement answered. He raised both arms as if to lift their fury with his own. "But this way? Maybe they learn their lesson and stay busy with their own people, right?" The mob began to shift, stomp, and cry out. He answered again with a roar. "Maybe they learn not to rob and enslave and kill! Maybe a thousand, *thousand* other people get peace!" His people were screaming now, raising their fists and their rifles. Spittle flew as they replied. "And that? That would avenge my love. That would avenge my Tiger." As his audience bellowed, Jackson knew they were far beyond his arguments now, that he'd run out of ways to stall. The Warlord's eyes glistened with darkness and sorrow. "It would avenge *all* of us. That is worth fighting for. That is worth dying for!"

The spear pressed harder.

The crowd beyond leaned in, chanting now for death, thrusting their guns over and over to the sky.

The beasts of war were hungry.

Jackson swallowed, heart hammering, shaking. He couldn't die.

No matter what. Surviving was his purpose, as Inoki said.

But betray his home?

"Prove your honesty," the Warlord said. "Answer." He raised his false hand as if to ask for respectful silence from the mob behind.

"The generators," Jackson whispered. "They're on the island called Manhattan—just off Times Square. You'll never reach them. They're on the roof of one of the tallest skyscrapers in New York, in the busiest area of town, broadcasting to the sky. Which is why you'll never make it. Hundreds of soldiers would be on you far before that."

The Warlord sighed. He drew his spear back.

"I told you," he said, "Not to lie."

With that, he thrust down into Jackson's right shin. The pain was a howling, horrible, snapping wave. Jackson sensed he screamed, couldn't stop it. He barely came back to himself, seeing only red and tears. The spear was withdrawn. He was bleeding profusely, and a numbness took root. His leg was far, far away, throbbing, bursting open.

"Where," the Warlord said again, "Are the Barrier-makers?"

Jackson crumpled into himself. *How…?* He didn't see how anyone here could know what he said wasn't true… unless…

…unless the dreams had shown him something? Unless Shark had seen something?

Gods, he didn't know.

"If you lie again, it's your heart. I will finish what my son started."

The weapon hovered dangerously over its mark.

And every part of him wished his death wouldn't matter.

"There's a power station on the east side of Manhattan," Jackson whispered, defeated. "By the Wards Island Bridge. That's where." He'd driven by it so many times, taking lazy weekends up FDR Drive, putting the car he and his father had fixed through its paces. The outgoing beam in the setting sun was breathtaking.

The Warlord smiled. He drew a small chunk of charcoal from his pouch, circled a mess of lines. "On… Harlem River, yes?"

"Yes." Jackson breathed, dizzy, the treasonous words rank in his throat. But he didn't intend it to end there. If he'd bought his life with that information, that was priority one. Now it was his responsibility to stop all of this, before anyone could get hurt.

Sure. Easy enough.

How much blood am I losing?

The thought was distant, almost academic.

And his chest was throbbing painfully over his scar. The line was there, tugging. He raised his head, a strange, warm feeling in his heart, despite the pain. *...Anna...?*

He didn't have time to look for her, wonder why she might feel so close when she was so far away. "Man of the city," the Warlord was whispering. "May your spirit go in peace." He was standing tall again. In his hand, he hefted his weapon high.

"Wait! I told you what you asked!"

"Yes. And for it, I pardon you of my son's death." The chieftain sighed. "But the man in my dreams still wants you—and it would be cruel to just let you bleed out from your leg. So I offer you to him before we go. Blood and vengeance. That's all we have now. All we must give to get what we want."

The crowd murmured its assent as one.

Jackson threw himself to one side, tried to squirm out of the way, reach for what little shadows there were.

The spear drove down.

⁕⸰⊱◈⊰⸰⁕

Anna flew. She didn't think about it. Didn't question it, didn't let logic interfere. She *flew*, and that was all the reborn Anna needed to know.

Another ruin. Another van. Open crates. Orange blocks, dangerous black exclamation points.

No one was here.

Still the line pulled her onwards.

The billowing line of smoke pulsed into the sky from her left.

He wasn't that way. She could feel it. Refusing to be distracted, she flew.

Down side alleys, she wove. Sometimes, on her turns, her feet kissed the earth for a mere moment, launched her in a new direction. Her hands slapped the walls to push them away. The bricks were a blur. She'd left Shark behind blocks ago.

A sudden turn and—!

Thirty backs to her. Thirty mumbled voices in assent.

An antlered crown. A raised fist. A spear.

A bound friend, struggling for his life.

Anna dove, not thinking twice, *never* thinking twice anymore.

She managed to aim her heedless hurtle and tackle the Warlord. Lights exploded behind her eyes. He gave a startled, rasping shout. The spear went flying. She was a ball of recklessness and fear, tumbling end over end away from him now, until she hit a brick wall hard enough to knock her breath out.

Stunned, quiet, she stared at the clan of onlookers.

Blood. There was blood on the ground. Jackson was—

The Warlord stood, hissing. In his eyes, she saw rage, pain, and madness. Somehow, his crown stayed on his head, and holding his side, he advanced, stare burning into hers. "Do not interfere."

"What…?" she managed, fighting through her dizziness. "…What is going on…?"

"He betrayed us," the Warlord growled. "He told the Coalition where we were."

"No!" Anna stood, wobbly, not believing it for a second. She turned back to Jackson, ran to his side. He looked up at her with glad, fearful eyes.

"Healer Anna." A second voice: Maya. The doctor had a shotgun, and it was leveled at them both. "Do not attack my Father again."

Anna backed up. She was frightened to her core of bullets, of that shredding she knew could rip through her body and end her life in heartbeats. But she did not move out of the way.

"Anna?" Jackson whispered, sounding far away, confused. "They're… they're going to bomb the Barrier. Their dreams… they're… we have to get out of here. We have to go."

Freezing, Anna felt an even colder finger of fear up her spine.

They… were going… to *bomb*…

Oh God. I carried their crates. I carried extra *crates.*

"Healer Anna," Maya tried again. "You've done so much good for us. You freed slaves. You fought. You healed. Those slaves? Were likely Coalition prisoners thrown outside, people they didn't care about, didn't want to feed anymore. It happens all the time. The Coalition are monsters."

"You can't," Anna whispered. "Even with what you're saying, attacking all those people…" She thought of parades, parks, and butterflies, of children, hopes, and dreams. "That city, they're not just military and—"

"*They are Coalition, only alive because of what they stole from us!*" Maya spat. "Your friend is loyal to them, Anna. Loyal to *slavemakers…!* They didn't need to set fire to those buildings, chase out the poor and sick and half-starved. They didn't know why we were there. They hate us because we aren't them, and that's all they need. But we're going to make a difference. We're going to make sure no one has to suffer like us anymore. Never again. Come with us."

It was then a gasping, panting woman suddenly burst in at the clearing's edge—Nyx, up and staggering after her friend, a faint ember in her hands. "Woooah, hey," she said, falling to her rear on the pavement. Her eyes were half-delirious with exhaustion.

And Shark was already standing there, eyes wide, silent. Who knew how long he'd been listening…?

It was then Anna saw the circling dogs, too. They began to rumble and growl displeasure at the interruption. The crowd's gaze locked with theirs.

Anna lunged in the distraction, grabbing the shotgun, yanking it from Maya's grip. Staring the woman right in the eyes, making sure most of the mob turned to her now, she strained her muscles, squeezing out every last inch of fear and disgust she felt. Her light flared. The shotgun bent with a squeal.

"No," she said. "Bombing a random bunch of people isn't the answer! This won't fix *anything!*" She threw the gun to the earth.

"Then you betray us too?" The Warlord's whisper seemed far louder than a shout.

"This isn't about betraying!" Anna tried. Jackson was sagging, but nodding his head to agree. "I've helped you! I want to help you more! But it's not like it's okay to try to execute my friends and people that don't have anything to do with—"

The Warlord stepped in like lightning, behemoth arm of metal and fury slamming into her side. She stayed on her feet, but reeled back.

The spear was in his grasp, and—

"Wait!" Shark's mournful voice finally broke the air like the crack of lightning.

The Warlord stopped his second swing at Jackson. His eyes flickered, uncertain, for just a second. Anna stumbled again to stand between him and his target.

"Wait," Shark said again, softly this time. He was clutching the pouch of seeds around his neck like a talisman.

The Warlord stayed his hand. He inclined his chin, a beckon.

"What proof is there? Of what the city man did?" Shark managed, voice low and taut, like this was far more than he was able to handle. Jackson was looking up at him with all the gratitude in the world.

"I… did not want you to see this." The Warlord bowed his head. "You vouched for him. I am sorry."

"The *proof.*"

They came together. The Warlord braced his spear under his false arm, reaching his true hand to Shark's shoulder. It was a comforting grasp to the man's shuddering—like a father might to a son. Shark tapped three fingers to his throat, gazing long and hard with his dark eyes into his leader's own, asking a hundred questions without words.

Then something strange moved between them. Anna had no words for the shift. It was as if the fury settling over the scene jumped like a lightning bolt from the Warlord's fingers into Shark's frame, like a strength of purpose swallowed Shark's very soul. The entire mob was seething with the same dark energy.

The sun disappeared behind the clouds. A chilled breeze raised the hairs on her arms.

Shark's lips trembled in impotent rage and sorrow. "I do not want to lose another friend," he said. "Not when the Coalition has taken most of us as slaves."

A rippling gasp lit through the mob like tinder catching light.

Anna reached deep for her magic and strength, skittered forward and kneeled, trying to get Jackson's arm around her shoulders, trying to lift him. He was shaking and weak, biting his lip so as not to cry out as one leg just sagged, useless, streaming red. But she didn't have time to heal him, not here.

"The ones that they captured at the camp," Shark said. "They took them to work the land. *Our land.* They took them because they needed farmers to grow their food."

Shark's wild stare turned to Jackson, one sharpened tooth drawing blood on his lips. Only his leader's hand held him where he was. "So did you… did you really…? Did you know that's what they would *do?* When I treated you like someone who might be our brother? When I defended you? Gave you water? Help? Protection?"

"No—" Jackson began, eyes fluttering.

The Warlord simply reached in his pouch, pulled out a little device. Anna's eyes narrowed. It looked like a walkie-talkie with an amplifying dish fused on top. A communicator of some kind...?

"The proof. He carried this," the Warlord said, "To tell his city everything."

Anna's stomach dropped. Shark's teeth dug deeper into his lip as his fists clenched and shook.

"No," Jackson rasped. "No! It's for Frank. It's for—"

"I had your back," Shark said softly. That fierce, feral rage blazed in his gaze. It was like a switch had been thrown by the words of the man he trusted most. His voice rose to a screech. "How *could* you?" His stare was liquid fire.

He whipped out his rifle in a smooth tidal wave of motion, unstoppable, consuming.

"How *COULD* you?!"

Jackson's eyes went wide.

The shot roared.

And Jackson flew from Anna's grip, a red flash staining the wall.

"No!" she hollered, eyes stinging, diving down.

"Oh hell!" There was a flash in Nyx's hands, of embers once more sputtering to life. Shark whirled and fired again, and from how he screamed, it was clear he couldn't see his target, only that it was a threat. A second red splash kissed the air. Nyx fell back too, shouting weakly, kicking and twitching.

Shark kept screaming, spinning, leveling his gun as if to challenge anyone else, looking for something to destroy. Finally, as if by chance, he leveled at Anna.

Anna knew then that he saw a stranger, saw a friend to a traitor, saw all the ghosts he'd ever lost to a place he thought she called home.

She held her hands up to plead, cold wetness on her cheeks.

That berserker rage stuttered for one shaking, merciful moment.

"Did you..." he said, his lip quavering. "Did you know...?"

Anna could only shake her head.

"I can't be sure of her," the Warlord spoke. He was staring too, as if scrutinizing all she was, wondering if she was worth it.

"Then... then you gave me my life. And I give you yours, glow-witch." Shark growled. "It is done." He thrust the rifle into Maya's hands.

"But—" the one-eyed doctor protested.

"*No.*" He cast one long, sorrowful look at Anna. "Like the city. Like their walls. It is *done.*" And with that, he stormed away.

The Warlord's breath whistled in the still air. "Unfortunate," he said. It took Anna a moment to realize he was talking to her. "Thank you for what you have done for my people. But here is where I must break my word to you. We must leave. Our fate calls." He tossed the spear down, almost looking disappointed he didn't get to use it. "Goodbye. Sing for your dead. One day, you will make better friends."

Just like that, a cloud gathered in the crowd's eyes, their ceremony ended. A dark and seething mass, they turned, soldiers stomping through the dust, no more words, no more waiting.

Like a wolf pack with marching orders.

The dogs at the edges, they slunk back into the shadows until they too were gone.

Jackson twitched in Anna's hands. His eyes were bright with fear and pain. Red blossomed down his shirt.

Her brain went inward, like it had in the healing tent. Blood couldn't matter. Pain couldn't matter. Now it was just her and her magic.

The bullet had gone wide, perhaps in Shark's haste and fury. It wasn't dead center, and it might have missed his lungs. Her light told her the way.

"You're okay," Jackson mumbled, somehow managing to look relieved.

His blood smeared her cheek as his thumb brushed her face. "Hold still," she said. It had taken her several minutes to remove debris from Sergeant Waters's side not so long ago. But she was better at this now.

Jackson suddenly groaned and shook. Her hands flared. With an awful squelch, a metal glob forced its way up and out of his bones.

She was right, her light told her. Vital spots had been missed. If she'd been given to believing in divine intervention…

The injuries began to close once the bullet was gone. One more wound was left. One more point where…

Her light flickered. Jackson cried out in agony. Her vision stuttered black for just a moment, and the chill, it seeped up her legs into her core as it had never done. A wave of exhaustion followed.

Too much. She'd been asking too much of herself.

But she couldn't stop. His leg was oozing blood so, so fast. The bone had been shattered. She moved her hands and began again. The leg creaked. It solidified. It mended. Bone splinters melted into nothing. The torn artery, it stopped gushing.

The world was a rush of relief. But then came the chill again. Jackson lay back, gasping, eyes closed. He was no longer in danger.

She stood and wobbled over to her other fallen friend, spots in her eyes.

"Don't. Don't!" Nyx hissed.

"Shhhh," Anna whispered. "I know it hurts. Let me fix it."

"No, Anna, no… please… you're going to hurt yourself. You can't, it's just, you can't, I'm not worth it."

She tried to wriggle away, tears of pain on her cheeks, but Anna held her fast. And under her hands, she felt an almost dangerous heat. Nyx's skin was burning despite her magic being spent. A new shoulder wound now spurted blood, like an artery had been nicked. That wasn't all. Another wound had torn open in her thrashing, the thing she hadn't let Anna look at in the night, the thing she'd brought back to the camp. A whole chunk of flesh was missing near the base of her neck. It was like someone had dug it out violently with a knife.

"Don't don't don't don't," Nyx sobbed, squirming, bleeding. "I lied to you. It's my fault. It's all my fault. I'm not worth it."

To be frank, Anna didn't really care what she was talking about. She engaged all of her very, very powerful muscles and held down. *"No one else,"* she told the universe, "Is dying on me."

She filled herself up with light. It sang through her veins, told her of infection in Nyx's skin, of damage and sickness and bullets, and all of it could be fixed. The bleeding slowed. The bullets oozed free. Slowly, the fever-heat dissipated. The flesh knitted.

Anna laughed, dizzy, cold. She wasn't going to lose any of her friends ever again.

And she would find a way to fix this mess, tell Shark the truth, stop the bombs, and…

"Anna, stop!" Nyx called.

The light dwindled, emptied from her.

Then bone-deep, frigid darkness filled her up in its place.

CHAPTER SIXTEEN
Journey

Jackson was only lifting his aching head when he saw Anna go down. Nyx was dragging herself to her knees. He staggered to them both, body still flaring with pain, and he knew *exactly* what had happened, knew this was her comatose sickness all over again.

"Anna. Anna." He kneeled, cupping her face. She didn't respond.

"Dumb, stupid, dumb…!" Nyx scrambled over.

Jackson finally found Anna's breath, so soft it barely registered on his palm. Her skin was icy. Her eyes weren't even moving with dreams—she was statue still, stiff. He'd thought she'd been bad before, but now… this was like touching a dead body.

"Nyx… I…" Jackson tried.

The fire mage's mouth was a grim line. Some of her wounds still trickled blood. The bullets that had been wrenched from her flesh were at her feet. "Okay. Okay. This is… bad. Very bad. She tapped out her life force. I… I…" She shook her head, gasping, empty clouds in her eyes. "Jackson, what the *hell* was going on here? I'm not… not super present."

Jackson tried to gather himself. Nyx was shaking, looking ready to drop. "They're going to attack New York. Bombs. I carried gods-damned bombs for them in their supply crates. They're going to try and take down the Barrier."

"*What?* They… they can't. I mean, those facilities… no one gets in. They were built to survive anything."

"Yeah, I know, but… I think there's something else. They took a massive Coalition-guarded shipment on the road. I don't even *know* what was in there, what they could have stolen." Jackson shook his head, deflating, resting Anna's head on his knee. He only had the energy to figure out one crisis at a time. "How do we fix Anna? How?"

Nyx screwed up her face, biting her lip. She slammed her hand into the concrete. "The hell were you thinking?!" she yelled at Anna's unconscious face. "Trying to fix me! Trying to fix everything! Gods, you're supposed to be smart!"

"It's my fault," Jackson whispered, feeling the weak pulse of the link to her in his chest. "I should have been able to figure all of this out sooner." His frustration wound his throat shut.

Nyx pulled at her hair. "Yeah, well, we've got plenty of fault to go around, believe me." She suddenly stood. "We'll beat each other up later. Okay? We… we gotta do something for her. Maybe they left something behind where we were sleeping last night. Maybe it can help. I'm sure they've all driven off by now." She looked around, her eyes lighting on an old board, splintered and angry at the edges. She rose and dragged it over. "Alright, I've got her arms… if you've got her legs… one… two… three…!" Together they strained. Anna was a limp stone. After they moved her onto the board, they lifted again.

A couple blocks away, and Jackson's body was screaming. His chest was on fire where the bullet had hit. His right leg kept wobbling, sending up knife pains with with every step, forcing him to limp and stumble.

Part of him had thought to walk Anna all three miles back to the city. Nyx was shaking as badly as he was, and he realized those three miles might as well have been thirty.

He guessed Anna had tried to only fix what was necessary, to spread her power just enough between them—and it was still too much for her.

"Far enough," Nyx finally gasped.

"Yeah," Jackson wheezed. He gently lowered their friend back down to the earth.

This place seemed familiar. Yes—there was the empty spot near the abandoned shops where the van had been, where she'd healed his dog bite. A couple crates were still scattered there. "They were in a hurry. Thank the gods." He dug into the boxes, finding useless orange explosive bricks.

The Warlord had left some of his bombs behind. That was... troubling.

And it was a problem for later. At the bottom of the last crate, underneath the bricks, he found two blankets and a first-aid kit. The medical case was mostly looted, but there were still two little packs of hand warmers—that's what he wanted. He cracked them, feeling them release their blessed heat. Diligently, he taped them to Anna's chilly body, both against her major organs.

She didn't respond.

For the first time ever, he wondered if he ought to pray.

Thunder crackled overhead. Jackson looked up at the sky in defiance. A drop of afternoon rain burst above his eyes. "What? No. No! Come on!" He sagged. "Please help me out here."

That was all the prayer he had in him. He fell silent.

"Give me a hand," Nyx called. Nodding, Jackson did. Together, they carried Anna into a nearby building, out of the wet. A dingy pizza sign hung cheerfully out front. It seemed as good a place as anywhere else.

The corrosive rain began to fall harder.

With the storm, the temperature slowly dropped. Jackson sunk his head in his hands, and he bound up Anna tighter in the red blankets he'd found. Nyx said nothing. His dearest friend's soft wheezes filled the air until she was drowned out by the downpour.

Finally, stone-faced, his quiet mage companion lit a small fire that hovered just over her palms. The heat slowly seeped through the tiny space. Even a beady-eyed rat in the ruin crept closer, taking it in, not getting close enough to come to harm.

"It's my fault," Nyx whispered.

"…What is?" Jackson massaged his aching leg, though it felt like he was stabbing it.

"I'm the reason the Coalition found the camp. That everyone had to move. That they were given one *more* reason to hate the city. That Anna's…"

She stared at her toes.

Perhaps it was Jackson's wishful thinking, but a little bit of color seemed to be returning to Anna's face in the warmth. He readjusted the blankets to make sure no cold could get in. "What do you…?"

"My locator chip. I… I didn't escape from prison. I didn't just *happen* to get picked up by slavers. My old bosses started Project Esper again. Like what they did to your friend—that Tony kid. And this time I've been… enlisted."

Jackson's heart grew as chilled as Anna's hands.

"They sent me out to help them locate the damn slave markets near Foxhole. They were gonna follow me to wipe everyone there out—they needed someone who could go in without guns, someone who could still stay safe. And I was… pretty. A good undercover plant. But you guys found me instead, and then it all just went to hell. I thought I had at least a day before they were supposed to come. I thought maybe I could help you all out for a night and then get out of there before morning. But…" Nyx closed her eyes. Her hand went up to a deep, lacerating scar above her collarbone, one that seemed freshly knitted. "After they turned up… look, I'm not squeamish. I found something to dig the chip out before I came to find you again. But I should have run the second you set me free. I was just so happy to see her, to see you both… and I saw her struggling, and I couldn't imagine what it would have been like if no one ever helped me, gave me answers for my magic."

Jackson nodded. "Yeah…" It was the same reason he'd stayed with Anna at first, too.

"I just wanted to do right by the both of you after everything that happened… well, because of me. Because of the people I used to work for."

Jackson swallowed, processing. Finally he managed, "You said something about beating each other up later."

A ghost of a laugh flitted through Nyx's throat.

"I don't think this could have been avoided. I think one way or another, the Warlord was going to get out here, blow up that procession, try to kill me, and tear off for New York. It's all…" Jackson sighed. "Fate. There's something bigger pulling the strings. He's being guided by something very bad… very old."

Nyx did not appear to be comforted by this prospect.

"Anna…" Jackson leaned down, brushing her now-sweat-slicked hair from her forehead. *She's getting that fever again.* He slowly pulled off the emergency warming packs. But in an instant, she went back to feeling like ice. His eyes widened. "The way her temperature is fluctuating… are you sure there isn't anything we can do?"

Nyx shook her head. "I… I don't think she's gonna make it…" she whispered, sorrow leaking through the cracks. "Using up your life energy… it's not like you just go recharge your battery once it's empty. Once that fire goes out, you can't light it again."

The flames in Nyx's hand crackled in Jackson's ears. It was hard not to think of funeral pyres. The Archmage's prophecy rung in his mind. *There is* nothing *you can do to save her.*

No. *No.* There had to be something a damned Chosen of a *god* could do.

"Another healing spell?" he asked.

"What? No!"

Jackson blinked. "Why not?"

"Alright, so for one, *life energy*. Magic needs equivalencies. Save a life, take a life. I can't sacrifice *you* to… look, I don't even know how! It's not my domain. And two, frick, man, I'm doing the best I can, alright? It's not my fault my domain is… is… just gods-damned useless unless I want to hurt someone!"

Jackson blanched. "I… I didn't mean that. I don't know magic. Not like you."

Nyx's nostrils stopped flaring quite so wide. She breathed, long and slow. "Sorry."

"She's almost died saving me twice now," he wheedled. "If you can't do it, can I?"

"What?"

"I'm not just going to sit here watching her turn into a corpse."

"No!" Nyx dropped her fire orb, looking like she needed her hands to talk. It flickered into nothing. "If you can't even do a ward… you'll hurt yourself. Badly. A healing gift is *so* rare. And you're… look, I'm not saying this to be mean, but I get the sense you've got a lot to learn."

"Anna didn't know what she was doing, but she—"

"I've never even seen anything like her before. What good is it to her if, when you try to use this *crazy-rare* ability, you burn yourself out too?"

"I don't need to completely manage it," he said, one ear open for Anna's breathing, so faint, so slow. "Just need to give her enough of a boost that she'll be able to hang on, until her own magic can recuperate. Right?"

He received a dubious look, but she didn't say *no*.

So, Jackson placed one hand under Anna's collarbone, at her center. The line between them flickered, wrenched at his heart. He clung to it, remembering when it forged itself, remembering the feeling of her energy entwining with his. He tried to reach through the line as he'd done back then, back when his lungs had been flooded and she'd given him air. The shadows, cool and dark, shifted around him. The crackle of magic raised the hairs on his neck.

"Jackson…?" Nyx started. She seemed… confused. Surprised.

Anna, in her fevered sleep, smiled… just for a moment.

Then it faded.

Jackson pressed at the line. It kept slipping. The warmth he'd felt from Anna back when she'd healed him… it just wouldn't come. "No. I've got this. I've *got* this," he whispered.

"Jackson…" His name, this time, was infused with *pity.*

His shadows roiled, cold, directionless, and frustrated.

He knew he couldn't do it. The Shadow wasn't who the Atlantean mages prayed to when they'd wanted a medical miracle. He sagged, letting the magic go, unable to hook onto what he needed.

Her breathing… it was getting dimmer. More ragged.

He slumped.

Nyx pulled her knees up to her chin, voice small. "I didn't know you two had a sympathetic connection. I…" He gave her a questioning look, but her eyes welled up, and she shook her head. "I'm just… I'm sorry. Maybe one of us should check on that Coalition procession you mentioned." She stood. "Maybe we can find out this Warlord's plan, right? Road where all that smoke was?"

"But… Nyx…"

"I'm a former agent. Kind of. I'll know what to look for." She grabbed another old board, putting it over her head to protect herself from the rain. "You should stay with her. Maybe… maybe look at your book. See if you get any more ideas."

Jackson blinked. "I don't know if…" He fished it out of his bag.

But Nyx was hurrying, busying herself, voice cracking. "Do something if you can. And if you can't… just, hold her hand, okay? Be with her. Don't let her be alone."

Jackson guessed then why she was running, giving him ideas to keep busy.

Perhaps she couldn't handle goodbyes.

"I'll find something that will help," he argued. "I promise." He let the pages fall open, connecting with their energy. Most were empty, just waiting for a trigger to fill with knowledge. Perhaps... a question. He squinted, thinking, turning inward and talking to himself. "I might not be able to heal, but there are things I can do. Shadows. I can use shadows. I can... befriend extinct birds. I can have useless nightmares and endless insomnia."

Something shifted then, a small whisper in the interplay between his magic and the page.

Dreams, a word whispered across the top. *To walk in dreams is to walk close to Inoki's heart. In dreams, you are anywhere, with anyone, seeing all possibilities. In dreams, you can travel a thousand miles with only a thought. —Balthazar the Preserver, 10ᵗʰ year of the Fallen City*

Jackson stared, for just a moment feeling the presence of a boy he walked with not so long ago. Despite everything, he was relieved that at least one person who was a Chosen had lived. "If, Balthazar, you are suggesting I can call on a medic in my dreams and convince them to come out here..."

"*Balthazar?* Dreamwalking?" Nyx was halfway out the door, but she stopped, wrinkling her nose.

"...This is something you've heard of...?"

"I... yes. I mean, it's one of the foundational... but how did you...? I..." She shook her head. "Look, I guess that doesn't matter, but you couldn't go directly to a doctor. You'd have to find someone who'd remember you, who might be concerned enough to check if their dreams were a message. Someone who can help with magic problems. It's also advanced work to try—not everyone can. It's risky."

Jackson's heart pounded painfully. "No. Out of everything, I think I can do this. How do I start?"

"First you'd need to go into a trance sleep. I'm not good at those, and I sure as hell have never successfully dreamwalked. I always needed assistance even with…" Her eyes widened. "Oh! Oh gods, I've got just the thing for a beginner."

She reached into her pocket, pulling out a handful of dried, worn mushroom caps. It seemed she'd gotten ahold of some of the stash Jackson had found in the slaver caravan.

"…You're kidding." A chill crept down his spine. He'd tried New World Nightcap once as a teenager. It had been, all things considered, an *awful* trip: nightmares, visions, and cold sweats. He hadn't been able to sleep well for weeks afterwards.

"Don't worry. Just take the small one."

Jackson didn't like it, but he was already reaching out a hand. "If I have to do this to save Anna, I will. But is there anything else you can tell me?"

"You just have to dream with *intention*. That's all magic is. Look… if you make this work, the person you need to try and contact is my partner, Jaden Walker."

"Agent Walker? Are you serious?"

"*Yes*. He's way more than just some government flunky. He's in there to change things for the better. He'll do anything you need if he knows I'm asking. And if you hurry… I think it's, what, almost noon? City's still cycling those power shut-offs with the problems at the plant. So about now, Jaden and most everyone else is probably…"

"The noontime siesta," Jackson finished, the realization hitting him. "Until the electric's back on."

"Yeah—so move it. Tell him about the Warlord's people and their plan. Tell him to pull any connection he's got to find a magical healing expert." Her eyes burned. "And tell him I'm safe. Tell him I love him."

The mushroom was sour and dusty, sticking in Jackson's throat. He quickly chewed it, fighting it down.

She smiled. Kneeling again, she made a ring of concrete debris, spoke her magic. A fire lit in the center, filling the old shop with a faint warmth once more.

"I'll be back once I've seen what's out there," she said. "Good luck." With that, she was running headlong into the burning rain, leaving them to whatever might come.

Minutes passed. Jackson's stomach began to cramp.

Don't think about it. Keep it in.

He'd been advised once that chewing on ginger could ease this nausea. However, he'd have to make do. Sweat beaded on his neck. His back made a painful twinge, reminding him of the grimy and cracked tile beneath him. But he stayed still, breathing impatiently.

The truth was, he thought the drug could take up to an hour to take effect, and this would be the longest hour of his life.

But this nightcap, it was fresh. It was potent.

Suddenly, one side of his body felt heavier than the other. His head lolled. Gravity went uneven.

At once, the world *changed.*

His ears buzzed. Colors surged. They went so far through his eyes that he felt he could taste them. Red! Red sprung out like a pouncing beast. It was in the palette of the blankets, brighter than any shade he'd ever seen. It was in the fire, dancing in the bright. It was on his clothes, bits of his life force. Reds swam into his eyes like a strobe light.

There was a croaking and cawing on the breeze. The song of ravens. Voices on the wind.

The shadows on the walls, they were moving... like people. Like dancing, watching *people...*

A shuddering paralysis overtook him. He slumped beside his unconscious friend, limbs weighed down with iron.

And for a moment, he looked at the fire, and he saw a man seated there surrounded by the dancing shadows: a man all in red. Their eyes locked, the other's a golden, reptilian stare. It was his dead once-friend, his guardian demon. Tony smiled. "Jack?"

It's not real. Jackson closed his sight to the red, to the noise, to everything. He couldn't focus. If he stayed conscious, he was going to hallucinate wildly, and he didn't want to waste the Nightcap on that. Not on more birds and riddles and ghosts.

Instead, he willed himself inward, sinking into his own mind. He was still. He was calm. He could feel his heartbeat.

"Jack? Have you been listening? We need to talk." Tony's whisper came again, but now it was far away. So far.

In this altered state, entering his own head was easy, like turning the lock on a door and stepping inside. It was familiar. Warm.

He was floating in the shadows of his mind, going downwards. He was adrift in a hammock. He was sailing on the sea.

"I think I have to walk." The words oozed slowly from his mouth, the world fuzzy and strange. He didn't recall how he'd gotten there. He remembered… red. Everything had been red. Blood?

Anna.

Like ice, it all came back. He froze midair, gasping, wondering at the formless black.

Am I dreaming?

He flailed in the zero gravity, clenching his jaw. *Okay. Okay. Willpower. Intention. That's what magic is.* He grasped at the shadows with his mind, felt them wrap around his body, tugging him to stand. Miraculously, when he let them go, his feet pressed into invisible earth. He took a step forward, then another. The shadows were pulling back to let him through.

He swallowed, pressing out with his mind as best he could. All the red was still there, creeping in at the edges.

He couldn't think straight.

He needed to—

And suddenly, the black wasn't formless. It was night: crisp, clear, sweet-smelling darkness. This was a wood, untouched and old, like the ones at the beginning of the world.

Pressed only inches away were two eyes, glittering stars in their endless fathoms.

Jackson reeled backwards. There was Inoki himself, barefooted and perched like a bird, though still wearing a fine black suit and tie. A mischievous, boyish hunch was in the spirit's back, his long fingers drumming against each other. He was a near mirror for the Atlantean statue on its ancient basalt pedestal—even the raven stood on his shoulder.

But unlike that statue, this Inoki was not smiling.

A chilly wave of enormous presence rattled Jackson's bones.

"Dreamwalking," the god whispered. "You reach so very high... so very *soon*."

"I..." Jackson felt his mind slipping again under that stare. He shook his head. "No, I'm sorry, I don't have time to talk or play games or whatever it is you want. I have to go."

"But you prayed to me today—something no one has done in *so* very long." The smile reached wider. "What a terrible prayer! Do better. But regardless, you called to me. And I wonder: do you finally understand what I want of you in return?"

"Yes." The words echoed. "You want me to fight your brother. His monsters. And I will. But first, I need to help Anna." He swallowed, throat dry and sour still. "I need to find Agent Walker."

The raven rustled its feathers. Jackson couldn't help but wonder, *Atropos? Or some other Chosen who was once human?* It opened its beak and made a harsh, tittering laugh like it knew what he was thinking.

"Your choices revolve around *one* woman." Inoki scowled. His voice fell rife with a grave cold. "Do you not understand how far the world is falling?"

"Agent Walker is the best I can do, both for her and the threat against New York. The rest is out of my hands right now."

"It is not. And you choose to risk precious time on her... risk your very life. Dreams are dangerous. Who knows who you might meet?" The god snickered. It was not a nice laugh.

"Whatever you're trying to say..."

"What if her fate is for the best?" That tone was velvet-wrapped brass knuckles. "I wonder, child, did you learn what it means to be a hero? If you answer well, you may pass."

Jackson braced himself, feeling nothing but cold sweat. "Fine. They fight. They don't give up. They *win*."

"Sometimes."

"They're kind. They matter. They're the best of us." He knew exactly who he spoke of as he said it: both his father and his friend.

"And? What happens to them?"

Jackson blinked, staring. "They're loved."

"And?"

"They…" Jackson heaved a sigh. "They die."

The proclamation fell like a hushed blanket through the trees. Even the wind stopped.

"But—" Jackson said.

"No. Think. She wanted to save everyone, didn't she, back in her time? What did it get her?"

"But—"

"And she wanted to save you. She almost gave all of herself to do it. Had my Lady Sun not pulled her back from the brink…"

"No, look—"

"Then, just days later? The moment she sees her friends in pain, she rushes to give it all up again. I rarely see mortals martyr themselves so quickly, so *often*, but I think this one has a suicide wish!"

Jackson caught his breath. "So you want me to leave her out here to die alone?"

"It seems to me that dying is *exactly* what she's fated to do. And she will drag the very last of my Chosen line down with her if he keeps getting involved." The lights in his eyes were frigid. "I will not have it."

"So that's it, then?" Jackson sputtered. "You'll just order me not to care?"

Inoki closed his eyes, as if in pity. "You will recover. Love is fleeting for your kind. It can easily change. Come now. She does not even want you."

Jackson's flash of white-hot rage was almost blinding. "That doesn't matter," he bit off.

"It most certainly *does*."

"No, it—wait." Jackson's eyes widened. If this was the crux on which Inoki's annoyance spun... he let out a rasping yell of anger. "This isn't just about going into danger with her. Because *everything* I'm being put through is dangerous. But I'm the last of the line, and maybe, if I'm only watching her... is that it? Do you want me give her up because she won't continue the damn genetic line for you down the road?"

"It is something we must consider." Inoki shrugged as if he was discussing how good the tires were on a used car. "To be honest, you make a lot of bad choices in this space. So strict about protection! No sowing your wild seeds! Some of the mates you've chosen don't even have proper wombs—it's like you *want* everything to fall apart and die."

Jackson's hands ached to mar the god's perfect white teeth. "Back off," he spat, his breath misting the air. "She might be trouble. I know she is. But she's worth saving. All of that children crap? Let me worry about that later. She needs me *now*."

"No! Turn back. It is your duty to me. It is your duty to your role in this universe!"

"*No*." Jackson set his jaw and stared the god down. The oppressive aura around him turned crushing. He had to fight to get his words out. "I didn't ask for this job. I'm not going to shut up and dance to whatever fate or destiny you—or anyone else—dictates for me! I'm not going to abandon my past, my commitments, *who I am*, just because you told me so!" Jackson gathered his will and broke free of the cosmic stare, of the cold disapproval weighing down on his bones. "If you want me as your Chosen, then you get everything that comes with me. And you just better hope that what I want to fight for is what you want too."

With that, Jackson marched *around* Inoki, so angry that fear barely touched him anymore. If he had to struggle off into the dark wood by himself, then so be it.

He didn't expect the laughter, elated, buoyant. "Such a good boy! So unlike the rest. I *am* proud of you. Turn right up ahead. You will find what you seek."

"*What?*" Jackson spun. The rock was empty. The night was still. His spine shuddered.

When he turned back around, the forest was presenting him with three paths.

He had the unsettling sense he'd been getting tested, and he didn't like it, didn't have *time* for it. But if that was the case, and Inoki had actually given him something… *helpful*… then right was as good as any direction. So, to the right his feet went. The trees parted, a rush of wind on his face as if he was entering a clearing…

…A stale snap of air hit him. He was no longer in the forest. Instead, this was a smooth concrete hall, cold, sterile, flanked with dozens of doors. He spun. This place stretched into infinity. There were strange sigils painted on the walls, graffiti that looked suspiciously like dried blood.

Something about this place felt distant, slippery, like it was actively trying to push him out. The sense of being unwelcome was tangible on his tongue. Jackson swallowed and tried a door on his right. It didn't budge, a lock inside clacking in protest. "Hello?" he called. There was no reply.

When he looked back, the forest had disappeared.

Then, there was a click of shoes to the right. He spun again, certain no one had been there before. Now, a man of stoic face and clear Japanese heritage was there, a sheen of sweat under his black military hair. Black glasses shielded what felt like a piercing stare.

"…Agent Walker?"

The Coalition man made a thin-lipped frown. "…What? Dovetail?

What the hell are you doing here?" The agent's shoulders were squaring, his frown deepening, his fingers inching for the firearm placed at his waist.

Jackson held up his hands in peace. Could dream guns still threaten? "Look, I don't have much time, but I'm dreamwalking, and I'm looking for help."

Walker's scowl sunk deeper. "You're dreamwalking? That's impossible. My mind is shielded. I'm—"

"This is your *mind?*" Jackson looked around. "Oh. A long, boring hallway. Very government. Right. I believe you."

On that, Walker closed the distance, getting in his face, examining him. "How… yeah. It's you alright." He prodded Jackson's chest with his finger, his voice rising. "You smug bastard—tell me how you got past my wards."

"I don't even know what you're talking about. Look. Anna is very, very hurt. Nyx is with us. She said you'd be someone to talk to. There are raiders making for New York. They've got explosives."

"*…What?*"

"So one thing at a time. Nyx said you could give us a magical healing expert. What's wrong with Anna… it's something a doctor isn't going to fix."

The agent's mouth worked, his eyebrows in a stunned arch.

"Where do these doors go?" Jackson turned away, thinking of Frank, of a possible backup plan should Walker not come through. "Will they let me jump—like I did to you?"

"How many raiders?" Strain colored the words.

"Around thirty. They're heading towards the tunnels, to get in under everyone."

"Are you certain?"

"*Yes!*"

"Which tunnel? What's their target?"

Jackson gave the locked door an exasperated yank again, which didn't budge. "I don't know the tunnel. Probably Tony's old haunts. But they want to take down the Barrier facility on the east side of Manhattan. So you need to send everyone you have there, now."

Walker's brow furrowed. "There's no way they could—these are just some *raiders*, you're saying…?"

"Don't underestimate these people," Jackson warned. "Really. Don't. There's something metaphysical going on with their leader. And he's had everything taken from him—by *your* people. He has nothing to lose."

Walker considered. "Where are you, Anna, and Nyx, in the real world?"

"We're not far off—Bronx River Parkway. Three miles. There's an *extremely* well-guarded Coalition procession that's now a smoldering pile of wreckage just a couple blocks away. You find that? You'll find us."

The agent processed. Then, he bowed his head and heaved the kind of breath that a person takes before delivering bad news. "I'll certainly pass along this information. But I'm on leave. I'm being investigated, with the Antonio Bertinelli incident. And—"

Jackson swore.

"And…" Walker continued. "I can come out there, alright? I can try to help. I can bring a medic. But I don't know anyone who can magically heal. Not a single person. Not anymore."

Jackson stared. He put his head in his hands and slid to the floor, back to the wall. "Gods damn it, Walker, what the hell can you do?"

Walker made an agitated grimace. "Look." He put an awkward hand out. "The Order are the only people with those kinds of connections right now. They have the magical population locked down. Since the first Project Esper… they have not made things easy. Not that I blame them."

An angry, fiery ball was in Jackson's throat. "The Order, you say."

Deciding, he closed his eyes. He wanted to think of Frank: balding, angry, uncle-like Frank, smelling of shoe polish and rose-flavored candy. He wanted to think of that final shoulder pat between them, the understated way he never said goodbye.

Having his advisor would have been a great comfort.

But his most faithful couldn't help him, so he didn't let himself be drawn in to the thought too far.

"Nyx told me to pass on her love, and that she was safe," he whispered.

Walker jerked in surprise.

And Jackson thought of ice and anger and roiling magic.

It was easy to slip away from Walker's thoughts, the place expelling him like oil sliding through water. He hadn't needed the doors. All he'd needed was intention.

The air was different again.

Everything was darkness once more. It was as if he'd stepped back into his own mind, at the beginning of his dreaming. Still, the shadows slid off him in unfamiliar ways. As he walked, the sound of cold stone clicked under his shoes.

His palm brushed a wall, freezing, damp. Nervous, he peered at it—for just a moment, the darkness peeled back. There was a stylized eye encircled in ivy on its surface.

His heart shuddered.

"Unwarded dreamwalking." The hiss came from over his shoulder. "Foolish."

Jackson spun. There stood the Archmage, eyes glittering, leaning on his cane. The glowing pommel stone bathed him in an eerie red light.

"Just who I was looking for." Jackson tried not to shake. "I guess even *you* like the noonday nap."

The wizard growled. "Did you come to accept my offer? Or are you just mucking around with that book, heedless of the consequences?"

Something about him seemed angry, unsettled—almost surprised. Jackson wondered if he'd broken through this man's "wards" too. The thought of keeping the mage off-balance for once filled him with a grim sort of pleasure. He reached out into the dark—he didn't know if the shadows would abandon him a second time. But Anna needed him. New York needed him. Maybe even the gods needed him.

The dream shadows here were slippery and hostile. But this time, he managed to draw them to himself, squaring his shoulders. They were cagey, but they *obeyed*. "I'm not here to trade threats and insults. I'm here to talk about what I want."

The Archmage raised articulate eyebrows, mustache twitching. "My, my. Look who's learning to crawl." He stepped forward, cane tapping. His left hand eked out a strange pattern in the air. His eyes began to shine an ominous red. "You're desperate about something. What could that be, I wonder?" The strange glow in his eyes blinkered. "Oh dear. Your *poor* Anna. She's hurt, isn't she?"

Jackson's lip curled, his spine prickling with wariness.

"You remember my associate Claire, don't you? She was the woman who kept you breathing on Tony's behalf after your little cage match. She's the only mage in this Order with that talent. Useful. How nice it is, to know the only healer on the Eastern seaboard is loyal to you." He made an amused sneer. "I could send her to you if you like, right now. Anna's life would be in safe hands."

"And what do you want for it?"

"Don't waste my time. You know my price. Do you want her life guaranteed, or not?"

Jackson clicked his mouth shut. Part of him hoped there could be something else the mage could want beyond the pages from his book. Part of him hoped he wouldn't be forced to make Faustian bargains with objects he barely understood. *I...*

"Well, why don't you just think about for a little longer then, hm? I will send my agents along. And as she's dying, you can be wishy-washy about it, telling everyone in person just how little you're willing to give up to save her. How about that?"

"What?! Wait—"

The Archmage snapped his fingers.

With a sudden rush of whiplash, Jackson was thrust back into his own mind. His eyes fired open, and he took a great, lurching breath.

The abandoned pizzeria was above. The mid-afternoon sun burned through the windows. His lungs gasped for air. The rain had stopped, but the wet chill remained. The fire was out. His fingers and toes were numb. Where was Nyx?

Desperate, Jackson heaved himself to one side, feeling like his tendons were cut. His head was blurring dangerously, floating away. *The Nightcap's still…*

His thoughts were sand swirling through his fingers. But there was a soft wheezing in the air, steady, if faint.

She was hanging on.

Managing to scoot himself an inch closer, Jackson lifted the blankets and pressed a hand to her forearm. Her skin was still freezing cold.

He tried to call for Nyx, but his throat just wouldn't work.

The drugged weight was pulling him back down. He began losing seconds as he stared at Anna, trying to figure out what to do.

I can't do anything. I just have to wait.

Jackson closed his eyes, then settled his body next to Anna's, keeping her close. All he could do was share his own heat, hope it could help her in some small way.

Before he slept, he touched his fingers to hers, finding some small comfort in that. Perhaps he just imagined it, but… maybe she was a little warmer.

Perhaps it could be enough, to cling to a shred of a hope.

CHAPTER SEVENTEEN
Daybreak

The last thing Anna could remember was blood on her hands and a betrayal in wild, dark eyes.

Something in her head snapped when she'd fallen. It was all a thick, painful fog, and it tasted like copper and fear. The horrible thing was, it was very familiar.

"Anna!" Jackson's voice rang out.

Oh hi, she thought. She was happy to see him, happy to not be alone again, but her mind was on a ship, and he was at the harbor. She was pulling away, taking up anchor. *That's my name. I'm Anna.*

Jackson was cupping her face with one hand, the touch like it was on someone else's skin.

"…Very bad. She tapped out her life force…." Nyx's voice whispered, like smoke leaking through the cracks.

Don't be silly. Who can't go a month without dying twice?

"Anna…" Jackson sounded lost… scared.

But she was fading, and could no longer see him.

She drifted in and out, a bundle of pain and misery. Sometimes, there was a warm hand around hers, a comforting touch telling her she wasn't alone. Once, she caught a flicker of sunlight before she had to close her eyes—it all hurt.

For long periods, her mind would go quiet, floating in a void. Every time her consciousness came forward enough to feel the hard ground under her back, she was afraid that the next time she slipped into nothingness, it would be the last.

She'd done that before. Just… slid away.

And she was teetering over the precipice again right now, losing her footing.

Once more she brushed against the waking world. She shook with chills and aching fire. Her eyes opened, burning and blurred.

She was in a ruined building, the air quiet and still. She'd been bundled up in blankets. The barest of sunlight was pressing back dark rainclouds in the sky, the tiniest kiss of warmth in the breeze. It felt like a caress, a hello, even as it shot her through with pins and needles.

She couldn't turn her head, but she felt a body snug against hers. Jackson: she knew even without seeing his face from the weak pulse in her chest. His breath came even and slow. She shook, feeling the damp, rainy cold, realizing he'd been trying to keep it back. She wanted to squeeze his hand, let him know she was still there, but her arms were numb, her muscles too weak to move.

And her vision blurred. She was sliding away again. She couldn't stop it.

No. Please no.

The ruined ceiling blurred and bled, filling her eyes, morphing color and texture.

Sky. It was nothing but sky, bright and crisp as only the dawn could be.

Anna wept. She knew the process the brain went through as it shut down, flooding itself with emotions and chemicals. Now there was grass under her back, the scent of lavender in her nose. Now she heard a gentle stream. Now there was the rustle of a peaceful wind carrying leaves overhead.

This was her vision of paradise before everything went black forever.

It looked just like a painting, a meadow of endless green and flowers. The sky was vast, so clear, something she could fall into. Soft, puffy clouds melted overhead.

Yet, there was something alien about the sight. After a moment, she realized what it was: the world was awash in daylight, but there was no bright sun to give it.

A swelling noise built in her ears, jarring her sadness.

There was music.

There was a song.

The world grew brighter, brighter.

And a woman appeared standing above her. She hadn't walked up, hadn't made a sound. She'd merely blinked into existence. Anna reached out, tears leaking down the sides of her face.

Help me. I'm not ready to die. Not again. Please.

The woman above kneeled down, the dawn shining through her hair like it was a dark frizzy halo. She was naked as the sky beyond, her skin a warm, earthy brown, her smile wide and gentle. From her throat came the insistent, rolling melody that had been following Anna for days.

Then her humming stopped, but in Anna's mind, it kept cycling in the wind.

"You've made a mess of yourself," the woman said gently. "There is so much more you could have done."

Anna could barely talk, unable to articulate her sorrow that once again, she was growing cold and scared and weak. *But I decided to live!* was all her mind could manage. Her second chance had been hell so far, but it had been short, too short.

"Shhh." The woman's soft touch came to rest on her forehead. She was silent a long moment. "You are afraid."

Anna sobbed.

"I would save you," the woman said. "Believe it with all of your heart. I would."

Anna did believe. The way the words fell, they rang full and pure, like their speaker had never told a lie in her life. Even so... "...You can't?"

The woman's face crumpled. "I am not as strong as I was, child. It took so much of me to do this but once. You have called me time and again, to save those around you, to save those dear to your heart." A tear rolled down her wide nose, plunking onto Anna's cheek, leaving behind a tangible surge of sorrow and love. "Now... without aid... I am so sorry. I need time, and we do not have it. I can only ease your passing to the other side. It... will not be long now. And all of your loved ones, they wait for you there."

"No... no, *please.*"

The woman shook her head and squeezed her hand. "There will be no more pain. That much, I can promise."

⁕

A hard toe sunk into Jackson's side.

"Tch," a dispassionate woman's voice rang in his ears. "Here he is, clinging to the girl, just as predicted."

"Don't be rude, Claire."

Jackson rolled over, struggling to get up. There, as the Archmage promised, was the cold-eyed woman who had healed him in Tony's underground. She was in a black skirt-suit, rectangular glasses severely perched on her nose as she evaluated the broken tables and ancient chairs. She looked like she'd been on her way to some important corporate function—at least, before she took the wrong turn into this desolate alley on the backside of New York's bones. "I'll be rude if I want. He's going to make me late for work. So shut up, old man. You're just my ride." Her heeled feet tapped out an impatient rhythm.

In the pizzeria doorway was also a stout, nervous figure Jackson knew very well. His deep brown fingers fiddled with the gold buttons in his waistcoat. In his grasp was a crystal of some kind, a soft blue light emanating from within.

"Huxley," Jackson snarled, fighting to get the words out. "And... and you. Claire. So he did send you."

"Yes or no, Dovetail?" Claire hissed. With one hand, she drew a disc from her pocket, something that glittered golden inside her thin white fingers.

There were several retorts on Jackson's lips. But that was when his ears registered a terrible sound.

His head whipped back.

Anna was silent.

Something cracking in his chest, he reached out with a trembling hand. Her skin was so stiff to touch. "Anna?"

She wasn't wheezing. She wasn't breathing.

Balance addled, Jackson lightly shook her good shoulder, tapping her face with one hand. *Anna?*

"Did she die already?" Claire sighed. "Huh. The Mind's Eye's visions are rarely wrong." The tap of the shoe on the linoleum grew stronger.

Jackson felt for the line in his chest, for the *connection*. It was faint, rapidly slipping through his fingers like sand. In its vacuum, his heart began to collapse. "N-no..."

The healing mage's voice was a knife-edge. "No as in, 'get out, I need to say goodbye to this dead woman?' Or, 'no, please save her?' Be clear."

Jackson felt like a bug pinned under glass. The price for her life was irrelevant, wasn't it? He'd pay it. Both Inoki and the Archmage were right about him. "Save her. Please."

The woman clicked her tongue. "Payment."

Frantic, Jackson dove for the book. Any page would do? Fine. One out of a thousand would hardly make a difference. And Inoki would just have to god up and deal with the fallout.

But fate twisted in strange ways. Perhaps it was destiny that saw the book fall open to one page in particular.

There it was: Huxley's image burned in ink, howling in anguish. The wretched, tormented thing looked nothing like the cowed, nervous creature at Claire's side.

I hope you choke on this.

Jackson reached up to the seam of the page, wondering if such a thick, waxy thing could even tear like paper—vellum was hide, after all, and—

He needn't have worried. In all magic, intent was what mattered. As Jackson reached, his fingertips began to glow a sick, strange violet. A purple seam split under it in the book, a searing, stomach-turning smell following after. The page came free with a mighty *r-r-r-r-rip*, and for a second, Jackson saw no page at all, but a brilliant, intricate web, a billion stories, people, and songs, shredding, splitting, the sound of the page coming free rattling his mind and soul. He felt his own consciousness flicker, blackness washing over his eyes, but he hung on. *The universe has been torn!* his mind screamed, irrational as he knew it was.

When he came back to himself, thick tears were clouding his vision, as if he'd done something unforgivable.

There was an aged yellow page in his hands.

And there on the vellum, the ink began to peel and flake. It lifted up and out, flecks of blue-black dust glittering in the afternoon light. They swirled through the air, spiraling, and Huxley's imprint obliterated itself.

The ink motes, as if an angry swarm, made a beeline for the mage's face, exploding in a sparkling, violent *poof.*

They were gone.

Huxley blinked.

Claire blinked.

Jackson wept.

"Well, whatever," the healing mage said as she snatched the

outstretched page, slipping it inside her blazer. She scooted inside and kneeled on the blankets, all business. Then, she drew a knife, dug it into her palm. From the welling blood she dabbed her fingers, tracing a sigil on Anna's forehead, something that made Jackson nervous.

An eye: the Order's mark.

Claire settled the golden disc on Anna's sternum. Both her hands and the blood she'd painted began to glow.

⁕

Anna was fading in and out. Sunlight swelled in her sight, almost swallowing her, along with the vision of the meadow and the naked stranger at her side who promised no more pain.

"I don't want to die," she pleaded.

The woman lifted Anna's shirt, putting her hands on her abdomen. "Let go of your fear, child. I will ease your passing." Her eyes fluttered closed. "Wait. I… I see." Her sorrowful frown suddenly split into a smile. "No. It is *not* over! Be not afraid! The dawn comes for you after all!" Heat began to pour from her hands. It shot through Anna's belly, arching her back. It curled around her organs, splicing through her legs, her arms, her toes and fingers.

Something came back to Anna in a rush: the dream where she'd been pulled into the fire. She was lanced with the memories of the horrifying soldier specter, the laughing man with stars in his eyes, and the burning under her skin before she'd woken again to the morning. She thrashed as the flaming touch seared across her stomach, into her back and bones.

The tears ran hotter, faster.

The fire passed. Her body uncoiled.

The bruises were fading, her wrenching aches gone. So was the horrifying shredding nothingness in her core. It felt… how could it…

Her mother's voice was in her mind now, something she'd said so, so many years ago. *Everything's right as rain.*

"How...?" was all she could breathe.

The woman was smiling, but her warm brown face was dulling, growing sickly. There was a clamminess to her hands that wasn't there before as they lifted from her belly. "A bridge opened, an infusion of power. It was all I needed. I am glad for you. Glad indeed."

Anna lifted herself, feeling her strength returned, and reached out, wanting to touch, wanting to know if this miracle was real. "Thank you. Thank you so much."

The woman laughed, a genuine twinkle lighting her eyes despite the exhaustion. She drew Anna's hand in to rest on her cheek next to that expression that could lift the most jaded soul. "Do you remember me?"

Anna was certain she would remember such a beautiful, powerful presence. And yet, she had no memory... no... memory...

Wait.

No.

She did.

The Mojave desert had been in her lungs, pain and blood, sadness and desperation. The sun had been burning her eyes. Then, the light above had simply swallowed her, and that had been her last moment in her own time, in her own place. There had been a singing woman in that light, giving a sad smile, murmuring a sad apology. There had been a caress in those words. There had been a kiss on her cheek, a gentle vow in her ear. It was all a blur, flashes and feelings.

"Child," the woman spoke now. "You remember what I said to you, don't you?"

Anna did, and it made her eyes sting, her chest seize, overwhelmed.

The woman had whispered a song to her before she'd woken in that box so far from home. The song had words now, words she recalled.

I name you hope, and I give unto you myself.

"*You* brought me here," Anna said. "You made me like this." She struggled to understand. "Who are you? *Why?*"

The woman's voice was soft. "Because you tried to save everyone, even when you knew you couldn't." She straightened Anna's shirt, dusting her off, like a mother would for her young. "Because I knew the world was about to die. Because I watched you try to do something about it." Her touch shot thoughts through Anna's mind of things growing in the ground, celebrating life, basking in joy and comfort. "The lives in this time, they need someone like you. I am so sorry to cause you so much pain. I am so sorry I did not let you move on. I should have, perhaps. I should have."

"No, I…" Anna swallowed. "I wasn't ready."

"Good. Because they need you. And I know you can help save them."

• • •

Anna's entire body was shaking under Claire's grip. With a sickening, puckering quaver, the blood on her forehead spread, seeped into her skin.

It vanished.

The weakest of pulses answered Jackson, deep in the link to his chest.

A great, gasping breath rocked Anna's body. The healing mage grunted and pressed her firmly to the earth, an annoyed strain locking her brow tight.

Suddenly Anna glowed brighter. *Brighter.* Claire tore her grip away with a shocked gasp. The magic subsided, as quick as it'd come. Anna's skin was now ruddy and healthy, as if she'd always been whole and well.

Jackson realized he was squeezing her hand so hard that his fingers were numb. He tried to relax his grip, but it was difficult. A relieved, quaking sob wracked his chest.

"That should… should do it, then." Claire eased her hands by her side. She appeared to be forcibly shoving the shock off her face, replacing it with a trained dispassion. Jackson wondered if something had happened she hadn't controlled, and he rushed to check that Anna's heart was beating. He could feel it! He could hear her breathe.

"And of course, I got blood under my nails," Claire muttered. "That's great."

Jackson had been about to offer some words of gratitude, but they suddenly stuck in his throat. The mage was already walking away. "Professor Huxley, if you'll do the honors." She wrinkled her nose at her hands. "I have a page to deliver to our master, and a shower to take. Hurry it up."

Through the mist of relieved tears, Jackson saw something else quite strange, something new.

Huxley was sagging.

"I… what?" the old poisoner muttered. He slapped his face as if trying to wake up.

"Old man. You." Claire's heels tapped out their impatient rhythm. "You've got the soul stone for the teleporting. Not my domain, you remember? Now come on. Don't let the dementia set in too early."

Huxley squinted. "Claire? Is that you?"

"Who the hell else do you think it is?"

Great, Jackson thought. *Huxley's lost it.* He found this idea a tiresome note; he rather wanted them both to be gone so he could worry about the consequences of dealing with them later. And, he wanted Anna to wake up. Now.

Huxley adjusted his spectacles. "Where *are* we? What are you wearing?" His confused squint found focus. "And who is…? My boy, you seem awfully familiar… one moment, I…" A shocked look began to dawn. "Jackson? Jackson Dovetail? Why are you… what is all this? *How are you so old?*"

Jackson stared. Claire was turning white. "Oh shit," she whispered. "You clever goddamn Chosen. You… shit."

What is…?

But that was all the explanation he got. The healing mage darted forward like a rabbit, wresting the softly glowing stone from Huxley's fiddly grasp. She touched her fingers to Huxley's brow.

A design lit there in blue flame: an eye. It was a mirror for the one she'd drawn on Anna.

The old man grunted, arms flying out like a windmill. He shook his head, crying out in pain. "What's happening?" he sobbed. "Why are you… you're in my *head…!*"

Clair seized his collar. Her frigid stare turned Jackson's way. "You're going to pay for this," she snapped. Then, an uneasy string of incantation-babble flew from her lips, a bright burst of light swallowing them whole.

Two screams of pain hovered in the air for a disturbing second— both Huxley's and hers.

But they were gone.

Jackson bowed his head, shaking. Something had just happened that he couldn't understand, something he knew one day might come back to haunt him. But for now, he only held Anna's hand up to his heart, cradling it in both hands.

He would be here for her when she woke.

⁂

The naked woman was wearily bowing away.

Able to move again, Anna followed that limp stare. To her surprise, there in the wildflowers lay Jackson. He couldn't have been sleeping, because his eyes were wide open—but they were unseeing, black as night, filled with tiny, dizzying lights, stars in the darkness. Her heart beat faster. She reached out, touching his arm. He didn't respond.

"He cannot hear you. He is not here," the woman said. "Though his heart is. He is the one who brought help from the other side so my will could complete its work." She smiled. "Always a clever boy."

Anna held her right hand fast to Jackson's arm, not sure what to say.

"You asked who I was. I have been called many things, and all of them true. All of them said that I was *Sun*." She rocked wearily, as if about to fall asleep.

"Sun?"

She rose, woozy, hesitating. "I must go. I do not have the strength to walk this world for very long anymore…" Despite the drag in her steps, she was still elegant, as if her feet were made for dancing. "I cannot intervene again, Anna. Never again. The magic of the world is failing. *Life* is failing. But you can help in my stead. You can be hope. That is all that's important. All I want of you. Be hope."

"Wait!" Anna said. "I don't know how to use this magic. It is magic, isn't it, what you gave me? I don't know anything about… anything!"

Sun turned, smiling over her shoulder. "Don't worry. You'll learn. Your magic… it is *honest* magic, and you'll fulfill your purpose just by being you! It is easy, no tricks. You already know it. Just look your power in the eye and command it, when you feel the sun at your back and hope in your heart. You will find truth, spread life—heal what is broken. You are the darkness's equal. Never forget that."

Anna had more to question, more to cry out, but she blinked… and the woman was simply gone.

The grass under her palms became rough blankets. The scent of lavender gave way to dust and old smoke. The sky became crumbled concrete. Sunbeams spilled through long-broken windows.

Anna gaped. Her shirt was hiked up where the woman had laid hands on her. The air felt cooler than it had a moment ago, like an autumn wind had begun to spike the season. She fought herself all the way up, breathing hard as if she'd been running. There were still tears leaking out of her eyes.

Jackson was kneeling overhead, where the naked woman had once been. His eyes were damp, shining, and a little bloodshot—dark, starry pools no longer. He grasped her hand delicately, and the smile that cracked his face was as bright as the dawn outside.

"You're awake," he said, like he was announcing the most important thing in the world.

Wordlessly, Anna moved herself so she was resting on her knees, then pulled him into a tight hug. It was a bit like hugging a startled coat rack. But slowly, he relaxed, and she felt his arms wrap around her. There was confusion and relief in the connection in her chest. "M'sorry," Anna mumbled into his shoulder.

"You're sorry? Are you *okay?* You were going to *die—*"

"M'sorry for making you worry." She shuddered, and despite her confusion, there was still something beautiful shining through it in her core—something that made everything alright. *I'm alive. I'm here in this time because I'm meant to be. I'm here because... I'm needed.*

This was the deepest truth she'd ever felt.

"You're *healed,*" he was whispering. "Thank the gods."

Gods.

Anna trembled inside the hug. "I... Jackson. You're going to think this is *crazy.* I had this vision. Or dream. I saw this woman... she fixed everything, then vanished. She said she was the one that brought me here, and she was weird and beautiful and kind, and... and... she was full of light...!" An uncomfortable laugh burst from her chest as she started hearing what she was saying. There was no way anyone would believe it, not even if she felt all the conviction in the world.

"The Sun," Jackson whispered. He pulled back just a little. His eyes were strange, as if looking far away, hands still on her shoulders.

"*What?*" Anna froze. "That's... that what she said... how did you *know?*"

He licked his lips. "There's a lot I need to tell you. But..."

She bowed her head. And slowly, she fidgeted with her shirt fabric—damp and cold with old blood. "Shark and his people. New York."

"I got in contact with someone who's going to help, but..."

Anna perked her head up. "Where's Nyx? Is she... she's okay, right?"

"I don't know. I thought she'd be back by now."

Blinking, trying to shake off the wooziness, Anna staggered to her feet. "Okay. Real world problems first. Magic lady problems later."

He chuckled. Then, like he'd been fighting with himself, he hesitatingly pulled her into another embrace. It was a comfortable feeling, and she wrapped her arms around him right back. "I'm so glad you're okay." There was a rippling, warm feeling in her stomach as he pressed his lips against the top of her head, nestling his face inside her hair.

She closed her eyes. This was good. This wasn't complicated. "Thanks for whatever you did," she whispered into his neck.

Slowly, he let her go. His face was flushed. "I'd… I'd do it again."

His words curled around Anna's heart. She was wrestling with a response when a third person's voice shattered the silence. "Guys!" Bounding across the ruined asphalt was Nyx, dark hair flying behind. "Anna! Anna, you're up! You're…!" Anna caught a flash of a brilliant white smile just before she was tackled into an arm-crushing second hug that smelled like dust, copper, and sweat, one that shook with happy laughter. "Jackson, oh man, I'm never gonna doubt you again—did you see Jaden? How the hells did you—"

"I made some deals that might be a problem later," Jackson rasped. This hung in the air in an awkward, heavy way—Nyx raised an eyebrow. "But I did get to Agent Walker. I'm guessing he's going to do his best to warn someone about the attack." His brow scrunched. "But his first question was, 'just some raiders?' If his bosses take the same tack… and he's been put on leave, on top of that…"

Nyx groaned. "Shit. Leave? No, they aren't going to take him seriously at all. He must be getting investigated. Probably regarding everything that went down with you two, Bertinelli, and me. And…"

She made a helpless gesture with her hands, pointing off into the distance. It was the same direction, Anna realized, as the column of smoke that had been rising on her arrival to the area.

"Did you find something?" Jackson asked, eyes growing sharper.

"I've been keeping one of the soldiers company that the Warlord's people didn't finish off." Nyx stared at her feet. "He… didn't want to be alone. At the end." A silence stretched after her words, and Anna bowed her head too, understanding. Her friend's voice rattled, "Look, he knew the dangers of his job. It is what it is. But even knowing he was dying, he wouldn't tell me why anyone would want to rob his caravan. Tried making me swear not to look at the back, told me to just get the hell out of there after he was gone."

Jackson leaned in. "What would he be guarding that could be worse than all of the guns and explosives the Warlord has *already?*"

"I don't know." Nyx looked to Anna. "It's probably treason to find out. And I can't get in by myself. So. Who wants to toss one more felony on the pile to lend me a hand?"

CHAPTER EIGHTEEN
Defuse

The Coalition cargo truck had skidded and toppled into a cluster of pines. It was turned on its side, though beyond a few scorched tires, it was mostly intact.

Anna told herself that if she focused on details like that, she wouldn't notice what used to be the retinue of soldiers once protecting it. This almost worked. When she was done heaving, she kept moving, shaking, but trying anyway.

Nyx guided them through to the wreckage. The truck's back was already smashed in, scorch marks and wrenched metal framing an entrance. Inside, it was pitch black.

"Hurry," Nyx urged. "There's no way word hasn't gotten back to the city by now—this road isn't used much, but if any transport misses their two-hour reporting window... I'm sure backup's already on the way."

"Point taken." Jackson pulled himself into the dark. "It's fine!" he called. "No one's here."

His hand stretched out of the hole to assist. Anna, still queasy, stepped up, letting her friend help tug her inside. Her ankles thwacked cold, heavy metal on the floor, making her stumble—guns. In the crash, a nearby rifle rack had fallen. She fought the shiver up her spine and braced herself by Jackson's side, helping him lend Nyx a hand too.

Much further in, it was too dark to see. Anna, wary, called to her inner light, hoping it wouldn't cost her like her healing. Thankfully, it didn't. The glow rose and illuminated the hold. As it did, a cold, slimy sensation oozed across her brow, just between her eyes. She blinked and reached up, wondering if she'd been hit by a dripping liquid.

Her fingers came away clean.

The feeling wouldn't go away.

She shivered and kept looking around.

Beyond the mess of rifles, there were papers and teal-blue radiation suits scattered at her feet. She remembered Jackson's mail truck and tried to hope these kinds of supplies were normal. Two Geiger counters were also fastened to the wall, now her floor.

"What is it you needed me for?" Anna whispered. Something about this wreckage demanded a respectful hush.

Nyx pointed. "I want to know what those are."

A long cargo rack stretched across what was now the ceiling. Fastened up there was a row of black-shelled cases, each about the size of a suitcase someone might have brought to the airport. A sensor system at the far end seemed to have locked them firmly into place.

Jackson reached up, tapping each container before coming to rest in an empty slot. His eyes met hers. "This must be what they took."

Anna silently agreed. The space's clamps were mangled, hanging loose. It was almost as if a creature with unimaginable strength had just torn the cargo straight out.

How they'd managed that, she didn't want to know.

"Okay, here I go," she whispered.

Wrapping her hands around a different case above, she strained. It was no good. Her weight just wasn't enough. So Anna channeled every last shred of gravity-defiance magic she had. She awkwardly curled in her body and floated her feet up to brace against the ceiling rack.

The blood rushed to her head as she crouched upside-down.

"Careful," Nyx warned.

Lodged and ready, Anna sent her mind even farther away, to that sunshine-filled field and the beautiful woman clothed only in hope and light. Her muscles seemed to know *exactly* what she wanted. She dug in her stance and pulled. Her back screamed, the vertebrae popping—there was a screech of metal, a snapping groan.

The clamps gave.

"Woah!" Anna tumbled, the case thudding heavy into her chest. Two sets of arms caught her before she smashed to the floor. She smiled at Jackson and Nyx both, then rocked herself up, dizzy, setting down the container by her feet.

A keypad stared up at them now. She rolled her eyes, ignoring it, and applied as much pressure as she could to the locks. They sprung free, one ricocheting into the wall and denting it, making her wince.

"We're gonna be workout buddies after this." Nyx chuckled nervously, and even if it was hollow and false, Anna felt better with laughter there. She opened the lid.

Her jaw went slack.

Familiar, bright yellow-and-black warning signs were staring up at her—as if anyone who handled this weight needed reminding that it was dangerous.

Far away, she felt her face growing cold. Her blood was falling away into empty shock.

Nyx and Jackson were both leaning over her shoulder. "The hell…" Jackson whispered.

Anna's head bowed, emotions warring between sorrow, anger, and bitter, roiling disappointment.

"No way." Nyx said. "*No.* This… this is *illegal.*"

Anna's voice cracked an octave too high. "Well, yeah, digging out a government's *suitcase nukes* is probably—"

"No. We don't *have* nuclear tech here. We just don't. It's against the Charter." Jackson looked as if he'd been punched. "The Coalition was bringing these into New York? Holy *shit*."

"Why?" Nyx kneeled. "Why would they *want* these?"

A distant, academic part of Anna's mind wondered the same thing. *My world died from these. I died stopping these. And they made more.*

If her stomach hadn't already been emptied, she would've thrown up again.

In her time, there'd never been accurate reports of a viable nuclear weapon being built that was so small. Soviet-era legends abounded, but… nestled inside all of this case's foam, this thing was only as wide as a folded shirt going on vacation. The gleaming metal was cool to the touch. The wires were carefully concealed, as if such a death-dealer needed to be aesthetically pleasing too, freshly rendered from some well-polished blueprint out of Silicon Valley.

They made more. They've made so many more that they've gotten GOOD at—

Her jaw clenched. She bit her lip *hard*, a bright stab of pain, but she couldn't stop. Her hands started to shake.

The only thing between nuclear fission and them was another little keypad. It was covered in thoughtful, accessible Braille.

"This is built for terrorism," she said, tone flat and distant. She almost didn't know who was talking. The old Anna, over a century ago, dreamed of decommissioning nuclear weapons. Everything inside her wanted to rip these devices off the ceiling. She wanted to destroy them, one by one.

But she didn't know how to do that. These weren't her missiles. She'd never seen anything like them before.

"You have something this size…" Her voice spiked, hollow and helpless. "It's not meant to level cities. It's not meant to make a big, flashy, war-ending point. You carry these into secret places, and you detonate them, and you take out a couple blocks. Like, these all *have* to be half-kiloton payloads or less. But the fallout…" Her breath hitched. She closed the case, as if it could make it go away. Her hands wouldn't stop trembling. "It goes a lot wider than that. You make people sick. You cause *horrible* suffering for… for miles. In a tiny area like New York… with wind… and on the *water…*"

Jackson was ramrod straight. "Oh gods. That's why he didn't care if he left behind some of his mining explosives. We need to go. Now."

Nyx too seemed to understand. "We gotta talk to Jaden."

"He's not going to be asleep again. We can't wait for—"

"Radio," Anna interrupted weakly. Her mind kept whirling. Her numbers for calculating this bomb's power were assumptions over a century old. Anything she thought… it would be *worse*. Did the Warlord really understand what this would do?

"The cab," Jackson said, darting out the back, stumbling on his injured leg. Anna's eyes welled, overwhelmed.

"But there's not…" Nyx covered her face with her hands. When she pulled them away, her lips were thin and resolved. "Up front—the radio's burned out. I looked."

"Maybe one of the other cars?" Anna tried.

"Yeah… there too. The Warlord… it didn't look like he wanted anyone sending for help. We… we should actually get out of here." She waved a hand to the racks on the wall. "I know you probably don't want to run right now, but… I thought, at worst, we might be looking at… I, I don't know, just not *this*. If we're going to inform anyone about this, we need to be smart and not get arrested at the scene of the crime. Because no one's going to listen to us then."

Anna rose in agreement.

But the sound of shoes clapping the asphalt again made them pause. Jackson was back, bursting around the side of the cargo doors. "Someone's coming!"

"…And, there they are." Nyx sighed, rubbing her hands together. The barest of glimmers sparked. The exhausted look in her eyes yawned wide open.

"Don't you dare," Anna said. "We can't fight, not like this. We'll hide, see who it is, then we'll figure out what to do."

"They're in one of those spook vans!" Jackson was shifting from foot to foot.

Nyx paused. "Wait. One? *Only* one?"

Anna dove out of the claustrophobic cargo space, leaving the bombs behind. She lingered to help Nyx down as well. Then she was off, aiding Jackson in stumbling along, hustling to the side of the road, to the abandoned buildings beyond.

But he wasn't the only one moving too slowly. Nyx kept lagging, fiddling in her pocket, bringing something out—

"What are you doing?" Anna cried over her shoulder.

A paperclip was swinging on the surface of the fire mage's compass. It pointed insistently down towards the city, but this time, it was shuddering, near alive with energy.

Nyx smiled, and she stopped. "Wait."

Jackson most certainly did not wait, and was trying to drag them both behind the nearest cover, a cluster of pines. Anna hesitated, stopping, torn.

The van she'd hoped was still a decent ways down the road seemed to actually be doing almost a hundred miles an hour. It came to them with an ear-wrenching screech of brakes. In a haze of fog and burning rubber, the vehicle skidded and squealed, swinging to a furious stop next to the truck.

Solar panels lined its slick black roof, and up top, a series of antennae blinked. It was utterly unmarked, the dark windows giving no clue who was in command.

There was no time to reconsider. All Anna could do was fall behind cover where Jackson lay.

But Nyx was turning around entirely.

She was shuffling towards the van, arms wide open as if to embrace it.

Anna's jaw dropped. The passenger door fell open, and out came

Agent Jaden Walker. His shoes flew above the ruined asphalt in rapid bursts. When he reached Nyx, he lifted her into the air with a swing and a bear-hug, a bark of joy coming from his throat.

Jackson was swallowing, owl-eyed. "Walker…. he… he came through?"

Nyx was chattering, waving her hands, and pointed excitedly to where they were hiding. Chagrined, Anna could only stomp down her reservations and hoped her friend's trust was well-placed. She emerged slowly, curious. But instead of sending another cheery welcome, Walker became a flurry of beckoning. "We need to go!" he said. "Now! NOW! They're just behind us!"

Anna reached for Jackson's fingers. There didn't seem be time to argue. He didn't look happy, but he came anyway, jogging, leg shaky. Walker threw open the rear van door, and together, they dove inside. Nyx leapt after. There were no seats in the back, only what looked like a row of radio and video equipment.

The door slammed shut, and Walker pounced into the passenger chair. "Go, go!" he shouted.

The driver was a stubble-ridden old man with a glimmering gold cross hanging heavy against his chest. "I swear, this is the last damn favor I owe you," he grumbled, voice thick with Brooklyn.

He slammed the gear shift, wheels peeling out. Anna fell into a heap against Jackson, who fell against a computer, letting out a stunned, "Ooof!" Nyx found her balance with reflexes that seemed born of habit, crouching like she was riding a surfboard, clutching hand straps nailed into the ceiling.

Flurries of chatter filled the air over a radio's staticky airwaves. The driver was clicking buttons on his dash as he tore back the way he'd come.

A glimmer of blue lay before them on the horizon.

Suddenly, five trucks blew past. They were armored, black monstrosities, gun turrets on full display.

"What the hell?" the driver said. His lip curled as he faced Jaden. "They didn't even hail me. What kind of freak emergency have you gotten me into?"

"I… they… *bomb!*" Anna finally burst. She didn't realize she was crying until her eyes started to blur.

Agent Jaden Walker really had come through, and she didn't care how or why he was there. He could help them stop her worst nightmares from coming back to life. He could help save both the Warlord's misguided people and his own.

She clung to this fiercely, begging him already in her mind.

The agent's dark eyes turned to meet her. This was the first time she'd seen Jaden without sunglasses or a radiation helmet—just civilian clothes, a short-sleeved shirt and cargo pants. For some reason, her hopes began to sink. "Dovetail mentioned explosives," he said. "Is there more intel? I reported it, but I couldn't give my source." This was trailed with a meaningful look. "They've got the Barrier plant on lockdown for inspection. But it's probably only going to be for twenty-four hours. I did get a guy to listen to me that took his platoon out to barricade the tunnels—you remember Sergeant Waters? Man you saved?" Anna nodded, startled. "He was a little more ready to go out on a limb for this than most. So thanks for that."

She smiled gratefully at the news. It almost made her sag in relief that a life she'd rescued was now their ally too, for whatever needed to be done. But she held up a hand, knowing that was not enough. "That truck that was attacked: it was a weapons transport. It—"

The driver made a strangled noise. "No! No, I don't want to hear *anything* else!" He unhooked a pair of headphones from his dash, put them on, and fiddled with the volume. When he waved afterwards, it was like he was giving permission.

Walker nodded. He met Anna's eyes. "Go on."

The van made another squealing turn down the road, and Anna struggled to stay up. "Nukes! Suitcase nukes. The Warlord, he… he took one."

The agent's face puckered in confusion and horror. "I... what? That's... what do you mean *Warlord? Nukes?* What the hell is going on out here?"

Jackson was fighting to sit straight too. His Adam's apple bobbed, but his voice was cool, pointed. "To keep this short, Walker: the Coalition's manufacturing carry-case size nukes, and was *bringing them into New York.* Then they managed to piss off a band of survivors out here with absolutely nothing to lose who despise the city for all it's done to them. Plus, lucky for us! Their leader gets *magical premonitions.* He knew what was in that truck, he took it, and now he's taking his entire family and all of the monsters they've picked up on the way to break down our door. So. There you go."

Walker stared. He processed. He slowly turned sallow. Then he looked at Nyx. Gently, he raised a hand, taking hers. "Love, I'm glad you're here too, but... how...?"

Nyx made a pained face, and Jaden fell silent. "Yeah. Project Esper sent me to clean up the slave markets. Don't worry. I dug my chip out. I'll be fine."

"I'm... I'm really glad to see you." He closed his eyes for a moment. "But... *you two.*" Jaden pointed to Anna, then to Jackson. "How did you get mixed up in all this—why are you even *out* here? I talked to that Frank of yours, you know. Several times, trying to find out what happened to you. And he just keeps finding increasingly creative ways of telling me to fuck off."

Jackson smiled ruefully, genuine affection in his voice. "He must want a raise."

"It doesn't matter why we're here, right?" Anna whispered. "Jaden, we can't let this bomb happen."

Walker wiped the sweat from his brow, and to his credit, wasted no time. He snatched the headphones off his companion's ears and began wrestling with the dials.

"Hey!" the driver said.

"Waters, do you copy? Sergeant Waters? This is Agent Walker. I repeat, this is Walker." His face fell neutral, listening. "Waters, are you out there?"

Suddenly, his back stiffened. Jackson gave Anna a sidelong, concerned stare. Anna, in turn, looked at Nyx, hoping for some kind of interpretation. She only got a wide-eyed shrug.

It was a long, long minute before Jaden spoke again. "Understood," he said. "We're on our way. Be advised: the explosive they have. It is likely nuclear.... No! ...No, I didn't have clearance to know that, and I'm sure you don't either. I'm sorry, Sergeant. But we need to get that information to the plant. They need to evacuate." Another long silence.

"*Manhattan* needs to evacuate!" Anna rapidly tapped his shoulder. "Hey! Anyone within a couple miles of that plant! Okay?"

Walker stared. He was sweating harder. "I can't..." His eyes unfocused. "Yes? I'm still here, Waters. No, I know. Did you hear that? Can you do it? We need to get as many people as we can out of—" He suddenly cursed, fiddling again with the dials. "Sergeant? Do you copy?"

The headphones came off. "He stopped transmitting. There was gunfire. And what sounded like..." His expression scrunched, confused. "Animals, or something. *Howling.* Waters said his people had the main group pinned down, but a few of them broke away—*big* guys. It sounds like they were carrying something. I don't know if he got them."

"I'd bet he didn't. They've got some kind of magic." Jackson cursed. "It's not going to be easy for untrained soldiers to deal with. We..."

"*We'll what?*" the agent snapped. "Is there something you can do about this? Because if so..."

"I don't know." Jackson fidgeted.

Anna rested a hand on his knee. "Can you drop us off where Waters went? So we can make sure he's got all the info he needs? Probably best we don't go through that city checkpoint anyway, right?"

Jaden slouched. "Alright. Yes. It's best. And it's best if I try again to get word to the higher ups about a needed evacuation. Nyx—"

"I'm going with them." The woman pointed. "It'd be way better if that evacuation isn't needed after all."

"But you just—" His brow crumpled a little.

"*Honey.*" Sweet as anything, she smiled. "What do I do?"

He sighed, looking argumentative. "You kick ass." It was like he was finishing an inside joke.

"Damn straight." She ruffled his short military hair. "Do your best. Yank the Director by her damn ear if you've got to."

Jaden just nodded, swallowing what looked like several objections. And after a few more minutes of going a hundred miles an hour, dodging down odd little makeshift paths, the van screeched in a furious turn to a hand sign the agent waved. The driver wordlessly zig-zagged right through a few interconnected and empty lots.

Finally, Walker raised a closed fist. "Here," he said. They stopped. Up ahead, there was a steep drop in the concrete. A furrow was there, excavated from the earth. "We've been re-mapping these tunnels, but it's been slow. Waters said he thought the best place to set up was about a half-mile in from this entry point. That's when he ran into trouble."

"Got it." Nyx nodded.

"Wait. Take this." Walker unhitched a metallic clip inside his pocket, slipping it into Anna's confused fingers. "Friendly signal. The sergeant gave it to me just in case. You carry that, his people will know you're coming. They'll probably think twice before shooting you."

"Do I get one?" Jackson asked dryly.

Nyx chuckled. "What? No. You're not pretty enough."

Jackson made an offended huff, and even if it didn't *break* the tension in the frightened space, it eased it. "What? You don't think I'm pretty?"

Jaden stared. "How are you all even friends?"

"It's my charm." Nyx slid open the van door and hopped out, face singing bravado. Anna wished she felt the same.

"Hey." Jaden's voice held her back. Quietly, just so her and Jackson could hear, he whispered, "Please keep her safe. I can tell she's not in good shape."

"We will," Anna agreed.

Jackson's lips were a thin line. "We'll *try*," he allowed.

And together, they stumbled out of the van. As soon as Jackson closed it up, it squealed off again without another word.

CHAPTER NINETEEN
Underground

Jackson hobbled to the cracked concrete furrow, pain shooting through his leg with each step. He barely thought of it though, one eye to the wall of blue energy just blocks away. This entrance into Old New York's aqueducts looked like it used to be entirely underground. Heaps of rubble were piled here—someone, maybe a long time ago, had blasted in. It was all clear now.

He stumbled along quicker, getting dizzy.

"Your leg," Anna whispered to his left.

"It's okay," he said. A ripple of nausea cut through his stomach. "We don't have time to—"

"Wait." It was Nyx. She trotted in front of Jackson, reaching out, perking his chin up with her palm. Squinting into his eyes, she frowned.

"I'm fine." Jackson cringed away.

"Uh-huh. Your pupils are dilated. Still." She sighed. "But I guess you *do* have to be fine. We don't have time to sit and get better." She gave Anna a pointed look. "No healing. Not for a long time. Got it?"

Anna rubbed her hands together, opting, it seemed, to stare at her toes. "…Okay. You're right."

"And you." Nyx turned her stare again to Jackson. "If you start feeling a second wave from that Nightcap, you say so. All three of us are probably magically exhausted. Do not engage if you can help it—we are *delivering information.*"

Jackson suddenly felt very much like a soldier from whom a "Yes, ma'am," was expected. But what else was there to do, drug in his system or not?

His skin prickled. His magic-senses buzzed. This was a rather unpleasant and lingering trip.

Still, he nodded that he was ready.

"Then in we go." Without further ado, Nyx hopped down onto the decrepit waterway. The pipeline under the streets was more than wide enough to allow her to stroll inside. Anna frowned, held her breath, and followed. Jackson was last. The duct made way to another ancient access hatch. It was already wide open.

Even in the dim light, he could see both women fighting back their gag reflexes, just as he was doing.

Onward they pressed. Beyond the access hatch, there were stairs burrowing down, and beyond that, tunnels. Hollow dripping echoed in the moldy dark.

Then, a sudden punch of gunfire came from further down the labyrinth. It was heart-stopping in its proximity, terrifying in its sudden cease.

Silence.

"Light it up," Nyx whispered. Anna nodded, her glow a slow burn. In it, they had just enough to see. Decay marked this place, stones long crumbled, blocking the walking path. The only way through was wading down a corridor of waist-high stagnant water.

"Promise me we're gonna go get a shower and see a doctor after all this." Anna's whisper accompanied a light squeeze of Jackson's fingers.

He realized that maybe there was a place after all for his uncertain promises for the future. "I guarantee it," he said, forcing in every last shred of pretended confidence he'd ever staged.

Nyx was already wading in. "Shark," she was whispering. In her hands, firmly above water, was what looked to Jackson like a cobbled compass. Her eyes were narrowing as the pointer spun and spun, never landing. "Frick, that name's all I have!"

"What is...?" Jackson shivered. The water was icy, slimy, and now, it was in *all* the cracks.

"Tracker." Anna rubbed her forehead like muck had dripped between her eyes. "She needs a real name, maybe some things about the person."

He reached in his pocket, drawing out a long-range transceiver he'd palmed from inside Walker's van. "Try Baldur," he said.

"Who?" Nyx blinked.

"The Warlord. Father of Tiger, leader to his people. But his real name: it's Baldur." Jackson began to fiddle with a few dials on the communicator's surface, careful to pull it away from the gentle waves and splashes at his elbows.

Nyx began to whisper again.

Her compass spun, whirling.

Then it settled. The arrow pointed inexorably forward.

"Got you, asshole," she muttered. "The sergeant will definitely want to know this."

Jackson ignored her, extending his new transceiver's whiplike antenna. Quietly reciting a frequency to himself, he fine-tuned the sounds of static. Frank once forced him to memorize several channel designations in case they were separated. And now, these numbers were a wonderful tool to cement his focus.

The shadows around him were bending strangely in Anna's light, like a mess of living creatures, like lean, breathing, waiting people.

He was certain he was never going to touch Nightcap again for as long as he lived.

"Hey," Anna said. "What's...?"

"Radio." Jackson found the right wavelength, a thin hiss of static answering him. Slowly, he tapped the buttons, sending through slow

Morse beeps, the only ones he knew—a distress signal. *Please answer. Pick up. Come on. Pick up.*

"That's not gonna work much farther," Nyx cautioned. "And that gunshot didn't sound too close yet, but…"

"Trust me," he said. "It's important."

It was then the static and crackle began to part. At first, it was just strained clicks, shuffling and catches of voice. And then, it was if the heavens opened, a man descending from on high to grace them with his warmth and social charisma.

"Who the *hell* is this?" the voice demanded, ricocheting off the broken bricks.

Jackson sighed in relief, eyes stinging at that gruff, agitated snarl, turning down the volume. He pressed the communicator to his forehead as if it was holy. *Missed you too, you old bastard.* "Frank," he whispered, voice echoing hollow. "It's good to hear you."

There was a silence on the other end, the sound of a man's mind pivoting. His next words were quiet, laced with urgency. "Boss. Tell me what you need."

Jackson swallowed back his emotion. "I'm back in the city. Under it. Tony's old tunnels. The sewers."

"What…?"

"Camping didn't go well."

"You tell… *bzzt* …where you are. *Bzzt*… coming to get you."

Jackson could imagine that: the big man, almost in his seventies, grabbing his shotgun and galoshes, storming off into the mildew-and-cockroach laden underground.

"I can't," Jackson whispered. "Frank… I'm calling because something very bad is about to happen. I'm about to use all of my magic to try and stop it."

"Like *hell* you… *bzzt!*"

"No. We need to do this. Now, if Anna and I escape, we're probably going to end up on the East Side. Maybe near the Barrier plant. And if not there, a duct outside the dome, near Bronx River Parkway and the checkpoint. Can you keep some eyes out above ground for us? Just in case, so the militia doesn't get us before you can."

A fury-laden stillness bloomed in the silence that followed. "I don't care what's happening!" Frank finally growled, "You get out of there *now… bzzt…*find somewhere safe to wait!"

Gunfire broke the silence of the tunnels again. More this time, answering reports.

Jackson swallowed, an iron ball in his stomach. "Frank, I can't run from this. It's… it's fate. If I can help, then I… look, I want you to know that—"

"Boss, don't you—!"

"—I appreciate everything you've done for me. You're family, and I need you to—"

"Kid, you stop *right now—!*"

"—take care of Dad's company. If anything happens. I know it's in good hands."

"Wait!"

"I really hope I see you soon."

"*Jackson—!*"

Jackson silenced the radio and breathed, a snarl of emotion roaring in his chest. A sopping wet arm was suddenly around him, the warm leaning of a head on his shoulder. Grateful for the silent solidarity in their march, he returned Anna's half hug as best he could.

The rubble blocking the dry paths was past. Nyx was hauling herself up and out of the chilled muck and wet, back onto the walkway alongside it all. Anna was up before Jackson even had time to blink. Her warm, softly glowing grasp extended to him in turn.

His resolve steadied a little. Taking her hand, he managed to pull himself up, too.

"That was Frank McSheffrey?" Nyx held her compass a little higher. The pointer was ridged and trembling, as if its target was getting closer.

She picked up her steps.

They all started to jog, stumbling, hurt. Jackson slipped the communicator back into his damp pocket. "Yes, how did you…?"

"Hey, we kept tabs on you. But good choice. You probably don't know half of what that old guy's done to keep you safe." Nyx paused at a tunnel bend, then took the right-hand path.

Startled, taken aback at this acknowledgement of surveillance, Jackson had to ask. "…What all *has* he done?"

But he would not learn.

As they rounded the tunnel, the Coalition was upon them. Seven men and women in gray-and-black fatigues sprung from dark crouching places like well-oiled machines. The whites of their eyes flashed in anger and fear. Rifles snapped up in a millisecond.

"I *said*: they've got a friendly signal!" someone hissed.

The guns wavered. But the soldiers' faces were trembling too. They were bloodied, dirty, and looked about ready to snap.

"On your side!" Jackson said as Anna took Walker's device from her front pocket, holding it up as if it was proof.

He did not like this desperate, hunted look on these new faces. Not at all. These were not soldiers that were winning.

"This one's wearing an antler-sign!" One of the troopers pressed a rifle deeper into his chest.

"*Woah*, hey." Nyx narrowed her eyes. "At ease!" Another gun pressed closer to her. "Agent Jaden Walker sent you all out here—and Waters, right? You're doing this with Sergeant Waters?"

"Guns down! Down!" A haggard man came from deeper in the shadows, wiping his night vision goggles up as he entered Anna's circle of light, resting them on his tightly kinked black hair. Disbelief rocked his tone, as if he'd discovered the intruders were, in fact, penguins. "… Dr. Matthews?"

Anna stuttered. "Y-yeah! That's me!" Despite everything, she even smiled.

The man inclined his chin sharply at Jackson, then at Nyx, a gleaming question in his harsh brown eyes.

"With me!" Anna added. "Both of them."

"Guns," this man repeated, "Down."

Slowly, *very* slowly and with much shaking, the guns really did fall.

Jackson realized this must be the sergeant that Walker spoke of. That squared jaw and severe stare—this was clearly a military man for life. "I hear," Jackson tried, nervous, "that Anna saved your life too."

There was a friendly flicker in that gaze. As Jackson hoped, it seemed Anna made friends wherever she went. "That's right." The gleam disappeared. "And you couldn't have come at a better time. My people are… look, I don't even know *what* we're dealing with here. I was told there was *thirty* of them, and most seem real young or *real* old, but they fight like… like…" His voice was thick and rough as sandpaper as it trembled. "It's like that goddamned Bertinelli. Like the whole world's gone crazy."

Jackson's heart fell into his shoes.

And then, as Anna's glow spread a little farther, as she tried to illuminate the entire group, a dizzy red lanced the corner of his eye. It drew his stare upward, ever upward.

They were now standing in a junction where the ancient aqueducts were dissolving into the earth. It was at this place, Jackson suspected, that the Old Bronx ended above, and that the city proper began.

Someone had left a sign here on the cement up high, letters a foot tall in paint flaking, dark, and blood-red.

THIS IS MY CITY.
THE RULE IS THAT YOU MUST FIGHT TO LIVE.

Your destiny, Jack. Tony's voice rose unbidden in his mind.

Jackson shook his head, bowing it. Magic still buzzed a little here, sick and strange. It was as if this place's former master had seeped into the walls like smoke, insidious, inescapable.

This underground was still his arena. Killing the ringleader didn't make much of a difference.

Jackson trembled.

And a flickering golden eye bobbed in the dark—down the tunnel, stretching back into the abyss.

No. He forced himself to remember reality. *Tony's dead.*

It was only the reflective gleam of another against Anna's glow. A person was running to meet them, waving, clothed in soldier-gray.

Breathe in. Out. It's not real.

"Someone from B team made it…!" one of the soldiers whispered, smiling.

Jackson wrenched his brain into the present with a vengeance, to boots echoing on wet stones.

"I wish I could help heal you, but…" Anna was explaining.

"We're mostly here to advise." Nyx crossed her arms. "The one with the skull's their leader. There's also a big guy with sharpened teeth, and a woman with one eye—she's a medic. Those are the two the Warlord delegates things to. I'd wager one of those three is the one carrying the bomb. You probably already know they're desperate. This is personal, and they've got a whole pack of nasty attack dogs they've managed to tame."

A separate conversation was getting hissed between the sergeant's team. "I know dogs. Those were not *dogs*," a young man's voice twanged painfully—he couldn't have been more than eighteen.

"Dogs don't scream." Another man shivered. "They… they don't scream like that. Like when Hailey got—"

"Button up," the sergeant whispered. Only he seemed to be keeping one eye on the new arrival. Everyone's mumbling ceased.

The approaching solider was a woman, hair long and ragged, holding her rifle close. She was just twenty feet away when Jackson saw her reach into her pocket, saw her right eyelid was oddly wrinkled and sunken.

Was that eye… missing…?

In Anna's wavering light, he remembered a woman's face lit in candle, a medic ushering him into an apartment under a storm-wracked sky.

"*Got a present for you, city scum!*" Maya screeched in her stolen uniform.

"SHIT!" Jackson reached into the darkness, not caring who saw him do it. The plentiful shadows *seethed* under his hand. Charging Maya was wrenched off her feet. The thing in her hand went flying into the water.

The muck erupted.

"Grenade!" a soldier yelled at the blast geyser of slime.

"Goddamn—!" Waters bellowed. He drew his gun, started to fire. Maya rolled agilely, springing down a side tunnel. The bricks exploded into dust where her head had been not a second prior.

The sergeant's eyes blazed. "Sons of bitches!" he barked. "They've tracked us; we need to move!"

"Sergeant," Nyx managed. "Are there any more of you? We gotta regroup—"

"Where do you think she got that uniform and friendly signal?" he snapped. "We've been trying to take them out for the last hour! B team *was* our backup!"

A baying echoed bleakly through the tunnels. All the guns rose.

Maya's laughter floated eerily from gods-knew where. An entire chorus of chuckling was rising with her. It was impossible to know from which direction either the warriors or the dogs were coming.

And it was clear that this frightened these soldiers a great deal.

"MOVE!" Waters roared. He dove down the left-hand route. His team hustled behind. Jackson was swept up in the tide along with all the rest.

So much for just delivering information.

The sergeant was yelling into a communicator. "Team C, do you copy? They've found us! They are in pursuit! Target not found! Give me your sitrep!" Only static answered. "Team C, do you copy? We are bearing west to find a defensible position!"

No reply.

The group kept going.

And suddenly, as they rounded a bend, a wasteland wolf sprung from the shadows. Its sinewy legs scrabbled furiously against the wet stone, its eyes lolling, stained teeth glistening with hunger. The soldiers fired. It grunted, flopping back into the still river. There it sunk with a splash.

But it wasn't alone. Anna's light caught a flicker of tawny movement in the dog's wake. This new beast's muscles were oiled stone, coiling, its claws razors, eyes amber. It was some kind of *cat*—big as a motorcycle. Two dagger-like teeth extended over its lips as it snarled.

"The *heck...?*" Anna shouted, backing up.

Jackson agreed. This wasn't a creature the Warlord had picked up outside.

It was something he'd sensed in the dark forest at the dawn of time.

When the thing opened its mouth, its screech was a woman tortured. Like a cannon firing, it sprung. Bullets went wide as it streaked past. A paw as huge as a man's head slammed into Waters, raking his chest. The sergeant collapsed against the wall.

The youngest soldier got off another shot, burying it in the wildcat's thick leg, eliciting a second soul-rending shriek. Yet, it didn't seem to *care*, more bullets slicing across its flesh. Pouncing again like lightning, jaw wide, it closed its teeth around another soldier's throat. The woman seized and struggled.

The wildcat bounded off, dragging its prey into the dark like her weight was nothing.

"Ramirez!" a soldier hollered. He fired down the tunnel where his comrade vanished. Bullets echoed off stone.

And from the direction the cat had fled, now there was only the storm of pounding feet. A near-unholy shriek of purpose resounded from every direction.

A team of people surged up and out of side tunnels, from every direction except behind. They all bore the antler sign over their hearts, and they wailed like the desperate and damned that they were. Their bullets tore open the tunnel rock.

Coalition hands pushed Jackson, Anna, and Nyx back behind the bend again, into cover as they returned fire. Two of the Warlord's charging army fell, a flash of blood against their hides and tattoos.

Their frozen, pained faces flashed through Jackson's memory. He saw a man and woman he'd helped drag from a burning building.

The wastelanders suddenly parted and scattered—except one, who they'd been shielding. She kept charging as if her very will could part the seas: Maya. Battle-lights blazed in her stare as she threw another grenade. "SURVIVE THIS!" she screeched, then dove behind a rotting pillar.

"Woah!" Nyx barely slapped it into the water before it went off. Slime showered down. Jackson's hearing rang into nothing. His panicked breath seized. The world seemed to slow, unreal.

Nyx shoved her compass closer to Anna, reading it in her light. The pointer swung insistently back the way they'd come. "They're herding us the wrong way!" she yelled, voice fuzzy and muffled to Jackson's ears. "They're stalling us, picking us off! Warlord isn't even *close...*!"

Waters's eyes were swinging around. There were six soldiers left in his team—Jackson could see the man mentally count. Six, plus the three unknowns who'd brought them intel.

His hearing crept back into focus. The tunnels echoed only with the sound of dripping water again, like no one had been here in decades.

Then somewhere, seemingly far away, eerie laughter floated to greet them once more.

"Gone." The sergeant swore and gasped, wincing as he touched the shredded claw tracks on his chest. "Guerrilla strike tactics. These goddamned animals… how did these people even get them…?" He panted. "We need to smash through to whoever's got that bomb. That's the only way we're ending this. You've got some way of tracking their leader?"

Nyx awkwardly held up her locater. "Yes."

"Good. I don't care how it works. You're now key to this mission. And we're on our own—command isn't responding. The team I sent to get word out stopped answering."

"Backup isn't…?" The teenaged soldier wavered.

"Don't think about that," Waters interrupted, stern as the grave. "Think about how we're going to save every one of the half-million lives up there." He jabbed a thumb to the heavens, holding the teenager's stare.

Eyes went wide. "Yes, sir!" the soldiers chanted as one, growing in resolve, even though their voices still trembled.

Jackson swallowed. Was he himself worth more than a half-million people? Were they worth magic leaving the world should he die? Who could even wrestle with a question like that, put a simple price on it?

But would Inoki have given him the book and this fate if he were meant to simply lock himself up, away from harm he could prevent?

"I can help cut a path through," he whispered. Afraid though he was, this was home. He wasn't going to walk away from this city so easily. "If you can protect me."

"Jackson." Nyx gave him a warning look. "Know your limits. There's no way your reserves are gonna be much stronger than mine right now after dreamwalking…"

"No. I can do it. I feel…" He thought about it. Deep in his core… well, he was exhausted and hungry, and feeling more than a little sick. But magic still flowed on his skin. It swirled in the shadows around him. Buried in this darkness… even if it buzzed foreign and strange…

This part of him that was connected to the place called the Shadow was not even the least bit tired.

"What are you going to do?" Waters demanded.

"Anna," Jackson said, more sure of this than he'd ever been of anything. The story of the Sun flickered in his mind. "I need you to really shine."

She nodded like he only needed to ask, even if she didn't understand. "No one put on their night vision goggles," she said. And then, she closed her eyes. Her light burst. It flared up and out, like a new star rising—almost painful to look at, and too beautiful to look away. It cast warmth, drying the unpleasant damp clinging to Jackson's clothes and skin. For a time, this sewer, far underground, was awash in pure, comforting daylight.

I'm glad that if I fell in love with anyone, that it was you, no matter what happens now. Jackson silently let his heart thud in this wash of gentle magic. In his mind, he felt the shadows spreading dark and long in her wake, including his own. They rooted him, extending all the way to the light's edge. His mind tumbled down through his shoes, through his shadow, connecting to everything beyond this ring.

"The hunters will run from the light," he explained. In his voice, he heard a strange thrum, almost an echo. "And I think I can handle the rest, if you all can stall the warriors."

"…Sir?" One of the men looked to Waters. Jackson wasn't insulted by their uncertainty. Even he was guessing.

"I trust him," Anna said. Her pupils shone a sparkling blue.

The sergeant drew his gun up, clearly set on ignoring his pain. "And I trust *you*."

Nyx squared her shoulders, looking reserved, though she was biting down her questions. "Then I'll lead the way?"

Waters nodded. "Do it."

Nyx rose, setting off in a jog down the tunnel bend. Anna followed, the soldier team following, and Jackson fell to the fringe, keeping in lockstep with the bubble of sunshine, feeling out the black.

If he felt carefully enough, approaching paws were like flies landing on the surface of a spiderweb, disturbing the tension. He poured every last ounce of himself into listening for these disturbances in his magical field, extrapolating what the book had taught, combining it with strange, shifting instincts that were rising in his blood.

Almost immediately, as they ran, they were met with two howls—an attack dog bred true and a reedy wasteland canine, both waiting in the tunnel and vibrating with hostile intent. Jackson swung his hands in an arc. His shadows reared like snakes. They tripped the first dog, sending it reeling and skidding uselessly into the water. The second dug in its claws, flailing. But with a furious yelp, it was torn back into the tunnel from whence it had come.

"Left!" Nyx called. She banked, following her compass like it was the only thing in the world. The group pivoted with her as one.

A scream! A young wastelander, tangled hair flying, barreled from one of the side tunnels ahead. He peppered the air with rifle bursts. Jackson and the team dove behind a rotted column for cover.

His face was familiar—a teenager from the planting fields. A lone serpent tattoo coiled around his torso and back. Perhaps he'd only had his first rites.

But his reedy yell echoed desperately in the dark: "I WON'T DIE ALONE!"

He shrieked like a descending banshee, four other warriors joining him as he made a new charge. It was the same group that had attacked alongside the wildcat. At their rear was Maya, stare grim, spit flying as she screamed.

Her fighters knew their guns well.

The column shielding the group exploded in dust and debris, getting pulverized

With no choice, the Coalition men and women threw themselves to meet their enemy, returning fire, using the wall of their bodies to protect. Slugs punched at their chest armor. They were blown back.

But they'd bought Jackson all the time he needed. He shoved with his mind. The darkness rippled in a wave. Three of the attackers lost their footing before they could dodge. The other two tripped over their startled companions, falling in a bundle of skins, stolen black boots, and fury.

The sergeant and the recovering soldiers wasted no time taking advantage of the scramble. Their return onslaught was absolute.

The boy toppled with his friends. His teeth were bared in an unrepentant snarl. His eyes were white with fear, angry tears leaking from them and mixing with blood.

Anna let out a horrified cry.

The five bodies ahead quivered as the frightened soldiers unloaded round after round. All five looked long dead well before the shooting stopped.

Jackson tried not to see.

We... we can't save them all, he reminded himself. These people had come here to fight and die, to pay back wrongs with blood and vengeance. When their bomb was in hand, that would be the right time to consider if killing them was ultimately moral or just.

His stomach turned anyway.

"Go!" the sergeant snapped, voice hazy in the ringing, numb silence.

Slowly, the Coalition group started to advance.

And just as they began to step over their victims, one fired to her feet right next to them, *shrieking*. Her only eye was filled with the righteous rage. She was covered in blood, and none of it her own—all of her friends in front had been her shield.

To her chest, she clutched a third grenade. "FOR US ALL!" she screamed.

Guns fired again. Maya smiled as two bullets struck her legs and she dropped, simply holding her weapon to her chest like a new mother.

Jackson barely registered that he needed to flee.

Anna yelled with hollow sorrow and indignity, and she wasn't running anymore. She *flew*.

Maya went down with Anna in a tangle of screeching limbs. Together, they tumbled into the water. The tunnel was plunged into pure darkness.

"*No!*" Jackson ran to the water's edge.

A furious geyser of water blasted against his ears and face, hot, punching him back. Arms pulled him out of the way.

He couldn't hear. His eyes struggled to adjust.

Then, a glowing, blond head broke the water's surface again, almost out of sight down the tunnel. Jackson kneeled in relief.

The monsters in the dark were still as he breathed. They felt as if they were pausing, like they were unsure.

Watching. Waiting.

Spitting and choking, Anna hauled herself up. Waters ran forward and extended a hand. Nyx trotted up too, then helped Anna to drag a body… good gods. The body was Maya's, mostly intact, even. The woman's head lolled on her neck, her eyes closed. Blood was running from both of their ears, but from Anna's, it stopped, her cuts and scrapes fading inside her glow.

Anna sagged a little, but it looked like it was from relief. Jackson jogged to meet her. Slowly, his hearing was returning, more slowly than from the last grenade blast. Anna's warm glow engulfed him again, and she mouthed a weary answer to the question burning in his throat: "I'm okay."

"This one's alive!" Waters called. "Janda! Secure her! She's gonna be needed for questioning."

Maya's eye fluttered as a man ran forward, cuffing her hands together, binding her bleeding legs. Quickly, she was stripped of her weapons—and beyond the grenades, these seemed to be an ungodly number of knives.

"You kill me, you cowards," she spat, dazed. "You kill me. No slave. Never again. *Never.*"

Anna knelt, reaching out a hand, and Maya flinched away. At first, Jackson thought to make a concerned noise, but he needn't have worried. It seemed Anna was going to ignore the worst of the wounds. "I'm sorry I can't heal your legs," she said. "But I think the bullets went through. You'll be okay with some help. And I think I can manage your ears and that concussion."

Her palm glowed a little brighter, though she rubbed the center of her brow, like it itched furiously.

Maya's eye widened, clarity entering her gaze.

If anything, this made her worse.

"I'LL KILL ALL OF YOU!" she screeched, lunging. The soldier called Janda had to wrench his massive arms down to hold her. It seemed impossible that it should have been so hard, but twice, he was nearly thrown. Jackson only began to understand how she did it when Maya's eye flickered black and hollow, a sick sense of magic rolling over her. "DON'T TOUCH ME! GET OFF! I'LL KILL YOU!"

His mouth dried in that blind fury, and he believed that even without her weapons, she would have tried.

"Make her pipe down," Waters snapped.

"Wait," Anna said.

"She's going to raise the dead screaming like that, and—"

"Promise me," was all Anna replied. "That you aren't going to stick her in that slave program up north."

The sergeant blinked at her. "The *what?*"

"Promise me!" A tear streaked Anna's cheek. She jabbed her finger forward. "You have to *promise* me you'll ask her whatever questions you want, but you're not going to throw her into a slave program!"

Waters looked taken aback. "Miss… Dr. Matthews. What happens to her isn't up to me. But the Coalition doesn't *have* slave programs."

"Whatever you call it," Anna said. "She's not going there."

Maya actually quieted. She looked up at Anna, gaze war-weary and sad. "They lie," she rasped. "You should have helped us. They *always* lie."

"We're clear!" Two soldiers jogged up. Jackson barely realized they'd broken from the group to go scout ahead.

"We keep moving," the sergeant announced. Nyx held up her compass again. It looked like it was tugging her on. The soldier named Janda nodded, taking out a pouch, tagging a little device to Maya's uniform. Then he dragged her to where a rotted bit of pipe jutted from the wall, securing her cuffs to it.

The woman's stare bore into Anna, and only Anna, the entire time. She was gone again, eye black and cold.

"You know what they will do to me," was all she said. "You *live* with that."

Janda extracted a rag, soaked it against a chemical bottle from his pouch, and held it to Maya's face. The furious medic fell silent, her gaze drooping, her form sagging into unconsciousness.

The only sound left was Anna. "Promise me you won't send them there," she whispered, sounding defeated.

Waters was staring at her, stern, seeming… confused.

Then he waved the group on, and there was nothing left to do but go forward.

CHAPTER TWENTY
Vivat Rex

Anna's sides throbbed in pain as she ran. She kept her light up, kept the group safe, followed Nyx's compass—because that was what she had to do.

But a bitter, angry streak of tears began to fall.

They were passing bodies now. Some were Coalition soldiers. Most were people she'd just met and healed. She'd just learned their smiles, and now here they were, half-starved, twisted up in threadbare cloth and hide… growing cold.

Some were partially eaten.

No one here deserved to die. No one should have lost their homes. No one should have been sent up north and chained into forced labor.

And maybe these soldiers really didn't know anything about that.

Maybe the Coalition buried their sins deep.

But that was irrelevant. Everyone here would die just the same, angry and empty and hoping their deaths meant something that they wouldn't.

And she could do nothing but run, hoping she could stop as much of it as she could.

The tears were helpless, and they were growing faster by the second.

Nyx sprinted ahead, darting down another tunnel, audibly gasping for breath.

In the air, suddenly, a cracking, thundering roar of disintegrating concrete echoed. It vibrated the stilled water to her left. Loose rubble tumbled from the walls.

Anna's heart leapt in her throat. If that was the *bomb*—

An eerie series of howls floated in the sound's wake.

Then silence.

Anna ran harder. If that had been the nuke, the sounds of destruction would have gone on for much longer.

Jackson was staggering behind, barely keeping up at the edges of her light. He made no noise of protest though, his eyes shining reflectively. Whatever watchful magic he was doing thrummed up the line to her chest, quiet and sure.

And the beasts were staying back, as he'd promised, though they never went far. Hordes of flickering eyes darted down the tunnel behind and to the front. They were running thick now, in packs, blood on their maws. The soldiers took pot shots now and again, getting answered with furious yowls and yips.

The animals parted, tails between their legs, only growling in warning.

Like they were waiting.

Nyx suddenly skidded to a stop, and the ceiling vaulted upwards. The tunnel had punched into something new.

Anna stared as her light feebly tried to touch the furthest reaches of this cavern, fading into nothingness. Hollow, metallic drips echoed through the air. Flashes of pipes shone briefly as her sunshine bounced off walls and pillars. This space was huge and open, part natural and part manmade, mud and decayed cement slushing underfoot. Before her, several tunnels branched. In her lungs, the air hung stale and dead.

The breathing of animals hung here too, rank, moist, and hissing. Here was where they'd all gathered. Hundreds of paws shifted on ledges, slunk away from the light as she led the group past.

One of the tunnels before her was collapsed. Bricks and cement lay in a heap before it. Dust shimmered in the air here, as if the collapse was recent.

Was that the explosion sound…?

Suddenly, amidst the animals, a bright curve of bleached antler reflected in her light, just for a moment.

Anna's breath jerked.

A freight train of a man barreled towards her.

A grim laugh echoed in her ears before her head burst with blinding pain.

Jackson limped, senses bursting and overloaded. He felt the disturbance in this cavern's pool of magic long before he saw it.

But not soon enough to warn her.

Anna went flying, a rusting steel arm flashing in the light, following her arc in its brutal swing.

Her light ripped away from them all.

It was as if the animals knew this was their signal. They descended in a mob.

Jackson's cry stuck in his throat as three chittering, maned canines pounced from a ledge above in a wailing, speckled flurry. A soldier's bullet caught one. His shadows flung the second. But the third, it fell on another soldier while screeching in triumph.

Jackson wrapped his magic around the wild dog's midsection, trying to yank it away. Its prey screamed. The beast only dug in deeper. More of its friends were gathering on the ledge now too.

A massive paw suddenly slammed into his side. A great, rumbling bellow filled the air. He flew back into the wall, breath collapsing, stars blooming in his eyes. He lost his grip on his magic—heard the attacked soldier scream again. A new monster towered over them all on two legs, shaggy brown fur bristling, claws like daggers. It was built like a tank given life. Behind it, the laughing canines advanced.

Streaks of blood and wounds dotted the behemoth's flesh. Its stare was dead like Maya's, like it was only the ghost of an angry memory. Its skin seethed with insects.

"*BEAR?*" The sergeant made a shriek of surprise, then turned his rifle on it. The shot punched the titan clean in the neck.

The thing called *bear* only turned its head to the troops and bellowed again, *angrier.*

Jackson dashed to his feet. A wasteland mongrel surged from the black, slamming its jaws shut where his leg had been not a moment ago. Ten more pairs of eyes glimmered behind it.

He ran. The wolf pack followed.

Then another nightmare slid in his way—the saber-toothed wildcat from before. Its eyes lit with joy. Its bobtail twitched as it readied to spring.

But a burst of fire exploded in its face, embers scorching its flesh. Jackson leapt over it as it howled, stress sharp in his lungs, the heat brushing his shins. If he hadn't been so intent on not being eaten by the pursuing wolves, he would have thanked Nyx.

Anna's light suddenly welled up before him, letting him know where she was. He dodged into her protective circle. His arcane shadow strengthened in her wake, and he sent back a rush of darkness in a suffocating wave. It wobbled through the canines as they pranced, and they reeled, barking in pain. A few tripped. They scrambled over each other, biting their own comrades in a panic.

Anna herself leaned against him, stumbling to her feet, face bruised, nose bleeding. "Where did he…?"

Jackson felt the Warlord's presence with his inner senses again. It was a violent surge of magical purpose in the cavern dark—like the man had become a living home for raw, ancient power now, like the book, like the field. He'd marinated with purpose in this death trap for hours until he'd become an extension of it.

It lanced up and down those antlers, a crown of fury and vengeance.

Baldur, whoever he'd been, was gone.

The chieftain howled above his bestial horde, crouched before the caved-in tunnel, arms spread wide. And here, he delivered his final proclamation:

"KILL THEM ALL!"

Anna fell back to defend the group. Her sunshine burned as the darkness crushed down. The soldiers were easy to find again—Nyx stood by their side shouting, hurling bursts of embers at the oncoming army of fur and claws and hunger.

Some of her fireballs were fizzling out before they reached their targets. Desperate strain clouded her face.

There was blood washing the soil. One soldier lay totally still.

And as Anna reached them, a thundering cry of a monster whipped her head around.

Her mind refused to process this new creature.

A bear.

An entire… bear. Under New York. Next to hyenas. Wildcats. Wolves. Beasts she'd never even seen in her life.

The bear's form flickered strangely as it bore Sergeant Waters down, like it wasn't fully there. But it raised its dinner-plate paws to crush. The thing only hesitated as the light reached it—suddenly, it drew back, as if in pain.

"*Yaoguai*," Jackson said, agonized breaths gasping behind her. "The Warlord… the monsters, he's *summoning* them…!"

Five soldiers yet stood. Another round of bullets roared from their rifles, and that was all Anna could hear of Jackson's words.

Screeching laughter peppered her ears then, inhuman. Void-eyed, maned canines trotted in a noose-like circle around her light. Joined in their ranks were the dogs from the wastes, and all the other impossible beasts, flowing like liquid as they stalked, all pressing in, trying to get past to the flagging soldiers.

She was the only thing standing between these people and that circle of slaughter.

The animals wound tighter.

They were getting *used* to her light.

Bullets answered the wave, flying past, sending up spurts of blood and shredding bone. Fire raged across the beasts' backs, catching a few in a blaze like living tinder. The monsters didn't seem to care. For each one that fell, a new one flowed in to take its place, another nightmare demanding flesh.

She screamed in horror and frustration, realizing they were trapped.

Jackson's hand yanked her wrist back, and she spun. He forced her to face him, urgently signing just beyond the pack—to the Warlord far beyond.

Jackson mimed antlers over his head. His lips said one word she couldn't hear, over and over, but she understood.

"MAGIC."

He made a motion like he was crushing it in his hands.

Anna's chest tugged.

The beasts, as one, finally found their courage. They stormed together past the line of sunshine.

Jackson's hands made a trembling wiggle, like a man tuning a well-loved instrument. His eyes flickered shut, but not before she saw an almost-light shining at the back of his pupils, blue-violet, strange.

"RUN," he mouthed. He pointed the way forward. The bond between them sang, as if she was part of a whole.

Anna's heart stopped.

She did what he asked.

The shadows surged around her, blood-mawed monsters scrabbling and snapping teeth, saliva flinging as they were shoved out of the way by Jackson's dark reach.

The Warlord tilted his head as she tore for him, as if in surprise. His muscles gleamed with sweat, his fists curling. Air was puffing in front of his face, a cold mist. It had an irregular cadence—like an animal scenting its hunt.

It was coming through the *skull's* nose, not his.

The temperature of the cavern dropped.

The crown wasn't just hiding his eyes anymore, creating some dark illusion. It had fused with him. His very pupils had disappeared into its black pits—just like his monsters.

In those depths was endless rage.

"Echo," he said. The way it rattled through the air was like a curse.

He lunged so fast she didn't have time to react. The false arm came up like a club, crunching again into her chest.

"ECHO!" he bellowed.

Anna tumbled to the side, crying in pain, feeling like at least one rib was broken. Breathing was agony. She righted herself though, knowing there wasn't time. Her bones knitted and began to heal, melting together under her skin.

She grabbed a chunk of cement and threw. It glanced off the Warlord's antlers, sagging his head to the left. Something's teeth grazed her leg, but not enough to stop her from diving forward at her target in a full-bodied assault.

It seemed that was the last thing the chieftain was expecting. His antlers almost gored her neck, but she flung herself into close range, fists wrapping around the helm of bone. The iron-heavy prosthesis that was his right arm swung around useless, unable to reach inward. His good arm caught her in the chest, trying to push her out.

Still, she held fast like she'd wrestled with the hood of that swerving semi-truck.

"ECHO-O-O-OOOO!" he howled.

It was like pulling free a bond made of *cement*.

With a great swing of his torso, his neck snapping like a bull's, he threw her. The side of her cheek sliced open under an antler's sharp tip. Her back crunched into the collapsed tunnel rubble.

The man screamed, the beasts behind him howling in unison, the soldiers crying out in despair. His metal arm smashed where her head had been not a moment prior. The jury-rigged sheet of metal that was his hand squealed on its makeshift wrist, hanging battered and broken from abuse. She painfully wrenched to the side and out of the way.

A furious, giant wolf barreled from the left. In a flash, there was Jackson. He was stumbling from the swarming predators, two soldiers flanking him, keeping him safe as his shadows roiled and flung the beasts away from them all.

He was protecting them.

For now.

As Jackson's magic rose, his glowing eyes were wild. The feral wolf charging Anna was ripped off its feet, bound up in ribbons of darkness, eyes lolling, throat gurgling as it was flung into a decayed pillar.

Jackson staggered. There were gashes up his arm, across his chest.

Gunfire punched the air, both beside him and from behind.

Nyx's fire no longer flashed through the black.

The pack fell on them all again. Anna cried out as her friends disappeared in a flood of teeth and fur, as the line in her chest vibrated with consuming horror. A wolf knocked Jackson down. It was straining against the shadows for his throat—

The Warlord was on her, catching her under the jaw. His cold roar froze her sweat into frost. Steel sent stars through her brain.

His other hand darted in and closed around her windpipe.

"Urk!" she choked, pain and red exploding in her sight. He slammed her back into a wall, making her arms drop in a numb explosion.

There he stood, towering over her, smiling. Her vision started to blur. *Can't breathe…!*

Yet as her sight flickered, as she struggled and kicked, she made one last desperate swing. Her right fist glanced off his skull again. His grip loosened as he reeled. Air entered her lungs in a throbbing, lancing burst. She tore free.

And then, she saw it. Where she'd thrown that punch, there was the smallest of new cracks. They radiated out from an old bullet hole.

That awful club-arm of his rose a second time, about to brain her.

Anna barely managed to dive low, letting the swing go wild. Ducking under his other arm, snatching at his antlers, she yanked. With her left fist, she jabbed. It connected to the broken bullet circle. Numbness exploded in her knuckles like she'd punched a wall.

"ECHOOOOO!" The chieftain screamed his battle-cry, trying to wrench back. Water was falling from the skull's eye hollows like tears.

There was the slightest bit of *give* in the helm's movement on his head.

Roaring her own rasping terror and pain, she swung again and again at the helm. Blood from her knuckles flew free, staining the bone.

A shattered crack was left behind.

She swung again! Again! The crack in the skull widened. The sound it made was like the earth tearing open.

"*Echo,*" the man sobbed one, last time.

The shadows in the phantom-hollow eyes flickered.

It broke, dust and splinters, a thing greater than anything Anna knew she could ever understand.

Around her, the frigid air shattered.

The beasts moaned. Their heads raised, like something distant called to them, something no one else could hear.

One by one, they began to disappear.

Anna stared, shocked, as the bear dissolved, its bloody paws still dripping. The hyenas became ether, the wildcats and wolves disintegrating into shadows too.

The wasteland dogs remained. But their tails tucked in between their legs. They instantly dropped, cowering, hackles raised—terror, not aggression. One by one, they began to scatter, confused, nipping at each other as if they were all strangers.

The howls and snarls faded as they fled. They were gone.

"Anna!" Jackson made a surprised cry from the ground. His voice floated lonesome through this now-empty place. One of the soldiers beyond him was sobbing in relief. Another was cursing in shock.

An old man was crying before her too, on his knees, cradling two halves of a broken crown to his chest. His long hair was washed through all the way now with silver. His once-powerful body was riddled with lines, wrinkles, and age spots, bones a sharp relief against his malnourished frame.

He was... so small.

Was this really...?

She kneeled before him. His storm-gray eyes peered at her with such pain and questioning that she didn't know what to say.

"I'm sorry," was all she had.

He leaned forward, shaking, and rested his head on her shoulder, tears soaking her shirt.

⸺ ❖ ⸺

Jackson blinked at the empty cavern, bursting with pain.

He'd lost count of how many times he'd been bitten, how many times claws snagged his clothes and tried to tear and render and disembowel.

Much longer, and they would have succeeded. All he'd been able to see were yellow, snapping fangs inches from his eyes. All of his strength had barely been able to hold his attackers back.

The world still stunk of fur and mold and rank breath.

His brain could barely reconcile with the fact that they'd just... vanished.

He fell to his knees, laughing with relief, clutching at the muck like it was the finest earth he'd ever known.

We're alive.

I'm the luckiest damn Chosen Inoki's ever had.

"Do you know where you are?" he heard Anna whisper. Slowly, his head raised. She was kneeling with a wizened old figure.

This had to be the Warlord. Yet, this elderly man—back bowed, spirit broken—looked nothing like him at all. For just a moment, Jackson was reminded of the careworn creature that had given his true name by the side of a road, removing his crown like it was the heaviest weight the world had to give.

I was right. It was that thing that was channeling the magic.

This had been a pure guess.

Lucky, lucky. Tony's remembered voice floated to his ears.

Jackson shook off the memory and rose, leaving the soldiers behind as they tended to each other, shouting, tearing cloth into tourniquets. Slowly, he put a hand to Anna's shoulder, letting her know he was there, watching over them both.

The old man's mournful shaking was stilling. His head was rising. He did not meet their stare. "Yes," he said. "I know where we are." His voice was hoarse and riddled with deep regret.

"Where's the bomb?" Anna gently put a hand to each of his frail shoulders. The old man only gazed into nothing though, as if he was lost.

Jackson tensed, at the ready. Baldur may have been a shattered creature, but that grief had also almost killed them all not a moment ago.

"Echo was your wife, right?" Anna's soft whisper jerked the man's silent form out of his stupor. He didn't need to answer with words. The bright pain in his eyes did it for him. He softly placed the crumbling heap of his crown on the earth. This he regarded for a long, quiet minute.

The shouting of soldiers was coming up now. Jackson could hear their jackboots, the cadence of clipped, frantic orders. It seemed only one more of their own had been killed—a miracle in this situation.

"Innocent people are going to die," Anna said. "Not soldiers. Not people that did this to you, or that even know about you. Not Coalition people—just people that were born here with no choice. Like you were. People that might hate what the Coalition did, if they knew."

The man regarded the bones, trembling, curling into himself. "My wife was innocent, too."

The soldiers began to form a ring around them, teeth bared, guns drawn. Jackson tried, "The Fear. The man in your dreams. He got into you, and he gave you power, but he twisted up everything you wanted. Was this what your wife would have told you to do?"

Baldur's eyes went to him, hazy, bloodshot, tears staining his cheeks. "I... she... no, if I'd died, and *she'd* been given this gift... she would have... the *same* thing..."

"She would have thrown away all of your peoples' lives?" Jackson pressed. "All of them, like the ones left behind at your old camp, sent off to slavery because *your revenge* poisoned their minds? Because *you* didn't even stop your march to save them?"

The old man's eyes widened, his nostrils flaring, unsure. "I... I..."

The Coalition-gray sergeant broke the soldiers' half-circle, limping, leaning on bandaged, bleeding Nyx for support. "Don't move," he barked.

The Warlord's stormy pupils glimmered. "Yes. I should have led my people to a home. Not here. But here we are. And you will never catch my boy." His eyes flashed for a moment to the collapsed tunnel. "Even if we all die, even if I should have done everything else, this will... this will mean something...!" He reached out, suddenly grasped for Anna's hand like a man reaching for salvation. "It... it *has to...!*"

At the sudden movement, one of the soldiers fired. The bullet tore through Baldur's outstretched limb. Jackson jerked aside, pulling Anna with him. The Warlord collapsed, still alive. His hand spasmed, but it reached again, as if to close the distance.

"This all... all had to mean *something...*" he said.

The soldier fired again.

Baldur jerked back, coughing, slamming into the debris. His gaze rolled upwards.

Slowly, he smiled. "…E…cho?" he whispered.

And life left that storm forever.

CHAPTER TWENTY-ONE
Old Ghosts

"Stop! STOP!" Sergeant Waters was stumbling up now, far too late, still leaning on Nyx. Anna shook. She backed up into Jackson. He tried to brush her fingers with his, wanting to reassure her, knowing they needed to move. "Who the *hell* gave you orders to *shoot?!*" Waters knocked the rifle down from where it was still quaking and pointing at the dead body. The soldier responsible, Jackson noticed, had no bars of color on his chest: the teenager. The rookie.

"I'm, I'm sorry sir!" the boy stuttered. He was pale as the grave. "He, he just, he lunged, and those monsters were here with him, and I didn't know what he was, and—"

"Did you *consider*," Waters hollered, getting in the teenager's face. *"That he could get us to that bomb?"*

Jackson stared up at the cavern high. *His boy. He said his boy was down that tunnel.*

Tiger was gone, and there was only one man left that fit that description. It was someone with strong arms for carrying, someone who knew this maze well and could have slipped through.

"We have to find this bastard," Waters was saying, gesturing his rifle to the massive blocks of rubble in their way. Blown-out orange wrappings belied the explosives the Warlord used. "Can you find us a way around?" He looked to Nyx.

The compass was spinning in her hands. "It's... it's not GPS," she said helplessly. "I can't just find anyone, and I can't pull a *re-route* if the way is blocked..." Her eyes fluttered, and she collapsed. Waters couldn't catch himself before he went down with her. As they both sat in the mud, she began to shake. "I'm sorry... I think I'm just... just out of power..." The way her eyes lolled, it looked like she was fighting a blackout.

"We need to call the base!" One of the soldiers said. "Sergeant, they got away, and if they get to—"

"We have to get out of this hellhole before the call will go through." Sergeant Waters lifted his head. He too looked to barely be hanging on to consciousness. He started to undo the gear around his vest, fishing for his radio. This he passed to the closest soldier on his left, the one he'd called Janda. "You need to run back to the surface. Get that news out. If they haven't started evacuating..." He began to cough.

"We need to find a way around while we get help!" Anna edged towards an open tunnel. "What if we can still catch up to...?"

Jackson shut his eyes, trying to focus in all the noise. His head was sagging, his body exhausted, hurt, and full of questionable chemicals.

The sergeant rasped, "These passageways branch off in totally different directions. And that's only if the damn *pre-Bombings* maps are right! We are *blind* down here. At this point, the best we can do is confirm Walker's warning." He wheezed. "They're not ready for this. They think this is just a couple rats with C-4 at worst. God, I wish they'd taken the agent seriously."

Anna made a distressed keen, inner light flickering.

The shadows pulsed in time.

The way they vibrated called Jackson's stare, like they were crowds of living creatures again.

He shook his head, trying not to put much stock in it.

Champion! Tony's voice rose unbidden in his mind once more. *You won! You're the champion, Jack.*

Stop it, he thought. *Stop talking to me.*

And he realized everyone had fallen silent. He blinked. They were all staring at him. "Do you hear something?" Anna said.

"N-no," he managed. *Did I say that out loud?*

"Jackson's not doing so good, guys," Nyx whispered. "Don't worry about it… got more important things."

He wanted to argue, but he couldn't. As the group began to chatter again, as he shook on his feet, his eyes caught the Warlord's blood on the ground, the brilliant red. It was seeping into the muck. There it would go, deep into the foundations of New York—just like all the rest of this suffering.

You must fight to live, Tony's voice reminded him.

"Stop it," he whispered to himself, rubbing his eyes, trying to keep his voice very low. "No hallucinations. No time for this."

But Jack! Every champion deserves a prize!

Jackson snapped his head up.

Everything Tony's remembered whispers ever said were bits of prophecy and broken logic from their final meetings.

Except that. Tony had never told him that.

Jarred, disturbed, the blood red began leaking through his brain again. It was soaking the ground. It was marring his body.

It was on a man standing in an open tunnel archway, golden eyes shining.

"I know which way the big man went," Tony's ghost said, voice hissing. "I know all the hidden places in my city."

Jackson stared, then sat on the cold, wet earth.

A tug of magic was troubling him too, grinding at his brain.

The Warlord's pouch. A solider had dumped it all out on the ground.

A few ration bars. A couple vials of Quarantine.

An old book.

Jackson reached out, scooped it in. No one seemed to notice.

And as he did, its hum re-attuned to his body and senses. The trembling vapor of shadows began to overlay with wavering voices in the dark, voices long dead and gone.

Tony wasn't alone, he realized.

The shadows stood straighter, as if they were looking back at him. He'd thought they'd looked like a mass of people, and he realized: he'd been *right*.

A flicker of a smile in the gloom. A flash of a greeting wave. A shifting of hips.

Ghosts were following him, whispering in his ears, waiting at attention. The book was merely a formality, wasn't it? His tome might have manifested as an etched cave or a scroll or a thousand other things. But these hundreds and hundreds of souls were its real form, his guides, his protectors, his predecessors, all here waiting for the very last of the line to act.

His throat went parched, his hands shaking.

"Jackson." Anna was shaking his shoulder. "Hey! *Jackson.*"

"Chosen."

"We are here."

"We will always be here."

"We're waiting for you."

"We're listening."

As he recognized them for what they really were, the shades became clearer. He could see their features, see faces he'd never imagined, glimpses of long-lost times and secrets. He saw the canny stare of an old man and recognized Balthazar in his heart. He saw Atropos beside him with raven feathers in her hair, stare keen into the past and future. He saw Magnus hulking in his furs, face lined with regrets, and Xīng too, strong and brave, challenging him.

Tony stepped forward. "Jack," he whispered, sounding pleased. "You finally hear."

"Yes," Jackson greeted, letting go of excuses, breathless, brain humming, alive.

"You were always meant to come back," the ghost said. "Your destiny is here in this city." He looked about wryly. "*Your* city. It was my city, I guess. You killed me. It's yours now. Those are the rules."

Jackson shuddered, remembering the feel of driving a knife into a man's chest. But Tony only smiled, and the disconcerting thing was, it was confident and pleasant. The mad lights in his eyes were gone. There was only clarity now: conviction free of damaged wiring.

The ghost continued, striding forward. "The dream man by the fire told me a story when I was little. He said I was to have a best friend, someone who would help me if I kept writing him the letters. He said my friend would save me when I needed it most."

Jackson swallowed, recognizing his guilt. "I'm sorry I didn't. That they turned you into..."

He received a blink, long, slow. "You did." Tony tapped his ribs, right where Jackson's knife had come to rest. "They wouldn't let me kill myself. Those are the rules too."

To that, there was nothing Jackson could reply. His heart beat far too loudly in his chest. Someone was shaking his shoulder still. Anna? Everything seemed so far away. His voice was an octave too high when he spoke. "Were you a Chosen? Like me?"

"No," Tony said, echoing and strange. "Not all of us are. But I did have a job. I'm always supposed to show you the way."

A raven fluttered from the dark, landed on the phantom's shoulder. It made a soft croaking noise in his ear.

"Mmm. Yes. Not much time now," Tony whispered.

"My guardian," Jackson said, understanding dawning. "Inoki gave you that magic just to protect me."

A nod, frantic and pleased. "Yes, and I had a great time. Now, eyes forward, Jack!" The ringleader cheerfully tipped his hat. Then he turned, all the exaggerated grace and sweeping arms of a man dedicated to being center-stage.

The crowd of specters parted, as if inviting him through. Jackson wobbled to his feet. Some reached out their hands, frowning, as if they wanted to help, wanted to touch, even though they couldn't.

One man in particular had eyes shining with sadness and regret. He was far back in the gathering, but Jackson knew that mustache, that suit, and it made his heart hammer with relief and love.

"Dad…?" he whispered.

Peter Dovetail's smile widened with relief and pride.

Tony's voice was alarmingly far away. "Run, Jack! You must run! No time!"

Jackson wanted nothing more than to run headlong into the shadowed mob, to fling his arms around his only family. It tore him in two to turn away. *I… I promise I'll find you again, Dad. I'm sorry.* He looked instead to the darting ghost in red—he'd nigh vanished into an open tunnel, a vapor unbound by physics. Jackson gasped. He picked up his feet, knowing if he lost this chance, New York might never see another.

"Everyone!" he yelled, book under his arm. "You need to follow me! I know the way!"

"Jackson…?" Anna called after, alarm wringing her voice.

"No time…!" he yelled back. "Follow! Follow!"

When he glanced over his shoulder to her, the ghosts were gone.

But he still felt them, and that would need to be enough.

Now, his shoes clicked against the reverberating tunnels, clattering against debris, sending it flying. Not everyone was following, but Jackson didn't have time to care. The glimpse of red and gold and gleaming teeth was far out of reach every time he turned. Tony's shade was a mad will 'o the wisp, picking directions seemingly at random. It even went through a *wall.* And as Jackson stood there gasping for breath, despairing, leg in agony, he reached out, and realized… there were no bricks there, in actuality. A tangle of sick, buzzing magic washed over his skin. It was an illusion.

He dove in headfirst, not thinking twice about it, feeling like he'd been dragged through cold slime.

And there taunting gold eyes were again, a hundred feet away down another passage.

He stumbled and sprinted, still following.

Anna was there too. Her breath was even and easy by his side, though he grew more sharp and ragged as the minutes passed. His head blurred and spun, but he threw himself into the labyrinth again and again.

Finally, his flailing feet tripped over stones. He stumbled to his knees, exhausted, realizing he was about to lose the ghost forever.

And Anna caught him. She looked at him with wordless understanding and urgency. Her strong arms were under him, scooping him up like some kind of movie hero from the film classics. Her feet left the ground, and she was *flying*. Flying! He hung on for dear life.

"Left here!" Jackson barely remembered to guide her, stunned, but understanding what she intended. He'd lost so much breath he was almost unable to talk. But they couldn't stop. They *had* to press on.

Oh gods, she was warm and *powerful*. If anyone else was following, they'd be left in the dust.

Tony's ghost almost seemed playful now as they darted through the air, stuttering through twists and turns like he'd been waiting the whole time for them to finally get serious.

Until he halted. Anna barreled clean past him and straight on down another tunnel. "Wait!" Jackson gasped. "Wait! He stopped!"

She looked at him confused, but managed to drift to a halt. Gently, she eased him back onto the ground, his legs almost giving out.

Tony stood, grinning, pointing up at an access hatch. "The Coalition doesn't know about this one," he snickered. His face turned deadly serious. "Like I'd ever let them find me again."

Jackson tried to shake off his sweat and find his second wind. "Th-

thank you," he managed.

"You're welcome," Tony whispered. A note of sorrow kissed his tone. "Goodbye, champion. Was I… was I a good friend?"

Jackson didn't know how to respond.

But just like that, the smile in the dark was gone, evaporated into nothingness. No more red. No more snake eyes. Nothing.

Jackson knew, deep down, that Tony's last job was done. Maybe his voice too would forever go beyond the veil.

He hoped so.

"Jackson, I don't know what's going on with you, but it's super creepy." Anna's hands were on his shoulders, tugging him back to reality.

He winced. "That's probably true."

"But this is the way?"

Nodding, it struck Jackson that she wasn't even questioning him. *She trusts me entirely. She believes.*

She was already halfway up the ladder, ready to take part in this destiny of theirs, and he was on her heels, believing in her too with everything he was.

CHAPTER TWENTY-TWO
Sacrifice

A rifle was in Anna's face the moment she emerged from the manhole.

Shark's eyes pierced hers. "How…?" He was standing there before her, almost like he'd been waiting, a bundle of wonder, hostility, and trembling nerves. Muck covered his limbs, his breathing coming in short, sad gasps.

Anna's eyes darted between him and their surroundings. Jackson was pausing beneath her on the ladder, quiet breath on her ankles. This narrow enclosure above ground was cast in shadow from looming buildings with broken windows and abandoned rooms. It was a strange, cramped courtyard time had utterly forgotten and built up around. At one end, a rusted, twisted, iron fence prevented easy entry, piles of old refuse blocking the view through.

But it couldn't block the sky. On the horizon, a blocky, gray structure sprawled, surrounded by high walls and barbed wire. From its top, an extraordinary beam erupted into the sky. It was sapphire-rich, like a geyser of gemstone, up, up into the clouds, where it split and spiderwebbed, a latticework of energy and beauty.

Anna remembered she needed to breathe. Soft, undulating, humming waves were dripping through her, speaking to some fundamental instinct of safety and peace.

So this was New York's savior: what kept the radiation at bay, what helped them weather this new world.

Shark was kneeling before it too, weeping. Beside him was the heavy black case.

"I... I should have known you would try and follow, glow-witch," he sighed, voice oddly hushed. "But how you did, I don't know."

Perhaps he hadn't armed the bomb yet. Perhaps he didn't know how.

"Hey," Anna whispered, voice thin.

Shark frowned. The gun didn't lower. His other hand fidgeted with the seed pouch around his neck, almost like it was full of prayer beads.

Anna put her hands out, palms up. "I don't have any weapons, alright?"

"You are weapon." His accent stuttered in the pressurized, humming air.

"I... well, okay, that's fair, but... have I ever hurt you?"

He bit his lip, looking like he was considering. It drew blood. Rivulets were already on his chin, mixing with stubble and sweat.

"I'm just gonna come out of the sewer. Really slow. Okay?"

"Fine." He did not budge.

Far away, she could hear cars. She could hear someone playing music, mellow guitars: the surreal sound of the city, full of life... not evacuating.

They weren't evacuating.

Walker and the sergeant, Anna realized... they hadn't gotten through yet. Or no one believed them. Or the Coalition refused to discuss the existence of their secret nukes. It could have been any one of those things.

"Jackson's here too. And, um, it'd be great if you didn't shoot him. Again." Anna rose like each step was on a land mine.

Those terrible teeth bared in warning.

"I promise, he didn't have anything to do with what happened back at your camp. I *promise*."

"You… you saved him, didn't you?" Shark snorted, resting one hand protectively on his cargo. "Of course you did. Can't believe I… I should have checked…!"

Anna tensed. "He's innocent. Your leader… I know you loved him, I know he protected you, but there was something happening to him… he wasn't right—"

"You know *nothing* about him." Shark's eyes flickered down to his free hand. "About us. Baldur is like… like father I did not have! He is good. *Loves us all.* Would not lie. Not to me." The gun pressed his point forward. "Why did you even follow, eh? You could have just stayed out there! *I gave you your life.* I… I…"

A sorrowful stare finished what his words were struggling to say: *You don't deserve to die.*

Anna saw Jackson's head peeking ever-so-carefully up over the edges of the concrete now. Shark grimaced at this, and yet, didn't move his rifle from Anna.

Either he was listening, or he considered her the bigger threat.

"When did you know you were all going to attack the city?" Anna spoke, trying to keep his attention.

The big man snorted. He shrugged, as if to ask if it mattered.

"You didn't act like you knew your leader was going to kill Jackson," she pressed. "Did you really want it to end like this, with all this death?"

"Why would I know what Father was going to do to him?" The scout waved his gun, exasperated. "I knew city man would maybe have good knowledge. Good idea to bring him. Okay? What Father chose to do…" His eyes narrowed at his feet, as if he was ashamed. "No. I thought maybe, after what city did to you both, you would both help us. You would *understand.*"

Jackson made a catching breath, like he was weighing his words, about to speak.

"Don't care now if you betrayed us or not." The man hung his head even more. "End of journey. Shark's job is done. Ran the way you told Father to go, city man. His dogs found this ladder. Good, secret place." He looked up at the sky. "Clear. No clouds. Good day for harvest."

Anna's nerves made her jitter to her feet, and Shark's gun rose warily again. "You can't do this," she said, loud and clear. "You need to give us the bomb."

He squinted. "What you do with it, eh? Is already set. Just ten minutes or something now, probably." He sighed. "I got here faster than he thought I could."

Jackson's fists clenched, an alarmed gasp in his throat. "Who gave you the code?"

Shark only shrugged. "Father Warlord knew many things he shouldn't."

Anna's heart hammered faster. Dizzy, the new reality of this situation slammed into her. If the bomb was armed, then the man before her needed to *move*. Or him and everyone else here would die.

"No," she said, and then she said it again, shouting as loud as she could manage. "*No!*"

Shark rose too, eyes dark and angry.

And Anna heard the sounds she'd been hoping for.

Jackboots. The plant's security.

"Someone's back here!" A woman yelled, voice full of militaristic purpose.

The big man made an exasperated groan. He slammed a huge hand on the case's shell. Anna winced. "I... I walked here. All the way here. And it's hurt. And I want it to be over now." Tears welled in his eyes. "I've lost everyone. Don't you understand? I've kept walking, so, so far! Please. I want it to be *over*. So what are they going to do? Kill me? I don't care anymore."

"Yes. They'll kill you," Jackson said, a tremulous feeling in the link to Anna's chest. "And you'll have died for nothing."

"You need to go," Anna urged. "We don't have time to fight. It's pointless, almost everyone that came here with you is *dead*, and the leader you loved regretted it. I saw it in his eyes. Now *move*."

Shark scowled. Then he sat—right on the bomb, glaring, defiant.

Anna saw the dark energy in him that she'd seen in Jackson's execution mob. She saw the fury like she saw in the Warlord's hunched back, the gritted teeth, the black flicker in his eyes. Like Maya. Like the beasts.

Whatever it was, that void-eyed madness had killed enough.

"Blood," Shark said. "And vengeance." He brought the rifle up, finger on the trigger and ready to pull.

There was a cool brush by Anna's cheek, a tug in the line in her chest, and she turned to Jackson. He only nodded. She trusted the promise in his eyes without words.

Just as Shark pulled the trigger, Anna dove forward. A shadow spun about the gun barrel and the arm aiming it, yanking it to one side. The blast tore wind and pressure across her left cheek, obliterating her hearing. But the bullet missed. She collided with the huge scout, wrenching his arm up the rest of the way. The darkness of the courtyard wobbled disconcertingly, and Shark's feet stumbled too, sending him toppling. He roared in berserker fury.

Anna knew she could smash his face in if she wanted, stun him before the soldiers came.

More death in this war.

Instead, she reached in, touched the seed pouch still strung around his neck, just for a moment. Her light came forward. She thought of Sun, of things growing and new.

Shark scurried back, kicking the bomb protectively out of her reach. She stayed where she was as he raised the gun again. Jackson moved the shadows a second time, but Shark's power was relentless, dragging the sights up, digging in his feet, aiming it while spittle flew from his furious breaths.

"*ARGH!*" Jackson yelled in frustration and strain behind her, his shadows breaking. "*Stop this!*"

A huge book hurtled over Anna's shoulder, beaning Shark directly between the eyes.

The book slid off.

Shark blinked, stunned. The furor shattered, confused.

And a tiny vine touched the giant's cheek from below. Anna sagged, weary, hoping he was present enough to see.

He gave a startled glance to his chest, then snapped the twined pouch from his neck. "What...?" Roots were snaking through the fabric, green poking through the sides. A plant twisted up and around his grip, reaching for the sky.

A bulb bloomed at the plant's head, brilliant yellow, reaching for the sunlight with all its might.

"Life from death," Anna said. "That's what Baldur really wanted, right? Not blood and vengeance. Life from death. Remember? *That's* who you are."

A hazy, clouded sorrow entered Shark's gaze, his lips trembling.

The blood-mad rage... it didn't return.

A platoon of Coalition soldiers rounded the bend then, colliding with the ancient iron grate. "They're here!" one bellowed. "Freeze!"

Another shouted, "Ram it! Take it down!"

An engine was roaring.

Anna's eyes flickered to the bomb behind her opponent, who still remained gazing mutely at the miracle in his palm. "Some of your people are still out there, you know that, right? You're not all dead."

Shark's neck creaked up so he could stare at her.

"They'll be stuck forever if you don't go." The ghosts of her own past moaned in her ears. "You know that to keep walking... it hurts. But we do it. Who will save your people up north if you die here?"

The tears began again in those eyes. "I'm... I'm sorry," he said. "I'm sorry. I didn't... I didn't want..."

Anna's voice cracked. What she said next was truth. "It doesn't matter. Maybe you should choose to live. Because most of us aren't."

"But... but I..."

Her tears were falling freely again, her stomach churning. "Maya's down there, chained up in one of the junctions."

Jackson was leveling his gaze, following her lead. "As long as there's life," he said. "There's hope, right?"

Soldiers were still screaming. "Get these walls down! Now! NOW!"

Shark jumped, looked at all of them.

"Go," Jackson prodded.

The titan dove past him, sorrow and confusion and rage still in his stare, the fragile sunflower bloom still in his hands. He leapt underground, and he was gone.

Anna kneeled by the dark case. Jackson knelt beside her. "Please tell me," he said softly, "That you were lying. About the most-of-us-dying part."

She broke open the locks, looked down at the bomb.

Shark had been right. There looked to be about three minutes to go.

She was still crying. But her soul was quiet. She looked up at the sky.

"You're not lying," Jackson said. "Okay. Okay, what do we do? Can we throw it underground?"

Anna shook her head. That wasn't far enough—at this range, it could still destabilize the plant when it went off, or contaminate the water supply.

The iron grate suddenly exploded inward. Wrenching, screeching bars toppled at their feet, and over them rolled what looked like the closest a van could get to a tank. Anna held up Walker's friendly signal device like a talisman over her head as soldiers filled the cramped courtyard, rifles clacking.

"Who the hell are you?" one demanded.

Anna barely noticed the gun leveled to her. There'd been so many of them lately that it almost felt like a matter of course. "I'm Dr. Matthews, and we need the code," she said. "It's nuclear."

Color drained from the soldiers' faces.

She knew then she was right. They didn't know. Or, maybe, the Coalition wasn't owning up to this, was withholding incriminating data that could save their own city.

"What is wrong with you people?" she couldn't help but wail.

"Anna!" Jackson said. He grabbed her arm. "We can let them take care of this. We should get to safety!"

She dug her feet in and didn't move.

The only safe place for a thing like this to detonate might be in the *stratosphere*, providing it was outside the Barrier blue.

And that was only possible if someone in this city could fly it out.

She smiled, fearful, eyes stinging.

The bomb *clicked* against her palm. She yanked her fingers back with a small shriek.

No. It wasn't ready yet.

"Anna...?"

She'd been plucked out of time, averting a nuclear disaster.

She'd been given these powers so she could stop another.

Perhaps the universe was being neat. Tidy. But, her heart was fighting to tear out of her throat. It didn't have time for philosophy.

I don't want to die I don't want to die I don't want to die.

I... I want to be here now.

She was shuddering and cracking. Jackson stepped forward, wrapping his arms around her in silence. She shook. He held. And as soldiers squeezed around their battering ram, shouting at each other, full of confusion and fear, she smeared tears into his shoulder, letting herself, for a moment, just *be*.

Someone was shouting for a bomb expert. There wasn't time for that.

These were people with families. Futures. Loved ones were waiting for them to come home.

She was only a visitor, right?

It was time to go.

So she reached up, wrapped her fingers in messy black hair, and slid Jackson's lips softly against hers. It was a kiss that surprised her as much as it seemed to surprise him, borne of terror and tenderness, a need to feel close and a need for courage. She didn't mean it to last. She didn't mean it to be much more than goodbye. Whatever this was between them, whatever it could have been... it wasn't going to get time or space to grow, but she cherished all he'd done and all he was. More than anything, she wanted him to know it.

Her heart suddenly jolted. Something strange overtook her, something powerful and flowing and strong. It smelled like lavender and summer, like ozone and earth.

I met you in the first dawn, it said, *and you gave me everything, half of your sky and your world and your heart.*

And I will always love you.

She pulled back, stunned, shaking.

For a second, she thought Jackson's eyes were dark, yet full of starlight.

No. They were just brown and wide with fear, were searching for hope... were moist with resignation.

He wasn't stopping her. Why wasn't he stopping her?

"Anna... be safe. Come back. Please, come back."

She turned, closing the case and scooping up the bomb before she could think about it anymore. As she dug her hands into the shell, her heart was suddenly silent. Strong. She was believed in. Maybe, she was even loved. And that? It was all she needed.

If she was going to die again, at least she wasn't alone.

Someone yelled at her to freeze, but she sure as hell did not. She flung herself up in the air, and with all her force of will, the breeze helped her rise. No shots fired after her, just as she suspected they wouldn't— after all, who would want to shoot an explosive?

Anna climbed faster and faster. The people down below were shouting and fading. Her luggage sagged, slippery in her arms. But she dug in and kept flying, up, up, gathering it as tightly to her as she could, refusing to look at it, afraid her instincts might find it too dangerous to hold, and then, she'd drop it, and they'd all fall.

Instead, Anna stared up at the sun.

Strange. She could gaze directly into it and didn't need to look away.

The orb was bright, hypnotizing, the metallic weight in her arms pulsing and clicking as she ascended, like some kind of nightmarish infant. The high rises of glass and stone fell away. The skyscrapers' spires slipped past her toes.

There was only the bright blue of the sky.

The white-hot blaze of the light.

The Barrier was a thin film of raw energy, hot and crackling, whining in her teeth as she approached. Anna never even questioned that she'd be strong enough to pass through it. It struck her like an electric fence, sharp, furious. The smell of broiling hair filled her nose.

Then she was past. Her skin itched and burned. Her hair was gone.

Her only misgiving was her cargo. She glanced down… it was glowing. Like she was. The metallic casing shrugged off the energy wave, like it had become part of her.

She smiled, relieved.

The wind on her skin was growing colder, frosting the sweat on her neck, her thoughts spreading thin as the air did. The blue expanse was starting to fade, now dispersing ever more to black, and she knew she was rocketing like an uncoiled spring, faster than she had any right to fly.

Her lungs constricted in pain. Her throat tightened in the frozen air. She couldn't breathe.

She knew she shouldn't even be conscious up here, but she'd known she would be, just like she'd known how to heal Jackson when he'd been bleeding out on that street.

What she didn't know was how long she could stay awake.

Take it as far away as possible.

Stay awake.

Stay...

A great click resounded through the metal beast in her arms, thrumming through her chest, like a monster inside was knocking, knocking, ready to get out. Anna smiled, feeling a hysterical shudder bubble up, even if her body was in too much pain, held too much ice for it to leave.

Part of her thought of the EMP that was sure to result from this blast. Would the Barrier be able to absorb all of that?

Still better damaged than broken forever.

Part of her let herself daydream, think about what a nice thing it would have been to really live in this world for a day, no cares, no radiation, no pursuers. Even a place as shattered as this... she had no doubt there was great beauty out here somewhere too. Just like Jackson said.

Maybe she would have tried to figure out love this time around, and surrounded herself with her friends and purpose and joy.

She felt she deserved that.

But, the universe operated on cold, hard physics, not warm, fuzzy deservings.

There was a whining in her ears, perhaps the result of the atmospheric shift: hills, peaks and valleys. The whooshing of the wind gave way to dizzying, deafening pressure and tinnitus. Wait. No... it wasn't *whining*. It was *her*. She was singing again. That beautiful song from inside the dream fire. That song... the one she could now understand...

Be hope.

The bomb resonated with its click against her chest once more. The beast inside the shell was knocking harder.

She thought of gentle brown eyes, of Jackson's tentative and warm hand asking to dance.

She thought of Nyx's belly laugh, of her resolve and fire.

She thought of the smiles and wonder of those she'd helped, of those she'd lost.

Anna held them all close.

And the world shattered in a white-hot, suffocating blaze.

CHAPTER TWENTY-THREE
Drowned

Jackson felt his heart lifting up and away, leaving with Anna into a bright, beautiful afternoon.

She was only a speck now. It was like the sky had swallowed her, like—

And then, the world above lit up with fire. The burst billowed furious, savage, red and orange and white and smoke, burning out and out forever. It seared his eyes even as he screwed them shut.

It consumed the connection in his heart. It burned and it choked.

And it fell away into nothing, empty, cold. The home inside his chest beat tentatively, alone, no echo, no answer.

The shockwave hit. There was nothing but ringing. The Barrier surged, the sapphire trilling, crackling with white. It rippled and seethed as he'd never seen, a stormy, deadly sea. It held, but it *roared*.

An entire city fell silent. An entire city was nothing but ringing ears and stopped hearts.

Slowly, the blast dissipated. The sky puffed with smoke and ash.

The sun broke through the clouds, serene.

The Barrier blue remained.

Jackson fell to his knees.

A furious shout broke the pall of his stricken ears. It was… it was *joy.* The soldiers were whooping and cheering, clapping each other on the back.

"Was that... was that the Angel of New York? From the datalink?" one shouted in wonder.

"Yes," Jackson whispered, so low he couldn't even hear himself.

The Barrier above wasn't returning to normal. It still crackled and warped, angry, sparking, like someone had stuck their finger in a rippling electric lake.

And a man stepped in from the crush of soldiers, one in agent-tailored black, sunglasses before his eyes. One arm was shriveled against his chest. It wasn't Walker. This one's name tag read *Reeds.*

"To attention!" an officer barked by his side. The soldiers ceased celebrating. They fell in line.

Jackson realized he couldn't breathe. He sagged against the wall, paralyzed. His chest was seizing with wracked attempts at sobbing, and he bit his bottom lip so hard it bled.

"Can't believe..." Agent Reeds was hissing. "Five attacks! Around the *world*...! What the *hell* kind of conspiracy is with these damned filthy raiders?" He barked to the man on his left. "I need sweeps of the area, and I need prisoners to question. I want that asshole Walker interrogated. I want every Barrier tech on the coast out here *now*, before Beijing claims them! We're going to need to shut down power to the city and reroute to this plant for... Christ, who knows how long."

"Sir." The man saluted. "Where will I be able to find you?"

"Outside. I'm going to see if there's any bits of Anna Matthews that can be recovered. Maybe we can get *something* out of this."

And in that moment, this *Reeds* became the raging red center of an unfair universe. The shadows hardened and twisted under Jackson's hands. Hot tears coursed freely down his cheeks. The agent's delicate windpipe was *utterly* within reach.

The warm line in his chest to Anna... it was cold and dead.

So was he.

"Oh," Reeds added, jabbing his good thumb in Jackson's direction. "Arrest that one. *Dovetail.* I want him taken to our maximum security wing for questioning too."

Jackson let out a furious roar he didn't even know he could make and lunged for the callous-tongued agent, the shadows moving with him—but his head exploded with pain as a rifle slammed into his skull, whipping to him to the side, carrying him into a graceless fall.

"I got this one, don't worry," a soldier's voice flittered in the background. The man's eyes seemed almost apologetic.

"Coalition bomb," Jackson rasped, vengeful. "That bomb was *yours.*"

The soldier recoiled in surprise.

"Shut him up!" Reeds snapped. "Get him out of here!"

Jackson groaned, clutching his head—he saw blurred faces, and he saw the Barrier up high, flickering, sick. Just beyond, yes, there was the pale, distant sun, so, so far out of his reach.

He crumpled into unconsciousness, drowning in his anger and grief.

And when he awoke, his tongue was thick, every bone in his body tingling, sore, clumsy. The world was blurry. Sour.

Drugged. Sedated. I'm…

Jackson pulled his palms under his body, trying to get up, scraping himself across unblemished and frigid concrete. For one, blissful moment, he didn't know what had happened or where he was, and he took this new place in without truly understanding. His brain sloshed in his skull.

He'd been stripped of all his clothes. The too-short undergarments left behind were unfamiliar, scratchy. It was as cold and dark as the world before the dawn, and silence hung like a moldy shroud. There was nothing except the faintest outline of four tight walls and a bare mattress.

It was the reinforced door that told him everything he needed to remember.

She's gone.

The emptiness slammed into him again, burrowed into his chest until he couldn't breathe. Breaking, he collapsed, curling his aching knees to his chest. He started to shudder, the empty sorrow threatening to overwhelm him, to drown him forever.

Anna, I'm sorry, I'm so, so sorry...

His hope was lost.

But as he lay there, his knee brushed an object, a sturdy rectangle, a whisper of leather and vellum.

Jackson's pained gasps slowed. He reached out, curled his fingers around his book. *You...* It had returned to him again. Tugging it close to his body, he felt the voices, the magic, the stories of those that came before.

They would always find him, right?

The kiss of the darkness was a palpable thing in this prison. It descended around him, cradled him, comforted its wayward child so far from home.

Anna wouldn't have wanted him to lay down and die.

Anna never gave up. She was a hero, right?

Still, he couldn't move, couldn't think, could barely *breathe*. So he lay quiet, just trying to exist.

And there was a warmth in his chest. It was small at first, but then it bloomed, stronger and stronger, a tiny star against his ribcage.

The... book?

It was the magic the book had drawn in from that field where he'd found her. It was so different from the rest, something he'd barely felt before, but now, it was all he could sense. It was the touch of the Sun: the promise in the dark that it would rise again come morning.

Get up.

Jackson closed his eyes, gathered his power, and tried to remember how to stand.

Get up, the voice repeated, powerful, sure. *This is not over.*

Gasping, Jackson realized truths without words. He saw a light in his mind's eye, warmth and hope and promise. He stood, pressed his palms to the door, to his cage.

A bit of Sun had come in here with him, and like Anna, it wanted him to rise.

He'd been told he'd been in a cage all of his life, cages of everyone's making, even his own.

I swear to you, he told the woman he'd loved. *I swear to you, I won't give up.*

I'll break free.

CHAPTER TWENTY-FOUR
Pawn

Somewhere, far away, a woman gasped in answer.

Anna woke, jolting up into the chilled black.

Her body was shaking from shock, her skin icy and wet. Her mind was frantic and spinning. Her chest throbbed like someone had reached in and torn a massive hole right where her heart was meant to be.

The first thing she realized was that she was in the dark. Cold stone was beneath her. Everything ached, and her stomach was close to dry-heaving from nausea. The second thing she noticed was that she felt alone: utterly, completely alone. The link in her chest... it was gone. No answering heartbeat. It was astounding how quickly she'd grown accustomed to her connection to another, and how shocking it was to have it ripped away. The imbalance almost gave her vertigo.

But why was it...?

She moaned with dawning horror. Had she not gotten the bomb far enough away? What if he was...? What if *everyone* she'd tried to save was...?

A wave of cold water doused her without warning, flooding her mouth, choking her. She sputtered and spit, scrambling, trying to summon the light under her skin so she might see. It refused her, not even the faintest spark coming to her aid.

"Ah." A soft voice floated from her left. She whipped her head to greet it. "Finally."

Two reflective eyes peered back at her from deep in the dark: two tiny moons.

She trembled, frigid, weak. "…Jackson?"

"Oh no, my dear. *Never* him." This soft voice was tinged with England, laced with menace and condescension.

"Get away from me," she hissed. "I'll fight you if you get any closer."

"I'm sure you will."

"I *mean* it."

"Right now," the Archmage hissed, "You're unable to fight much of anyone, cut off from your source of power."

Anna's muscles were quaky and gelatinous. But her mind had *always* been quick. This felt just like when she'd been trapped underground in the Coalition facility.

The Sun. She needed the Sun.

That meant that the longer she was down here… she would only get weaker.

Fighting back the sickness, knowing this man could not mean her any goodwill, she tore to her feet and lunged for him.

Then she fell, right through the space where those two eyes briefly reflected in the dark, passing through nothing but cold air.

There was a soft, malevolent chuckle. It seemed to surround her, drilling into her brain. She didn't care. Nothing was tying her down. She ran, and she ran hard.

SMACK!

Her hands hit frigid rock, her body following through. The wall smashed her nose and knocked the wind out of her chest. Startled, she staggered back, then placed one hand to the stone and started to sprint, tracing the wall's length, looking for a door. Warm blood dripped down her face.

"There's no exit," the Archmage said, tone bored. "This is one of the places where I keep the things I don't want found."

Anna's head spun. She fled blind, feeling the wall curve.

It was a circle. She was running in a *circle*.

He sighed. "I brought you here with magic, and that's the only way to leave. So you really should stop before you use up all of the air in this chamber. I have to make an *effort* to bring in more, and I'd rather not."

Anna kept running. No break in the stone tripped against her fingertips.

Then, she stumbled. A leg met her ankles in the dark. She fell, jarring her elbow, crying out in pain.

At first, she thought the Archmage had done it, just a casual cruelty. But the leg didn't move, and far away, she heard the sound of shuffling, like her antagonist was pulling up a chair and having a seat.

Frightened, she felt the leg, traced the form of a body. It was a short man, large around his belly, though she could feel a fluffy, handlebar mustache on his face.

She could feel a chain around his neck, too.

A weak, rasping voice greeted her touch, like it belonged to someone long denied water. "Run," the Order mage she knew as Huxley pleaded. "Please, run. *Don't let him catch you too.*"

Anna rocketed to her feet, horrified, confused.

But she was trapped. If the Archmage was telling the truth… there wasn't an escape. Unless… maybe he had something on him. Something that could be used to get her out of her.

And this prisoner of his.

No one deserved this.

So she turned towards the place where she'd heard someone sit, peering and straining to see. She wouldn't beg. She wouldn't insist he let her go, because he wouldn't. "What do you want? Why am I… why are *we* here?"

"Your gratitude for saving your life is overwhelming."

She could tell there were no hurt feelings. "You teleported me from the blast."

"Yes. Your death seemed wasteful at this juncture. So I burned up a number of souls in my collection to get the job done… then I set a few wards, blocked your ties to the outside world. You're alone. I know you can feel it. No one is coming for you. No one can even know you're alive." There was an unpleasant smile in his voice. "And I wouldn't rely on Huxley there, either. He's almost spent."

Her stomach was a rock. *Burned up… souls?* She thought of Nyx's friend A'laria, screaming inside a stone, drained like some sick battery. "Fine," she snapped, trying to sound brave. "Tell me what you want."

"Your complete and utter obedience."

The hairs on her neck prickled.

He continued, "And Jackson's, of course."

"In what?"

There was a long silence. "Do you know how old I am?"

"…No." She didn't know why that was important.

"I don't either. Not anymore. I stopped counting after my four hundredth year."

Anna licked her cracking lips, treading carefully as she tried to find his exact location, suspecting this was just one more madman on the pile of her life. "Well, you don't look a day over forty. Tell me what you want. Let me go, and maybe I can help."

"Forty? Really?" This actually sounded like it irritated him. "Never mind. Do you know how many I've killed, in all these centuries?"

Her ears had almost pinpointed him. She crept forward on wobbly ankles. "No. How many?" *Keep talking.*

"Every so often, a new Chosen child surfaces, some fresh pawn in this wretched game. And I've murdered them. I've done this for centuries, girl. *Centuries.* I've waited, suffered, as every year crawled by, for one of the gods responsible to come forward, to leave themselves open. You know what it's like, of course—your life a plaything. *She* brought you from the dead, and she gave you powers, and then she cast you out into this cruel world, expecting you to break yourself, to sacrifice it all for her. Like you just did. Like a fool."

Anna swallowed. Sun hadn't seemed so callous. She'd only seemed kind and sorrowful, and so, so heartbreakingly beautiful. "I think maybe you've got the wrong idea."

"Oh, no. I don't." He gave a hollow chuckle. Anna felt a puff of air across her arm. She'd found him. "But when you came here, I realized things changed. The game is different for the first time in millennia. You're going to bring the gods just close enough to touch. And I'm going to end this millennia-old, world-destroying grudge match once and for all: Inoki, his so-called wife, his brother, *the whole wretched lot.*"

Anna leapt at him, certain of the voice, swinging at the shadows.

Nothing! Nothing but air!

A cold wind iced her neck, all of her hairs rising as she whirled.

"Don't even think for a second that you can fight me in the dark."

How had he gotten behind her? She hadn't heard—

Something seized her midsection, wrapping around her like a python, squeezing her insides until they were agony. She cried out, gasping to breathe.

"I've never lost in the dark." His voice was low and furious. "I am of the Shadow, and you have no idea how many of souls I've imprisoned, how many bones I've *burned.*"

Anna struggled, but the coils around her just squeezed tighter, white spots exploding in her blinded eyes.

"Now are you going to behave?"

She wheezed, tears mixing with the blood on her lips.

"I'll take that as a yes."

Suddenly, she dropped, smashed to the floor gasping, trying to stay conscious.

Cold, thin fingers pressed on her forehead, between her eyes. What felt like a brand lit there, began to *burn.* At the same time, it oozed, cold and slimy, like blood. It was like his fingers were pressing right through her skin, through her skull, straight to her brain.

"You're going to bring my dear Jackson in line," he whispered, and his voice curled through her ears, drilling itself into her mind's recesses. She hissed, squeezing her eyes shut, trying to pull away. "He trusts you," the whisper continued, winding about her like heavy blanket. "And so will many, many others in this city."

"No!" she cried out, struggling harder now, fighting the fog the Archmage's fingers wove around her in the dark.

"Yes. You're going to help me take down the very gods, Anna. And you'll thank me when this is all over. You will. Even if it kills you. Everything is going to be *fine*, you see. Everything is going to be *okay*."

The mental fog leached into her being.

"Repeat after me," he wheedled. "And you'll be free to go." His hands were so cold. His scent reminded her of death. "Everything is going to be fine. Everything is going to be okay."

Let me in, the voice in her head whispered.

"Everything's fine," she heard her vocal cords articulate. "Everything's okay."

Anna recoiled, unable to control her words, and she beat back the voice as fiercely as she could. It was like keeping back air itself. It crept and snuck and bled through the cracks, begging her to embrace its message.

"Don't bother," he threatened. "You've already let me in once. I've broken so many minds, girl. Yours is no different."

Anna reached deep inside herself for the tiny flame of courage and strength that she'd claimed since her journey began.

And her mind slipped, went placid and cool like a peaceful lake, sending her beneath. The fog of his voice roiled over the surface.

Perhaps days did pass. Perhaps weeks. She did not know. She couldn't feel anything.

Everything's going to be fine, an inner voice reassured her, and she couldn't tell anymore whose it was.

Everything's going to be okay.
All you need to do… is just listen to me.

EPILOGUE

An old man named Frank McSheffrey stood straight and tall in southern Gravesend, Brooklyn, watching the sky.

The Barrier's sapphire field was twisting with lightning, nerves snapping, lashing out. The explosion had been hours past. It wasn't getting better.

His neighbor was on the curb, kneeling, reciting prayers from hundreds of little slips of paper. Incense burned by her side as she gestured at the sky, wishing health to the force above that protected them all. Little pockets of spiritual vigils, like this one, had sprung up in every borough.

The Coalition had yet to offer a statement.

Frank's expression was unreadable.

He returned indoors to his spartan apartment. One hand brushed an enameled box scribed with Hebrew letters on the wall. This was a decades-old habit. He wasn't going to bother praying. He'd yet to see it do anyone any good.

Ancient furniture and mottled flower-print wallpaper was all that rested here with him, old dust and smoke in all the crannies. At his mantle, he paused, taking in a shelf of pictures—the only real personalization this home had ever known, yellowed from cigars and flood damage. In one, a mustached man had a protective arm around a fidgeting, black-haired pre-teen: a newly adopted son. A younger Frank loomed unsmiling behind the two Dovetails, captured in the photograph as if by accident.

The Frank of the present blinked rapidly at his family, then reached up over the pictures, taking his shotgun off the wall. He returned to his table where a long-range communicator sat, thunking the gun down beside it. Cleaning brush in hand, he got to work.

The radio lay silent.

Frank disassembled the shotgun bit by bit, smoothly polishing and checking each component.

After long, agonizing minutes in the quiet, he had to stop. His hands were shaking too hard.

The hours kept passing. The power around him flickered off. Darktime. It was earlier than it should have been, much earlier. Were they re-routing electric to the damaged dome?

Not a single word had come through the city's emergency channels.

No peep from the people he'd sent to find Jackson, either.

Frank fell asleep in his armchair, waiting, wrapped up in dreams of his mistakes.

Two days passed. Messages began to pile up from the company. Sabbatical, he'd told them. The youngest Dovetail was on sabbatical for his health.

He glanced over at the picture of the boy and his adopted father often.

His arthritic hands shook harder.

The power never came back on.

It was four in the morning, days after that, when he awoke to pounding on the door. The hinges rattled, the pictures falling from their perch. The shotgun was in his hands before he knew it.

They've come.

He'd been waiting. There'd been no point in running.

Not if Jackson and Peter were dead.

The paper trails were burned and buried, though. Not a single illegal thing they'd done would *ever* come back on the Dovetail name. The news would say the smuggling operation hiding in the delivery company was orchestrated by one bad egg, some old, pointless guy who'd confessed to everything before taking himself out.

Frank waited breathlessly in his armchair for the militia to break down his door, holding the gun in a business-like way to his chin.

Silence.

The minutes passed.

No one was entering.

Growling, Frank rose, lowering his weapon.

And a small flare of optimism niggled in his heart, no matter how hard he'd tried to kill such things.

Jackson.

He hustled to the entryway, holding himself to the wall out of line of sight. With one hand, he undid his many locks, carefully jimmying the handle and letting the door drift open of its own accord.

No one was there.

Confused, Frank stuck his balding head outside, staring into a dark hallway. His visitor seemed to have fled. Then, he looked down.

There was a woman curled up on his doormat. She was unconscious. Her clothes were bloodstained, and tufts of burned, blonde hair sprouted from her head like a halo.

"Well, *shit,*" Frank said. It was the way he'd greeted Anna the first time they met too. Here was trouble, once again.

And here was hope, burning brighter.

Slowly, he kneeled, scooping up her prone form and shuffling back inside.

⁂

An old manhole in the wasteland pulled aside, scraping rust into asphalt.

From the ground rose two people. One was a giant, his face tattooed red, sorrowfully reading the empty, desolate road for signs. The other was a one-eyed woman curled up in his strong arms, legs wrapped and bleeding. Both were dirty, gasping for air.

The giant gently laid the woman on the street, then slowly transferred her to his back. "I've got you," he said. "Shark got you, Maya. Don't fight."

Her eyes were dazed and bleary. She weakly allowed him to carry her. "Where are we going…?"

"Home." He trudged forward like a man used to walking with burdens.

"It's… no, it's…"

"Still, we go, eh? We fix this."

Maya only wept on his back.

Eventually, the blocks passed. Her tears quieted. "We're all that's left, aren't we?"

"No." Shark wasn't even close to tired. "Many of us are alive. Up in Sunrise now. Like I said, we go home."

The medic closed her eye, resting her forehead in the small of his neck. "The Coalition will kill us."

Shark's pointed teeth gleamed to the road ahead. "Hope, yes? As long as we're alive, we are hope."

Maya shuddered. From one wrist, handcuffs still dangled. Her companion had torn the pipe clean off the wall to which she'd been chained.

But for the first time, she noticed the seed pouch around her rescuer's neck. From it sprouted a flower, curled around his head and up behind his ears. Bright yellow petals spread wide and welcoming against his hair—a crown arching for the light above.

Something like a smile touched one end of her stern lips.

"Father Shark," she whispered, touching the sunflower's soft center.

His laughter came in a surprised bark. "Yeah?"

Maya reached inside, found the hard-worn resolve that the world could never steal from her. "I will follow you to the end."

The giant smiled wider. One foot went in front of the other. Together, they walked down the broken road, away from the city.

They never looked back.

TO BE CONTINUED

HELLO, DEAR READER,

I hope you're enjoying *Inoki's Game*. Don't worry—this isn't where these stories end. The sun waits to rise once more.

I'll see you soon. Be prepared for more dark machinations of humans and gods in Book Three, *The Mind's Eye*. Our dear friend, the Archmage, is about to unveil his grandest schemes and most terrifying sins. Sign up for notifications at ia-ashcroft.com to be notified of the release.

But if you have a moment more to spare...

Readers like you make or break a new book. I would be deeply grateful if you would consider leaving a review on Amazon: the parts you loved, what you'd like to see more of, what you're looking forward to—anything! It would only take a moment, and it would mean the world to me as a writer.

Thank you. May you have pleasant wanderings as you return to the waking world.

- I. A. Ashcroft